DIM SHORES PRESENTS

Second Dim Shores Original Edition, June 2020
DS-025TP

ISBN 978-0-9991430-0-1

Cover and interior art uses images courtesy Pixabay and Francesco Ungaro/Pexels
Frontis image courtesy Kaitlyn Jade/Pexels
Layout by Sam Cowan

Dim Shores
Carmichael, CA
DimShores.com

Printed in the United States of America

DIM SHORES PRESENTS

VOLUME 1 / SUMMER 2020

CONTENTS

MANY LIVES THEORY
Christopher Burke

There are many lives you live that are not the life you were meant to live.

The dark, rust-tinged smoke extends from the Company's factories and disperses over the town like tendrils of corruption granting their smirking blessing upon the inhabitants below. Motors deep within the heart of the Company drive pumps and conveyor belts, an industrial vascular system whose reach extends into every home in town and far beyond into places alien to the inhabitants. Expelled waste product is managed and disposed of by persons whose primary function in this mechanized body is to adhere to environmental standards and regulations.

Every day, the first thing you do is wake up and the second thing you do is grapple with the fresh realization that you have to live as the person who just woke up. You know you were meant for more than this, and you know also that you were meant for nothing at all. This nothing has sensed the vulnerability of your grief, taken you over, and now uses your fingers to press buttons for people wealthier than you and as distant as ghosts.

I am the you that we both wish wasn't true.

I am the you that still has Gem. And Elizabeth.

The days pass you by so quickly that they've disappeared into a dream-life of the past before you've awakened into each late morning. I am the you that exists by moving backwards through time, back to Gemma. I am the old you that is waiting for its own shambling future ruins to come back, if only the world and those who control it would simply permit the journey.

Patrick Wolfe sensed eyes upon him.

There was no detectable air displacement or other vague sensation that would normally alert one to the presence of another. His skin prickled.

Patrick looked around the quiet area near "his" cubicle (not his, really; everything here was the Company's, of course). Everyone else had left for the day, as was customary by this hour. He'd taken to working a later shift due to difficulties at home that had made it too challenging to come in at the usual 9:00, and he was often the last of his department to leave for the day. He was grateful to his Manager, Alison, for permitting this. He realized it was an inconvenience, that he was an inconvenience, and the Company kept a close eye on inconveniences to ensure they didn't become significant enough that they'd have to excise them.

He minimized the word processor window he had open on his computer and went back to the spreadsheets and data, looking for answers in numbers and relationships, and numbers of relationships. The data spread its tendrils over every part of the Company and every worker who existed underneath it. Somewhere on the other side of the third floor's cubicle farm, sandwiched between the other farms on the second and fourth, a light turned on, activated by the overhead motion sensors.

"Hello?"

The normal faint, ambient buzz of lighting and other life processes of the third-floor farm grew louder in his perception in contrast to the lack of response. Patrick stood up and looked around, heard the faint noise of someone retreating toward the exit, and then the click of the door in that distant section.

The eyes were still there, though, he was sure, as he looked over his shoulder. Patrick hesitantly got back to work, but he'd lost his concentration and didn't regain it. He fired off distracted answers to e-mails from his Manager, long since gone home for the day.

His lonely walk across the floor, down two flights of stairs, through three hallways of the labyrinthine office building, and out to the parking lot felt like an eternity under another set of cameras eager to learn all it could of the world that fell under its gaze.

———◆———

Gemma.

A dim part of him knew that he was dreaming. That it was one of the terrors. Even subsumed by the darkness and slow viscosity of nightmare, he knew that Gemma was still gone. But someone or something was telling him otherwise from a distance unknown.

In the dream that wouldn't end, he was lost in a house utterly alien and cold that was not his home even though it was. Dimensions were slanted, the floorboards dusty, cracked and barren, unrecognizable, littered with ceramic detritus bordering walls riddled with holes in unfamiliar wallpapers behind which lurked eternities necessitating loss, and none of it looked like the house in which the brighter part of him now slept and quickened his body's breath, the respiratory system performing its duties semiconsciously.

Gem was in here, somewhere, even though she couldn't be. There were hints of a voice that might have whispered such assurances through the wallpaper holes or broken floorboards, that might have wailed hints of such from the far side of the broken building. He sensed hints of eyes that were tracking his steps through this not-home. He knew she was gone, but he also knew this was a cruel lie told by the disease.

A small, brighter part of him sleeping on the bed redoubled the effort to breathe heavily, desperately, through the suffocation of nightmare, hoping it would be enough that Liz would wake and rescue him from his paralyzed slumber, from this other life that couldn't exist.

"Hey. Hey, wake up. Pat!" Liz was shaking him. He was already crying before most of him was awake. "I'm so sorry," she said, her brow furrowed with concern. "Was it the same one?"

He couldn't speak but nodded as his breath slowed back down to normal. In the dream, Patrick was usually in some deformed building. It was always different while always being the same one, a vague sense of a home into which one was reluctantly displaced. *The many lives of houses,* he found himself thinking often. *Always the same in their differences.*

He always awoke dimly into the dream already inside the not-home. It was silent, but he always knew Gemma was in there somewhere, lost, free of her disease, and needing to be found. There were always obstacles, impossible dimensions, and a sense of constantly receding interiority; the further he went into the depths and heights of the building, the closer he got to finding Gemma and the less certain he felt he could get back out. He'd never seen her nor heard her voice in the dream, and after its recurrence more or less weekly for the last three weary years he no longer expected to. That was the worst part: confronting again, from always-new perspectives, the reality that he wouldn't see or hold her, that he had long since begun to forget the specificity of her voice and distinctness of her movements. Patrick knew this to be a betrayal for which he couldn't forgive himself.

Liz sighed and her head dropped back down to the pillow.

Fifteen minutes later, while Patrick sat at the kitchen table with a cup of coffee, the uneven, creaking floor announced Liz's presence well in advance of her arrival. The muted television in the corner displayed the earliest parts of the news cycle, a scrolling caption beneath an unnamed face summarizing the body count from a shooting at a mall that had occurred the night before. Liz poured a cup of her own after a tired glance at the screen and sat down in the glow of the numbers as they ticked up in a methodical death march.

Patrick wasn't sure which of them must look more exhausted by the last few years. They both felt as run-down as the house looked. Liz grimaced as always but refrained from her customary criticism of the cheap coffee he'd long since gotten used to.

"Sorry I woke you again," he said.

"It's fine," she waved his concern away. "I have to be up for work anyway. Do you want to talk about it?"

He shook his head. "I want to forget it. More than just about anything. We've talked about it plenty."

Liz looked at him with her usual weary concern.

"But…" he hadn't realized there was going to be a "but". "This time I think there was someone else there. Not Gemma, but someone at the beginning, some vague voice trying to guide me…"

Liz raised her eyebrows.

"I thought you didn't want to talk about it," she said.

"Well, I don't, but…I don't remember seeing anyone else, just sensing something. Like a pair of eyes or a muffled voice or I don't know what, but I don't think it's been there before. There, I guess we talked about it."

Liz looked at him with a mixture of sympathy and exhaustion born of more than just a single night's interrupted sleep. The kitchen was filled for a few minutes with silence interrupted occasionally by the sound of mugs being picked up and set down before they went their separate ways to prepare for the day.

———◆———

LIZ:

The creaks in this house precede me everywhere, as though I'm following them. There are supposed to be young, growing feet pattering around it, the healthy sound of laughter. I smell only dust and entropy, neglect and an inability to keep up with life while it runs on without us. The dirty sun peaks at us through dirty windows, and when I look at them I feel nothing more than the exhaustion and defeat of a future whose call I've stopped hearing.

But how much of this is because Patrick is swept up in dreams rather than futures? How long must this go on before he will let us see a future through clearer windows? He is still horrified by the idea of a future without Gemma, but so am I, and he alone seems incapable of being equally horrified by the dust and creaks in this dying architecture that used to be a home. Maybe he's grown accustomed to it, but I cannot. Of the halls I can see to walk down, all seem to be gradually constricting. All of them have only a door to loneliness at their end

———◆———

After the rusty tendrils leave the Company's smokestacks, they disappear into the clouds, and are later expelled from this paradise to flood the Earth below. Carving their way through and etching new arteries into the spinning orb of life and death, they create a new paradise, blessed by fertility but condemned to impurity. The arteries strangle the world and in so doing push up new corruptions, new organisms, new diseases. Its position in spacetime is a fluke, an accident, a stumble. The organisms create systems that carve still more arteries into the world to carry newer versions of life and death.

———◆———

The way Gemma's disease made her cough and cry out in pain, Patrick typed in "his" lonely cubicle, and then impulsively deleted everything but *"Gemma."* He minimized the window as he heard Alison's door open and close a few dozen feet away.

"Do you think you can have the Project Solaris reports done for tomorrow?" she asked on her way out.

"Oh, yeah. Yeah, that's no problem," Patrick said. "I can send them to you in a couple of hours. I just need to get some info from the field teams."

"All right, great. Let's connect and review them in the morning. Have a good night!" she said in her usual chipper voice. He watched her head float over the cubicles toward the exit until the door opened and closed. He turned back to his computer, ready to start compiling the requested reports.

An e-mail notification appeared in the corner of the screen. He muttered to himself, minimized the database, and then opened the new message.

From: Patrick Wolfe <pwolfe@████industries.com>
To: Patrick Wolfe <pwolfe@███industries.com>
Subject: GEMMA

The body of the e-mail was blank, but there was a video file attached.

He wondered for an instant if it was malware; the subject and his name would be easy enough to harvest from older e-mails if the right program had gotten onto the company network and begun circulating with whatever infection it might carry. But he didn't care at the moment, and curiosity got the better of him.

Patrick put his headphones on and opened the video.

It started as a blank screen with a sound like some warped cousin of white noise. Soon the edges of the display began to color with gray, curved pulses of light, and inside them was a vague shifting blackness suggestive of forward motion through a tunnel.

Fading in and swimming up through the noise, a sound like an anguished wail emerged, followed by the first semi-distinguishable image: a sudden confusion of unrecognizable humans, or rather, portions of them as though shown at an extreme close-up on various parts of their bodies that branched off at impossible angles as though they were being broken or built. He stared, mesmerized by the strange, inexplicable scene, and then felt his stomach start to heave when the noises were cut off suddenly for a few seconds of silence. Then arose a loud embryonic ambience accompanied by something loudly gurgling and a crunching as of teeth on dry cereal, amplified to a point that caused distortion in the recorded audio track. He winced but kept the headphones on.

The footage cut abruptly to a room so crammed full of people in suits that it would be impossible for them to move, and the audio track faded except for the crunching sound. This continued for only a second or two, and then appeared the face of his wife and daughter from a vantage point above a bed on which they slept, Liz with her arm protectively over Gemma.

Gemma.

He recognized his wife and daughter. He didn't recognize the house they were in, or their clothing, or the decorations he could see in the periphery of the video. A floral-patterned vase stood on the nightstand near Liz's calmly sleeping body. The slivers of wallpaper that he could see were unfamiliar. And then the camera cut again to a close-up of a face, breathing rapidly under apparent distress.

His face.

Patrick's stomach heaved again, close to expelling its unhealthful contents.

"My life," Other-Patrick began. "I mean, the Company's— Shit!" The video stopped abruptly, its runtime complete.

He stared at the blank display while his stomach settled, but as it calmed down the tears started to surface. He felt pathetic, frightened, and confused in a way that hadn't been quite so acute since Gemma's death. The slow march to her end had featured countless such moments, and afterward over time they'd tapered off to a level that would permit him to mostly function. Despite that, Patrick always expected strangers with whom he interacted to see through his facade to the nervous anguish in his gut.

Now it all spiked back up to a volume louder than anything he'd experienced since Gemma had died and Liz had stopped welcoming his arm over her at night.

That night, Patrick dreamed again of a different not-home that was broken and twisted, extending itself at impossible angles, the creaking halls carving illogical pathways. That night, he sensed again the vague suggestion of another presence. That night, he awoke again in terror amid a fresh sense of loss and Elizabeth's attempts to comfort him.

He could not bring himself to tell her about the video. He couldn't hope to explain it to her when he didn't understand it himself. They had enough to worry about at their counseling sessions.

I am the you that doesn't feel terror and loss each day and night. The you that doesn't have to do any of this anymore. The you that never had to do any of this day in and day out for all of existence.

I am the you that looks in the mirror and sees the same person that exists in his mind instead of unrelated images.

I am the you that still knows when and why he began working at this place. I am.

A new e-mail notification flashed on the screen and he quickly minimized his daydreaming.

From: Patrick Wolfe <pwolfe@████industries.com>
To: Patrick Wolfe <pwolfe@████industries.com>
Subject: 7:00 PM

In the body of the e-mail was a familiar diagram of the company's campus, but it indicated a floor and room of one of the manufacturing sites that he'd never been inside. Startled by the strange message, he stood up and looked around the empty floor, unsure what else to do, searching for the eyes he'd sensed the other day. He knew about the security cameras in the office, of course. Those had been there all the years he'd worked here, and he'd long been accustomed to them.

He clicked "Reply", typed "who is this?" into the body of the message, and sent it. It immediately bounced back as undeliverable. Confused, Patrick created a new message as a test and sent it to himself. It immediately showed up in his inbox.

It was 6:30 now, and the location in the e-mail was on the other side of campus. It would take at least 20 minutes to get there on foot, and he wasn't sure he'd be able to find the room quickly. He printed the diagram and quickly left the silent cubicles. A small, distant part of him wondered what Liz was doing and wished she could be here with him. He was unsure if she would even want to be.

Their next counseling session was scheduled for tomorrow night, and he felt a sense of fear about that almost as much as he feared whatever awaited him at Plant C.

The polluted violets of the sun cast over him somber visual allusions to the disease that had taken Gemma as they beamed down now. Her skin had taken on a similar hue toward the end. Patrick felt as though he'd stepped into some transitory limbic zone that operated outside of the rules that bound him to the mundane world of offices and computers. The concrete path that had been carved through the carefully cared-for corporate "forest" was littered with shadows, which felt as though they were seeping into him. The trees inexplicably radiated a quality of never having been born or growing, of having emerged from a factory fully formed.

Gemma's voice spoke in counterpoint to his echoing footsteps, a dying jumble punctuated by the stabbing pain and cruel clarity of the word "daddy."

Patrick's feet felt as weary as his soul, which he could only envision as a diseased halo of grief that attempted to guard him from having to live. Soon, the manufacturing plant and neighboring warehouse appeared out of the tangle of anomalous trees. The last remnants of smoke from the day's production trickled upward from the stacks. He drew closer to the building where the company's products were stored. He couldn't recall which products were stored there. He couldn't recall which products they made. He couldn't recall why they would make them. He couldn't recall how he had come to work at this place, or how he had existed before the Company, or if there had been joy before. The crunching sounds and white noise from the video arose in his mind, adding to Patrick's disorientation even as it seemed to push him toward the plant.

Its distance attained the proportions of his dream and now seemed both a footstep and an eternity away. He felt as though he had stepped back into the nightmare now, that these buildings were also his not-homes, the unplaces among which he spent most of his waking hours.

The gray concrete at the base of the factory was stained with soot and rust colorations that faded up from the dirt, suggesting to Patrick that it had been here for an incalculable length of time, some natural outgrowth emerging as a result of the Earth's processes. His head began to throb, and his mind immediately went to a vision of Gemma when the headaches had first begun to overtake her, some unidentifiable toxin coursing through her veins and arteries and corroding her brain. Not for the first time, he worried the disease would find him next.

How she had grasped at her skull, desperate to pull the pain out and discard it somewhere out in the world that had spawned her.

He looked up in awe at the smokestacks and silver ductwork extending upward and off into various directions suggestive of a cosmic staircase to nowhere and of which he could see only a fraction.

Patrick opened the door and peered into the lobby.

It was deserted, as though it was the middle of the night rather than just the end of a standard day of production.

He felt the empty room seep into his body and become a part of him just like the tree shadows, and in turn it welcomed him as a home to which he was returning for the first time.

The crunching in his ears faded even as he felt it too becoming part of him. Patrick proceeded to the abandoned production floor and walked its length, a journey almost as long as his walk through the corporate forest that sat atop vast networks of tunnels and piping used for the disposal of waste.

Over the gnashing teeth in his ears, he thought he heard the ghostly sounds of the factory in operation, but at a time and place diagonal to this one.

As he approached the end of the production floor, he opened a red double-door and stepped onto a staircase that wound down to the basement, and then the sub-basement, and then a place that had been forgotten behind a cheap door that belonged in a barn rather than a high-tech manufacturing enterprise. A sign, written in faded black marker on a simple white background, said "BOARD" in child-like, sloppy print.

The door opened onto a kind of concrete service tunnel, which looked as though it had been constructed haphazardly with equipment that couldn't possibly have been brought down here. It had the character of a toy bomb shelter whose rear wall extended into a darkness that grew out of the gray. It was the route indicated on the map. The gently curved cement walls framed his vision as he walked cautiously forward through this strange artery.

He felt as though just beyond the persistent, cosmic crunching sound in his mind, he could almost hear his daughter's voice. He pictured her in the video, sleeping in Liz's arms on an unfamiliar bed. And he pictured her in his memory, sleeping in both their arms as she'd died in a building that had stopped feeling like home to her, and that could only be home to his grief now.

The tunnel turned to the right and then began a slight decline. He walked and walked, outside of time, outside of the life that could not possibly be his.

The repetitive crunching sound no longer felt confined to his mind. It now seemed to be emanating from somewhere still further down that was pulling him along like a heart beckoning the blood to return, a future calling for the diseased past to catch up to it.

Patrick heard Gemma's voice wailing briefly through the receding darkness of this not-dream, and then he began to run.

———•—•———

After several twists and turns in the grayscale underbelly of the Company, Patrick stood anxiously in front of what he believed to be the room indicated in the e-mail. His fingers clenched the knob and turned it.

He crept over the threshold into a dark room with unmoving outlines of unknown objects registering as different shades of black. His hand felt around unsuccessfully for a switch on the wall.

One of the outlines disappeared before his eyes, and his ears felt the slight discomfort of a shift in air pressure.

"Hello?" he said softly.

"Shh!" hissed a voice from the darkness.

"Wha–" he began but was cut off by another hiss.

The crunching sound rose again through the walls that separated him from the main hallway where he'd been moments ago. It reached a volume that was almost deafening even from a distance, and then it faded.

"I once overheard someone, or something, say, 'The Company doesn't begin or cease. It just is. Its emergence into existence is a byproduct of its existence." The speaker's voice had an irritating quality to it that he couldn't quite describe to himself. He just knew he wanted it to stop, or to speak more softly.

A dim light came on and Patrick found himself blinking at Other-Patrick from the video, clad in a gray custodial suit.

"I don't know how I got here, exactly," Other-Patrick said. "Other than I woke up next to… Well, I've been hiding down here for awhile. Months, I think. I've seen you many times. Many yous. It keeps happening, and it's tearing me—us—apart."

"Is this some fucking joke?" Patrick said. "What is this? Who are you?" He let his abject confusion be pushed away by his anger at the incoherence of the moment. At the incoherence of a world in which this moment had become not only possible but possibly inevitable.

"The Company isn't what you think it is," Other-Patrick continued, unfazed. "Understand that, first and foremost. Though I don't suppose it matters, the way you feel. You might in some way even now be simply fulfilling a preordained function. You balance numbers all day, right? Preserve a sense of order in the system, even if only in a very small way. You don't have to be able to see the end product to know that. The depth and breadth of information, the tendrils it all creates…"

Patrick squinted at his not-self, and then his mind returned to Gemma. Her death had really been the initial incoherence anyhow, he thought.

"I don't know what the hell this is, but where is my daughter? Take me to her. What the fuck was the video?"

"I will," Other said, with a hint of hesitation. "Soon."

"Now."

"First, you have to understand," Other began. "There's no easy way to say it or hear it, but your daughter isn't really your daughter.

"What the hell are you talking about?" Patrick snapped.

"I mean, she is, but-"

"Just show me. Tell me how you took that video."

Other-Patrick ignored him.

"We're here as part of an ecosystem. A series of processes that fulfills some greater function. But do you even know what it is we do here? Why, or how, this place exists to pump useless objects out into the world? The products create their own demand, which gives the products a reason to have been made. Surely you can grasp that bit, at least. That there's a foreordained mission that exists in a self-justifying loop. What role do you play in it all? The cycle it all makes? The endless cycle…"

Patrick stared at him.

"I'm going to show you something that can't be described, but afterward you'll understand, at least a little. It isn't a bridge, or a consciousness, really. I don't know what it is, but I know that what we see here is only a tiny fraction, a partial cross-section, of the realities that have emerged from it."

Another shelving unit disappeared.

Patrick looked back and forth at the now-vacant space and the Other, fighting off his stomach's inclination to dry-heave at the impossible reality of this particular moment.

"Follow me," Other said.

"You'll be decommissioned in a year or less at this rate, is how it usually goes. You're already showing signs of wear. Atrophy. You'll find yourself too lonely, unable to derive fulfillment from work, that sort of thing. Lethal conflict or suicide is usually the result. A way of naturally recycling the parts when they've outlived their usefulness. Think of it like a T-cell no longer able to respond to foreign entities within a body. Might as well repurpose it, break it down into reusable resources just like the Company does with its materials. Who knows where the waste ends up."

"Are you familiar with the idea of the hyperobject?" Other asked.

Patrick shook his head.

"It's a conjecture that an object, or large-scale event more easily conceived as an object, could possess properties that affect spacetime in ways that seem backward to us, that reach back into the past and move it towards itself. An effect causing its own cause. I've existed in a few of these cross-sections now, due to some glitch, I think. I've met my not-self countless times, and we've all had our sorrows. Remarkably generic but experienced as the most painful of specifics."

Patrick could hear the faint sound of running water somewhere beneath the inexplicable tunnel as the artery wound its way beneath the campus. The floors above them where machinery churned and reshaped and expelled waste. The endless cycle, Other-Patrick had said. He felt a momentary revulsion as the thought of Gemma's disease flashed into his mind, evoked by the unsettling experiences of the evening.

They walked for what felt like hours, progressing further down into the Earth.

"The Company's reach extends far beyond—and behind—its grasp, you might say."

Patrick remained silent.

"There are lots of other Gemmas and Elizabeths. We're not so uncommon either." Other-Patrick held up a phone, the light from the screen cutting through the darkness. "I can show you more. Stop here."

They were at a door constructed of old, rotting wood that looked like it would cave in any moment. Other-Patrick held up his phone again and began taking video with its camera, then pushed on the door. Despite its decrepit state, it opened silently onto a metal walkway in the upper periphery of a vast, dim space. They proceeded down the path to their right as it stretched into the cavernous room. Patrick heard again a distant hint of water, unsure whether or not it was just a part of the natural subterranean ecosystem or in some way connected to the Company. The nausea started to return.

"We should be fine, but stay quiet," Other-Patrick whispered.

After walking hundreds of feet, they descended a staircase and found themselves confronting another factory space. Industrial machinery churned out unidentifiable items, pumping them out onto conveyor belts that took them to the next stop on their journey to life, consumption, waste. The endless cycle. Dozens of massive pieces of equipment operated in impossible silence.

Patrick and Other-Patrick were dwarfed by the metal titans, and their function seemed simultaneously obvious and completely inscrutable. No other living presence seemed to haunt the subterranean factory. Several machines emitted a vapor cloud that resembled equal parts water and rust.

Other motioned Patrick around a rotating turbine attached to a large machine with tubes sticking out like a spider's legs. They walked for another few minutes around and among the industrial behemoths, winding their way toward the center.

"How did all this get down here? And why?" Patrick asked quietly. There was a peculiar quality to the words as they left his throat; they were quieter even than he'd intended, as though their force had been drawn away faster than normal or he'd spoken them into a nearby vacuum incapable of conducting sound.

Before Other-Patrick could answer, the first sound he'd heard other than a whispered voice faded quickly into his ears, eventually culminating in a nauseating POP. Other-Patrick pointed his phone off to the right and caught a portion of another turbine system appearing from nowhere. It spawned in between two other machines, as though it had been meant for that slot all along. It immediately linked the two and began operating silently.

As Other-Patrick approached the center of the factory-cavern floor, Patrick through the half-light could see a spherical object hovering near eye-level, radiating a grayish glow. The closer they got, the sharper Patrick's nausea felt, and he had to pause a couple of times in fear that it would overtake him. They drew within a few feet of the glow.

Without thinking, Patrick stretched his hand out. Somewhere in the back of his mind was a vague notion that this was what would get him to Gemma again. Wherever she was, this would take him there, or nowhere. Either way-

"Don't touch it!" Other-Patrick hissed. He continued filming. After a moment, he whispered over the glow's negating effects, "I think this is its heart, or something like one. Everything seems to emerge from and return here. I don't know where it goes, but I know it opens somewhere. This is not the only..." he motioned at the factoryworks all around, still silently running and emitting its rusty steam.

"The Board–" Patrick began.

"What??"

"Is this the Board?"

Other-Patrick opened his mouth, but Patrick couldn't discern the reply. Within the nebulous boundaries of gray was a field of vantablack that was somehow as painful to look at as a bright light. The gray varied in shade, pulsing with a cold vitality, but the darkness inside negated every hint of life existing at its borders as soon as the gaze passed over it. His sense of time left him, and with it his sense of spatial dimension. The cavernous floor seemed so enormous that he felt constricted. Minutes and hours passed while in thrall to the Company's heart.

The orb began to emit a sound, a low rumbling that soon resolved into a muffled version of the awful crunching Patrick had been hearing.

The combination of the cereal slew and the nausea he'd been combatting became overwhelming. He turned and vomited onto the floor, the splash inaudible over the orb.

"Come on, we should leave while we can," Other-Patrick said into his ear.

Patrick tried to look back into the orb. He'd felt himself drawing closer to Gemma, somehow, even as he felt the black spherical heart intensifying the empty longing of his own. A tug on his arm broke the spell.

"Now."

❦

"I don't know what drives it. I don't think there's anything operating the controls, so to speak," Other-Patrick said after they'd finished the long walk back to the supply room.

"How do those machines just appear and disappear?" Patrick said.

Other shook his head.

"It's not just those."

After moment, he continued.

"Might as well ask a worker bee to put into words the scent instructions they get. Some instinctive thing? I don't know. It's some kind of organism-complex, I think, driven by motives it might understand just as poorly as I do, or possibly unaware even of itself entirely. Maybe no less absurd than anything we do or the systems we create. There are systems of organisms that make us who we are and our bodies are their entire universe. Without them we're nothing. Without us they're nothing. It's not so outlandish to think that maybe we're part of something else we can't realize. In any case, here we both are. This place might really just be one arm, and it has countless other limbs stretching into other realities. I don't know if the Board sits at the head and guides it, or if it's the other way around. But there is something more to them. Have you seen them, walking among you and your colleagues?"

Patrick shook his head.

"They only appear every so often," Other-Patrick said. "And if you see one…" he reached behind him, opened a drawer, and pulled out a handgun. "They're at least partly flesh and blood, I think."

"This is my last one, Patrick," Liz said later that night at the kitchen table. "My last session. We're not going to be able to make this work, and I just don't have it in me to keep trying anymore."

He stared at her. The muted television was informing anyone who could hear that they were receiving reports of a gunman with a manifesto who had opened fire on a congregation.

"It's been 3 years, Pat."

"No, it hasn't," he answered softly.

He felt a breaking inside, distantly, but it was only a partly new sensation. It overlapped with Gemma's absence. An endless cycle of fresh absences.

He stared at Liz.

"And what you said in there tonight! It's one thing to make that kind of shit up for me or yourself, or to have some kind of escape, but in front of our therapist? This isn't right and it can't go on. I've been trying, I really have, but I just can't. I don't even think you remember what it's like to not be the main character in this. It used to be 'us,' and for years now it's been 'you' and 'me.' We don't even know each other anymore."

Patrick couldn't decide what he should think. Maybe Liz was right. Maybe not. He felt as though he'd never be able to pick a side in the battle that had been taking place between the two of them. He didn't remember it starting, only that it went back to Gemma.

The silent mouth on the screen informed the audience to be cautious about upcoming cell phone footage recorded during the shooting.

Patrick looked around, wondering if there were other hims ghost-walking the deteriorating halls somewhere nearby, still blissfully ignorant in their sense of wholeness.

He knew he should fight her in some way, or at least say something, anything really. That was what was supposed to happen at this part of his story.

Patrick didn't dream that night, of Gemma or of anyone else. When he awoke in the darkness, however, he groggily wondered if the lives he was not living could say the same.

I am the you that still knows how to relate to Liz, to other people. I am the you that still feels like he has something in common with his colleagues and friends. The you that still knows something of life.

Patrick saved the file and e-mailed it to his private account.

A new e-mail notification appeared on his screen. He opened it.

From: Patrick Wolfe <pwolfe@█████industries.com>
To: Patrick Wolfe <pwolfe@█████industries.com>
Subject: CLICK NOW

In the body of the e-mail was a link that opened up a live video stream. The gray tunnel appeared in fast motion, suggesting Other-Patrick must be walking swiftly or running.

"Sometimes the disease tricks the body into attacking itself," he muttered. "Sometimes the body attacks itself to kill the disease."

Other-Patrick stopped at a door that they must have passed without noticing when Patrick had been down there. Inside were rows and rows of tall shelving units stretching back as far as the camera could see. The view proceeded down one of the aisles, displaying large glass containers on all the shelves. The camera turned and inside one of the containers was Gemma.

Patrick stifled a scream, his eyes widening.

More containers were brought into the field of vision, showing more Gemmas. Five, ten, two dozen Gemmas, at least. There were other bodies of unfamiliar people, some unique and some duplicated as many times as his daughter's.

He stood up and ran to the exit, paying no heed to the few pairs of eyes that followed him from other cubicles.

The organisms that circulate through the arteries etched into the world carry out their duties, monitoring and sanitizing, attacking foreign bodies, helping new cells to generate new life and systems. There is an equilibrium present, but only from certain vantage points both spatial and temporal. From others, it appears as a vast asymmetry that never balances, never resolves, and never ends.

Patrick ran, huffing, down the corporate forest path toward the factory. The desperation sidelined the strangeness of what he'd just seen, but a distant part of him struggled to figure out what he'd do when he got there. He crashed into the BOARD door and kept moving quickly down toward the tunnel.

When he found the supply room, he discovered a different layout. Some shelving units were missing, others were present in different configurations.

"Hey!" he called out. No response.

Patrick frantically searched until he identified the desk with the gun, grabbed it, and studied it for a moment, unsure if he'd be able to actually fire if necessary. He burst back into the tunnel to the sound of running water and continued searching for the door from the video stream.

After several frantic minutes he gave up and headed for the underground factory, hoping the other Patrick would be there so he could force him to answer more questions. The crunching sound returned as he saw the door. He opened it and crept cautiously along the metal walkway on the route they'd taken previously, but this time as he arrived at the first set of steps he could sense activity below.

Patrick quietly descended to the floor, trying to use the equipment as cover. The gray glow at the center of the floor became dimly visible between the machines as he moved. On the opposite side, hundreds of feet away, he could vaguely discern a series of pneumatic tubes that stretched from the ceiling and halfway down to the floor before each bent and fed into one of the machines. He could occasionally see a blur of motion shooting through the tube and disappearing into the machine.

Then he glimpsed more movement, but this time it was on the floor below the bend in one of the tubes.

There was a sudden loud POP near the glowing vacuum orb, and three humanoid figures emerged into the space just beyond the gray light. They were taller than anybody Patrick had ever seen, and vaguely shaped like people. Their faces were unusually thin and tapered. They wore suits that looked painted onto their strangely proportioned bodies as camouflage.

From one of the tube-machines emerged a young child. The boy hopped down from an external tray that jutted out from the machine and walked rigidly toward the three suited figures, which bent over and seemed to inspect him. Finally, they each spat a gob of gray, viscous liquid onto him that distributed itself evenly from head to toe, and in a few seconds it was absorbed into his body.

The boy blinked and walked into the gray glow, then proceeded to slowly dive into the vantablack center, his dimensions shrinking as he plunged in and disappeared.

Patrick stifled a cry as he saw Gemma descend from the machine next and walk toward the three silent tall figures.

Then he heard his own voice, muffled but shrieking from behind the machine that had expelled Gemma and the boy. Other-Patrick charged toward the Board and Gemma, bellowing uncontrollably. Patrick was frozen with fear. He knew he should be charging them, trying to save Gemma from whatever bizarre fate was in store for her. He should be trying to save his not-self.

The tall things immediately turned toward Other-Patrick and fell upon him. Their thin mouths open as much on a vertical plane as a horizontal one, and they bit into him like wild animals with an unsettling silence. Other-Patrick's screams were still muffled by the dampening effect of the orb. They tore him to pieces in a matter of seconds as Patrick's heart beat faster, circulating the blood through his arteries at impossible speeds fueled by desperation and guilt at the cowardice that had frozen him into inaction.

The Board walked back to the orb-heart, surrounded it, and opened their mouths again, this time expelling pieces of Other-Patrick into its center. The wads of chewed flesh shrank and disappeared into the darkness. Then the Board turned back to Gemma as if nothing had happened.

That got Patrick moving. He ran toward them, unsure if he should fire into the orb or the suited bodies. Gemma stood still, ten feet from the orb and fifty feet from him, seemingly unaware of anything. He took care to stop in a position that wouldn't put her in danger.

Filled with the dueling profound revulsions of having lost his daughter and never having had the daughter he'd thought, Patrick raised the gun and started to fire.

Later that day, reports began to trickle into the news cycle that another workplace shooting, and possibly an explosion of some kind, had occurred. Details were scarce, but a portion of the Company's factory had sunk into the earth, creating a fissure on the main production floor that destroyed countless products and some of the machinery that generated them.

According to these reports, the alleged shooter was a white male employee who, after opening fire on some of the Company's board members, had been shot dead by armed security personnel responding to the scene. The reports indicated that the shooter's wife had recently decided to file for divorce. News anchors informed the audience that they had been experiencing financial difficulties in the wake of expensive medical bills incurred by their daughter's illness and eventual death.

"I was just doing my job, neutralizing a threat" stated one of the responding security guards in front of a camera for the whole town to see. "I just want to put this behind me so we can move on, though. I don't know why a senseless thing like this occurs."

At a press conference, a Company spokesperson expressed shock and regret at the incident.

Surviving coworkers described the gunman as "nice," "amicable," "professional." They shook their heads and trailed off, unsure what more to say.

The shooting received a day of national coverage, and then the news mostly moved on in its endless cycle. The Company only showed up in local coverage when there was relevant new information over the ensuing weeks, such as an anomalous finding in the autopsy of the gunman indicating apparent severe animal bites from a species unidentifiable by the coroner or available experts.

Mentioned in another update a few weeks later on local news was the release of information about a journal the gunman had kept, titled "Many Lives Theory: A Manifesto." The full text was not made available to the public, but Elizabeth was asked several times by authorities if she could provide any insights that might help investigators determine its significance.

LIZ:

After all these months I pace these halls now and smell a life in them that I can't remember before. Gone are the incessant phone calls and letters, finally. Gone the sense of activity punctuated by the stillness of the missing. After all this, I no longer hear the floorboards creaking. There are no ghosts here any longer, if there ever were at all, and it isn't the same house. But I have to carry the ghost of who I used to be with me to whatever home awaits me. I don't think I know this person who used to be me, but I feel a sense of sorrow when I try to look into her eyes or ask her a question. We wouldn't understand one another even if we could speak directly. But I no longer have to see Gemma's empty room and think that her ghost is in there rather than in me. I do not see sickness in her bedroom.

Thankfully, there are many houses that are not this one.

There isn't a future for that me, maybe not really for anyone. If there is, it's already in the present at all times, and the present is nothing but the atomic limits of a knife's edge, which cuts into us and infects us every day with its contagions. What can it even mean to speak of futures?

When I look through these windows in between the hours I'm at the office, the sun doesn't seem to break down into its usual old sickly hues, which were never beautiful to me, like it used to. I don't know if this is a change in my perception or a change in reality, if there's even a difference, but that is all that can be said of anything.

I am no longer haunted by the sensation of being seen by a man who isn't there.

For all of these things, I'm grateful, but I know my gratitude will one day end and the contagion that is grief will begin again to rush through these veins back to my heart.

VACUI

Jane Sand

Graciela was sweeping. David had talked about getting rid of her — said we couldn't afford her and I needed to pick up more slack around the house. I guess my departure meant he'd changed his mind and kept her on.

Charlotte sat on the bottom porch step, feet barely reaching the ground. She was picking her nose with increasing confidence and skill, finally fishing out a perfect snotflower on the tip of her finger, which she contemplated for some while in awed wonder.

I sat beside her and watched. Before, I'd've been trying to make her stop, to distract her, worrying that it would become a habit, that other people might see. Now, I didn't mind, just enjoyed the sight of her wide blue eyes, her curls flashing true gold in the sun—David's child all over, almost nothing of me there. I suppose not having a body anymore means that anxiety (heart quickening, muscles tensing, gut fluttering) had no place to take hold, and didn't plague me anymore. That fearfulness (she'll be hurt, she'll turn out wrong, I must watch over her and be certain at all times) that I'd always felt about Charlotte was gone, leaving only the love.

And yet, sitting here beside her, watching her, amused, loving her—I feel more like I have a body again. I feel more clearly than before that I am actually *sitting* on these steps. I can feel the rough wood under my fingertips, feel the warmth of the sun, even the clothes I would've been wearing (cut-offs and a t-shirt, feels like) if I had a real body to sit here in. I feel myself smile, reach out to stroke Charlotte's hair.

Her curls stir as if in a breeze. She flinches away, gets up and trots across the lawn to Graciela and hugs her bare leg (oh dear, those sticky hands).

"Que pasa, mami?"

"S'cold!" answered Charlotte, evidently disapproving.

Graciela looked up, wiping sweat from her upper lip. The breeze stirred her hair, too, and the leaves of the lilac behind her. "Un viento maluco," she murmured, looking uneasy.

I moved back, feet becoming indefinite, drifting back instead of walking. The breeze died away.

Me?

I drift about the kitchen like an orphaned thought balloon in a comic strip panel, without a character to attach to. I usually have no feeling of having a body, walking with it; drifting is definitely the right word. It doesn't really bother me. It isn't that different from the way I spent most of my adolescence, often feeling barely there, unaware of myself except as a disembodied floating point of view. There were times I'd pass by a mirror and feel startled to see someone reflected there.

My tackle is gone from the counter—the pump accessories, the glucose monitor. No insulin vials in the refrigerator; I see the gap when Graciela takes out the rice for dinner. Once upon a time seeing that emptiness would have set off a panic attack—I used to count each vial obsessively. Now — no palpitations, no shortness of breath. I am splendidly indifferent. Of *course* he threw them out; why be reminded?

Charlotte is coloring at the table. I watch from the furthest corner of the kitchen. I've been avoiding getting too close to Charlotte; I don't want to scare her. Charlotte's gripping the crayon better than she used to. I remember the warm weight of her on my lap, my faint, weary pleasure as we scribbled together. Charlotte looks almost three. Time has passed, but I feel no urgency about it. It's not just not having a body to feel distress with that keeps me so calm. I *should* be distressed. What am I doing here?

David. I want to see David. But then his voice resounds sharply from the next room. He's berating someone on the phone—a client, from what I can hear. Charlotte looks up, frowning. I remember how

I used to cringe at that tone, knowing that he often would go too far and drive away the client...always for good reasons, which he would *always* explain exhaustively to me afterwards, and he'd take that same tone of voice with me if I ever — however gently — questioned his interpretation. I'm not cringing now, but I'll wait until he's calm, when I can look on his face with unalloyed pleasure. I drift through the ceiling with disembodied ease.

The attic's stairs end right under the roof peak. When I walked to the top of the stairs I could stand straight with my head barely clearing the roof. When David came up the stairs he would usually crack his skull on the ceiling unless he remembered to duck. The attic was my place, my desk up here under the window. Before Charlotte was born I would design websites and (when I was lucky) paint illustrations and a book cover now and then. All freelance, of course. When I wasn't paid for a few months (as usually happened) I would sic David on them. He would send threatening letters in his best legalese, which would often shake the money free. We had an easy camaraderie then, at least until David's fledgling practice slowed down and we actually started *needing* what I earned.

I didn't come up here for at least two months after Charlotte was born. She was so heavy (almost eleven pounds at birth; a sugarbaby, the doctor called her). I was afraid to carry her from the start; she seemed so unwieldy. When I held her I felt like I was balancing a line of crystal goblets along my arm, fragile little skull, rib cage, pelvis, legs, all precariously lined up and seeming ready to slide one way or another. Surely I would drop her, I would shake her, I would damage her, often I could feel *nothing* but fear toward her. And I was so tired, the first few months, lugging Charlotte around, like a big white larvae slimy with saliva and tears weighing me down. Climbing the stairs to the attic with her was unthinkable.

The sky is cloudless afternoon blue through my dormer window. Funny, it was evening down in the kitchen. I suppose time passes differently for me now. There's a lovely patch of sunshine on my desk. My paintings are stacked around it; David's stripped them from the walls and brought them up here. My Macbook is gone. Did David take it? To use himself? To sell on Ebay? I didn't mind. I'd never liked the damn thing, though I had to use it for most jobs. I worked in light pencil and watercolors, and only scanned the paintings to clean up the imperfections in Photoshop. People in the illustration business like the handmade look, but won't tolerate too many flaws. It was the drawing and painting that I loved. I look at my watercolors, at the pencils still sharpened like spears. For a moment I wonder if my love of art will remake my arm to grip the 6H pencil—my favorite for drawing an outline that wouldn't smear with watercolor. The number 2 sable brush. But they stay still, and I drift bodilessly about, and don't care. The pencils don't leap up and start to draw on the dusty hot-press paper. I don't feel the faint ache in my fingertips from gripping too hard, and in my back and neck from hunching, though I remember them vividly. And yet as I look at my desk, the window above it framing a perfect summer sky (cerulean, shading to delicious cobalt) I *do* feel the bated-breath excitement I felt when a drawing or painting was coming out really well, each hesitant stroke a line closer to what I had in mind, forgetting myself in the wonder. I am drifting toward the window, I realize, toward the sky, feeling that soft, quiet joy, moving toward an immensity of richest expectation...

I jerk myself back into the house. I don't want to leave. I flee downward, to David's study...and yes, the picture's still there, the only one he kept where he could see it, the only one of my works he loved even more than I did.

He was so beautiful. Always so beautiful.

———◆———

When I was five and our parents were friends, he and my brother would sneer down at me from the lofty age of seven, and leap into the deep end of the pool without me—golden-haired David looking like a Renaissance *putto* with a bratty smirk. I disdained them in turn, preferring David's teenage brother, a good-natured, muscular young Thor in Speedos, who could sometimes be persuaded to give me piggyback rides. I clung to his neck, enjoying my imposing height, and admired his blonde hair, which had darkened to a lovely fawn. I was myself a moderately cute kid with russet-brown hair, sturdy and strong, and thus perfect in ways I didn't appreciate at the time.

I stopped trusting my body around age six, when I'd started feeling weak and ravenous, and peeing a lot (sometimes involuntarily). Having public toiletry accidents more than once at school did not make me popular with my first-grade peers. Even when the problem was diagnosed as Type I diabetes and treated, things didn't just clear up, either medically or in my social life. I had to learn to stick my finger and draw blood every day to monitor glucose, to use the insulin syringe, eventually the pump. My body was an adversary I had to watch over with deep suspicion.

As for school, I discovered that while dropping a tear was infallible bullybait, serene indifference *could* eventually bore taunters if you could simulate it long enough, convincingly enough—I'm talking *years*, here. My parents alternated overprotective coddling with vague resentment, as if I'd deliberately become ill to reflect poorly on them. I learned to keep my head down, grimly manage my illness, be ever inconspicuous. My parents were relieved to boast of my bravery and leave my care up to me, turning back to my flawless brother. At school I did my best to blend into every background and stay invisibly reading and drawing while I rebuilt my dignity, with an iron determination *never* to be humiliated again. My family moving to another city when I was twelve made things easier, leaving behind the people who'd seen me at my worst. David and his family never had; we went to different schools even before we moved, and my family cut down on the socializing a *lot* when I became ill. We didn't meet again for a long time.

I survived high school, had life down to a manageable task by then. In college I really came into my own, as many do. I was as healthy as I'd ever been since I was first diagnosed. I was thin without sickly scrawn; even the port on my flat belly had a cyborg-like charm (or so Brian, my first boyfriend, told me. He came later, though.)

I'd learned the art of draping myself over sofas and chairs in elegant attitudes, and staying so to conceal the fatigue I still often felt. I would draw people and toss the drawings at their begetters, and occasionally let drop carefully rehearsed wisecracks. (They sounded impromptu, as they should. They would occur to me while I listened to conversations around me, and I would save them till the right moment, which would always return. People say the same things over and over, if you really listen to them. Missed an opening? No matter. Hang out with the same people long enough, and your chance to briefly shine will come again).

People liked the laughs, and the drawings. However much they protested that that wasn't what they *really* looked like, they were flattered that someone had truly *looked* at them...and the drawings got better, over time.

I made a few cautious friendships. Lacking natural instincts for social interaction with one's preferred sex, I invented Great Truths to guide me, my (limited) experience distilled into wisdom. The First Truth I don't remember—which probably means it lacked essential Truth. The Second Truth was "Never eat an ice cream cone in front of a dirty old man"—and I will stand by that as an Absolute Truth till the end of time. The Third Truth came later, after David.

David transferred to my college in my second year, after he changed majors and his parents told him to go someplace less expensive. I'd been vaguely conscious of David and his family through social media, I recognized him when I saw him again, but to see him in the flesh—I'd faked Apollonian detachment long enough for it to feel real to me. My loves till I saw David were all for heroes of books and movies and TV (I was a champion fanfic writer and illustrator); all perfectly safe targets. Seeing David in the flesh threw me rudely back into my body and made me feel and want with it, want something terrifyingly possible, a love theoretically, frighteningly attainable.

By instinct I did exactly the right thing—immediately hid every indication of what I felt. I presumed on our long acquaintance to treat him with condescending sisterly bonhomie, which amused a guy who'd never actually *had* sisters. It was partly the old reflex to avoid humiliation by exposure, but I think I also had an intimation of the Greatest Truth I ever learned, even then. I knew in my bones that if I let him know what I felt, made myself vulnerable that way, he might laugh at me good-naturedly or even take me up on it a time or two, and let me drop—but he'd *never* take me seriously.

He gave me lifts in his dad's hand-me-down SUV, and sometimes he would drive too fast, to scare me. He'd shit himself laughing as I slid carefully into theatrical prayers and screaming hysterics—and though I *was* somewhat scared, I was also giving a performance of what I thought he wanted. He enjoyed it, I'm sure.

We were in summer semester that year—he to catch up, me to graduate early. He made friends fast, expanded my limited social circle. In return, I would occasionally host gatherings that his dorm wouldn't accommodate. I had moved into my parents' basement apartment; they had semi-retired and spent a lot of time in Florida (I think my parents always *wanted* to be old). I staked out a comfy corner, a watercolor kit propped up beside me on the ratty old couch (well stained with previous spills). It was there after a barbeque on a sultry hot day that he stretched out on the carpet near my couch, shirtless after sweating over the grill.

I've found that ugly people are easier for me to paint than beautiful ones—in Life Drawing classes I always tranquilly addressed myself to the challenge of sketching the ninety year old man, carefully rendering his liver spots and pacemaker without a qualm. But beautiful people always put me under pressure—they move me more, and it is so much harder to do them justice. And David, lying there beside me—*David*—

I hastily scratched the outline of his body with my pencil as he lay stretched out, avoiding his gaze when his blue eyes sleepily opened on occasion. I sketched his features, working quickly — this wasn't Life Drawing, he might not stay still as long as I needed. While correcting a few lines with eraser I fumbled the pencil, which went spinning to the floor. With a deep breath, I took up my brush and began to paint.

A mix of Yellow Ochre and Burnt Umber with just a touch of Alizarin Crimson, diluted to a thin wash, to paint the first glaze of skin and hair, leaving just a few spots white for the glints in his eyes, his hair, the places the sun from the window highlighted him. Shadows, with more brown, to shade the jaw and cheekbones, to round out the arms and torso and outline the muscles of the chest and belly. He takes on solidity and dimension. God, I hate the words 'abs' and 'pecs'; so lame. They don't convey the fluid strength and softness. Even the Latin... *Pectoralis major...abdominis rectus* doesn't sound good enough without being modified by words like *gracilis. Formosus.*

Washes of Cadmium Yellow and Raw Sienna to add more gold to his hair. The thinnest wash of Alizarin Crimson, just enough for the flesh to take on warmth and life. Another coat for the face, the hands, which always flush more. His colors were pale, misty, as if I had exhaled him in a delicate film of colored frost on a windowpane. But then I painted the background around him a darker green-brown. The elderly shag carpeting he lay on was faded to that color, but I darkened it, dappled with lighter patches, as if he lay in a forest glade. The paleness of his flesh became a virtue; with that dark cool color around him his figure sprang to greater life, as if on that tree-shaded mossy ground he had been caught in a stray sunbeam, gleaming rose and gold.

I added the last details. His eyes are the blue of a spring sky with gray streaks of cloud. They make a startling contrast with his golden brown skin and hair—he's the rare blond who tans well. Our gazes met for a moment—he'd noticed what I was doing, was mildly curious. I turned back to my painting. It was the best thing I'd ever done, I knew. When the paint dried I peeled the drawing off the pad. I wanted so badly to keep it. But I negligently tossed it at him.

I heard him draw in his breath as he looked at it, but when he glanced up at me I was already turning away to retrieve my pencil, as if that were the only thing on my mind. He liked it, I could tell when I risked a passing glance. I saw him looking at me with new eyes before returning his gaze to the picture, which he did frequently for the rest of that night. Paulina, his girlfriend, looked over his shoulder and made a great fuss—effusive Russian Paulina, who was going through an Anglophile phase and wanted to be called Polly, pretty Polly. Paulina loved the painting, and immediately demanded one of herself. She volunteered to do it topless as David had, and pulled off her shirt to whistles from Brian and Craig, which drew David's attention from the picture. He besought her to cover up with a laugh, though there was a bit of an edge to it. Polly appealed to me as the artist to decide. I split the difference and told her one tit was enough, and posed her draped with a blue afghan for proper contrast. She let me; I'd acquired some authority I hadn't had before.

All credit to Paulina, she was an excellent model, and yes, beautiful. But I felt much more confident, as if that painting of David had been an apprenticeship in itself. Technically, Paulina's painting came out even better than David's; she posed longer, I kept hold of the pencil and could render her in more sharp fiddly detail. She loved it; I still saw it appear now and then on her Facebook feed years later. But David's picture had more power. He knew it, too. I had won some ground with him, and had to act as if it meant nothing to me. It hurt to give up the picture, but it was a gamble that ultimately paid off, wasn't it? I got the picture back, eventually. Here it is, in my house, on the wall of David's study.

I lost my virginity because of David. Not *to* him, *because* of him. Brian, who was a nice guy I mildly liked, asked me into the back bedroom just when David's eye happened to fall on me, at another party. I gave Brian my hand, and went. I divined it was best that David think of me as desired—and maybe, eventually, desirable. It dismayed me to eventually brush off Brian, who clung harder than I'd expected. I hurt his feelings in a way I hadn't meant to, thus proving my Third Great Truth of Human Relationships: "Indifference is the greatest aphrodisiac. Unfortunately, it cannot be faked."

I stand by it as now the Greatest Truth, all the more because my relationship and marriage to David almost, *almost* proved it wrong.

I hear David's voice now, only his. He's on the phone. I'm too far away to hear the words, but I know that sweet cajoling tone.

I got to know that tone after I graduated, while he was in law school. He was still with Paulina then. They came apart gradually, with melodramatic explosions punctuated by smashed glasses, interspersed with reconciliations, often in front of an interested gathering of friends. Their audience was dwindling, though; people going off to jobs or post-grad school. I stayed around; the graphic design job I'd picked up paid horribly but let me work from home a lot. I hadn't taken up with anyone after breaking up with Brian (I sincerely didn't want to hurt anyone else that way, and guiltily hid from myself any other consideration). I was convenient.

I listened to David. He really *had* been having a hard time; he'd been cut from the soccer team even though he'd once had hopes of turning professional, the band he'd been playing bass with came to nothing (justifiably, I thought, though did not say). He'd finally come around to pre-law, as his family had wanted him to do to join his father's firm. Though it ultimately suited him best, it had been hard for him to give up other choices. Paulina had chafed at his increasingly boring lifestyle as he finally graduated and plunged into law school (he was bright and driven, when he felt like it).

I'd learned David by observing him. You *could* convince David he was wrong by questioning him sidewise, gently joking about the missteps he'd taken in reaching his conclusions. If done delicately enough, he sometimes *did* give in, with a rueful laugh at his own pretensions. But if you told him flat-out he was wrong about something he'd decided, he'd dig in his heels and double down. And it was just not in Paulina to do other than tell him he was being an idiot and demand he go with her to California where she hoped to find designer work, or Europe, or somewhere else - her plans changed from one argument to the next, though not his answer.

He would call her, his voice wooing her back. When he failed, he'd angrily hang up on her and turn to me to complain. I judged their disagreements with severe evenhandedness, telling him when I thought Paulina was at least partially in the right. I'd also tell him they were both being horribly tedious, sometimes amusingly enough to get a laugh out of him. My behavior was impeccable. In all their fights I was never blamed for being the third person that each accused the other (often justifiably) of having. I barely admitted even to myself what I wanted. I passed up many chances to say something, at moments when he was vulnerable. There was guilt about it, yes, but also a sure deep intuition. Wait long enough, and your time to shine always comes again.

They finally broke up in one last spectacular fight, ending with her move to the West Coast, which hurt him more than he'd wanted to let her know.

He told me instead. His friends had mostly gone in different directions after graduation, and law school didn't leave him much energy to seek out the ones left. I was there. I listened, sometimes late into the night. And one night, especially late, I lazily held out an arm to him, the same sort of casual, negligent gesture with which I'd tossed him the painting, as if I didn't much care whether my offering was accepted or refused.

It wouldn't have lasted between us if I'd done it sooner, or later. We started at just the moment he'd decided to settle down and get serious with his life, and before he started feeling disillusioned by that. Our families liked each other and were glad. Things started to hitch when he argued with his dad soon after graduation and decided he would go into practice on his own. But even then we got along well enough, and I heard that sweet wheedling tone from him after our arguments.

Everything went to hell after I got pregnant. The birth was difficult, my recovery long and weary. My blood sugar went out of control during the pregnancy, and never really went back to normal afterwards. After my third visit to the ER with either a faint from hypoglycemia or sugar too high to register on my home meter, my endocrinologist shrugged his shoulders. Probably stress hormones were causing the in-stability. There was nothing he could do besides recalibrate my insulin dosage over and over, and prescribe antidepressants which my mother and David's mother agreed I ought not to take while breastfeeding. Quailing under their critical gaze, I did without them. The thinness that was willowy grace when I was healthy turned lank and slack and strengthless. But I really think the worst thing was letting David see my façade crack, letting him see I needed him, telling him how leaden and tired and hopeless I felt. He helped when I asked at first, but I could see the disappointment in his face, the gradually increasing impatience, the realization that I was not what he'd thought I was. And then, after noticing that Paulina said on Facebook she was coming to the city but David didn't mention it at all, I heard him using that tone on the phone. Then he left the phone around, unlocked and open to his text messages.

My temper blows every seven years or so. The blast is exhilarating and shameful. Finding out about Paulina was the angriest I ever re-member being. Half the dishes on our wedding shower wish list got broken that night.

I never aimed at his head. Really, I threw most of them at the wall as I screamed, and the worst I did was wing him on the hip and ankle. The involuntary grin that kept flicking across his features, his grace-ful dodges, his non-apologies that were so shittily self-serving that he seemed to be willfully *trying* to further piss me off—it all convinced me he was enjoying it at some level. He finally carried me to bed, where I left scratches up and down his back. It was the most intense it had ever been, but I had a sick migraine the next day as I swept up the smashed porcelain (no way was I going to explain that to Graciela). If that was what he wanted from me, I couldn't give it to him. The next time I found his phone open to his texts, sitting enticingly balanced on the edge of the bathroom sink in the middle of the night, I accidentally on purpose knocked it into the toilet and went back to bed.

I avoided confrontation after that, at all costs. I meekly agreed to cut Graciela's days to twice a month — the economy had taken a downturn, David's fledgling practice was slow, and I had to pull my weight. I admitted every fault as soon as blamed for it. I groveled, I apologized at all times, I was a world class competitor at the Olympic half-cringe. I grimly narrowed my focus to doing what I could with the energy I had, keeping Charlotte fed and clean while calculating how much housework I could manage to keep David's complaints to a minimum without melting in tears with exhaustion. Some distant day, when Charlotte was finally toilet trained (perhaps while doing her graduate thesis) I might gather enough will to look squarely at my situation and decide what to do. Till then, I lived day to day. Mostly I kept things quiet and uneventful between us. I would turn away when I felt tears spring to my eyes (God, how I *hated* to cry) lest David see and give me that get-*over*-it-already look. Once in a great while, I still would complain. One morning after a sleepless night (Charlotte was quiet, I just couldn't sleep) I found myself telling him exactly how much insulin, of which different kinds I could put in a large syringe and inject precisely *here* on my abdomen port, to go into a coma and die.

It didn't start a fight, or make him angry, the kind of anger that would make him scream at me and harangue me for hours until I damned well admitted he was right and I was wrong. He just looked at me and said, briefly and effectively, "Do it if you really mean it, and if you don't, stop fucking whining. I'm sick of it."

A faint rattle, like a handful of dice thrown on the parquet floor. I can't hear David anymore, he must've hung up. I drift off to investigate the source of the noise. It takes a while to find it; I amuse myself by rising to survey the living room from heights never attained in life. Looking down from the ceiling, I spot what made the sound; a knick-knack has fallen. It was a creepy plaster sculpture of disembodied hands clasping, a wedding gift from one of David's cousins. I'd told David it looked like two Things from the Addams Family. He laughingly agreed to put it at the top of the bookcase where we could point to it if his family asked about it, but otherwise never have it within our line of sight. Now it lies in pieces behind the bookcase. I doubt anyone will notice for a while; only one or two fragments have fallen far enough to be visible to the living room at large. Graciela might miss it while sweeping. Both she and I are (I *was*, anyway) a bit slapdash about that kind of thing when cleaning, a fact both David's mother and my own never failed to point out when they visited.

———— ◆ ————

Charlotte is mewling in her sleep—a familiar sound; even after she started sleeping through the night, she would often get nightmares. I walk down the corridor toward her reflexively, as I did over hundreds of nights at that whimpering sound, urgently wanting to soothe her before she got loud enough to wake David, before she got loud enough to jolt me with that pang of mixed anger and guilt her full-throated cry always set off in me. I remember trying to crush down my resentment at being awakened *again* when it was so hard to get to sleep at all in those months, so dazed that I twice made the turn into her room too early and smacked into the wall face first. But I feel no anxiety or irritation now. I go to her with a sense of well-being that I rarely felt before.

I hardly notice out of the corner of my eye my silhouette as I pass the mirror on her closet door in the night-lit room. I feel my arms stretch out to her. I feel my lips smile. I slide my hand under her head, feeling her sweat-damp curls. I put my other arm around her and pull her close, a gesture so natural that I don't even wonder at the bedclothes shifting under my touch. A little rocking and a soft croon would usually soothe her without waking her all the way up. She went quiet, as she usually did.

But as I lift her (I'm *lifting* her) I see she's not asleep. Her face has paled, and her eyes are gleaming in the faint glow of her nightlight. They are bright, so bright because they are open wide, and her spine beneath my hand is bent backward hard, a rigid bow. Her breath is a faint whistle, growing fainter, and stopping, stopping completely.

She slips from my grasp (not hands, I don't have hands anymore as I back away), and falls back to the mattress with a thump—I'd only lifted her an inch or two. She finally draws in a great wheezing gasp, and squeaks faintly on the exhale. I've backed to the door when she draws in another breath and lets it out in a drilling shriek.

I shrink away from David as he comes stumbling into the room, turning on the light, still mostly asleep. Charlotte's shriek has winded her, but at least the wheeze is fading when she draws in breath to scream again. David picks her up and rocks her a little. He looks more puzzled than alarmed. Charlotte's color has returned, and she has enough breath and presence of mind back that she can scream words, or a word. *"Cold!"*

David looks around, sees her bedroom window is open a crack, slams it shut. She clings to him with arms and legs, and starts shrieking again when he tries to put her back to bed. With an exasperated sigh, he carries her back to the master bedroom. As he moves toward me down the corridor I shrink further away. The sight of him, his tired eyes, the faint light shining on his hair—even from the other end of the corridor that I've withdrawn to, it makes me yearn, want to cry with the eyes I suddenly feel I have. He'll tuck Charlotte in beside him. He won't have much of a problem getting back to sleep, he never did. He joggles her gently in his arms, murmuring soothing nonsense words. He's such a good dad.

I flee to the attic. Once there, I'm calm again. It all seems equally unreal as I mull things over, drifting in slow circles like an errant dust-mote in a sunbeam.

And Atys with his bloodstained knife were better than the thing I am.

Oscar Wilde, wasn't it? I can't exactly look it up, though the books are still on the shelves, just where I left them. David doesn't read.

I don't remember what the poem was about. The poet was express-ing self-loathing, I *do* remember that. *The thing I am.* The thing that doesn't feel horror at what it just did to Charlotte. There is a distant regret. But it seems self-loathing just isn't the same without the pound-ing heart, the grinding of teeth, the roil of nausea and the caving in of your stomach.

It's more than that. Parts are missing from me. The part that *should* be revolted at what I've done. The part that *should* feel scalding shame at the things that seem clear to me now, like the fact that me keeping far from David despite my yearning means I love him more than I ever loved Charlotte. Before, I would have hotly denied it to everyone, to myself. But looking at it now, I accept it serenely as the truth, and am hardly bothered by it.

Why is this happening? And though things are missing from me, other things are left. Because my mind, seemingly sharp as ever despite the lack of a cerebrum to house it in, goes calmly to work on the question.

Why *cold?* Why do they sense me as cold when I feel I radiate warmth and love when I'm near them?

I was no STEM student, but I used to be a bit of a science fiction buff. I remember that when the space traveler's ship has a hole blown in the hull, the people in the ship may *perceive* the cold blackness outside to be willfully and malevolently pulling them outward to death. But in fact it's their own warm life-preserving atmosphere that is rushing out to try to fill an infinite emptiness, and insensately taking them with it.

When I'm near them, I feel I have a body again. I can feel with it. I can even touch them, *move* them. When I'm near them, the body I've lost remakes itself, its breath and strength and sinew. And isn't it a fundamental law of the universe that you can't make something out of nothing? Am I *taking* something from them when I touch them, to do what I do? Something important, vital? I remember suddenly, very clearly, Charlotte's pallor, the faint bluish tint around her lips as I held her, her unnaturally quiet breathlessness, her convulsively arched back against my arms.

A theory; maybe in life I never got quite enough of the love of soul and body together. No, I don't *mean* to hurt them, certainly, when I touch them. But the way I lived, my wraith's existence, feeding my desires on art and moonbeams, looking at life and love from outside for too long, and losing them too soon after tasting them briefly—maybe it left an emptiness. And when I get too close to them now, the life and the warmth I craved and never *quite* got enough of rushes from them to me, to fill that infinite emptiness.

I love them. But what is love like, without conscience, without remorse?

I notice it is evening, and that I am in the living room, the furthest corner. I stay scrupulously back as I look toward the entry, where David is handing over Charlotte to Jessica, my sister-in-law. I like Jessica; she adores Charlotte and was always happy to babysit, though she and my brother live too far away to do it often. She and David exchange a few stiff words. I always got the impression she didn't much care for David (and vice versa) but they are civil and Charlotte is glad to see her aunt. Jessica takes the small bag David's packed and leaves with her. David withdraws to his study. He calls someone, I hear again the caressing tone in his voice.

I withdraw to the attic. I remember waking up in the middle of the night with a chill on my midriff, blinking sleepily in the dim light as David fumbles with my insulin port, the flash of a syringe in his hand, me looking on in dazed incomprehension (or complicity?) I remember also preparing the syringe myself, lying in bed rolling it in my fingers as David snored faintly beside me. Both memories share the same dream-like quality. Both were things I fantasized about, in the days of my exhaustion and David's resentful looks. Though I remember clearly the feel of the bedclothes on my limbs, the sleep weighing my lids, I feel no emotion relating to either memory. Neither of them seems real, or particularly important. Maybe neither ever happened.

I look around the attic. My window at this late hour frames a beautiful midnight blue sky with a crescent moon, but I don't feel drawn to it. For better or worse, I'm staying, and I'm staying for the soft sweet murmur of his voice in the bedroom below, under my feet.

I walk (I *walk*) down the attic stairs. I feel my body again—not the tired woman of the last days, furiously wiping her tearful eyes as if they were shameful weeping sores. Not even the guarded college girl in her carefully careless pose, vigilantly and ceaselessly enacting poise and wit and strength that she never really felt as hers. I've never felt better than right now.

The voices have died down. The bedside lamp is on in the master bedroom. They are asleep. It's Paulina with him in the bed. Because of course it is.

I smile at him. I feel no anger...how could I blame him? Love wells warmly up in me. The woman sleeping next to David doesn't matter. It might not even be Paulina, though it *does* look like her; the pale skin of her back, the brassy assisted gold of her hair. Regardless, she's unimportant. What matters is David, here, now. His thinning hair, the lines etched on his forehead barely register. All I see is the beautiful golden boy I painted, my Endymion.

I listen raptly to the soft rhythm of his breath, ebb and flow like waves on a beach. I am barely aware that I can feel the carpet beneath my feet, feel my bare skin tingle in anticipation as I move closer. If I looked down at myself I know I'd see my own body, proud and curved and strong, not wasted and bowed with weakness, nor scarred and stretch-marked.

But I only look at him, at him as I draw closer. His tan skin, the faint fuzz of golden hair gleaming delicately in the light of the lamp on his arms, his chest, low on his belly. I feel the warmth of his skin as I reach out and run my hand over his chest, as I climb into bed with him, straddle his thigh, savor the tickle and scratch of his beard stubble, the warm scent of skin and sleep as I kiss his cheek, his lips, feel his body arch galvanically beneath mine, and hear his breath catch. I see the beauty of his eyes as they open wide, so wide, the blue of a spring sky with gray streaks of cloud, and I feel the most poignant joy in my heart that I have ever felt, of coming home, of really and truly coming into my own at last.

WALLS OF WHITE
Chiara Nova

Day 23

If you'd ask me for how long I've been here, my best guess would be around fourteen days. I didn't know how long I had been unconscious, so it was hard to know whether I started counting at day one or day three or day two hundred and fifty-five. I just decided to start at one.

It's really hard to keep track of time in here. There are no windows and the light is always turned on, a bright, blinding white. The walls are white too. There is no door. There are no cracks through which I can get a peek at the world outside. There is nothing but these four white walls.

I haven't been given anything to eat or drink in all this time. I don't seem to need it anymore. Nor do I need to sleep. I feel suspended, stuck in time, as the not needing to drink, eat or sleep make my sudden misplaced existence even more surreal. All the things that make me human have been ripped from my hands. Sometimes I wonder if I'm even still alive.

Though I don't seem to need or get these things anymore, it doesn't mean I'm comfortable. Far from it. The most unsettling thing is the thirst. I'm not exactly thirsty, though I'm never *not* thirsty either. It feels like I'm always perched on the edge of thirst. It's extremely uncomfortable, though I suspect that that is what this entire room was built for.

I trace my finger over the structure of the wall, willing the wall to fall away or to turn into a door, but it never works. There's the smallest sound coming from above and I go still, my finger stuck on a tiny hole. I strain my ears, trying to catch as much of the sound as I can. But as soon as I hear it, it's gone, and it's like it was never even there at all. I feel that about a lot of things these days.

I know it was the sound of a dying scream, but it comforts me. The truth is, the scream eases my mind. It's the sound that tells me I'm not entirely alone in here. That something still exists outside these four white walls. It reminds me of that philosophical question, of whether a falling tree really makes a sound if there's no one there to listen. I am here to listen to the others' screams. I am here to listen to them fall. And I can only hope that someone will be there to listen to me too. That someone will have heard of my existence, no matter that it was dying out. It reassures me to know that I have been real even when I'm not.

I know the nature of the sounds is not too promising, but at least I know what to expect now.

I quickly discovered the walls have holes. They're small, about the size of the tip of a needle. Not nearly big enough to have any illusions that the tiny holes could become bigger holes which would eventually lead to my freedom. But big enough to regulate the air in here. And big enough for a strange substance to come through once a day. At least, I think it's once a day.

Every surface of the tiny room is covered with the holes. They're in the ground, in the ceiling and in every one of the four walls. They're spaced at regular intervals and there are no hidden messages or codes or anything else that may lead to my escape. I checked.

There are two hundred holes in every wall. The same number in the floor and in the ceiling. That makes a total of twelve hundred holes, and something comes through every one of these tiny holes once a day. I don't know what to call it, although I clearly remember the first time it was released. It was the first day and I was sitting on the floor in the corner, examining the walls, when it suddenly got impossible to breathe. My eyes bulged and I gasped, trying to get as much air as I could, but there simply was none. It was as if all the air had been sucked from the room. It was over after a second, but just as I regained my breath and air flooded my lungs, it started all over again.

I got up and tried to move to the other end of the room, anything to get away from whatever it was that was keeping me from breathing, but it was just as hard to move as it was to breathe. Whatever it was, it was everywhere. It felt like the air had turned liquid but at the same time as if it had solidified, and still it felt like there was none at all. The air got harder, denser. I tried to walk but it was as if I were walking through the ocean where the water resists you every step of the way. But this was a million times worse and I was only able to move my arms and legs an inch at a time. Finally, when I felt that I couldn't hold on for much longer, the air became air again and I could move and breathe again, immediately falling to the floor and gasping for breath.

I hoped it would be a one-time thing. It wasn't. It returns every single day and I dread every minute of it.

It did get me thinking. The mist—even though it's invisible, the name seems fitting—probably explains a thing or two about why I'm in here. I can think of no other reason than that they are running experiments on us. I say us, not because I have developed a multiple personality disorder—though that wouldn't come as a surprise to anyone—but because I have to believe I'm not alone in this. There are the screams, the only thing I can hang on to, but with each scream, I never know whether it will be the last of them. Whether the next scream will be mine.

I think they want us to hear the screams. I think the threat of the screams is biggest in what you *don't* hear. But as long as I can believe others are also suffering this fate, as long as I can pretend I'm not completely alone, I might be able to live through this.

As for the nature of the experiments, I can only guess. There have been rumors about the walls of white for as long as I can remember. The truth is, once you go in, you never come out. But everything else surrounding it is a haze. I think it all comes down to immortality. Our never-ending search for bigger, for better. For more. At this moment, we are closer than ever to achieving that. It all accelerated when we figured out a way to access the brain and everything in it. Personalities, skills, intelligence, memories, and so much more, everything that defines you as you, can now simply be accessed through a computer.

We never have to memorize anything again. Pictures? Unnecessary. Everything we see is automatically stored in our files. The next step is new bodies, so that when we outlive our old ones, we can simply transfer everything to a newer, shinier model.

I don't know why we ever thought it could work.

The original intention behind the downloadable brain was to make society safer. And it did. What better way to catch a bad guy than to look into his head? You prevent locking up innocent people and you make the world a safer place. Crime rates went down dramatically, cold cases that hit a dead end twenty years ago were suddenly solved. Killers were caught. And so was I.

But we strayed from that intention a long time ago, always looking for more. We humans can never be satisfied. We will go on, until we outlive humanity or until we destroy ourselves. I think the latter will come first. We want to be immortal, though we can't even handle mortality, and that happens to everyone. We search for a solution that's so much bigger than the problem it solves. And the problem, to us, seems so large, so insurmountable. How then would we ever be able to survive immortality, a solution that much bigger? It's like defeating infinity.

I'm ripped away from my thoughts by a sudden lack of air. It never fails to take me by surprise. I struggle to close my eyelids and hold my breath. There is nothing I can do now but sit and hold on until it passes, feeling like I'm slipping over the edge but the air is preventing me from falling, my screams locked up inside.

⸻◆⸻

An eternity later, the mist is gone. They are probably assessing my every brain wave right now. My responses to being locked up, alone, in a room without stimuli, my reaction to the mist. I wonder what it is exactly they are experimenting with. If it will harm me, soon or in the distant future. If it is *meant* to harm me, to torture me in some way.

I strongly suspect that the mist takes care of my body's needs, and that that's why I haven't had to eat, drink or sleep since I came in here. Stripping those basic needs away makes for an extremely boring existence. One in which I had plenty of time to think about why they would need such a substance. The things I came up with frighten me. The thing that scares me most about it, though, is that the substance seems to be able to sustain me indefinitely. I can be stuck in here forever, until my hair goes gray and my skin wrinkles up like a raisin, simply existing, with nothing to do but wait. I won't even be able to starve myself to death. That's quite a depressing thought.

But my fears go even deeper than that, further and further, until they touch bone. It's scary, the things that surface when your mind runs loose for too long. What if the mist won't even allow me to age? What if it takes even that away from me? What if I won't even wilt away, not even be able to die of old age? Will I be stuck here indefinitely?

I try to ease my mind by telling myself that that probably won't happen. That it's just my imagination running wild, my mind straying. But stranger things have lived there that have proven to be all too real.

Ever since my sentence, I found myself tumbling further and further into a darkened rabbit hole, though I never expected the end of it to be so blindingly white.

Day 45
Outside

Heels click on the marble tiles. The sound echoes through the cavern, bouncing of the stone walls. The hall is dimly lit but for the excruciating white light coming from the boxes stacked in the middle of the room. She walks along the boxes, the people within trapped in agony. A pang of regret and anger shoots through her heart, but it's not enough. It doesn't even scratch the surface.

It would be easier if the light would just cease. If the room would dissolve into darkness and take everything inside with it. Until the room, until the world, ceases to exist. The thoughts darken her mind as she passes the walls of ice. She shivers. It's cold, but it's not the ice that's giving her chills. It's mainly what's inside. The things inside represent an entirely different species of agony.

She forces her gaze away from the ice and pins her eyes on the control room. Nathan is on monitor duty today, which makes her heart and her feet even heavier with reluctance. He glances up at her approach and his gaze instantly chills a couple degrees, coldness dripping from the edges. He looks back towards his screen, lips tightening disapprovingly.

She opens the glass door and enters.

"I brought the new batch."

"Put it on the desk."

The atmosphere in the room feels as cold as the rows of ice outside. The room used to heat up when they were together. They had been in that fragile state of almost-dating when more important things forced themselves into their lives and the thing dwindled down, out of existence. She's glad it did. It was around the time everything had started to unravel. Around the time they asked her to make a new aerial. And ever since everything started spiraling down, she had gotten a closer look at the person he really was. She did not like what she saw. It felt like something behind his skin was missing.

She takes the file from his desk and is already halfway through the door when she opens the cover and frowns. It's empty.

"What's this?"

"Change of procedure."

"What do you mean?"

"No more files allowed outside control. You'll have to monitor from here."

"That's ridiculous. First no more access to the system from my computer and now I can't even take the files with me? What's next? Disabling the memory cells of my Nucleus?"

"I don't know, Mara, I just follow orders. Pick it up with someone else."

She sighs and settles down in the chair at the other end of the room. Him mindlessly following orders is what she can't wrap her head around. How can you simply proceed, not giving it a second thought, when someone orders you to kill a bunch of people? She knows she's not exactly in the right place to judge him for following orders and killing people, she knows that she herself is not a hair better. But at least she tried to do something. She wages a mental battle with herself every day. Her conscience is eating her from the inside out. All the while, he's just fine. He can sleep at night. They once had a discussion about it, when everything first started going wrong, and it had been the first sign that something about him was not quite right. There probably has to be, to survive in this world.

She tries to focus on the report on her screen but soon finds her gaze wandering throughout the room. She regards the cavernous hall, with its walls formed by rock. This was something beautiful once, before humans took over. She remembers the first time she came here, her first week on the job. She had been amazed by the cavern and its potential, and excited by all the possibilities of everything they were doing. She had felt like she was holding the future in her hands. And she was. Until everything slipped through her fingers.

She had started out eager and ambitious, had been living in a kind of dream. Then, slowly but surely, shreds of that dream were ripped away. She woke up and had to face the realities of what they were doing, too. And those realities became all too real all too soon. So many people had to suffer, had to be surrendered for the greater good. To achieve her dream, their dream. Now, there is only a tiny shred of that dream left and she wonders where it is.

The whole thing has broken her, left her in half and at war with herself. So many people have died because of her.

And now, she has yet again delivered another batch that delivers people to their death.

She can't bear it, hasn't been able to ever since they asked her to develop a new aerial. And then another one, after that. The intention used to be to let the prisoners out after completing the trial, let them serve out their sentence in a normal prison. But that was a long time ago, before it stopped being about the greater good and strayed to control and paranoia. Before the need to kill arose.

She had been uncomfortable enough with the fact that the sustaining aerial was so uncomfortable, so painful. But that was something she believed in, something for the greater good. These other serums she can't justify. The government's claims are simply not enough. She doesn't buy that this is the only way to guarantee a crime-free country. That this is the only way to eliminate terrorism, control prisoners. The only way to defeat death. They simply don't see that their perfect society is not free from crime at all. That, now, things have shifted and they are the ones committing the crimes.

She had refused to do it at first, but then had let herself be swayed by the promise of good. No good came, and her hands got only redder and redder by the blood that spilled from the bodies she killed. Then, she tried to resign. Her superiors had let her know that they valued her and her work, that they needed her and could not let her go. Surely she understood that. They were working for the future of the country, of the world. They also told her, in a way that left no room for doubt, that they had no qualms about putting her in a cell of her own for a while if she refused to keep working for them.

"The future can wait for a while, of course. It will come no matter what. We have plenty of room here if you need to think some things over, reconsider your priorities." He nodded subtly to the white boxes. She knew there was no way out of that once she got in. "But we would expect your return, of course. And your cooperation. If some time spent... alone helps with that, we are happy to oblige." She had thanked him politely and said that that would not be necessary. His meaning was clear. There would be no return if she did not cooperate, no matter what he said.

That was the moment she knew she needed to get out, but heard the prison door slam shut behind her.

———————

She passes the ice again on her way out and a cold feeling of dread settles in her stomach. She can perfectly see the bodies inside, imagine them reaching through the ice. Creeping through the world. She can't even begin to imagine that, one day, these bodies will replace the ones they have now. They raise the hair on her neck.

She knows it's not a rational fear, that it's more of a distant fear, a fear for the future. And she knows it's not really the empty bodies she's afraid of. It's the empty ones of the living she fears. The ones that are living, for now, in the white boxes. So many of them have already died, she's certain that by now, some of them must be haunting her. And that number will only grow, until one day, she will be so surrounded by ghosts that she will be unable to move, unable to walk, unable to breathe. Then, it would be just as if she were living in her own walls of white. A white box of her own devise. And it feels like that box is shrinking around her, getting tighter and tighter, squeezing the air until none will be left. She's aware of how awfully close this image matches the truth of the boxes they're building.

Day 49

I can't think about what I did. I can't have my mind wandering to unwanted places. And I have to make sure that they don't know. That they will never find out. But today, it's proving to be more difficult than ever.

My hand wanders to the back of my neck and a sharp sting shoots through my head as my fingers graze the sensitive skin. I suck in my breath and grind my teeth against the pain, waiting for the throbbing sting to ebb away. I think that cut is the only reason I'm still alive.

I know that they have an idea of what I did—otherwise, I wouldn't be in here—but I'm fairly certain they don't know the extent of my actions. How I did it, or more importantly, how to fix it. The fresh cut confirms my hypothesis that they gave me a new Nucleus, and are now just waiting for me to slip up.

So I have to make sure that doesn't happen. I have to survive as long as possible if I want to have any chance of living.

The irony of the entire situation is not lost on me. That I have been captured by my own creation. That my own creation is now being used against me. That I am now seen as a criminal, even though I needed to make things right. I understand that, in their mind's eye, I did something wrong, illegal, even, and that they felt like I needed to be punished for it. In their view, I went rogue and tried to destroy everything they had been building for years. I crushed their life's dream.

But they have no idea why I did what I did. They have no idea of the consequences of their actions, of what this will mean for the future of every human, ever. They have no idea what they have unleashed upon the world.

But with me stuck in here, they will never know until it's already too late.

***

It suddenly occurs to me that something in the room has changed. I hadn't noticed it before, while trying not to think about everything that happened, but now I see that the room has changed its shape somehow. I can't quite put my finger on what it is exactly, but I'm sure that something has. Maybe it's just the stress and the painful memories playing tricks on my mind. I think I will close my eyes for a moment, try to doze a bit, and see if I feel better afterward. My body doesn't need sleep anymore but sometimes, if I'm lucky, I can pretend. I can pretend to leave the world and everything awful in it behind and lose myself in a world of made-up dreams. The whole thing feels fake, staged, like actors trying too hard to be funny, but it's the only thing I can do to hold on.

———◆———

When I can't pretend any longer and reality invades my world of dreams, I open my eyes and see that the room has shifted completely. I feel feverish. It's like the room has been warped, as if someone took the other end of the room and twisted it so that it doesn't follow the laws of nature anymore. So that it twists and twists and twists around itself.

I'm suspended in the air. I know I should be falling but I'm not, and for a minute, I think the substance is in the room again. But no, it's not, I can breathe, I can move. Everything is normal except for the fact that it isn't. I tentatively feel my way along the floor. I put my finger in the crease of the room, where the wall I'm clinging to turns into the floor. It again turns into something else when I touch it and lifts itself up until it is slightly suspended to my right. I try to move there, to see if I can climb from wall to wall, get to someplace safe, but I feel that I can't. The walls resist somehow.

My head pounds and I lie back down. I stare up at the ceiling—no, one of the walls?—and see it being twisted further and further, until the entire room becomes a large spiral and a reflection of itself and I find myself falling into the endless depths of my prison.

Day 49
Outside

Another day in the control room with Nathan. Another day of misery. She wonders if they can think of any new ways to make her life even more miserable. Every time she thinks they can't do better—or worse, actually—than this, they surprise her by coming up with new methods of torture. But she shouldn't be surprised. It's this awful inventiveness of torture that runs this whole thing.

Sometimes, she wonders if it would be easiest if she just... ceases to exist. No more new batches, no more new aerials. No more new deaths on her hands. But she knows she would never be able to do that, no matter how miserable her life gets. They will find a way to continue, eventually. They are already bringing people in to learn about her methods.

No, it's best if she just does it all by herself, remain in control of the situation. Or well, in what little control she still has left. She has been thinking about ways to make the substances difficult to approach by someone else. To change them somehow, make them less effective, ruin them, break them. Like one of their patients, Elin Miller, did with the Nucleus.

But it's proven to be almost impossible. Miller did it extremely well, and she was still caught. She can't even *think* too much about ways to resist, lest it show up in her Nucleus. Let alone act on it. And now with all the vultures skulking around her lab, keeping eyes on her and her methods, she knows she will never be able to pull it off. Not unless she wants to wind up in here as well.

And if she's sure of one thing, it's that she doesn't want to end up in the walls of white. Not any more than she already has.

Some have died horrible deaths in here. Once, the kill aerial wasn't released into the boxes before they shut down, thus not relieving the prisoners of their sentences and their lives before the boxes were terminated. The walls of white inched closer and closer and the prisoners were crushed to death. There hadn't been a spot of white left on the walls of those boxes that day.

Others killed themselves in the most inventive ways. Smashing their heads against the wall until the light went out of their eyes. Strangling themselves with their hospital gowns. Worse are the ones who didn't succeed. Who were left to live with their injuries, enduring the trials of the boxes until someone in the control room decided that their time ran out. Their agony was so palpable, even outside the boxes, that even Nathan was quieter than usual on those days.

Some tried to inhale the sustaining aerial, the one that filters into each box once a day, in the hope that it would take their breath and keep it. If only they knew that that aerial *gave* life instead of taking it.

Something on the screen captures her attention and she sits up straight. She doesn't immediately see what she's looking at, but something about it is significant. They administered the new batch, aerial H12, to a set of patients in Q56, and now, results are coming in.

They are responding well, exemplary really, nothing out of the ordinary there. Their own fears are nicely turning against them. But there is something odd about Miller's responses. Something expected, and at the same time, entirely unexpected. A memory has just come through. An old one.

"Mara." Nathan is sitting just as straight as she is, a concentrated look on his face, their animosity temporarily forgotten.

"I know."

That pang of regret shoots through her heart again. That Miller, who had accomplished some of the things Mara herself was too cowardly to do on her end, should be brought down like this, like an animal in a cage. And that she is the one who created most of Miller's suffering.

When they first brought Elin in, the problem of her Nucleus arose. She had tampered with the Nucleus system, which was bad enough in itself, but they needed to know who else's Nucleus she had tampered with. Her own Nucleus being faulty, this was a problem as they couldn't simply look into her brain to see what she had done. They could never restore everything to its state of societal perfection if they didn't know whose Nucleus' were faulty. They gave her a new one, in the hope that she would reminisce about what she did, that something would slip through that they could use. But she had been extremely careful not to think about it, not to trigger any memories that they could use. Until now.

During the first phase of the hallucinations, she had gotten unconscious, and in her state, a memory arose. It's blurry and tangled, events scattered and incomplete, but one image stands out very clearly. One person stands out very clearly.

"Oh my god." Mara mutters.

They look at each other, and Nathan reaches towards the phone.

Day 54

It's been some time since the room decided to change its shape and I'm still not sure if it was real or if it was all in my head. I wouldn't be surprised if it was. Stranger things have lived there.

Ever since I woke up, my head has been pounding but the room has kept its shape. The walls are the sturdy, non-giving things they always were and there is no evidence that the room ever had any other shape. I decide it was just in my head. That worries me. Is it something that came from *me?* From *my* mind? Or is it something that was put there, as part of an experiment? I don't know, and for the first time since I've been in here, I truly feel afraid.

Day 55

I wake up and I instantly feel that I'm not alone. I didn't even know I had passed out again, but there is a gaping hole where my memory should be. For a moment, my thoughts shift to my Nucleus and the things I saw before they put me in here. For a moment, I'm afraid the thing is happening, the thing I'm most afraid of. I have to force myself not to go there.

I open my eyes and everything shifts and turns. A cold feeling of dread settles in my stomach, dread at the room twisting its shape again. My vomit from the last time still decorates the corner. I close my eyes again and take a deep breath. My head is pounding, my stomach twirling. I could really use a glass of water right now.

I try to open my eyes again, and it takes a while but eventually, everything shifts into focus. The room has stopped spinning. But the relief is immediately replaced by that nagging feeling I had earlier, of not being alone in here for the first time in who knows how many days. I drag myself upwards and let my gaze drift through the room.

In the corner, opposite of the one I threw up in, is a young woman. She has tangled, long brown hair not unlike my own, and is looking at me with a wary gaze. She's wearing the same kind of gown as I am, and she's obviously distraught. In between staring at me, her gaze shifts through the tiny room, quickly taking everything in, as if she's afraid of something, as if she's waiting for something.

"How did you get in here?" My voice is shrill from disuse. If the situation were anything less than dire I would make a mental note to talk to myself more often.

She doesn't answer, just continues her search of the room. Something is wrong with her face, and she has this haunted look in her eyes, as if something inside has left. That's probably what you'd see if you looked into my eyes as well.

As the thought enters my head, I realize something about her strikes me as familiar.

I shift closer towards her. Her features are distorted, as if her eyes and her nose are trying to flee from her face, slowly drifting towards the sides. I didn't recognize her at first, but the realization comes sudden.

I'm looking at a broken version of myself.

——◆——

Throughout the day, more versions of myself wander into the room, each as broken as the first. I don't know where they came from or what they're doing here, but they're here. It was just the two of us for quite some time, her observing the room and staring at me. Me, talking at her and staring at her—my—deteriorated features. I wonder if that is what I look like now.

I move my hands towards my face and it truly feels as if my face has shifted. My nose is not in the place it belongs, and I swear that one of my eyes has drifted downward on my face and is now much lower than the other one. This gets me in a panic and I spend some time clawing at my face and crying in the corner. There are some periods of rage in between, letting out my fury over being trapped in here, over what they are doing to me, to my face, not even having a mirror to <u>see</u> what they did to my face. The space of the room, as little as there is, is pressing down at me and I can't get the air in my lungs even though it's all around me.

But I calmed down when the next version of me appeared.

She looks more like what I think I looked like, before, though something about her is wrong as well. As silent as the first, as loud is the second. She's in a rage, fists pounding on the wall, screams reverberating through the room and forcing its way into my skull. It makes my blood run cold.

After that, all I could do was squeeze my eyes shut and hold my hands over my ears until everything just stopped.

It didn't. The room only got more crowded.

Now, I am stuck here with more versions of myself than I am willing to count. They are pressing me against the wall and it has become hard to breathe. They're using up all the air in the room. One of them bumps into me and I lose my balance and crash against the wall. My head hurts and I try to calm myself, shut my eyes and breathe in and out, but it doesn't work.

Howls and screams and moans of pain fill the air and I just need them to stop. My head is filled with them, so much of them, of me, and I can't take it anymore. I beat my fists against the wall and start screaming and screaming, trying to drone them out, my screams occasionally taken over by sobs. My hands start bleeding but I don't care. I just need to get out.

Then, the mist comes into the room and stills me in my movements. The other versions of me just continue their wailing and screeching and beating and pounding, until all the fight goes out of me.

Day 56
Outside

There's a subtle change in the atmosphere of the facility. There's this cold hostility underlying everything. It's colder than before and she doesn't know what changed, what caused it. They haven't shown her the latest test results, saying there has been a delay but unwilling to tell her what kind of delay. Of course, there is no delay, it's all bullshit. It means they found something that they don't want her to know.

She eats herself up over what it could be. Was it something in the results itself that she's not supposed to see? Did they see something suspicious in her Nucleus? Has she finally outgrown her use?

Day 56

The no air thing came and went along with all the versions of myself and I'm contemplating the point of it all when I notice the wall at the other end of the room is boiling. There's really no other way to describe it. Large parts of the wall are forming these kind of welts, which pop open and then the remaining wall substance drips down. The wall keeps boiling and foaming like that and I quickly stand up. I think I feel the heat building up and I need to get away from it. The boiling gets worse and worse, and it spreads to the other two walls beside it as well. I stand back against the outer wall, searching the room for the millionth time for a way out, but I can't find any. Surely someone must be doing this, must see what's going on and save me? I press myself harder against the wall but then jump away as I feel a piece of the wall behind me bubbling and expanding until it pops and melts and makes a hissing noise.

I move back from the wall and towards the center of the room. Every wall is boiling now, the stark white getting brown edges as the walls move and melt and bubble and burst. The temperature in the room rises as the heat from the walls fills the room. The walls turn into sticky, gooey stuff, which reminds me of marshmallows that have been softened by fire. The boils keep getting closer and closer, and for a moment I consider throwing myself against one of the walls, hoping I can get myself through the gooey stuff and be free. I inch towards the place with the smallest amount of boils and reach my hand towards it. The wall scorches my hand and I yank it back immediately. Going through it is not an option, not unless I want to burn myself alive.

The boils come closer and the walls are closing in. I move towards the center of the room until I can't go any further. A drop falls right next to my foot. I look up and am horrified to find that the ceiling is now joining in as well. The boils above me burst with a loud pop, and some of the goo starts dripping downward. A drop falls onto my shoulder and I cry out in pain as it burns and blisters through my nightgown into my skin. There's another burn on my elbow, and I see that the left wall has come so far that it is now right next to me.

I bite down on my lip in pain as the boils keep closing in on me from all sides and the marshmallow walls drip onto my head. I get down and make myself as small as I can, trying to avoid the burning boils as long as possible.

To make matters worse, the air is suddenly gone and I can't breathe or move. But the walls keep on boiling and closing in on me. Air fills the room again and I take short, quick breaths, taking in as much air as I can and moving away from the walls before the next burst comes. When it does, I can't do anything against the burning goo to my left that is now bursting and spilling all over my body. Air is released and I scream out in pain and move to the right, only to encounter more of the same on that side. The ceiling is coming down, pressing down on me, and when the next burst of non-air comes, the walls are touching me from all sides. I can't move, I can't scream, I can't <u>breathe</u>. I am thoroughly panicking, and it takes too long for the air to come back in. I can't hold on much longer. And it *hurts*. It hurts so badly. I feel tears streaming down my cheeks and I am aching for air, aching for air that's outside this box, fresh air, and I just want the pain to stop. My skin is a bright red where the boils touched me.

The walls are clouding my vision now, they are less than an inch from my face. The boil in front of me keeps growing and growing, and then it bursts, the goo splattering all into my face and eyes. There's still no air, but I try to open my mouth anyway. I need air, I need to scream, I need freedom. Another boil bursts and it drowns me with burning white.

Day 63
Outside

Nathan is monitoring the patients when something beeps on one of the screens. Incoming progress report.

Aerial H12: 100% successful. 99% reliability. Ready for use.

His face lights up. They had been working towards this for months. This means more than just the application of the hallucinatory aerial. So much more. This means they can finally get rid of Mara. Sure, the kill aerial is not yet complete, but a substance that kills is far less complicated than a substance that is meant to turn your mind against you. A killing gas requires less finesse. Which means that Mara has just become disposable.

He hears the slam of a heavy door and moments later, the tell-tale sound of heels on tile. Think about the devil.

She enters the control room and he can't stop himself from smiling. This may be the last time he sees her.

"Why are you so happy?"

"No reason."

She stares at him, a dead look in her eyes. She still knows him. It's as if she sees right into his soul, dark as it may be, and it's something that has always irked him.

"It's a nice day, that's all." But his smile now feels forced as his boiling hate for her hijacks his happy mood.

She settles down in her chair and starts to work.

"Mara, I need you to drop off the latest batch of cubes." He knows she hates that task. Hates to be confronted with the consequences of her actions. The blood that is inevitably stuck on her hands forever.

Her face drops. The haunted look that she tries to hide is now written all over her face. She doesn't let it out often, but when she does, he can't help but feel satisfaction. Satisfaction, and a little bit of victory.

She quietly stands up and walks away. A moment later, he hears a bang and a shriek and he sees that her hands have actually turned red. For a moment he wonders whether he is hallucinating, but no, one of the pristine white cubes is seeping blood all over her. It splattered on her clothes and covers her hands, and her face is a distorted mask of anguish.

The seeping cube drops to the floor and forms a dark red puddle on the floor, streaming around her shoes as she stands there, paralyzed.

———◆———

His thoughts about Mara and the seeping cube are disrupted by the sound of an alarm. A red message flashes across the screens: Breach in Q56.

A breach. A breach in one of the cubes in Q56.

He types in some commands on his keyboard, trying to localize the breach as fast as possible so he can shut down the right box. The computer thinks for a moment but then comes up with no results. The breach can't be identified. He frowns. That's unusual.

He quickly decides to follow protocol and to shut down all four boxes in Q56. He checks the boxes' occupants and halts, finger hovering over the button that shuts down the entire quadrant. Elin Miller is one of the occupants. Shit. She's their most important patient. The one they are supposed to keep alive.

He contemplates his options. Follow protocol and shut down all four boxes, risking the wrath of his boss about losing Miller but containing the breach and preventing further aerials from spilling out. Or letting it run its course, cut off the aerial supply to all four boxes and wait it out. Wait until the aerials have dissolved or are sucked away by someone from the outside. They would lose the ability to control the occupants as no more aerials could enter the boxes. It would fail the experiments. But they would still have Miller.

He knows that's what they would want him to do, seeing how their priority is to keep Miller alive, at least until they have gathered sufficient data from her. But something tickles in the back of his mind. Something he can't ignore.

He glances outside. Shutting down the quadrant would mean killing the occupants and allowing the killing aerial to spill into the cavern. His boss won't be happy about losing Miller, but her new memory gives them enough to work with.

The more important thing is that Mara has become disposable.

And Mara is still outside.

He smiles as he realizes he knows just what to do.

The blood pools around her feet, but somehow, she can't get them to move. It's on her clothes and her hands are stained with it. She stands there, staring, her gaze fixated on the redness around her. Then, an alarm as red as the blood shrieks through the cavern.

The alarm tears her from her thoughts. She turns away from the cube and the blood and the terribleness and hurries over towards the control room, blood dripping and trailing behind her. Nathan is inside, with a peculiar look on his face. He doesn't look as panicked as he should and she realizes that something is wrong. Something is terribly wrong.

In her hurry, she stumbles and falls, her heels slippery with blood. She crawls towards the door and reaches for the handle. She's close, so close, but then, all the air gets sucked from the room. Her arm freezes in midair and her lungs are empty where air should be. She moves her arm, excruciatingly slow but it's as fast as she can go. She needs to open the door, get inside. Get away from the aerials that spill into the cavern. Why isn't Nathan helping her? He's staring at her from inside the room. Why doesn't he open the door?

Her arm moves further downward and the coolness of the metal handle is a relief on her skin as black spots start appearing in her vision. She pushes her hand down with all her might, and it moves-it moves!

But the door doesn't budge.

The door doesn't open.

The door is locked.

The black spots are taking over and she slumps towards the ground, her last conscious thought a wish for her killer to save her.

Day 63

A light shines on the wall to my left. It's the first thing I see when I open my eyes. I'm surprised I'm still alive. I sit up, my head pounding, and I look at my arms. My skin is a light tan, as it always has been. No signs of red, scorched skin. I look at the walls, and they are restored to their normal state again. Except for the fact that one of them is now slightly see-through. I sigh and close my eyes for a moment, rubbing my hand across my brow. So it was another hallucination. One so powerful that it made me pass out. I wonder again about the state of my health, the state of my mind. I can't see how any of this could work out in the end. Everything is only getting worse.

I stand up and move closer towards the see-through wall. If I move close enough, I can see inside the building. I'm in a cave. It's filled with stacks and stacks of the same white cubes, all of them I can look into. I guess the walls are made of a special kind of glass that you can look into, but not look out from. Except for today. I see figures slumped inside, some banging on the walls, screaming, others just sitting there in defeat. And at the other end of the cavern, new cubes are being built.

On top of every finished cube sits a white platform, with on top of that an unconscious person. Some kind of mechanical arm slides a piece of wall to one side of the cube, while another comes from the other side. It seems like they build the room around the person. That explains how I got in here and why I can't get out. The realization sinks my heart and the tiny shred of hope I had left. The rooms were never built to let someone out once they had gotten in.

My suspicions are confirmed when I let my gaze wander along the rest of the warehouse. There are a lot of motionless forms in the cubes. And there's blood, too. The specks of red can be clearly seen among the pristine white of the rooms. Some of the rooms with red seem to be smaller and are *shrinking*, caving in on the deceased. Creating a nice, small package of death. It reminds me uncomfortably of the day my room was changing. Maybe it wasn't entirely an hallucination after all.

I turn around and am confronted by a face trapped in a scream. The box next to me is shrinking with alarming speed, the man inside screaming and slamming his fists on the wall, terror written all over his face. He tries to turn around but the walls are closing in on him and he can't move. I look away as I realize what fate awaits him. Nausea builds in my stomach and I force myself to look away from all the boxes, away from the pain, the horror. I feel numb, paralyzed, but I know it won't take long before my paralysis is shattered by reality. I fear what happens then.

On the ground, there is a woman, crawling very slowly through a pool of blood. I frown. Did she escape? She's not wearing a gown like all the prisoners inside the boxes. She's crawling towards a glass wall that separates a kind of control room from the rest of the cave. She reaches for the door handle but then slumps towards the ground. She stops moving.

Suddenly, there's a flash of light to my left and a line of text appears on the wall.

Elin Miller, thank you for your participation. You will now be freed from the program.

I frown. *Freed* from the program? That doesn't make any sense. It doesn't work with my theory that the boxes aren't meant to be opened after a person has gotten in. How would they-

My stream of thought is cut off as the air is sucked from the room and the mysterious substance takes its place. My breath hitches in my throat as there is no more air to breathe in. I realize that freeing someone can be done in other ways. I realize that, this time, there won't be any relief in the bursts. No air will be released in between to save me. I fall towards the ground in slow motion, the substance slowing my fall. For a moment, it feels like I'm flying.

I softly hit the ground and dark spots appear across my vision. Deep inside me, there are two sparks at war. One feels relief, relief that all of this will finally be over. The other feels regret. Regret for all that ever was and all it could have been, but couldn't at the same time. I don't know which spark I want to win, and I realize that it doesn't matter. I will never be able to find out. All that remains now are these endless walls of white. And I am left to wonder whether my soul will be stuck in here forever.

A surge of panic comes over me as I realize I'm unable to scream. No one will hear me fall. I might as well have never existed at all.

The black spots take over, and everything goes dark.

SILVER BELLS AND COCKLE SHELLS

Richard Staving

The crone appeared from nowhere. Her long, tattered cloak the color of wet earth and rainy skies. A hood covered her features. Except her hooked nose. Except her cracked lips and yellow teeth.

She spoke to the girl. The old woman's voice was dry. Craggy peaks and valleys. But her tone was sweet. Understanding.

What is your name, dear?

Jennie.

Why, what a nice name.

No, it's not. There's two other girls in my class named Jennie.

The old woman chuckled deep in her throat. You're right. It's not fair.

Jennie blinked. Someone agreed with her. The old woman didn't parrot out what she thought Jennie wanted to hear.

Jennie and the crone were hidden by large maples that had just burst spring leaves. They were a block away from the elementary school. Jennie tried to play basketball with the five boys at the courts. None of them picked her. They told her to go home.

But she was twelve soon to be thirteen, just like them. Going into the seventh grade at the big Junior-Senior High School. Just like them. She was even taller than the others. Perfect for center.

But no.

Grow a dick and we'll let you play.

They brayed like crows and asses.

Jennie left. Face red. Jaw clamped tight enough to hurt.

She wouldn't cry, though. Screw them.

She sat under a maple tree and calmed down. Then the crone appeared.

The old woman looked down the block to the school.

They can't stop staring at your chest, can they?

Heat rushed to Jennie's face. But she was right.

Those boys don't take you serious, do they?

Jennie spoke through clenched teeth.

No. They never do.

The old woman reached into her cloak. The folds of the garment moved of their own accord. She removed a small wooden box. The cloak reshaped itself into its original position.

The crone proffered the box. Jennie studied the hands that held it. Wrinkled. Wiry. Ancient. The fingers, long gnarled branches.

After a long explanation, Jennie accepted the box. And the gift inside.

———◆———

Jennie stepped back to admire—

Well, what? It was unlike any flower she'd seen.

It looked like a shrunken sunflower with different coloration. The pedals were pearl white. The seeds in the center were not brown or gray but deep scarlet.

Be careful not to touch the middle, the old woman had warned. Like all flowers, it has teeth.

Jennie looked at her finger. A blood bead on the tip.

She had taken the box to her Secret Place, beneath an old oak tree in the woods behind her home. Not so far that she couldn't be called from the house, but far enough. Away from her mother. Away from her brothers. She opened the box and revealed a lifeless flower. Pedals wilted. Leaves withered. Seeds dried.

She planted it as best she could in the damp soil. She thought it brightened a little, but figured the old woman had tricked her. She went to touch the brittle pedals and brushed her middle finger against the center. A needle thrust into her fingertip. Blood seeped onto the flower. It exploded with color and life. She heard a deep sigh.

The tiny bud of a flower opened in her mind. Empty in the middle. Waiting to be fed. Eager.

Jennie felt this more than saw it. She knew if she closed her eyes and concentrated, the image would appear.

What do you do after you throw a coin into a well? the old crone had said. Make a wish.

I want to play basketball better than those boys.

Her limbs were awkward spindles. Unreliable at best. Her vision blurry. Wore glasses to read. Would have to wear them all the time, the ophthalmologist said. All that changed.

She was imbued with confidence. Muscles awoke and stretched beneath the skin of her arms and legs. Her eyes gained a trained focus unlike they ever had. She even forgot about the growing breasts stuffed in her ill-fitting bra.

She marched down the sidewalk lined with manicured gardens and gargantuan trees that painted the perfect suburbia. The elementary school came into view. The boys were still there. Stopped. One of them cat-called. He wore stained sweatpants. His face a pockmarked mess. He was in Jennie's class, but got Held Back a year. That labeled him for life.

Jennie challenged them to one-on-one. Each.

Okay, said the pockmarked boy. We'll only go to ten. Ya know. Cause yer a girl.

She beat them all. Danced around them, made layups with ease, shot the most three-pointers she ever had. She dodged elbows aimed at her head. Fists and feet meant to trip her up. One observer launched the extra ball at her head. She caught it mid-stride. They slunk away after the last point, mumbling until they were out of earshot.

A grin on her sweaty face carried her home. She didn't touch the ground. Not until something hard cracked the back of her skull. She saw explosions of light. Fell face-first to the pavement. Skinned her outstretched hands and her knobby knees. Hit her nose and knocked a sneeze to the fore.

Something heavy landed on her legs and locked them together in a vice. A hand pinned her left wrist. Another pulled her arm behind her back. Her shoulder shrieked. So did she.

Hot breath hissed in her ear. She smelled onions, garlic. The tang of wild testosterone.

Shut the fuck up.

The boy with the pockmarks.

His knees dug into her thighs. Something stiff pressed against his sweatpants against her ass. His breathing was heavy. Hitched a little when he moved. Her stomach twisted.

You ever, and I mean ever, pull shit like that again you fuckin cunt, I'll beat the shit outta you. Got it?

Jennie nodded.

He released her right arm. Punched her in the kidney. Pushed her face onto the pavement. Bloodied her nose.

He fled the scene, loose shoes scuffing the sidewalk.

Jennie sat up slow. Regained her breath. She walked away once the pain abated. Cut through a random yard to the woods. To avoid more confrontations.

She remembered one of the old woman's warnings. Clenched her teeth and swallowed the rage. At the crone. At the boys. At herself.

Be careful what you do, the old woman had said, or how far you push it. Boys of any age don't like to be shown up.

Dry twigs snapped beneath her feet. Birds of many ilk squawked. Squirrels and chipmunks, what her mother called grinnies, leaped from tree branch to tree branch. Jennie approached the old oak where she planted her flower. She felt rather than heard the entire forest pause, inhale, hold its collective breath. She held hers as well.

Three new flowers had sprouted to join the first. Arranged in a perfect square. She thought they moved in her direction. As if sensing her arrival.

No. She convinced herself it was just her imagination.

———◆———

Four years later.

Football has always been king in western Pennsylvania high school athletics. Boys basketball, distant dukes.

Jennie hit a three-pointer at the buzzer to break the tie and send the Boarshead High School Lady Badgers to the State Championship. The home crowd, which filled only half the gymnasium and included her mother and two brothers, roared. Jennie's teammates lifted her on their shoulders. Some of the teenagers cried. That night, the Lady Badgers sat tall in the high school sports throne.

All because of a stray cat.

One month prior.

Can't you do anything right? Dina said. What the fuck's wrong with you?

Jennie refused to call her Mom. It would imply someone who nurtured. Cared. Not the self-centered creature who carried Jennie and her brothers to term. Dina was the woman's name. Jennie called her that.

Dina had just returned from work. So she said. Jennie smelled the sweet and sour trace of alcohol. Dina had stopped at the bar.

It's a day ending in Y, she would say and cackle. Often from the payphone outside the establishment.

But Dina drank Jack and Coke that night.

If she had a few beers just to take the edge off, the rest of the evening would be tolerable. Perhaps even relaxing, if Dina fell asleep early. A few vodka and whatevers, Jennie would have to watch her step. Nothing major. Any brown liquor, though, meant trouble.

That's why I don't drink it anymore, Dina reminded her. Countless times.

Dina lied. Countless times.

Eddie. Jennie's father. Also a liar. Also a drunk. Left to go get smokes when she was two. Forgot to come home. Popped back in for just enough time to get Dina pregnant twice more and never returned. She still talked to him daily. Jennie wouldn't have cared if he lived next door. She wouldn't speak to him at all.

Jennie and her brothers came home right after school that day. The guys watched regurgitated sitcoms on TV. She read a book. Waited until seven, hadn't heard from Dina, decided to cook. Breakfast for dinner. They mowed down scrambled eggs, sausage, toast. After they cleaned up, Jennie started the dishes. It was her turn.

She heard the car pull up. Drew, the older of her two brothers and two years younger than her, poked his head in the kitchen.

Hurry up. She's here.

Jennie picked up the pace.

Josh, who was four years younger than her, followed Drew out the backdoor in the kitchen. Avoided meeting Dina coming in the front.

Jennie frowned. They escaped Dina's ire, as always. Maybe they were smarter than her that way, she wondered.

She refused to run. From anyone. She was the oldest. She had responsibilities. She wouldn't take shit from drunk Dina, whose moods, even sober, swung in wide arcs.

But Dina drank Jack and Coke that night.

The screen door slammed home. Jennie stopped the running water. There were several dishes left. She had to pause and gauge the inebriation. She stopped breathing.

Floorboards groaned under the thin, worn carpet in the living room. A loud, jangled THUMP from a purse filled with keys and loose change. Slow shuffle. Unable to lift her feet very high. Made her way through the small dining room and into the kitchen.

Jennie let out her breath. Hastened to finish.

Shitshitshit.

Looked up when she heard Dina stop. The woman leaned against the archway between the kitchen and dining room. Mouth ajar. Lipstick smeared. Dress wrinkled. Blouse untucked. An open eyelet at the bottom gawked at Jennie. A stray button hung loose at the top.

What made her drop the glass was Dina's eyes.

One was almost closed. The other open but unseeing. Glazed over. It surveyed the kitchen. The dishes drying in the rack. The girl standing at the sink.

Two thoughts, horrifying in their truth, whispered to Jennie.

Dina doesn't know you right now.

Dina will remember none of this in the morning.

The juice glass slid through Jennie's soapy hands. Exploded on the linoleum.

Nononogodno.

Recognition dawned on Dina's face. The closed eye opened. Slow. Wide. The anger built from her toes and rose to her red face and streamed forth in a torrent of slurred profanities.

Can't you do anything right? What the fuck's wrong with you?

Jennie said nothing. Knew by now that no matter the verbal abuse, no matter how exhausted she was of hearing the screams, it was best to let the steam pour from the kettle.

Goddammit. Why would you drop a good glass on the floor? Do you want me or your brothers to shred our feet? Clean that shit up. Jesus Christ.

Dina crossed the kitchen to the refrigerator. The glass forgotten. Rummaged through the containers.

What did you make for dinner, she said. A statement, not a question.

I made breakfast for dinner. Eggs and sausage.

Hmph.

Jennie heard more moving. Then an exasperated sigh.

What's this supposed to be?

Dina had removed a ball of aluminum foil. She opened it to reveal one sausage link. Let the aluminum fall to the floor. Held the sausage inches from Jennie's face.

Jennie closed her eyes. Cursed her brother Josh for bothering to put that in the fridge.

It's the leftover sausage.

I can see that. Did you think to save me any? Did you think for one moment that I might be hungry?

Well, I mean, I made the whole package. I only had two and the boys—

She knew it was a mistake as soon as she said it. She brought up her brothers. Mommy's angels. Though her wrath aimed at them was just as swift as with Jennie.

Don't you dare bring your brothers into this.

Dina smeared the sausage on Jennie's face. Hard.

That did it. Jennie felt a tense wire within her snap.

Fuck you.

She pushed her mother. Pushed her again. Repeated the refrain fuck you fuck you fuck you. Each punctuated with another shove. She continued even when Dina hit the far wall.

What's the matter? Didn't get laid? Couldn't get someone drunk enough? Why weren't you here to cook? Why aren't you ever here you drunk asshole?

Jennie took a wild swing. Connected with Dina's chin. Her head hit the wall.

They paused out of the shock. Jennie's eyes were saucers, her mouth an O.

She said, Dina, I'm sorry, I—

Dina lashed out and thrust Jennie to the floor. Bounced Jennie's head off the linoleum. Saw stars. Dina shrieked.

What the fuck's wrong with you, you crazy fucking bitch?

Jennie wriggled free and ran out the back door. She heard none of the verbal abuse. Her mind ran as fast as her legs.

Tears streamed down her face not from fear not from hurt teen angst but from blind searing rage at the injustice of her responsibilities, at her total lack of self, defined only by those around her, defined only by the suffocating conventional norms, defined only by the awkward stares by neighbors who turn their heads, ignore the fights, the drunken screams, the neighbors who think they're good people by keeping to themselves and say that poor girl, she'll get out one day, don't say anything to the authorities, that's not our business, she's strong, she'll make it on her own and find a good Christian man and things will be alright, they'll have a big family to take to church and she can be defined by all those children and some new overlord who will keep her in her place, just like her drunk mother and magic disappearing father, just like the rest of us sheep, blind leading the blind, world without end, in the name of the father, the son, and the holy spirit, amen.

Jennie stopped. She was at the old oak.

She didn't burst into additional tears. She growled deep in her throat. Roared at the trees. Shook her clenched fists. Collapsed on the cool earth beside her struggling garden. Another flower had joined the group. They looked sad. Wilted yet again.

Queenie mewed beside her. Rubbed against Jennie's bare leg. Purred. Jennie started. Lost in her own thoughts.

Queenie had no proper owner. Just the people in the neighborhood. Loved or loathed, everyone knew the feline and her trademark patchwork pelt. She strutted about as if she owned the street.

Jennie often left scraps for Queenie. She envied the cat. The lithe body. The freedom.

Jennie was thankful for the nonhuman company. Relieved to be rid of the specter of home. She pet Queenie while the animal groomed herself.

Queenie's head snapped to attention. Her hackles stood on end. She hissed. The newest flower in the back was angled toward the cat. The flower swayed. There was no breeze.

The smile that had played on Jennie's lips turned into a frown. Something was not right. She knew what would happen if she didn't scoop Queenie up. She hesitated. Then reached down to grab her.

Too late. The cat pounced.

Jennie said, Queenie don't.

Queenie landed in the center of the bed. Batted the pedals with a playful paw. Buried her snout into the flower and bit it. The flower pedals folded over Queenie's face. She tried to pull free but was unable.

Paused for a moment. She howled and cried. Shook her head. Frantic. The flower held fast.

Jennie jumped up and reached over to grasp Queenie but the other four flowers collapsed onto the cat. Jennie stepped back. Closed her eyes. Covered her ears. The noise ceased.

She surveyed the scene. Queenie had disappeared, as if she had never arrived. The flowers were renewed. Their colors all the more vibrant in the darkness. Four new buds had sprung from the ground. The entire bed pointed at her. Watching. Waiting. Expectant.

The bud opened in her mind. This one was larger than before. She knew it would hold a more substantial desire. But the reminder of the flowers collapsing around Queenie also emerged.

The shrieks. Christ, the screams.

The bud continued to grow. Pressed against the inside of Jennie's skull as if it had reached its spatial limit. Her head throbbed. She fell to one knee. Her vision blurred. Her breathing labored. She remembered another warning from the old crone.

Don't feed them unless you want something.

Dina.

One dark, hateful image surfaced. Jennie squelched it quick.

I just want to be appreciated, she thought. I want her to see it. My brothers, too.

The bud closed quick. Jennie gasped and blinked. The pressure had ceased. She knew then that her wish would be carried out, but she wouldn't know how. Not until the next day.

She was better than most girls on her basketball team. That week and in the month that followed, her athleticism was augmented. It carried her and the Lady Badgers to the state semifinals. Her brothers were there. Dina was there, less intoxicated than usual. They cheered her on. They waved. They celebrated as Jennie and the team exited the court of the Boarshead Junior-Senior High School Gymnasium.

Jennie returned home to find Dina and the boys waiting. Dina had baked them a cake. The first time since Jennie was five. Yellow cake with chocolate icing. Yes, from a box. But it was Jennie's favorite.

CONGRATS! read the message in Badgers' colors, blue and white.

Jennie later decided that Dina was a Mom on that night. One short month after smacking her daughter's head off the floor in an inebriated fugue.

One year later.

That college is too expensive, Dina said.

Jennie didn't want to hear it. Dina had come home late that evening. Stank like stale, moldy bread. And ashtrays. Jennie surmised it was a beer night. Payday was a week away. She was certain Dina performed some favors for a few rounds. She blocked any mental images.

I'm applying for grants and student loans, Jennie said. She tapped the paperwork in front of her.

If you didn't fuck up yer ankle, you'd be goin fer free.

Jennie winced. Blushed red anger.

She had sports scholarship offers to several Division I schools because of her basketball prowess. She twisted her ankle during the summer, however. When the season resumed after she healed, she couldn't run as fast. Couldn't jump as high. Her grades were good. Just not good enough. The offers vanished.

I'm not going to stay here forever, Jennie said.

That's a shitty thing to say, Dina said. Words mashed together.

Dina. I'm not living in this house until we get old and die. That's not going to work for either of us.

Dina pulled a beer from the near-empty fridge.

Yep. Someone'll sweep you off yer feet and take you the hell off my hands.

She collapsed into a chair at the kitchen table. Twisted off the bottle top. Took a long swig. Belched.

Jennie rolled her eyes. Turned her attention back to the paperwork.

I'm not going to be swept off my feet. I'm going to get the hell out of this shitty little town and go to a good school.

Don't you want a family?

No.

What about your brothers?

They can take care of themselves. When Drew's not at school, he's working with Mr. Potter. All Josh does is play video games.

Dina had the beer halfway to her mouth. Paused. Set it down.

What about me?

Jennie closed her eyes. Sighed. Dina was drowning. Looking for excuses. If it had been a liquor night, she would have erupted by now.

Any whiskey and they would have come to blows. Or Jennie would have avoided the topic altogether. On a beer night, though, Jennie knew she had the upper hand.

What about you?

Dina stammered. Expelled only noise and air.

Jennie said, Do you want someone here to cook your meals after a late night at the bar? Or make your drinks to take away your hangover in the morning? Or hold your hair back when you have one too many? Get one of your boyfriends to do it.

Why are you being such a heartless bitch?

Because it's a beer night, Jennie thought.

Because I learned from the best, she said instead.

Dina snatched the loan application and bounded to the kitchen sink in three clumsy strides. Fumbled in the pocket of her skintight jeans. Found a lighter. Lit the papers. Watched the flames gobble the sheets. Dropped them in the sink after they were engulfed.

There. Try to leave now.

Jennie watched with a passive face. Her emotions roiled with all the loathing she had ever held in check. Logic tried to prevail. She could get student loan applications anywhere. The public library. The school library. Her guidance counselor. The bank itself. There were any number of places away from home where she could fill out the paperwork and mail it. She was certain that Dina, as drunk as she was, knew this as well.

But the utter lack of respect.

Pure blind rage welled to the surface. The voice of the old crone whispered to her.

Jennie said, You're right, Dina.

Dina smiled. A little cautious. More than a little triumphant.

Yeah. I'm right.

Sorry I argued with you. Let me get you a beer. Can I have one, too? Mom?

Dina paused. Her lower lip shook. She nodded her head quick.

Sure. Thanks, sweetie.

They sat at the kitchen table. Jennie let Dina jabber on about work, about the people there, as if Jennie knew them all. She listened. Went to the refrigerator and replaced each empty bottle.

Dina talked about the men at work. The men at the bars. The men she slept with. The men she hadn't. The men she said she would never fuck but did anyway.

Jennie nursed her beer. Hated the taste of it. The not all flat but not quite effervescent feel on her tongue.

She said nothing but a few well placed Mmm Hmms, Sures, and the occasional, Yeah, I know what you mean. After the seventh empty clunked onto the table, Dina announced her plan to retire for the night.

Before you go, Mom, I have something to show you.

What is it?

A surprise. C'mon.

Jennie grabbed the Coleman electric lantern they used for power failures or Dina's failure to pay the electric bill. Jennie led her mother outside into the cool autumn air. There was no moon. There were no stars.

They were almost to the woods when Dina fell. She laughed. An inebriated cackle filled with mirth that Jennie had never heard before. At that moment, it struck her that Dina was a real person. She had aspirations once. Had told Jennie on many a drunk night, that one included. She was also in love once.

Jennie wavered.

But what about the next liquor night? said a voice not unlike her own or the old crone's. Or the next whiskey night?

The burning paperwork flashed in her mind.

Hey. Help me up, dammit.

Jennie whipped her head around to the neighbors' houses. Still all dark.

Shh, Jennie said. Keep it down.

Don't shush me, Dina said. Show me this fuckin surprise, whatever it is.

Jennie grabbed her mother's hand and pulled her up. Turned the lantern on. Guided Dina into the woods, away from the nosy neighbors, from her brothers, from the world and its view of how she should act.

They stood in front of the flower bed, now five feet by five feet. Jennie shined a light on them. They stared at her. They were discolored. Hadn't eaten a proper meal in over a year.

Jennie held her hand out to the flowers.

What? Dina asked. This is it?

Yes.

You brought me out here to show me flowers?

Yes.

Wait. Are you givin me these things? Cause I fuckin hate flowers.

No. This is mine. This is the one thing I have now. Basketball's gone. You're trying to take college away from me. I wanted to show you what I've done for myself. Without you.

Dina's face was blank.

Wonderful. Can I go to bed now?

Don't you want to smell them first?

What, those? Fuck no. They look dead.

Dina turned to leave but Jennie grasped her by the shoulders. Dina twisted from her grasp, forcing Jennie off balance. She fell into the flower bed. For a maddening moment she was certain that she would be surrounded and devoured. But no. The flowers provided a soft cushion to pad her landing. An idea sprung to her mind. She inhaled sharp through her teeth. Affected a pained tone.

Mom. Mom, I twisted my ankle.

Dina sighed.

Christ. Again?

Yeah, it hurts really bad. Please help me up.

Jennie held her hand aloft.

Another sigh from Dina.

Alright.

They locked hands. Jennie pulled herself up and kicked Dina in the back of the leg behind the knee. Dina toppled into the flower bed.

You bitch, why did you—

She stopped speaking. Started screaming. Jennie's eyes grew large, terrified that any residents near the woods would overhear. She did not run away or shield her eyes and ears this time. She had to see. Wanted to hear. Delighted in it. What little light shined from the lantern spotlighted the vanishing woman.

The flowers were lusher than ever. Luminescent. The bed gained two new rows. They faced Jennie.

She closed her eyes. Felt the bud open in her mind. Her plans for school, leaving, escaping, graduating college with ease, obtaining any career of her choice were placed inside the gaping flower.

Her dream was large, yes, but her sacrifice was as well. The old crone had told her they were connected.

The flower started to close. A final thought crossed Jennie's mind that she slid in before the bud squeezed tight. The desire that no one would ask after Dina. That she would be forgotten like an empty beer bottle. Discarded without a second thought.

It would be so. Jennie was sure of it.

The bud faded from her consciousness.

She returned home wearing a smile. She liked how well it fit.

Ten years later.

August stopped fussing and had fallen asleep. Only light static issued from the baby monitor. Soft snores drifted in from the living room. Chad hadn't lasted long in his armchair. Jennie's phone read 3:13 am.

She refilled her glass with cabernet sauvignon. She planned to use it for her Girls' Night with Chelsea that Thursday. But when Jennie fed August and tried to put her down for the night, the ten month old wanted no part of such nonsense.

It's not time for bed, Mother, don't you realize that? What are you, stupid? How about I shit through my diaper and all over the mattress? That'd really give you something to think about, wouldn't it?

August said none of this. She cried and cried.

The baby loved Chad more anyway. Jennie knew this. Knew that he was the only person to get August to sleep when she had one of her fits. Jennie wouldn't wake him. Not because of Chad's presentation or whatever the fuck work thing he had in the morning. Pride had taken over reason. She would get this kid to sleep if it took her all night.

Not that Jennie slept much as of late.

Sure enough, around three in the morning, Chad lumbered into August's bedroom. Griped about his presentation. Held August. She was asleep minutes later. Confirmed Jennie's suspicions about a preferred parent.

Screw Thursday. She needed that wine now.

Chad. Jennie met him while studying for her MBA at Pitt. Other relationships she had were superficial at best. Let's have fun, a few drinks, fuck, forget about each other. That worked for them. For her. For her plan.

She had things to do. Time for little else other than the path she mapped out in the woods by the old oak. By the flowers. After Dina.

Jennie had almost finished with her Master's when she got together with Chad. He had been there all along, a friend of a friend of someone else. He spent the night after their first date. Then they stayed at each other's places on weekends. Then for weeks at a time. They moved in together. Graduated. Worked in high powered managerial positions for several years.

Chad was a Good Guy. Said all the right things. Did all the right things. Treated her like an equal. She felt comfortable around him. Relaxed. Safe.

Most important, Chad did not derail the plan.

Is this love? she wondered one day. Did she deserve it?

He proposed. She accepted.

The morning after their first wedding anniversary. She knew something was different. Dinner and drinks were fine, the sex was great. That morning, however, she couldn't identify the malady. She knew she didn't like it at all. This was not part of the plan. This was not a branch off the path to another, more exciting route. A sinkhole yawned open in the middle. The path disappeared into an abyss. She created something she had not intended to.

Nine months to the day, August was born.

Chad wept when he saw August for the first time. So did Jennie, but for another reason.

They returned to Jennie's childhood home in Boarshead while she was still pregnant. Her brothers had maintained it while she went to school. They had never asked about Dina. They went about the business of living their lives. Older, modern Boxcar Children. Within a few years, they both moved away. Drew opened a construction business in Oregon. Josh went into the Army and was stationed in Florida.

Jennie loathed the place. It was still the cage Dina had constructed. But, as Chad reasoned when she protested, it was big enough for the two of them and the baby. And only a thirty-minute commute to work.

Not that Jennie worked much as of late.

After her allotted six weeks off, she called Tom, the director at her office. He had beseeched her not to take much time off. Begged her to work from home. Now it was Jennie's turn. She asked when she could return. Could hear the plea in her voice. Didn't care.

Oh, geez, Jennie, I don't know, Tom said. Dennis has really stepped it up here at work.

Dennis. That sycophantic fuck. Jennie gnashed her teeth.

Has he now? she said.

Yeah, yeah. Why don't you take your time with little, um, what's her name again?

August.

Yeah, yeah, August.

The Old Boy's Club, thought Jennie. Just stay at home in the kitchen, ma'am. We've got it all under control.

Fuck them, Chad said later. You can come work with me. Christ knows we need someone with your skill set. Maybe we can have one of those interoffice affairs they always talk about.

He wagged his eyebrows. Jennie rolled her eyes. He got her to smile.

We'll have to look into daycares or something, he said. Ruined the moment. Her smile faded.

She had been unable to connect with August. Ten-plus months later and her daughter was little more than some round-headed alien that insisted on being fed and changed. Every time Jennie held the baby, August squirmed to escape, to run to Chad, to pull him away from Jennie.

There was no competing. August had won. Jennie couldn't remember the last time Chad had touched her. Kissed her hard. Urgent. Slid inside her.

Jennie looked at her once slim figure in the mirror one morning. Now twisted, bloated, reconfigured. Stretch marks spidered around her enlarged navel. She saw Chad look from the corner of the mirror. Saw him frown.

She cried in the bathroom for an hour after he left for work. Emerged when August woke. Diaper full. Face red.

Stop feeling sorry for yourself, Mother. Feel for me. For my needs.

Jennie poured the last of the wine into her glass. She lost count of refills. Didn't care. Looked into the deep scarlet. It reminded her of the flowers. Reminded her of Dina.

She thought about the day that she and Chad had moved the last of the moving boxes into the house. She had crept through the unkempt yard. The high grass tickled the bottom of her round belly. Into the woods, under the old oak, the flowers were still there. Many had died, but the patch was still large. Maybe three by four or three by five. They shuddered to life. Looked to her. Hopeful. She had wept hard.

Jennie sipped her wine. Thought about her lost dreams. Her lost husband. Her lost life.

Chip off the old block, Dina, Jennie said to her drink. No one remembers you anymore. Just me.

Jennie lifted the glass to her mouth. The wine touched her lips. Then she set the glass down. The bud of an idea bloomed wide.

Babe. What are you doing?

She heard Chad behind her but ignored him.

It's cold out here. Why did you bring August outside?

He would soon forget. He wouldn't even know why he had followed her.

Babe? Babe? Jennie?

He shouldn't have come out at all. August started fussing once Jennie made it to the living room.

C'mon Jennie. I know you've been having trouble with this. We can get you some help. Please.

Maybe August suspected something was amiss. That's why she cried out. For help. For Chad.

Jennie. I love you.

Jennie set the child into the flower bed.

She turned to Chad. Tears coursed down her cheeks. A crazed grin covered her face. August wailed.

We can be together again. I can go back to work. I can find myself again. Just give it a minute and we can start over.

Chad brushed past her. To cradle the crying baby.

No, Chad.

Jennie took a step towards the flower bed to grasp him. He hadn't been in the bed long. She almost pulled him out. But the flowers shot up from the ground as tall as cornstalks. In an instant, they pulled Chad down into the earth. She heard muffled noise, then nothing.

She fell to the ground. Unable to move. Unable to think. Watched the flowers' resplendent return.

The small bud opened in her mind. Pressed against her consciousness. The air stolen from her lungs. A veil closed across her vision. Jennie imagined the future as she had once planned it. Her career. Her life. The path that had been destroyed. Everything she sacrificed for a family she wasn't supposed to have. A husband. Children. Then what? Grandchildren? Retirement to an assisted living facility? A home?

No. None of that.

She shoved the plan as it should have been into the mental flower. Threw every bit in as if gutting a house. As the flower closed, she wished no one would remember her husband and daughter, even Chad's parents, kind, loving, so unlike her own.

The bud closed. She opened her eyes. Saw Chad's glasses in the grass. She remembered August.

She remembered Chad.

No one else would, she knew. She neglected to alter her own memory. When the mourning would strike, and she knew it would, there would be no one to lean on. No one to relate the story. No one with whom to plead her case.

She stared at the flowers until the sun rose.

———◆———

Years later.

The girl sat against the tree. Cried. Her curly black hair shuddered. Her soccer ball forgotten beside her.

Jennie, now old, now near the end of a long, happy life, watched. She wondered if the crone who appeared to her had done the same.

She awoke that morning and knew it was time. Took a taxi northwest to Boarshead from her condo in Pittsburgh. Hobbled through the yard of her childhood home. It was still owned by her, but used only for storage. She peered in a window. It was filled with trinkets, furniture, the ghosts of her mother and husband and child, forgotten by everyone. Except her. She walked to the woods to the old oak. Pulled a wooden box and a hand trowel from her large purse. One flower remained. Wrinkled. Faded. Wilted.

Jennie sighed. Dug the flower out of the hard, rough dirt. Placed it in the box with care as if it were glass.

She left the woods. Wandered down the road to her old elementary school. It wasn't long before she witnessed a familiar scene.

A girl tried to play soccer with a bunch of boys from the neighborhood. They told her to go play with her dyke buddies. Shouted other insults Jennie couldn't hear. Laughed as the girl ran away.

Jennie followed. She approached after the girl's angry tears subsided.

What's your name, dear?

The girl looked up to view an old woman in an expensive suit. Her voice was dry. Craggy peaks and valleys. But her tone was sweet. Understanding.

The girl rubbed her eyes. Answered the old woman.

And soon accepted the gift.

USED CLOTHES
Paul L. Bates

In that faraway land where I lived as a boy—a twisted maze of wide ravines encased by inhospitable mountains and lingering storms— there came to my village each year a stooped and crooked figure known to all as simply *the ragman*. He emerged, a specter from the early morning mists, creeping along in his covered cart behind a shambling swaybacked roan. In a pathetic voice from which there was no escaping, he croaked, "Used clothes for the poor, used clothes for the poor." Soon he was collecting all manner of tattered garments fit only for a scarecrow from the village women in exchange for a few pennies.

The ragman would disappear the evening on the day he arrived, an animated shadow, his rickety wooden cart heaped high with whatever the village women had brought him. He and his ancient horse clopped off alone down those twisted streets awash in cold moonlight, back to whatever grim mysteries lay to the north. The mournful wail of a distant train whistle inevitably marked his passing.

I was certain from an early age that despite his lamentations to the contrary the ragman was no philanthropist, nor was he in the employ of other philanthropists. Rather, I felt sure, I knew not why, that the used clothes he gathered were never intended for the destitute in the great grey city to the north, nor anywhere else. In fact, I was convinced the kind-hearted women of our village had in some way been grievously duped, but I was unsure how or why. My suspicions—indeed, the ill will I felt as a child for this seemingly harmless vagabond—were predicated upon the smallest, perhaps even the shoddiest deductions my immature mind could concoct, yet I remained steadfast in my conviction from year to year that the ragman was up to no good.

The man himself was shriveled, hunched and swathed in a disgusting veneer of grime as if he tended a great furnace when not imploring old clothes from village housewives. His nose was long and thin, even filthier than the rest of his face, with pale streaks where he had vigorously rubbed it with his gnarled fingers. He wore a tattered felt hat, soiled woolen vest, patched jacket and trousers of some indeterminate dark shade, no better than the rags he solicited.

My conjectures about his purpose began as a simple notion that the used clothes he gathered were subsequently cut up and used as dust cloths, similar to those my mother made. They advanced to a more viable notion that perhaps the ragman himself picked the best of the lot he gathered for his own wardrobe, which accounted for the state of it; that he burned the rest in that furnace he tended. Other flights of fancy included the used clothes were meant for dangerous prisoners, chained in dank and forgotten dungeons; or for overactive lunatics wont to shred their own garments in moments of spastic agitation. I never imagined I would one day actually solve the riddle, the ghastly nature of the answer, nor the manner in which the solution would present itself to me.

As it happened, my father was in possession of an old shirt that was as dear to him as it was an embarrassment to my mother. The color was a distinct shade of yellow, not quite mustard, not quite ochre, with a pattern of thin pale blue horizontal and vertical lines intersecting every few inches. I had never seen another remotely like it. The shirt was, he boasted, hand made especially for him. I clearly remember he had worn it the night before to a dance at the local cantina. My mother had pointed out the badly frayed elbows and the wine-colored blotch on the pocket before they left me and my siblings in the care of my doddering grandmother. My mother begged him to dress, as she put it, *like a man of means instead of a beggar* but my father had obstinately worn it anyway. As I said, he loved that shirt, although who made it for him and for what occasion I never learned.

The next morning when the ragman's mournful cry reached our crooked street my mother snatched the shirt from the laundry hamper and marched to the door with it. My father, already off to that dreary stone monolith that cast its afternoon shadow across the entire village, could neither protest nor prevent her from giving his precious shirt to the ragman. I stood behind my mother holding my breath watching the garment change hands. The ragman turned his doleful gaze upon me as he dropped a pair of copper coins into my mother's open palm. His eyes met mine, brightened; his thin lips curved into a terrifying grin the like of which I had never seen. He tipped his hat, urged the horse on with a loud click of his tongue.

When he was out of earshot my mother smiled and said, "Congratulations—I've never seen him smile before. Perhaps he seeks an apprentice." With that she flung back her long black hair and laughed.

There was a scene the following week when my father discovered his loss, to be sure, but after the yelling subsided, he never made reference to the shirt again. So at the time I gave the matter no further thought, save for my renewed imaginings concerning the real use the ragman— or those for whom he labored—put the objects he purchased.

I turned fourteen shortly thereafter.

On that occasion my father took me with him before dawn to that frightful stone monolith so as the eldest son I might aid him to provide for the family. It was a dismal sweat shop, full of perpetually hovering dust, deafening noise, squealing pulleys, belts, gears, and ominous heavy machines that ground, bore, cut and stamped sheets and extrusions of assorted metals into parts for other machines to work in other places. Rickety open trucks that reeked of diesel came and went forever bringing more sheets and extrusions with them, taking away the parts we had fashioned. My innocence lost, I knew this sad state was to become the sum total of my existence if I gave in to it.

So when I was sixteen and of stronger heart—certain I had had enough of tending machines for six days a week in order that, presumably, others might do the same when the metal parts I helped to fashion were assembled elsewhere—I stole into the night, my few worldly possessions and half a loaf of bread pilfered from the kitchen stuffed into an old pillowcase. I made my way by moonlight across the potato, turnip and cabbage fields that surrounded our village, past bleating sheep and goats in the sloping pastures beyond. For the remainder of the night and all the next day I continued on until at last I came upon the imposing iron tracks with their black wooden cross ties, where I waited for that mysterious train whose doleful whistle I had heard each night for as long as I could remember.

I clambered aboard an open boxcar when the old engine, belching great clouds of churning cinders, struggled up the steep rise. I fell asleep to the clackety-clack of steel wheels grinding against the rails, let the train bear me to warmer climes and sunny skies. I vowed never to look back again.

What I did with my life has no place in this story, save that I eventually earned passage across the vast ocean to a fabled land of opportunity where I worked as a manual laborer by day, attended classes by night in an effort to better myself. Gradually, and with constant effort, my station improved. After decades of toiling ten hours a day in a tower of glass and steel I was promoted to director of foreign acquisitions. As I had never lost my mother tongue, my territory was to be that dismal faraway land of my birth. The irony of my escape from this place only to return to it decades later was not wasted upon me, and, as fate would have it, I was sent to that great grim city to the north of the village where I was born.

The city, whose name is nearly unpronounceable, even to its inhabitants, is almost impossible to describe to one who has never been there. Squat grey five story buildings erected centuries before teeter over the street at precarious angles, all nestled together like hungry beggars, each nearly identical to the next. Filthy cobblestone streets, both steep and narrow, that double back upon themselves innumerable times discourage travel to unfamiliar places. Perpetually dark featureless skies, where soot and water interbreed to wash the blanched buildings with a corrosive rain, etch the ancient stonework with a dogged resolve. And occasional rickety horse carts reminiscent of the one the ragman drove feel like relics from another age.

Still, I was treated as a visiting dignitary for bringing business from a wealthy land of opportunity to this decrepit place—a prodigal son welcomed home by an array of nondescript public servants who constantly watched over my commercial activities.

When the regional acquisitions office was up and running, the fees paid, employees hired, contracts in place, I made discrete inquiries concerning the fate of my family, for although I had once hoped to put them all, like the faraway land of my birth, well behind me, I still felt some kinship toward these people. Not to my surprise, my parents were both dead, as were all of my aunts and uncles. Like me, my siblings had immigrated to parts unknown. Only a few elderly and barely remembered cousins were left in that village with its surrounding cabbage, turnip and potato fields and the commanding stone monolith whose shadow fell across it each afternoon when the skies were clear.

Relieved by this news, I decided to forego a visit to the dismal place.

It was during an early autumn evening after supper in the dank city with an unpronounceable name that I came upon a bookshop on a street not far from my lodgings. The place was narrow, dusty, unheated, and dark. From the street I knew it to be a bookstore only by a faded placard leaning against the ground floor window proclaiming it as such—a placard I had not noticed before. The cramped interior was lined with sagging bookshelves and a small wooden service counter near the door where sat a rumpled man in a stained frock coat, his grey eyes made monstrous by thick lenses. He was painfully thin, reminded me of a cadaver, and made it a point to ignore me when I entered.

Perusing his seemingly haphazard assortment of histories, philosophies and novels I found nothing whatever to my liking. I looked up, suddenly catching his eye. He motioned with an ink stained finger for me to attend him, lowered his voice when I drew near, lest someone without be listening as we were the only ones in the shop. The acrid smell of unwashed skin, mildew and decay that clung to him gave me pause. I felt the urge to bolt as fast as my legs would carry me.

"You look to be a man of discernment, one whose education has come in part from books and in part from life itself. Am I right?" he asked.

I forced a smile, decided to play along lest the man be dangerous, nodded sagaciously, hoping my theatrics did not offend him.

"I have, for customers such as yourself, certain volumes—books not to be found in the usual catalogues; books not for those whose minds are closed."

I assumed he meant pornography, prepared to make my exit, but he placed a claw-like hand upon my wrist and held me fast, as if the shoddy underweight man I saw sitting across the worn counter were but an illusion concealing something monumental—something of enormous power and unimagined strength.

"What manner of books do you mean?" I whispered.

Smiling, he released his grip upon my arm. "Books," he said languidly, "filled with secrets; books that hold the key for one who can read between the lines; books that teach one with an open mind how to strip away the illusion; books for one who would see clearly what lies beneath. Are you interested?"

His words, echoing my own immediate fears, touched something within me, an inborn curiosity I had allowed to atrophy since the day my father brought me with him to that monolith of hopelessness whose shadow fell across our village—or perhaps it simply touched that growing sense that comes with age that nothing is truly as it appears.

"Yes," I averred, "I'm interested."

He slipped a filthy hand beneath the counter, removed a thin black leather volume that bore neither title nor image upon the cover or spine. It looked to have been read before.

"Start with this one. If it awakens anything within you—that is to say, if it is to your liking—come back again. Exchange it for another."

The price was steep, unbelievably so for a slender used book. I tried to haggle but he would hear none of it. As I was already bored with this dismal city of broken spirit and wished to be quit of the shop, I paid him, thrust the book into my coat pocket, bade the man good night, and hurried home.

The landlady made a pot of strong tea and brought it up to my rooms. I thanked her, changed to more casual attire, opened this curious volume. Entitled *The Crystal City*, it was written by someone using a fanciful pseudonym, a name meant to sound like that of a demon, or perhaps a fallen angle. It was, surprisingly, easy reading, putting forth the proposition that in the beginning all things were straightforward, intellectually transparent—that one had but to look to understand. Simple creatures with simple needs populated a world where time had no meaning, where space refused to obey the rules of physics—a world so unlike the one we know that it would be completely invisible to a modern man who had spent his life learning complex and obscuring lies in order to fit in—unless he were taught where to look.

I set the book down, sipped my tea, contemplating the supposition. It was fanciful, dark, oddly poetic—possibly an allegory, I decided. As I had the entire weekend to myself, I read on.

The book hinted at techniques for acquiring both the state of mind and the vision to see the ancient world, methods of breathing, eye exercises, visualizations and meditations. It further elaborated upon the effect of the modern world upon this first world, as the two were in no way mutually exclusive, although their seeming incompatibility was a paradox the earnest seeker must, perforce, decipher for himself.

It ended on an ominous note, stating that the reader, having learned of this place, would inevitably attract to himself the denizens of the primal world who would eventually judge him. It advised the reader to begin the practices meant to make them visible to him as quickly as possible, lest he be taken unaware in these uneven encounters, for his will was nothing compared to theirs. Further, it warned, when he met any of these old-world denizens, under no circumstances should he prevaricate.

I would have been amused, entertained, save for a series of somber and inexplicable events which shortly occurred that gave some small credence to what I had just read.

I finished *The Crystal City* before supper on Saturday. It was my first weekend free since returning to this faraway land of my birth and, as I have said before, from what little I had seen of it this entire city appeared depressingly homogenous with no distinguishing landmarks anywhere, save for an occasional church spire lost in the distance. So I asked my landlady, a grim widow with parched skin and too many petticoats beneath her frilly dresses what one did for amusement here. This earned me an icy glare. I rephrased my question, asking if there were any cinemas, theaters, or stadiums nearby, to which she replied cryptically, "There may well be, but I do not personally know of any."

My rooms, which were only a few blocks from my workplace, had been recommended to me by the first of several nondescript public servants who had overseen the establishment of the regional sales office, and who occasionally returned to make certain I was in compliance with their bewildering maze of laws. I had used the close proximity as an opportunity to take some exercise by walking to and from work, whatever the weather. So having never seen any public transportation during these daily strolls, I asked my landlady about the location of the stops, thinking some of them must surely be near the amusements I sought. But the concept of public transportation was beyond her understanding.

Once again I reiterated, citing buses, trolleys, trains, and subways as possible alternatives. Only at the word *subway* did I see a glimmer of recognition, and something else briefly—something I took to be pure terror. She shook her head vehemently and rushed back to her kitchen, the layers of petticoats swishing furiously.

That afternoon was oppressively overcast. From time to time the wind toyed with a few dried leaves or scraps of refuse in the street, half heartedly churning the stale air. I decided to walk the neighborhood, hoping to find what I sought—I had, after all, come across the book-shop quite by accident. The darkened windows I passed were mostly obscured by crooked shutters, yellowed curtains, or torn shades, with only an occasional small sign displayed on the inside announcing a butcher shop, green grocer, barber, or bakery. The smells were uniform-ly unwholesome, and apart from these intermittent placards, the build-ings I passed could all have been apartments, offices, or anything else one could imagine as there was little to distinguish one from the other.

After a fruitless hour I was ready to give up lest I lose myself in the labyrinth when an image from my childhood froze me on the spot—a battered wooden wagon, hauled by a swaybacked roan, a disheveled old man hunched over the reins, a mound of rags visible behind him. I could barely believe my eyes. It looked to be the same man, but I knew that to be impossible. I stood, my mouth agape, my back pressed against the stone wall staring mystified at the ragman. He passed me by without sparing me so much as a glance, rubbing his long nose with gnarled arthritic fingers.

In a trance I followed him, completely unmindful of where I was in relation to my lodgings. The horse clopped on, street after street, pulling the creaking wagon while I maintained a discrete distance be-hind it. It was only then I noticed how few pedestrians I passed, all of them heavily bundled with large brimmed hats concealing their faces, their eyes lowered. How long we kept at this I wasn't sure, but horse and wagon eventually disappeared into an uninviting arched opening just wide enough to accommodate it that led downward. I froze again, watching the top of the wagon sinking into whatever abyss lay beyond, remembering the terror in my landlady's eyes when I said the word *subway*.

I might have stood there forever had not someone taken me by the arm in a grip of steel. Startled, I looked down into the baleful grey eyes of the bookseller, enormous behind his thick spectacles.

"Have you read it?" he demanded.

I nodded dumbly.

"Do you have it with you?" he pressed.

Again I nodded.

"Come with me," he insisted. "You can use it in trade for the next volume."

The bookseller practically pulled me the entire way back to his shop. Neither of us said a word. During our walk the spider's web of streets imprinted themselves upon my consciousness, I know not how. I wanted to scream that none of this was real, that his book was a sham, but I could not form a single coherent sentence. Evening had settled upon the city like a drug-induced coma, punctuated only by the dim glow of the soot covered streetlamps and the occasional wan light from a window with the shutters left open.

Once we were both inside his shop the bookseller locked the door and quickly struck the kerosene lamp on the small black counter. A plume of soot balled its way to the ceiling as the dim orange flame rearranged his face into a grotesque play of light and shadow, menacingly predatory in every aspect. I fumbled within my overcoat, produced the copy of *The Crystal City*. He snatched it quickly, tucking it once again beneath the counter. Then, from a cavity concealed by several enormous tomes in the wall behind him, he removed a second leather bound book, also obviously well read. This one was a deep burgundy, the color of dried blood, twice as thick as the black one, and like it, bore neither inscriptions nor ornamentation. He whispered the exorbitant price and extended his hand.

When I asked about the exchange value of the first book, he shrugged, saying the second book was twice as large and he was charging me less for it. At a loss for words, I did not argue. With some difficulty I forced the book into my pocket, relieved to have gotten my bearings in this neighborhood at last, relieved at the prospect of returning to the relative safety of my rooms. I thanked him for his help and followed him to the door.

"When you are ready for the next book, you know where to find me," he said, pushing me into the street. He shut and bolted the door as quickly as he could behind me.

I dropped the book into the drawer in my writing table, donned my pajamas and slept for over fourteen hours. My dreams were filled with cavernous tunnels, dark and alive with gibbering voices of faceless things concealed within the shadows, the smell of dead fish. I felt the touch of cold appendages, rubbery and moist brushing against my hands and face. I awoke to find my landlady taking my pulse. She claimed to be concerned for my health but I think it more likely her concern was for the reputation of her establishment, should a tenant die, presumably from her cooking. She made me an odd smelling broth, told me it contained herbs to ward off what she called *the sleeping sickness*. Whatever the nature of her concern, I could see it was genuine. I thanked her and ate the bitter gruel with a piece of dry toast.

I lost myself to the demands of the new office until the following weekend, venturing beyond my lodgings for that purpose only. My landlady looked pleased with my return to a working routine, her wrinkled brows and tight-lipped frown gradually abating to a puckered smile when she saw me. I completely forgot about the second book until the following Saturday.

I had been thinking about the irony of employing the very facility in which my father had toiled for most of his life and from which I had escaped after only two years. The nature of coincidence reminded me of my wanderings the previous weekend, which in turn reminded me of the red leather-bound volume in the drawer of my writing table. Accordingly, after a small breakfast in my rooms, I settled into the easy chair, began reading by the grey light of the alcove windows.

The second book was called *Uncommon Things*. It was purportedly written by another author using one of those arcane pseudonyms that imply great mystical knowledge. Whereas *The Crystal City* had been a lengthy essay built upon poetic logic and wild supposition, ending with ambiguous advice, *Uncommon Things* was a series of first person vignettes—purportedly compiled through interviews—that read like ravings from a lunatic asylum. In each case some innocuous account began in a direct and unobtrusive manner but soon degenerated into snatches of delirium, wretched attempts at coming to grips with the impossible, ending with the narrator—or patient, as the case may be—unable to discern delusion from reality. It was a very disturbing collection to say the least. In retrospect, I am not sure why I read them all, but I did complete the last account just as the evening gloom settled upon the street. The night seemed to me to be unusually dense, so much so that even the pale streetlights beyond my windows struggled to illumine anything beyond an unnatural haze surrounding the sooty globes.

I put away the book, closed the shutters, joined the other guests at the landlady's table for supper in an extremely introspective state of mind. I returned our hostess' smile, nodded to my fellow lodgers who had begun without me—people with whom I had dined for over a month. To my dismay each one of them appeared to have developed the pronounced features of an animal—a rat, goat, rabbit, monkey, giraffe and so forth. I served myself a small helping of the mutton stew, stared into the bowl to reorient myself to the familiar. To my horror there were three pale eyes staring back at me from the sea of brown. They were, in fact, lumps of overcooked potatoes to be sure, but for just that moment, to me, at least, they were eyes. I ate in silence, thanked the landlady for her usual excellent fare, hurried back to my room.

By lamp light I read the epilogue to *Uncommon Things*, a short commentary that noted, rather than postulated, a common thread in the accounts purportedly related without embellishment. This thread, it went on, was how the slightest unintentional alteration to our daily lives could strip away the veneer we spend so much effort maintaining—an effort that we, by and large, are unaware we make. And when this veneer begins to fail us, we are privileged to gaze upon the world as it really is. Unfortunately, it concluded, most of us are of such weak character, that we immediately cobble together a second veneer, one which attempts to combine our former social veneer with the unfathomable we have witnessed. And we end up moving from a shared illusion to a lonely personal delusion utterly without hope. I let the book drop from my hands to the floor and sighed.

On Sunday, after a long internal debate, I returned to the bookshop before noon. The bookseller was waiting for me.

"Well?" he demanded.

"It's uncanny..." I started, unsure if I should share my experience of the night before with him.

"To say the least," he cut me off. "Are you in or out?"

"By that, I assume you're asking me if I'm up to experiencing the next volume."

"Ah," he purred, "you've chosen the right word. You're in, of course—most definitely in. Congratulations. Now give me back the red book."

And so I returned to my rooms bearing the third volume, a new white leather bound pamphlet, whose price was dearer than the other two combined. I knew better than to protest, or even ask why, for by then I had begun to accept the fact that whatever was happening to me was inevitable, and as such, it would be far better for me to prepare myself than to make any futile attempts to stem the tide from which no man may escape.

The third, and as it happened, final book, in the words of the book-seller, *meant to strip away the illusions*, was also without title or orna-ment on cover or spine. Entitled *How*, it was authored modestly by one who called himself simply *An Initiate*. It contained neither philosophy nor case study; essay nor vignette. Instead there were twenty-one tech-niques, explained in remarkable simplicity, with anywhere from one to five pages dedicated to each technique. These included answers to any useful questions the seeker might have—all other questions were, according to the preface, to be considered unimportant at best and dis-tracting at worst. The reader was instructed to master each technique before moving on to the next. In fact, the preface warned, to read the book in any other way was certain to bring absolute disaster upon the student and his entire house. After my experiences following my read-ings of the first two books, I took the warning most seriously.

Autumn sank into bleak winter. Recurring blankets of sooty snow were trod to slush by pedestrians and the occasional careening truck or wagon attempting to navigate those steep and narrow winding streets. Rivers of the filthy stuff gurgled beneath the same grey skies to an-nounce the onset of spring.

I had busied my weekdays securing the faraway land of my birth as a source of cheap labor and materials to maintain my affluent adopted homeland, my evenings and weekends mastering the techniques in the white book. I learned to sit in absolute stillness, listening first to the wash of my breath, then the melody of my heart, the chorus of my synapses, and lastly to *the silence of the night.* I learned to *breathe like a dragon*, fast, controlled, steadily, through my nose, for an hour at a time. I learned to conjure any image I chose before my mind's eye, by simply willing it so. I mastered techniques of vision, designed to peel away the layers one by one until I could look into the history and soul of any man or woman I met.

Unlike the first twenty, which were specific both in manner and goal, the final technique was utterly oblique. The twenty-first chapter consisted of a single cryptic command without elucidation of any kind. *Return to the beginnings, one by one, until the night's music delivers you to the Crystal City.*

Accordingly, the next day I made a point to stop at the bookshop on my way home from work, as it was, so to speak, the beginning of my mystical journey. I found, to my monumental disappointment, the placard gone, replaced by a badly scrawled sign proclaiming *fortunes told*. I popped my head into the doorway to the sad clang of a cowbell, found a foul-smelling woman with oily black hair and lecherous dark eyes who waved for me to enter, all the while leering through stubby blackened teeth. Applying what I had learned I watched her face transform itself from a choleric child, to a dour skinny girl, to a seductive young woman and back to the bloated thing before me, and then, beneath it all, I saw the hairy face and slavering tusks of a wild pig. Appalled, I shut the door and hurried off.

One of the bland faced public servants whose frequent visits to the foreign acquisitions office was required by law confronted me the following morning. As I stared into his round face with its fuzzy skin and small dim eyes, I saw a china doll, its pale features webbed with age—one that had been cleverly animated, but without volition of its own.

"Protocol demands," he informed me, cradling the massive black telephone on my desk, "your presence at the production center."

He unwrapped the sandwich he had been saving for his lunch, unable to wait another hour, spread the thick brown wrapper across the desk as an impromptu plate. The sharp scent of garlic and strong cheese permeated the entire office. Examining it for a moment, he beamed, took a large bite from the bulky dark bread and sausage concoction.

"Which facility?" I asked, truly puzzled by this unexpected demand.

He took his time chewing, swallowed with a sound akin to something striking deep water at the bottom of a well.

"The one where you worked as a boy, of course," his voice was almost scolding.

"When?"

"A car will pick you up at the boarding house tomorrow morning. There will be a small ceremony of appreciation. I'd tell you to dress appropriately, but you do that anyway."

He smiled paternally, went back to his sandwich and I heard nothing more from him.

The next day a massive boxlike limousine was waiting for me on the street outside my rooms. The landlady gushed with pride that such a vehicle should be idling before her establishment, puckered her lips into an approving smile as she held the door for me. The ride was arduous, and once we left the city, the roads ill kept. The unchanging view of peasants tending pale seedlings against the cold backdrop of black mountains was disconcerting. By midmorning the sky had cleared enough for a hazy sunlight to cast weak shadows. By noon the village I had hoped to leave far behind me forever rose before us like a tombstone.

"We're early," the driver broke the silence. "Is there anywhere you want to visit before we reach the facility?"

I thanked him, declining his offer. He slowed his speed, said nothing else. Staring at the back of his large head, applying the techniques I had learned, I watched him disappear altogether, until it seemed the limousine was driving itself. I shut my eyes, began breathing deeply and rapidly through my nose, for how long, I cannot say. I calmed myself—no I fortified myself, opened my eyes to see the rolls of fat on the driver's neck, the sparse hair jutting from his dark chauffeur's cap—and through the windshield, on the filthy rutted cobblestones, a covered horse drawn cart, with several women surrounding it bearing old clothes in their open arms.

"Does it feel like home to you?" the driver asked.

"More like a bad dream," I answered candidly.

His head bobbed slightly to his silent laughter.

The *ceremony* in my honor was a shabby thing. For the workers, it was a bewildering opportunity to stand about and do nothing. For the managers, it was a chance to blather and boast. And for me it was utterly mind numbing, standing there in the ill-lit dusty monolith where my father had toiled until the day he died, which, I learned, was not long after my leaving the village.

The ride back was interminable. Whereas there was no traffic whatever on the outbound journey, the roads were clogged with wagons hauling great mounds of reeking manure and I know not what else. As the evening gloom began to settle, these horse carts melted into the night, marked only by dim kerosene lamps bouncing at the front and rear. The chauffeur apologized for our lack of progress saying he could drive no faster for fear of ramming something in the dark. I tried to sleep but found myself wide awake with nothing to do.

All the lights were extinguished at the boarding house when we finally arrived. The chauffeur and I exchanged courtesies and he vanished into the night, his headlights illuminating a single cart approaching from the opposite direction. For the heartbeat the wagon's driver was bathed in light, I recognized the familiar shape of the ragman. I turned away, grabbed the door knob, twisted, pulled and shook it, but it was locked and bolted. My instinct was to hammer the door with both fists, shouting until I roused the landlady, but I knew such a singular display of cowardice would in no way deliver me from my fate.

I stepped from the stoop, sucking in my breath, my back to the cold stone wall. I thought to follow the ragman at a discrete distance, as I had done before, but with a tug on the reins he stopped the old horse before the rooming house. He extended a lanky arm, no more than a black line projecting beyond the vague silhouette of the cart, his gnarled forefinger curled beckoning me to join him.

Try as I might, using the techniques I had spent months mastering, I saw nothing save black on black, a chasm in the heart of the night. Silently, with the uncertainty of a blind man abandoned in unfamiliar surroundings, I climbed the wobbly wooden steps clutching a make-shift guard rail, pulled myself into the wagon. I sat beside him and he clicked his tongue against the roof of his mouth. The cart lurched onward.

The city whose name was nearly unpronounceable, even for those who dwelled within its dreary warrens, never smelled so foul. The air was suddenly thick and stagnant with the scent of boiled cabbage, greasy sausages, rancid stews intermingled with the inescapable stench of old unwashed clothes and horse dung. The decrepit streetlamps, never bright, dimmed, as if the night itself had become an impenetrable cloud of soot, with a dark volition that brooked no trespass.

The clopping of horseshoes against ancient cobblestones, the grinding of cart wheels, so ominous at first, became a lullaby—a soothing song to banish the fear and guilt of a lifetime spent callously scrabbling against the chaos that inevitably drained men of their paltry spirits. I shut my eyes and listened, saw sparks where the metal-shod wheels struck paving stone, the red cascade of cold fire as if I were floating above the wagon, a witness to a ritual whose meaning I could not guess.

I opened my eyes again as the sounds, amplified by the walls of that crude tunnel, the entrance to that *subway* which so terrified my landlady, jarred me from this reverie. Deeper and deeper the horse bore us until another light embraced us, an amber infusion that seeped through everything. Even the horse was no longer a horse, but the merest suggestion of twitching ears, a hint of swishing tail, a transparent husk that rose and fell like waves in a twilight tide. I turned to see my companion, and he, too, was little more that an empty shell, swathed in stinking rags. With great trepidation I looked at my own hands, but they remained as I remembered them, save for the amber hue that cast all things in a jaundiced light.

Deeper and deeper we descended until the tunnel opened onto what?—a cavern?—another world?—a mad hallucination? Try as I might, I could get no bearings, as there was neither up nor down. The amber light had grown much softer as we neared the source, no longer amber, yet still a golden infusion that defied one to find the heart of it. Creatures of all sorts shambled past us taking little notice, many of them like the horse and driver—suggestions of form, like a gleaming spider's web visible only against a shadow. Some bore shapes that were mockeries of the familiar, others were little more that assemblages of tentacles, wings, antennae, limbs bent at unnatural angles—quivering masses ever adapting themselves to some new awareness, some new sensation. All of them were making for the center of this place that was not a place.

The ragman nudged me and I turned. A whirlwind was emptying the old clothes from the back of the wagon, spinning them wantonly—but I felt no wind. At first as one, and then as individuals, the rags danced and pranced in an orgy of abandon, a sight to make one laugh save that every now and then there appeared an astonished face—like that of a terrified dreamer suddenly aware of the dream. Distorted visages, quivering bodies, wild groping hands, bare flailing feet filled the rags for a moment or two then vanished. With a lurch, the empty cart moved on.

Impossibly, we passed through the hollow creatures, without sensation, as if they were all illusion, or occupying another space altogether. And they themselves passed through one another, forging on like an anxious crowd outside a theater, scrambling to fill the seats within before the houselights dimmed. Old clothes, empty save for that occasional suggestion of their horrified and discombobulated occupants spun and twirled in their mad dance in an ever greater profusion wherever I looked.

How long this madness went on, I could not say, only that eventually we arrived at the center of this place, *that was not a place*, or so it seemed. Here the dancing clothes remained full of their former occupants. Once again the ragman nudged me, pointing with an empty sleeve at one particular assemblage of rags. A frayed yellow shirt, not quite mustard, not quite ochre, with a pattern of thin pale blue horizontal and vertical lines that intersected every few inches caught my eye, and within the floating mass of cloth the unmistakable form of my father, terrified beyond all measure. Dead or not, he danced wildly like a spastic marionette, as if there was nothing else he could possibly do until one of those shimmering creatures, whose seemingly insubstantial forms would now and then catch the infused light, wrapped a gossamer tentacle around him, lifted him gracefully toward its maw—a scene to be reenacted for all eternity in a time *that was not a time.*

Seen altogether the mad dance was no more than an endless chaos of jerking, twirling, leaping pandemonium without the slightest apparent rhyme or reason. As a whole, it was beyond deciphering. But each event when watched singly, each gossamer creature clutching a solid dancer in his tattered rags revealed an underlying purpose. Those simple creatures of the so-called Crystal City came here to feed. As I watched, the empty yellow shirt floated away, dropping beyond the chaos, toward who knows what lay beyond, and I knew beyond all question—don't ask me how—that the entire sequence when played out would repeat itself ad infinitum, although not necessarily in exactly the same manner as before.

Once again the ragman tapped my shoulder. I felt a gnarled hand take mine, open it, press the horse's reins against my palm. I watched the tattered felt hat, dark woolen vest, jacket and trousers dismount the wagon. And then the rags he wore simply slid from his transparent form, disintegrating into a glowing amber dust as he hurried to join the feast, the merest amber suggestion of a man becoming something altogether different—something beyond describing.

I pen the last of this account back in my rooms. I will tuck it into the drawer beside the white leather volume for whoever may find it in the hope it eventually reaches one, to paraphrase the words of the bookseller, who is of an open mind. It is the least I can do.

The landlady looked upon me aghast when I returned to her boarding house this morning. Only after I promised her to quit the premises forever before nightfall after cleaning out my rooms would she let me enter. I have no more interest in being director of foreign acquisitions for the company whose headquarters is the steel and glass monolith in the land of opportunity across that vast ocean—no more interest in books or amusements of any kind. I have been given a unique choice and I have made it without equivocation.

I burn the last of my clothes in the fireplace, save for the suit I am wearing. The old covered cart with its fat jar of pennies is parked just outside the front door, to the consternation of the landlady, who fears for the reputation of her establishment. The horse knows the route. I have no idea how long I must gather old clothes before I am allowed to feed, but I feel certain my reward will be well worth the wait.

OBSERVER/EXPERIENCER

Jonathan Raab

After a host of clicks, mechanical whirrs, and an arrhythmic crash of keypad-tone notes, something approximating human speech greeted Harris.

"Goblin Boys," it said in a slurry of competing voices. The voice was different every time Harris called the number. "We'll (*we'll*) employ flamethrowers to burn trash goblins off your property (*property*). This is [unintelligible] speaking, how can I (*we*) help you?"

Harris ignored the instinctual chill tumbling down his spine and clicked his pen. He began to work his way down the logbook's checklist, putting Xs in the appropriate boxes.

X – MULTIPLE VOICES SPEAKING AS ONE
X – ILLOGICAL OR ABSURD FRAMING OF CONVERSATION
X – REFERENCES MONSTERS, ANGELS, DEMONS, FEY, ALIENS, CRYPTIDS, ETC.

Harris had lost count of how many times he had called this number in the past few weeks, how many times he had listened to this chilling nonsense, filling out this same form in complete silence.

After a wave of static and half a minute of electronic-tinged heavy breathing, the voice on the other end continued.

"Very well-informed people (*people*) understand the danger of humanity's desire to return to the moon," it said. "Neil Armstrong and Buzz Aldrin performed a Masonic ritual (*RITUAL*) upon the Sea of

Tranquility, and left various objects of occult import along the moon's surface. Soon after, they were warned off."

X – REFERENCES THE U.S. SPACE PROGRAM
X – REFERENCES THE OCCULT

Harris had not known what "occult" meant until a week into the job, when Dr. Polan noticed he hadn't checked that box since starting phone duty. Shortly thereafter, the definition appeared in every booth in the command trailer, printed on plain white paper in a crisp, clear typeface and laminated onto the surface of every desk:

Occult
hidden, magical, supernatural, secret

Now, he ended up checking that box every time he was on phone duty. Of course, some smart-ass Observer/Experiencer had scrawled their own definition under the project's:

SPOOKY ASS SHIT

"Respond when spoken to, soldier," the voice said, voice suddenly singular and clear. Harris snapped back to the moment. He'd heard that rhythm and tone of voice often during his years in the Army; hearing it come from the other end of this freak phone line set his teeth on edge.

"Did I stutter, soldier?"

"Sir, no sir," Harris said, his words betraying him. He was breaking protocol by speaking back, even if the transmitter was disabled. But the outburst had triggered an instinctual response.

"That's better, troop! There's hope for you yet! We've got reports of Taliban massing on the ridgeline to the south. Word over SIPRnet is this is the big one, what they've been preparing all spring for. Now that the snow's melted—"

Harris slammed the phone back into its cradle, its coiled wire tangling around itself and bouncing with the force of impact. Breaking off the call early was against protocol, too, but he didn't care. Whatever was on the other end, it wasn't supposed to be able to hear him.

He signed off on the bottom of the checklist, scribbling in "Call terminated early, 5 min mark" in the NOTES box, then closed and slid the logbook away from him. He shuffled his papers back into his binder, then stood up and made his way out of the booth, one of several segregated by particleboard walls in the north end of the command trailer. Light spilled out from beneath a closed door, where another Observer/Experiencer sat quietly at a desk, ear pressed to a phone that spouted noise or nonsense or horrors in eight-minute increments.

Harris made his way to the entrance and then stepped out into the night, the air cool and fresh. A shaking hand sparked a cigarette and he looked up into the night sky, wide and black, starlight smeared over the heavens in vivid, vibrating colors. In the distance, a stretch of the Rocky Mountains was visible only as a collection of great shadows, looming over the valley and blotting out the stars at the horizon.

Harris couldn't shake the sensation that he had been under this same sky before, even if it had been on the other side of the world.

———◆———

They recruited Harris because he had a skill that the project needed: he could keep his goddamn mouth shut.

He'd proven that in the desert, a few years into his enlistment, when his fire team occupied a lookout over Barack-E-Barack for 48 hours. They were only about half a klick from the village, nestled in some rocks on a ridge overlooking the semi-improved road leading into the isolated Afghan settlement. Sergeant Villanueva saw it first, hissing at then-Specialist Harris to *wake the fuck up and bring me the goddamn thermals.*

To his credit, Harris had been awake. He kept the PAS-13 loaded with a fresh battery and easily accessible in his assault pack.

Sergeant Villanueva snatched it out of his hands and brought the eyepiece to his face, peering out toward the great mountain wall that rose beyond the killing fields of Logar province. Harris followed his gaze and instinctually shifted his body lower behind the small red boulders they used for cover. He didn't need the thermals to see the lights.

Red fireballs, bright and alive with dancing flames like the burning mist on the surface of the sun, floated back and forth between the distant mountain peaks and nearby cannabis fields, moving with a speed and grace unlike anything Harris had ever seen.

Villanueva radioed the company tactical operations center to confirm the contact, asking if they were flying drones, other air assets in the area of operations, weird-fucking-weather—*goddamn anything* that could explain what they were seeing.

"I count three—no, four airborne contacts," the young sergeant said. "Flying in a curlicue pattern over the valley. Fast as hell, too."

After a few desperate minutes of heated back-and-forth with the baffled specialist on radio duty, an unfamiliar voice broke over the net.

"Stallion Four-Bravo, you are to observe and record the targets' movements until you are recalled to Combat Outpost Altimoor," it said, cold and still as a frozen mountain stream. "But do not discuss this matter over the net again, by order of Sigma Six. Out."

Villanueva raised an eyebrow at Harris.

"That's the brigade commander's call sign, but that sure as hell wasn't Colonel Hobbs," Villanueva said.

The other two soldiers in the fire team joined them at the lip of the ridge, abandoning all pretense of pulling security—watching, instead, the push and pull of impossible lights doing their impossible dance.

The lights stirred something within Harris: a feeling of wonder, of simultaneous fear and attraction he felt as a small child, starring up at a clear night's sky and wondering what or who might be up there. He thought the Army had ground that wonder and hope out of him. But *here* was wonder, dancing before his very eyes.

Extraction came hours later, well after those gyrating flames faded into the red sky of sunset. Safely back at the company tactical operations center, they made their reports—individually, isolated from one another—to their company commander and another officer, a major none of them recognized. He wore a uniform with no nametape and with a crookedly placed ISAF command patch, meaning he could have been from anywhere. His eyes were a faded, light green, and his face was chiseled from stone. A recruiting poster come to life.

The major said nothing as Harris made his report, recounting the back-and-forth movements of those flaming orbs, feeling every bit the fool as he did so. The officers said little, save for him to not discuss the matter with anyone else, including his fellow soldiers.

And that was that—until three months later, as the brigade was preparing to return home, one battalion at a time rotating into and flying out of Bagram on two-week demobilization schedules. Between hours of endless PowerPoint briefings berating soldiers not to kill themselves, harm their loved ones, overindulge in alcohol, or otherwise embark on stereotypical mad-veteran rampages, there was plenty of time to hit the gym or blow money at the PX.

It was outside the Bagram PX—a palace of consumer goods and rear-echelon-mother-fuckery, that the major from the Barack-E-Barack debrief approached Harris. Seeing the major again, among the fast food trailers and overweight command staff soldiers that dominated the base, was a moment out of time, out of reality. Harris was so confused that he forgot to salute, the officer's sharp green eyes staring out at him from beneath a perfectly clean and crisp patrol cap.

"You like the infantry, Specialist Harris?"

"Sir!" he said, snapping to attention and finally offering that salute. "Absolutely, sir!"

"Great," the major said, not meaning it. "But if a new opportunity came along, one that didn't involve you sitting in the goddamn mud and sand all the time, one where you could do something a little more interesting, and paid better to boot—would you be up for that?"

"Sir," Harris said, processing. "I guess that would depend on the job."

"You didn't talk," the major said.

"No, sir," Harris said.

"Think you can keep not talking, even if you were to see something interesting—something like what you saw with Sergeant Villanueva on that ridge over Barack-E-Barack?"

Harris paused before he gave his answer. He wasn't quite sure what he was being offered, but he had a feeling he was being tested.

"I didn't see anything interesting with Sergeant Villanueva on a ridge over Barack-E-Barack," he said, carefully. "We reported no enemy activity and only sparse civilian traffic along that route that night. Sir."

The major nodded.

"Sign whatever they put in front of you back at Fort Drum. If anyone gives you a hard time, just act like a stupid specialist."

"That won't be a problem for me, sir."

The major smiled, then snapped to attention. Harris offered him a farewell salute.

"I'll see you in Colorado," the officer said, returning the gesture. He marched off and disappeared into the mass of civilian contractors and soldiers swarming around the marketplace, all in a hurry to get nowhere, to accomplish nothing.

———◆———

The separation paperwork waited for Harris at Fort Drum. His first sergeant had been livid, demanding to know why the hell one of his soldiers was discharging early. Harris offered muted, feigned surprise. After one profanity-laced inquiry to higher was answered with an invitation to discuss the matter personally with the division sergeant major, the first sergeant dropped it. There were a lot of discipline infractions, medical issues, and DWI charges to sort out in a demobilizing infantry company, after all.

A week later, when his paperwork was processed and his gear turned in to supply, the post shrinks cleared him—they cleared anybody who wanted to be cleared, Harris was disappointed to discover—and he found himself with a plane ticket to Denver by way of Buffalo.

When he arrived at Denver International Airport, the major—or the man who had presented himself as a major—waited for him, dressed in khaki pants and a blue form-fitting shirt, failing to blend in with the families and loved ones greeting the new arrivals pouring out of the terminal.

The man extended his hand and Harris took it.

"Welcome to Colorado. Are you ready to get to work?"

"What kind of work are we doing, sir?"

"You're not in the military anymore, and neither am I," he said. "So drop that 'sir' crap. This pays better."

"*What* pays better?"

"You ever been to Meeker?"

"No s—no, I haven't. Never been to Colorado before. What should I call you?"

"Briggs," the man said, stepping off toward baggage claim. "If you're hungry, we'll grab something to go before we leave the city. It's a long ride into the mountains."

———◆———

The ranch property, east of Meeker and abutting against the Routt National Forest in the shadow of the Rockies, was one of the most beautiful places Harris had ever seen, rivaling and echoing Afghanistan's incredible mountainous landscapes.

A rotting wooden sign declaring the property to be the "Nathan Ranch, Founded 1906, a Colorado Centennial Farm" stood where the quarter-mile driveway met the county road. The driveway led to outbuildings in various states of collapsing disrepair, three recently installed doublewide trailers, and a small, single-story white ranch house set within a grove of young spruce. Mobile light generators perched around the trailers, casting the overgrown yard in sickly floodlight. Beyond it all, miles distant, great mountains stood where the land rose up to meet them in curving ridgelines and imposing mesas, the canyons and fields between home to darkness.

Briggs guided their pickup over fresh gravel leading toward a metal gate, passing a pair of large, red-lettered NO TRESPASSING signs. Just behind the gate stood a diesel-powered roadside light array, illuminating two guards in blue coats and khaki pants—not unlike Briggs' uniform—brandishing AR-15 rifles. The eyes of the man and woman standing guard were hidden behind wide, black aviator sunglasses that reflected the failing light of the setting sun, and their flat-line mouths and smooth, confident movements implied military experience.

The man approached the driver's side and accepted the binder Briggs offered through the open window. The woman appeared at Harris's window, which he rolled down. He handed her his ID.

"You ever do duty like this?" she asked, scanning his driver's license with a handheld device that was all plastic and reflective foil.

"First time," he said. "Fresh fish."

She offered him a smirk—something approaching a pretty smile.

"Welcome to Disneyland," she said, handing back his ID. She walked ahead to swing the gate open, then waved them forward. That was when Harris noticed the cattle fence, stretching off in both directions away from the gate. Every dozen feet or so, white plastic pylons with black orbs at the tips stood affixed to those fence posts. A surveillance network, stretching for a mile or more across flat, open terrain.

Whatever they were doing here, they wanted to know if someone was trying to get in.

Or out.

A bright-orange-framed slide appeared on the screen, home to three logos across its top third. "DEFENSE INTELLIGENCE AGENCY / UNITED STATES OF AMERICA," it read, with twin orbits encircling a globe beneath a torch and stars; "MALTHUS PARA-ASTROPHYSICS AND TEMPORAL STUDIES RESEARCH CENTER," with its blue reflecting pool set beneath a night sky full of stars; and "PALLADIUM AT NIGHT RESEARCH AND COMMUNICATIONS SATELLITE PROGRAM," with a sinister, distorted dog's skull set behind a rocket taking flight.

Beneath all three logos:

NATHAN RANCH OBSERVER/EXPERIENCER PROGRAM (NROEP, "EN-ROPE")

O/E WELCOME BRIEF
SLIDES UPDATED MAY 2019
Adapted from "Meta-Cognitive Reflective Phenomena in Isolated Locations," D. Hyman, C. Slatsky, S.R. Jones, B. Holesapple. Malthus Para-Astrophysics and Temporal Studies Research Center Annual, July 2009.

"Take a seat," Briggs said, gesturing at the plastic-shell folding chair. "That notebook is yours." Harris sat and picked up the notebook—a custom-branded blue spiral-bound with "NROEP Observer/Experiencer" stenciled on the soft cover. It had a pleasant, factory-fresh paper smell.

"Rule number one," Briggs said, flipping to the next slide with all the enthusiasm of a man who had done this a hundred times before, "have a recording device, batteries, a light source, water, communications device, and paper and pen on your person at all times while on duty." Harris scribbled this down in shorthand on the first page of his new notebook. "While off duty, you are welcome to leave the ranch, but should you remain, you are not to venture beyond line of sight of this command trailer. The barracks, shower trailer, and this command unit are the only authorized locations. Do not go off onto the rest of the property unless you're on assignment and paired with at least one battle buddy. Understood?"

"Got it."

"It's also a good idea to carry an assault pack with extra food, water, and batteries, even if you're just on gate duty," the woman from the gate said, appearing at door. "When it gets dark and the fog rolls in, they'll do their best to get you turned around and lost." She entered the room and set a foam cup of steaming coffee on the table. Without her sunglasses and ball cap on, her brown eyes glimmered in the poor light of the room, and strands of dyed-blond hair poked over the sides of her ears.

"Harris, this is Dominguez," Briggs said. "She'll be showing you the ropes over the next couple of weeks."

"Good to meet you," he said. She offered him a smirk.

"You've got no idea what you're in for."

Briggs moved through the slides quickly. There were a dozen Observer/Experiencers—O/Es—on-site at various times, working in shifts. They were well-equipped, too: binoculars, night vision optics, advanced thermal imaging devices, Raven observer drones, MBITR encrypted radios, a small motor pool of SUVs and ATVs, 9mm pistols, a few AR-15s and tactical shotguns. The team here also had a robust camera inventory—passive trail cams, closed-circuit security cameras, 360-degree pylons, and DSLR handhelds.

"Batteries go dead all the time, just like that," Dominguez said, snapping her fingers. "Always carry extra, in case the ghoulies suck the life out of your camera or radio."

Harris waited for her face to break into a smile, signaling the joke. The smile never came.

"Reporting your experiences accurately and quickly is important," Briggs said, flipping to a slide with an image of a standardized report form. "Write down or record as much as you can, including and especially environmental factors like weather and atmospheric conditions, the phase of the moon, prevailing smells, odd noises, what you had for lunch. All of it.

"And I cannot stress this enough: do *not* censor your reports. Do not downplay what you see or explain it away as your imagination. Report it all."

Dominguez smiled down at him, enjoying the confusion on Harris's face.

"What's the craziest thing you've ever officially logged?" Briggs asked her. The veteran O/E thought about it for a moment, then smiled.

"The little blue-faced miner dudes with the pickaxes and lanterns, moving across the ridge to the north of here, about a month back,"

Dominguez said, eyes on Harris. "I shined a spotlight right on them from a dozen feet away, and they didn't even react. That was *weird*."

"Always maintain a two-person buddy team, minimum, whenever you're traveling away from basecamp here," Briggs continued, the slides on the screen zipping by featuring blurry photographs of people wearing black or dark blue shirts and khakis hiking through the mountainous backcountry. "You signed an NDA before you arrived, but the long and short of it is that you are not authorized to discuss any operations, experiences, or events that occur during your tenure here with outside personnel. Only your fellow O/Es, authorized staff, and the science group can be read in to anything you experience here. Failing to adhere to this agreement will mean forfeiture of your military benefits, honorable discharge status, and opportunities for future employment with our group, as well as possible criminal prosecution."

Briggs clicked through the last slide, and a block of glowing darkness covered the screen and half of his face. "There's no statute of limitations on this," Briggs said. "What happens here, stays here. Clear?"

"Crystal," Harris said, despite having more questions now than when he started. Briggs nodded to Dominguez.

"Our first patrol is in twenty minutes," she said. "Top off your water and coffee and meet me at the motor pool. I'm driving."

<hr>

Harris clicked his headlamp on during the brief walk from the barracks trailer to the motor pool, grateful for the sweeping, strong light produced by fresh batteries.

Another headlamp blinked on in the darkness ahead.

"It's me," Dominguez said.

"It's me," Harris said in response.

"Don't ever assume a light you see out here is someone or something you know," she said. "That's a good way to get yourself lost."

"Okay," Harris said. Dominguez popped the driver's side door open on a mud-spattered but otherwise brand-new pickup, one of several parked in a neat row on this far side of the ranch house. The light from the cab revealed her in the dark as she tossed her assault pack into the back seat. Harris followed suit on the opposite side. A shotgun stood mounted in a locked rack in the center console.

"I'll take you around the eastern perimeter tonight," she said as they climbed in. "Then up the low mesa on the north side. It's a nice night. Maybe we'll see some shooting stars. Or some weird shit."

"We're supposed to report 'weird shit,' I take it?" he asked.

"Somebody paid attention to the brief."

"The brief didn't say much."

"They don't want to influence you."

"I'm not following," he said.

"What you're expecting to see, you might just see," she said. "So try to keep an open mind." She turned the key and the engine roared to life. "Better yet, don't think at all. Easy for veterans, right?"

The truck pulled ahead, skirted around the driveway, and hung left onto an old dirt road paralleling the fence along the edge of the property. The dark waited for them.

———•———

The pickup's headlights struggled to illuminate the dirt road and field ahead, casting the terrain in a washed-out glow. The fence ran on their right, its posts ancient stalks of dried-out wood standing crooked in the dark. Harris counted: every five posts a plastic pylon appeared, tipped by an all-seeing black orb of a camera.

"We'll follow this path 'til we hit the switchbacks leading up the mesa over yonder," Dominguez said. She pointed ahead into the dark, at anything or nothing.

"What are we looking for?"

"We'll know it when we see it. Sometimes trespassers try to get on the property. We don't have arresting powers or anything, but I know how to be persuasive out here in Trump country." She tapped a pistol strapped to her hip. Nine-millimeter Beretta.

"When do I get one of those?"

"I'll qualify you tomorrow morning, then we'll request an issue," she said. "You shoot straight?"

"I'm better with a rifle."

"How fresh are you? From the sandbox, I mean."

"A month, month and a half," he said.

"Jesus. Maybe I'll let you cool down a little before I stick a gun in your hands and rush you out here to Spooksville."

"You were in?"

She nodded.

"Marines. Civil affairs. Iraq, twice, Afghanistan once."

"That's a lot of time."

"Sure. What about you?"

"Army. Infantry. Just Afghanistan, once," he said, something like shame at the edge of his words.

"Once counts," she said. "Here we are."

The path ahead cut sharply left and away from the fence, which continued into the darkness ahead. Already the ground was beginning to rise toward the brilliant night sky. Trees and scrub appeared out of the dark like the advance soldiers of a ghost army marching toward them. The dirt road continued straight for a few hundred feet, before sharply cutting right, then left, and then right again, zigzagging its way up the elevation of a rising hill that terminated in a flat mesa above.

"It's Maryanne," she said, suddenly, taking the final switchback to the open space above. "Normally this is the time you guys make a pass at me. So my name's Maryanne, but you can call me Mary, and no, it's not a particularly pretty name, so don't try that one."

"What?"

"Come on. A hard-charger like you, fresh out of the war and off active duty, alone with a pretty gal like me on a romantic night drive. Taking a pass hasn't crossed your mind?"

"I'm learning from you. Didn't seem appropriate. Also, I'm pretty rusty."

"Thank God. But give it a few weeks. I'm the only woman on the O/E team, aside from one of the research scientists, and those types tend not to fraternize with us grunts much."

"You're pretty presumptuous."

"Speaking from experience."

The ground ahead of them leveled out, revealing a plain of scrub and short, twisted trees in the faded wash of the headlights. The truck rumbled to a halt. Dominguez slipped it into park and rolled down the windows. She turned the key and clicked off the headlights, the silence and darkness rushing in to fill the sudden void. The only illumination was from the dim lights of the dashboard panels and the glimmering stars.

"The dark sneaks up on you out here," she said.

"Where are we?"

"You didn't tell me your name. Your first name."

"Jonah," he said.

"Alright, Jonah, we're on the mesa on the east side of the property, facing roughly north. A few hundred feet ahead of us the ground drops off to a canyon below, where there's a creek running through when the snow melt is heavy in the spring. During the day or when the moon is bright, you can see for miles."

"What are we doing here?"

"Waiting," she said, all the good nature draining from her face, "to see if they show up."

———◆———

Despite the coffee, Harris struggled to stay awake. They had talked for an hour—about where they were from, their time in service, what few entertainments there were to enjoy in Meeker and Rifle—but gradually they fell into silence. It was the silence shared between two people on a late-night watch, when there was nothing more to say and nothing more to do but wait.

A few beams of moonlight cut through the lingering clouds, revealing his hands still gripping the now-empty foam coffee cup between his knees. He blinked hard several times, catching himself nodding off.

"Harris," Dominguez whispered, suddenly. "*Harris.*"

"Hmm?"

She was wide-eyed and alert, her hands gripping the steering wheel, body pulled tight against it as she peered through the windshield.

"Looked like some headlights sweeping across the eastern side, then down the road that leads to the canyon," she said. "Look alive." She started the truck's engine, shattering the peaceful stillness of the night.

Their headlights swept across the great expanse of flat terrain, low growth, and the odd gnarled, desperate tree. The road was barely a road at all, all crumbling dirt, mud, and tall grasses trying to reclaim it. Low-hanging fog moved in slow currents across their path. Dominguez guided the truck through a winding maze of awful trees and ominous rock formations that cast terrible shadows in the tepid moonlight.

They reached the other side of the mesa, where the road became a series of tight switchbacks. The coffee roiled in Harris's stomach as they bounced over ruts, rock, and broken road. Finally, the road straightened out as the elevation eased down into a steady decline. The gnarled trees turned to healthy spruce, leaning over the roadway, obscuring what lay ahead.

"Jesus!" Dominguez slammed on the brakes.

A hatchback car suddenly appeared before them, emerging from the fog like a shape forming in a dream. The truck bucked to a halt, not a dozen feet from the small vehicle with its front half in the road, its rear tires in the weeds along the shoulder.

Harris popped open his door and stepped out into the night, clicking on his headlamp. A cone of bright light followed the sweep of his gaze along the derelict car.

"Could be campers, could be meth heads," Dominguez said. "Stay sharp."

"Aren't you monitoring the property's perimeter?"

"Sometimes the cameras go down." She reached over and spun the dials on the shotgun rack. The metal clips holding it in place snapped open. "That's you."

"Sure you don't want to take me to the range first?" he teased, taking the gun. He racked the pump back to feed a shell into the chamber. It felt natural to have a weapon in his hands again.

Dominguez stepped out of the truck and clicked on her own headlamp, sending a sharp beam of light splashing against the hatchback. It was a newer model, the kind of family ride you might see cruising along a cul-de-sac in the suburbs, not abandoned in the middle of a dirt road in the mountains.

They kept to the sides of the narrow road as they approached. They swept their gaze and lights from side to side, looking for ambushes in the impenetrable dark with the practiced paranoia of soldiers. Great, indistinct shadows moved beyond the road and its attendant overgrowth. Squat bushes reached out with thin fingers of bone-like branches to scratch and pull at Harris's clothes. Instinct told him eyes were upon him, boring into the back of his head.

He whirled around, kicking up dirt as he did so. The road beyond the pickup was dark—and empty.

"*Harris*," Dominguez hissed. He turned back and hustled up to where she stood at the front end of the car.

"Sorry. It's a little spooky out here."

"*Shhh!*" She grabbed his left arm, her hand an iron vice, and pointed. The cones of light from their headlamps revealed forms on the ground. Bodies—human bodies, clad in colorful hiking clothing fresh off the rack from some high-end urban outfitter—were scattered across the road. Arms, legs, and heads lay in the dirt or hung over in ruts carved by generations of passing vehicles. Harris swept his headlamp back and forth over the scene. Three bodies—no, four, five, with maybe more in the dark ahead.

The beam splashed against a shape ahead of them. Harris's brain struggled to make sense of it, landing on *cow* or *elk*, then dismissing those explanations as phantasms. The shadow rippled, giving the impression of movement. Two bright red lights emerged from the form, trailing vaporous crimson, like smoke passing before the setting sun. Eyes, locked on them both.

"Jesus Christ, Jesus *Christ*," Harris said. "Dominguez—"

She offered up a groan in response, not quite a word.

The body closest to them turned its head to face them, skin scratching against rock like ancient papyrus. Its eyes snapped open, revealing the same deep, glowing red of the shadow's terrible eyes. More points of red light appeared, hot coals smoldering in folds of darkness, glaring at them with a vibration of pure hate.

The bodies began to stand *up*, bones popping and muscles snapping like tree branches against the hood of a careening car, destined to spin out and crash on some remote mountain road.

A rotten egg smell hung over the air, nauseating and overpowering. Dominguez and Harris backed away from the impossible scene unfolding before them, weapons pointed ahead and quivering impotently at the corpses rising in the dark. Their headlamps captured a series of washed-out images between sputtering moments of darkness: pale hands, reaching for them; trees and brambles pressing in close; bloodless faces with slack mouths and bright red eyes; the impression of a great shape looming over it all, all stink and hair and menace.

That shadow-shape let out a roar, something from out of a memory of a creature feature seen in childhood, familiar and terrifying all at once.

Dominguez and Harris turned and ran back to the truck. Moving fast, not moving fast enough.

They clambered inside. Dominguez turned the key in the ignition before Harris slammed his door shut. The running lights came on automatically, revealing the horrorshow before them in bright, washed-out clarity: limp forms held upright in shambling repose, feet dragging with each purposeful step, limbs and faces of men and women stretched and blurry like distortions in a videotaped image. And that *thing*—looming behind the living dead, now among them, now closer to the truck, coming for them.

Dominguez slammed the shifter into reverse. Harris shut his eyes against the impossible terror bearing down on them. Dominguez turned and held the wheel tight in her left hand, guiding the truck backwards up the trail as the engine roared, mercifully drowning out the hungry bellowing of the creature.

She swung the wheel to the right and the truck's rear wheels led them off the road into a clearing. She slipped the truck back into drive and cranked the wheel in the opposite direction, then buried the gas pedal. The tires spun and spat up rocks and dirt in a shower of desperate traction until finally they were off, bouncing and slamming over the broken road back up the mesa.

———◆———

This time, the voice was a familiar one—its tone welcoming and jovial. Like speaking with an old friend.

"How's the ranching business?" it asked, its voice human, masculine—but possessed of a mechanical tenor, underpinned by electronic beeps and distortion.

Harris hesitated, pencil tip hovering over the checklist.

X – MAKES INDIRECT OR DIRECT REFERENCE(S) TO OBSERVER/ EXPERIENCER CURRENT LOCATION AND/OR DUTIES

"You smell like you've been *around a woman* (WOMAN)," the voice said, the words echoing and low and distorted toward the end of the statement. "How many women are there in your life right now? Ones you might like to have sexual relations with?"

X – ASKS QUESTIONS ABOUT OBSERVER/EXPERIENCER PERSONAL LIFE

"Does it get lonely, out there, on the *raaAAAAAAAaaaaaannnnnN-NNNch*—" That last word, stretched to painful lengths, twisted and curled back in on itself as a wave of distortion washed over the line, shrill klaxons and over-noise crashing in great waves of mangled signal. Harris pulled the handset away from his ear, and only returned it when the shrill chaos ceased.

"How's the *RAnCHinG BUSinESss?*" the voice said, its words warbling and corrupted.

———◆———

The cow's fleshless mouth leered at them, its teeth sharp and white against a red-stained jawbone exposed to the sun. Its matted, black fur stood in sharp contrast to the orange baked-clay earth on which the animal's remains lay. A cored-out hollow of wrinkled pink flesh where its ear should have been attracted flies, buzzing clumsily in the heat of the late morning. The cow's eyes were likewise missing, revealing pitted-out sockets lousy with coagulated blood. A great square was cut away along its abdomen, where open folds of flesh revealed a scraped-out cavity. Harris tasted sand and blood on the air.

"Anybody want a steak?" Dominguez quipped, hoping for a laugh.

"Take pictures, please," Dr. Polan said, walking up behind them. He wore a pristine white lab coat over black cargo khakis and a tan undershirt, eyes squinting in the sunlight behind thin-framed glasses. Polan seemed too young to be a doctor of any sort, medical or otherwise, but he moved about the dead cow's body, slicing flesh and collecting samples, with the confidence and skill of an experienced surgeon.

Dominguez and Harris did as they were told, snapping photos on their project-issued cell phones. Close ups of the cored-out wounds; then pulling back to capture the dead cow's body in the context of the empty field in which they found it.

"Mountain lion do this?" Harris asked.

"If that mountain lion did a surgery rotation at Johns Hopkins, sure," Polan said, scraping a bit of the cow's gum tissue into a plastic cylinder. He sealed the sample and placed it within a handheld cooler, then pointed a latex glove-covered finger at the cow's empty eye socket. "These wounds are inconsistent with mountain lion or coyote behavior. Precise cuts along various regions of soft tissue. Mouth, eyes, ears, udder, anus, vagina. These are the kinds of cuts I would make for sample removal, if I was studying, let's say, the progression of a pathogen in a given cattle population. Except it would take me a few hours, even with state-of-the-art equipment and a lot of practice, to make cuts this precise." He shook his head. "If predators attacked this animal, there would be bite marks, blood around the corpse, signs of a struggle. And they wouldn't leave so much prime angus to rot."

Dominguez snapped a final picture, one of Polan crouched over the corpse and looking back at them, then slipped the phone into her pocket.

"Were there any O/E reports of phenomena on this side of the property last night?" Polan asked. She shook her head.

"Not that I know about. We saw—well, we saw *something* about a week ago, but that was on the east side of the property, on the mesa road leading down into the canyon."

"The zombies and the wendigo," Polan said, nodding. Dominguez put up her hands.

"Hey, I didn't call them that. That was the worst I've ever seen it, and I've been doing this for a while."

"You've been here, what, a week? What do you think?" Polan asked Harris, standing up and pulling the disposable gloves from his hands. "Any theories?"

Harris combed his memories for some pattern, some explanation. Between this, the tableau of horror they saw on his first patrol, and the weird phone calls he had to make every other night, it didn't add up to anything sane or meaningful.

"Sometimes I wonder if I'm going crazy," Harris said. "Like, the war broke me or something, and this is all just a coping mechanism. Something my brain cooked up." Polan offered a quick laugh.

"Not a bad theory, and just as likely as anything else."

"Except that we're experiencing it, too, and I know I'm not a figment of your imagination," Dominguez said.

"That's what a figment of my imagination would say."

"Let's set that Nietzschean nightmare scenario aside for a moment," Polan said. "Any other ideas?"

"This place is haunted," Harris said.

"That's as good a word as any," Polan said. "But what would ghosts want with a cow's reproductive organs?"

"Aliens," Dominguez said. "I've seen them buzzing around." Harris shot her a quizzical look. "Don't worry, you hang around long enough, you'll see one of their ships."

"Does aliens explain what you saw last week? They sent a team out the next morning, and there were no bodies, no car, no wendigo."

Dominguez shrugged.

"What about you, doc?" Harris asked. "We're just the hired help. What do you think?" He wiped the sweat building up on the back of his neck. He wanted to be under the cover of shade—because of the heat, and because he suddenly felt very exposed under the wide-open sky.

Polan raised his eyebrows as his mind went to work.

"Could be we're not actually researching anything, but that *we're* the test subjects. Some military psychotronic weapon test. Or maybe this is an MKUltra offshoot, testing military veterans and DOD scientists. Or maybe it *is* aliens, *and* ghosts, and a hole in space-time, and this whole place is an Indian burial ground, and we're in *their* lab."

Harris glanced behind him, sure that someone was watching them. He saw only the sunbaked plain, where the wind kicked up little clouds of dust.

"I think whatever is out here is intelligent, or has the appearance of intelligence, and that it interfaces with the human mind, human consciousness, somehow," Polan said, his voice dropping to just above a whisper. "I'm still collating data."

"What does it matter?" Dominguez said. "The pay's good, and this beats playing IED roulette. Do you need anything else, doc, or can we get back to the A/C and make our reports?"

— ◆ —

"In 1954, your American President Dwight D. Eisenhower met with our emissaries at Edwards Air Force Base," the voice said. It was feminine this time, with fluctuations of deep bass reverberating through certain words, as if a sound engineer was turning knobs at random. "The official cover story was that he needed emergency dental work, or that he was golfing. These are bold-faced lies sold to a compliant and unscrupulous public in the years following the war crimes committed against the Japanese civilian populations of Hiroshima and Nagasaki."

X – REFERS TO HISTORICAL INCIDENTS OR INFORMATION

"It was the deployment of those nuclear weapons that brought us to your planet, and to an official, ritualistic meeting with President Eisenhower."

X – OFFERS SECRET KNOWLEDGE OF WORLD EVENTS OR HISTORY

The monologue halted for a moment, as a flurry of static erupted through the earpiece. Harris pulled the phone from his ear, then returned it as the grinding wash ceased and the warbling notes of an ice cream truck tune began to play. The voice continued, still feminine, but higher-pitched now, its words slightly sped up.

"The world is ruled by signs and symbols," it said. "Eisenhower thought himself the equal of the emissaries, meeting in fraternity and good faith. Such concepts are meaningless to us. The meeting was meant as a ritual of consecration, a gesture of our benevolence to the apes—we, the true rulers of your skies and nightmares."

A memory emerged, unbidden, from the depths of Harris's mind: a sweat-soaked summer night, blankets wrapped around his limbs, holding him tight. He's young, and small, and very afraid. He wants to turn on the light, but something won't let him. Something that rises up out of the cluster of shadows at the foot of his bed, something tall and menacing, growling, growling his name.

A bead of sweat rolled down behind his left ear. The shudder was sudden and involuntary.

The phone line went dead.

X – CONNECTION TERMINATED BY SUBJECT

———◆———

Harris entered the command trailer at 2100 hours, thirty minutes before he was due to head out on patrol with Dominguez. In the month-and-a-half he had been at the ranch, he had developed a routine of reporting in early to grab coffee and to talk with the other O/Es or science staff. But tonight was different. No one was idly watching ESPN or reading the paper. Three black-clad O/Es huddled around Dr. Polan, talking in low tones. Dominguez was among them. She waved Harris over.

"What's going on?"

"Briggs is an hour overdue to report in, and not answering on his radio," Dominguez said. "Cell phone goes straight to voicemail." Harris furrowed his brow.

"What's his last confirmed location?"

"Northeast side of the ranch, on the north end of that road where you had your first encounter," Polan said. The scientist turned to a large USGS map of the ranch hanging on the trailer wall. He pointed to the upper right quadrant. "Briggs was supposed to check some sensor equipment we have posted atop the property's northeast mesa."

"He went by himself?"

"Briggs does what Briggs wants," Dominguez said, shrugging. "Being on the project's board buys him some leeway."

"Maybe his batteries are dead and he'll show up any minute now."

"Maybe," Polan said, moving over to a row of computer equipment set on the nearby wall. "Except for this." He bent down to tap at one of the consoles and proceeded to move through a series of login prompts until he reached the project's custom user interface. A series of icons floated in a blue window before him. Images popped up, depicting great swaths of distorted light, like powerful rays of sunlight cutting through digital storm clouds. Blurry and pixelated, the images made little sense to Harris.

"The mesa array passively records audio, video, and still images on a continual basis," Polan said. "The AI analyzes the data for anomalous events, using routines adapted from deep-space radiological analysis. When the system flags something—an animal, a human face or form, a high-speed object—the staff evaluates it. We got a ping about fifteen minutes ago."

"So if Briggs is in one of the images, we'll know he reached the site."

"We think this *is* Briggs," Polan said. Harris squinted at the screen and leaned in closer.

"Relax your eyes, don't think about it," Dominguez said. She pointed to the center of the screen, at a bit of white contour in the pixilated noise. "This is his jawline." Her finger moved up to point at a pair of concave dark spots. "Eyes."

The cold A/C air of the trailer sliced right through his core. The face appeared suddenly to him, his brain putting the pattern together all at once like a *Magic Eye* image. The face—if that is what it was—looked toward the camera and just off to the left, much of its left jawline and skull curvature obscured by bright static.

"The cameras must be malfunctioning," Polan said.

"Must be," Dominguez echoed, voice flat.

Harris crossed the room and drew a shotgun off the rack, then grabbed a fresh MBITR battery from the charging station.

"What if the cameras are working fine?" he asked.

Dominguez's right hand went instinctually to the pistol on her hip. Polan clicked through the images, a parade of horrors before him.

⁕

The road itself conspired against them.

The ruts were deeper, the mud was thicker, and new formations of rocks had tumbled down from the cliff faces above, forcing them to swerve and drive slowly to avoid puncturing their oil pan, or worse.

They rode in a silence that turned sour, like blood on the air, when they passed the spot of their first patrol together—that tight stretch of dirt road, now empty. No abandoned hatchback, no bodies rising up like puppets on strings, no looming mound of shadow and red-eyed hate.

When they were past the spot of that dreadful encounter, they both exhaled audibly and with great relief, though neither of them spoke.

After passing through a labyrinthine path of dried-out creek beds and menacing, warped trees, they began their ascent of the northeast mesa. Harris called in their position to Polan back at the command trailer. The airwaves were heavy with static, pregnant with the interference of a coming storm.

The switchbacks carried them higher and higher. Dominguez took the turns slow, pausing to give them time to run a hunting spotlight down the edges of the sudden drop-offs, looking for Briggs's missing pickup on the canyon floor below. They found nothing, save a pair of cow elk retreating into the cover of overgrowth, spooked by the appearance of the unnatural light.

They reached the top of the mesa. It was a blasted heath, almost completely free of trees and scrub. A perfect viewing platform of the sky above and the canyons below. A few dozen meters ahead of them, built against an outcropping of great, speckled brown rocks, stood the observation equipment and power-control box. The equipment was an array of black orb cameras not unlike those along the property line, complemented by long, flat white panels resembling cell phone tower antennae, all built out of the wide, grey power box. Peeking out from the other side of the station and rock formation were the twin headlights of Briggs' truck, reflecting back at them, but otherwise dark.

Dominguez killed the engine but left the headlights on their brightest setting, their almost-blue glow cutting an illuminated triangle across the elevated, flat plane of the mesa and alighting the array.

They stepped out into the night, activating their headlamps. Even the crunching of their combat boots across rocks and dirt felt too loud for comfort.

"Check the truck," Dominguez said, her voice a whisper, but carrying over to him in perfect clarity. The chill wind rolled off of the nearby mountains, barely audible. No bird calls or the shiver of tree branches here.

Dominguez went for the control box, entering a combination on a digital keypad and popping the access door open. "No power," she said. "I'm going to cold-start the generator."

"Would that explain those weird images they were feeding HQ?"

"No," Dominguez said. "And I'd rather not be around if whatever that was comes back." She flipped some switches and began to pump a large hand lever up, then down; up, and then down again, a metal-on-metal whining noise and her own grunts accompanying each effort.

Harris walked around the rock formation to Brigg's abandoned pickup truck. The light from his headlamp floated over the hood and up to the windshield, revealing an empty cab. He bent low and swept the light along the ground beneath the truck's undercarriage, then checked the plastic-lined bed in the back. Nothing. He tried the passenger door and, finding it unlocked, opened it to search the interior.

Fast food wrappers, an empty foam coffee cup in the middle console, a plastic water bottle tucked into the driver's side door cupholder. Keys dangled from the ignition, tinkling softly as Harris moved about.

He put the MBTR handheld close to his face and pressed to transmit.

"Base, this is O/E Nine, over."

Polan's voice came back to him, awash with static and clipping in and out.

"Nine, Base, go ahead."

"We found O/E Six's truck, but no one's around. The station is offline, but we're working on bringing it back up."

"—roger, lost the transmission about five minutes ago. Must have—then," Polan said, his words overtaken by static. "Proceed to—give another—minutes. We'll—"

Mechanical sputtering morphed into a low hum, barely discernible in the dark. Dominguez must have restarted the generator. Harris stepped back and slammed the door shut, then made his way back around the rock formation, headlamp sweeping out into the dark beyond, hoping—and yet dreading—to see Briggs staring back at him.

A bone-white pillar of light shot out over the landscape from the south, originating at a point in the sky just above their truck. Harris's brain offered a competing series of suggestions: *floodlights, headlights, perimeter lights from the array.* None of them stuck. Dominguez stood frozen, staring up into the caustic beam trained directly on her, her skin gone stark-white, eyes wide, limbs pulled to her sides. She began to rise into the air, the toes of her combat boots pointing toward the ground.

A second beam appeared, just below the first, shifting over onto Harris. The sensation was akin to choking on a piece of overcooked steak, every breath a struggle as a great pressure built in his core. His arms were held to his sides and his legs dangled precariously over the indifferent earth.

He tried to scream, but the most he could manage was a pained *No.* He shifted his head and eyes to the left, finding Dominguez in his peripheral vision, her face pale and drained of blood, eyes shut against the radiant horrors before them.

A great mechanical hum reverberated through his skull, then declined in volume and intensity, like a passing helicopter. The lights shifted, accompanied by a great grinding and shifting of metal or rock or both, the noise an echo of the lights' movements, emanating from everywhere and nowhere at once. Omnipresent, and yet localized to Dominquez and Harris's brainpans.

Amongst the aural chaos, a sound like a door slamming shut—a door on their pickup truck, perhaps—and then footsteps, crunching toward them in the dirt, rocks kicked up and dry scrub snapping beneath sure footfalls.

A figure emerged from the light, tall and covered in shadow. It spoke to them in a familiar voice, calm and nonchalant, as if reality itself were not breaking down behind it.

"If a new opportunity came along, one that didn't involve you sitting in the goddamn mud and sand all the time, one where you could do something a little more interesting, and paid better to boot—would you be up for that?"

Those words were crystal clear, despite the thrumming of cosmic machinery and the furious hammering of Harris's heart in his ears.

The figure was only a shadow before him, shifting uncertainly in the overwhelming spooklight.

"You didn't talk," it said, a familiar statement, not a question.

The lights grew brighter, hotter, the skin along Harris's face beginning to thrum with the onset of a sunburn. Those lights shifted again, accompanied by the great grinding of industrial machinery, mechanical humming shifting tenor and rhythm, like the music of strange gods. The figure spoke again, but its voice was not audible in the air, but in Harris's fracturing mind:

Think you can keep not talking, even if you were to see something interesting—something like what you saw with Sergeant Villanueva on that mountain over Barack-E-Barack?

Harris struggled against the invisible bonds holding him in place. He experienced a sensation of slow descent, and the toe of his right boot touched earth again. He could shift his arms more, as if the coils of restraint were weakening.

I'll see you in Colorado.

"We're already in Colorado!" Harris said, shouting, that final word—*Colorado*—echoing back to him suddenly across the great elevated mesa, his voice, his *human* voice, the only sound in the suddenly pitch-black and still night. The lights blinked out. The grinding and humming of unimaginable machinery was gone.

Dominguez landed hard on her knees, coughing; Harris caught his balance, disoriented, but managed to stumble over to his partner. Placing a shaking hand on her shoulder and another on her arm, he helped her to her feet.

"Jesus Christ," she said, tears streaking down her face, reflecting the light of his headlamp back at him. "What the hell was that? Did you see him, too?"

"I saw something," Harris said, voice cracking. "It sounded like—"

"It was him. It was Briggs," she stammered, wiping the tears from his face. "But it *wasn't* him. It was like it was a reflection of him. An echo or something. Something pulled from my memories." She turned, the beam from her headlamp sweeping the plain before them with its bright light, revealing only their pickup truck, some scrub, and errant rock formations. "He told me we were coming here. To Colorado, to this ranch."

"But we're already here," Harris said. Dominguez shook her head, eyes locked with his.

"Are we?" she asked. "Are we, really?"

—◆—

The sun emerged from behind the mountains to the east not half an hour later—several hours early, according to their watches. Their cell phones regained life and signal coverage a quarter mile from the main property, telling the time true.

"Five hours," Harris said as Dominguez drove. She was hunched over the wheel, gripping it tight, eyes wide and staring at the road ahead.

"What?"

"We lost about five hours." He pressed fat buttons along the side of his digital watch until the time matched what his phone—and the rising sun—told him.

"First time?" she asked, her face hardening into a concentrated expression, a precaution against something welling up inside of her. Something she didn't have time for.

"Yeah."

"Me too."

—◆—

Papers tumbled in the early morning breeze, collecting around tree trunks or slapping against the side of the abandoned ranch house. The doors of the shower and housing trailers groaned as the wind kept them open for the passage of ghosts. Broken glass glimmered in front of the command trailer, all of its windows smashed out. Fractal shards of glass remained in the frames, like the teeth of a predator. A pair of cows wandered out from behind the housing unit. They considered Dominguez and Harris for a moment, jaws working over cud, then moved on to disappear behind the ranch house.

One of the pickup trucks was pulled up to the command trailer's front steps, idling. Dominguez kept her pistol at the ready; Harris kept the shotgun slung over his shoulder. Whatever happened here, it smelled like the violence was over.

Dominguez led them to the truck. She reached inside the cab and turned the key, the engine going out, leaving them in a sudden and restless silence.

Harris glanced toward the motor pool. The other vehicles—trucks and ATV utility vehicles alike—were gone. The empty expanse of dirt and struggling grass showed tire tracks and muddled collections of boot prints, but was otherwise empty.

A great crash of metal and glass sent them both to crouching against the abandoned pickup, hands over their heads in a futile gesture of protection. Metal groaned and creaked and, when they looked up, they saw the source of the crash. Not a dozen feet from their own pickup, four of the project's trucks stood stacked atop one another, crushed and compacted into an impossible junkyard tower, windows and windshields smashed or broken, headlights cracked or missing.

The compacted tower wobbled back and forth as if it had just fallen from some great height, threatening to teeter over and crush their vehicle. It settled in place with a great sigh of metal and crunching glass, mercifully leaning at a slight angle away from their truck.

Harris and Dominguez looked up, expecting to see a crane, an airplane, a helicopter—something, *anything* that could have suddenly dropped several metric tons of metal. The morning sky began to turn from black to red, with streaks of willowing clouds reaching like skeleton fingers from the horizon—but was otherwise empty.

"We should get inside," Harris said, but Dominguez was already moving toward the command trailer, whose open door tapped against the plywood handrail of the makeshift steps. Harris followed her up and in, grateful to be out from under the gaping maw of the Colorado sky.

Inside, the power was out, leaving the closed-circuit camera monitors and computer system screens blank and silent, the air noticeably absent the electronic buzzing that usually underpinned the atmosphere. Faint sunrise-light crept in beneath the blinds, giving the room a spectral glow. They turned on their headlamps.

Harris was about to step back outside to check the generator when Dominquez called over to him from a desk in the corner of the room.

He crossed the distance and found her studying papers: a long-form printout of technical data; marks and numbers arrayed in sequence, a line graph cutting up and down and across its many connected pages. It was an accordion of paper leading back to a large printer set on a nearby shelf. Over those many cascading sheets wound great black strikes and curves, black magic marker letters forming the scrawled words of a madman.

"This is Polan's handwriting," Dominguez said. She shuffled through the printout, following its course down to the floor and back up to the printer. "The fuck." She threw the papers down, the stack tumbling together in a soft crash.

"Is this a test?" she asked. "Is this part of NROEP or whatever? Some bullshit they're doing to us, see how we'll react? We served our goddamn country and they put us through *this?* How dare them. How *goddamn dare them!*"

"Talk to me, Dominguez."

"Are we observing *it*, or is it observing *us?*" she asked, her eyes going wide, sweat breaking out along her forehead.

Harris bent down and started to pick through the paper, clearing aside its own folds and pages until a stretch of it presented itself. Those large, black letters became legible, but his mind struggled to correlate their arrangement—until he realized that the letters formed words written backwards. Words that repeated over and over again, smashing in to one another across endless feet of printout.

...ODAROLOCNIUOYEESLLIODAROLOCNIUOYEESLLIODARO-LOCNIUOYEESLLIODAROLOCNIUOYEESLLIODAROLOCNIUOY-EESLLIODAROLOCNIUOYEESLLI...

Harris threw the paper snake back down again, the same panic rising in Dominquez beginning to crawl along his own mind. A familiar darkness began to pull at his awareness, drawing him toward considering some awful solution to all of his problems, all of his fear, all of his anxieties and frustrated hopes for the future. His shoulder and back felt the weight of the shotgun, and it comforted him in all the wrong ways.

A phone rang.

From down the hall.

One of *those* phones.

They weren't supposed to call *back*.

The ring echoed throughout the trailer, distorted and warbling. An exhausted alert, each shrill intonation a desperate gasp for their attention.

Harris started walking toward the source of those awful tones.

"No," Dominguez said, shaking her head but making no move to follow. "Absolutely not."

Harris found the door to the last room on the right open. A light clicked on within, despite the lack of power.

He leveled his shotgun at the door and sidestepped to see inside. Empty, save for a log book, the ringing, coiled-wire phone, and the desk lamp. The lamp offered a shrill buzz, lighting up the room. He wondered if the lamp was even plugged in, but decided that wouldn't matter. Not really. Not now.

Harris set his weapon down against the divider wall and took a seat. He pulled the phone and its square base toward him, the device giving up one final, exhausted ring as he set his hand on the handset. Before he picked up, he stared at the definition of that strange word, laminated onto the table's surface:

Occult
hidden, magical, supernatural, secret

SPOOKY ASS SHIT

He brought the receiver to his ear. A familiar voice spoke.

"Would you like to join us here, Harris?"

He flipped open the logbook to a fresh checklist. He traced his finger down the page until he found the entry he was looking for.

X —IMPERSONATES OR CLAIMS TO BE A FAMILY MEMBER, FRIEND, OR COLLEAGUE

"This isn't part of the NROEP investigation," the voice said. "Those efforts are complete, results inconclusive."

X — MENTIONS OR ALLUDES TO NROEP ACTIVITIES OR INVESTIGATION

"But there's a new (*new*) project. One I think you'd be perfect for, Harris. You were a good soldier, and you're a good investigator. You're the kind of guy I can count on. Dominguez can come, too, but she doesn't want to talk to me (*me, us*)."

"Would you go get her? She should hear this offer, too. It will be a promotion. For both of you. Was for me (*US*). Come back to the mesa. Tonight, when all the light has gone out of the world. I'll (*we'll*) be waiting for you. We'll take you in. Again. You can stay longer this time."

Harris's hand began to shake. He checked off another box.

X —CLAIMS THE OBSERVER/EXPERIENCER IS AN ABDUCTEE
X —OFFERS EXPLANATION FOR "MISSING TIME"

"Come on back to us, Harris. There's more we have to show you."

The line went dead. No static, no rush of terrible electronic noise. Just silence.

The desk lamp clicked off on its own, leaving his headlamp the only source of light, casting strange shadows on the wall before him. He checked off one more box.

X — OBSERVER/EXPERIENCER FEELS STRONG DESIRE TO COMPLY WITH THE REQUEST(S) OF THE VOICE(S)

There was no point in lying.

They already knew the truth, anyway.

THE DIVORCE OF DEATH AND PESTILENCE

Anna Tambour

They met at a bar. She ordered a Beyond Proof Absinthe. He, a Crème de Milk.

It was as amicable as a couple's split can be when each is self-made and unbelievably wealthy, and the boredom with each other is also equal.

"But what about the children?" said Death.

"They're old enough to look after themselves," said Pestilence.

"That's what I'm afraid of," Death mumbled.

Pestilence examined her nails. Death's under-the-breath talkbacks was one of the things about him that got on her nerves so much, she was perpetually jumpy in his presence.

"Like them?" she said, holding out two of her hands.

"Glitter becomes you. But why d'you have those stuck-on things?"

"You know I can't grow mine out."

"Oh, yeah. I forgot. Just as you're so peaky, you need blood for your anemia."

"You can talk."

"Why do you insist on arguing when you've got no defense?"

"Really. Like when—"

"Don't bother."

"Your supeeweeowity feel thweatened?"

The rest of the conversation went as well as many do at this stage of an amicable divorce.

Yeah, they still loved each other and all, but the talk of the town was: each thought it very unfair that the other didn't move out of town.

"This town doesn't fit you" Pestilence would have said. Death could have shot back, "You're holding yourself back here,"—if they'd still talked.

——◆——

Pestilence ran a hand up through her hair, looping a finger in a hand massaging her head. "This town is way too hip for him."

Corruption clucked sympathetically. She loved him for his touch, but he also had such a soothing bedside manner.

Greed was working other ends of her.

Meanwhile, Death walked to an appointment. As it is said of some of the world's richest, he lived modestly. The only time he flew or was chauffeured or took a taxi, or boarded public transport was when he had work in the vehicle. He preferred to walk.

And while Pestilence looked the same as she had before the divorce (the blushing cheeks, the super-glossy eyes, her supermodel height and the way her skin fit so well, it showed off her bones) Death was incognito.

For this appointment he was a cockapoo on the way to a children's ward. This was no contemplative stroll. He was being jerked along faster than he could walk. He yelped every time one of his uncut claws caught in the roughly cast concrete. He needn't have bothered. The woman who was leading would have noticed no protest unless it bit her. Nor would she expect it. She was not only the town coordinator for the branch, but the most active member of Visiting Angels. Her fridge was covered with photos of children at the moment they were given, due to the program, valuable minutes of the joy of a companion animal.

Today's visit turned out to be a disaster—

This was a new experience for Death. He'd never been a dog before, and was surprised at the power they have. He found himself licking the spot of an incipient, undiagnosed, operable cancer—the little girl bent over in bed, stroking his head and uttering sweet little-girl nothings—when he heard a high-pitched scream followed by a series of tortured squeaks. Death looked in that direction and saw a nurse burst into the ward and approach at gale force, stopping by the bed with an ear-hurting rubber-burning turn of heels.

The Angel, who'd been trying to stroke the little girl's resistant head, jerked her hands away, painfully pulling at Death whose lead was brace-leted to her like the cop and the perp in many movies but no real life.

"I told you, Deb!" The nurse's watch pitched and rolled on her heaving bosom. "Dogs frighten people. And they're as illegal here as they are in any restaurant."

The Angel Deb picked up and clutched Death defiantly. "They give joy. I'm taking this up with the Board."

"You do that, and explain the restraining order I'm taking out against you."

The Angel's grip on Death tightened so much, Death finally understood a phrase he'd only known as metaphor. The nurse reached out to the Angel, who recoiled. She put Death and the floor and walked out of the ward, viciously yanking Death, maybe to restore her dignity by proving she could make someone else's life a misery.

Death didn't know if the Angel had capable hearing, nor whether his current canine persona came with an extra whoomph for sound, but they were well down the hall when he heard the nurse say, "Filthy bitch."

Death, too, loves a good massage, and he sure did need it by the time he got home.

"She didn't even notice I filled in for her poor little Harpo," he said.

"That shouldn't discourage you. Does it?"

"Before you, it would have."

"But now you can look back and think of all the joy you brought that little girl."

"Joy!" He pulled his head away from two capable hands. "Tomorrow I'm going back as a surgeon. She doesn't need to die."

"Mmm."

"Joy!" he mumbled, lying back. "They've given her up. But that's ridiculous. I can remove it all. I'll be Doctor Wolf."

"Who's he?"

"A visiting surgeon who's really good. He'd know what to do, but they've already written her off, so she's not his patient."

Life leaned over him and kissed his forehead. "This is why I love you," she said, and smiled wryly.

He felt that. She might as well have poked him. "So why aren't you pleased with me?"

"You're so naive."

He rolled out of her grip and stood up, and even as he gasped with insulted pride, he couldn't help but breathe in her intoxicating scent—fresh grass, seedling oysters, rosebuds, cool springs, etc.—all the opposites of his rot and desiccation.

"You're cute, but," Life said. "If they've given her up, this Doctor Wolf hasn't got a chance of getting near her."

"But he can save her!"

"You know nothing about life, do you?" Life tossed her glossy locks. "Hospital protocol is inviolable."

"But don't you care?"

"Of course I care, dear. But you're all exercised about nothing. You think she'll die soon if that cancer isn't cut out. But you're wrong. She's got years more yet. Now let's get those kinks out of you."

He let himself be coaxed down after she reassured him that what she said about the little girl living wasn't a lie.

"You seemed almost fatalistic," he said. "If I didn't know you, I would have thought you wanted her to die."

"Never!" Her eyes watered with passion he couldn't see, but it would have made him feel all the more passionate about her.

He sighed with happiness and relief. As her fingers worked their magic on his wretched bones, he couldn't help comparing this marriage to his first. God, he loved Life. He told her constantly but she never seemed to need it said. It wasn't that she was conceited. She just worked so much harder than he'd ever known one can.

"I hope you're not selfless," he said.

Life laughed. "Do you think so when we make love?"

Meanwhile, Pestilence, Greed and Corruption had no misunderstandings in their household. Firstly, they were in no time, becoming enormously successful. They'd bought into the town's nursing homes and daycare—turnkey businesses—and had practically no reforms to carry out, making so much money legitimately, in this town, that Greed and Corruption were each worried about becoming impotent, their creative powers not being taxed at all.

Things looked up when, because they were, this threesome, so flashy and unapologetically crass, they were canvassed to run for office. Greed and Corruption were born to it and had already planned their victory speeches and run for President, when Pestilence stepped in. For some reason, she didn't want to. So they had to give the 'want to spend time with my family' excuse, which always just encourages hopeful hangers-on, but this aspect they kept from Pestilence who tended to have a one-track mind and no subtlety. Still, she had enormous power and a drive that neither of them had. And it was she who gave this trio the global awesomeness that they, in their relative pettiness, could only dream of.

Their neighbors admired their style, but could only imitate it to a small extent.

So that little household should have been blissful, but it was discontent.

Death shacking up with Life discontented Pestilence so much, she tried to deny it to herself, which worked as well as that sort of thing always does. Sometimes, Pestilence felt so feverish, she burned.

There was plenty of smoke before the split, as late one Sunday, Pestilence caught Death eyeing Life in admiration.

"She only looks younger than me."

"And smells it, too," said Death. "She makes an effort."

"It's just her genes."

"You're just jealous because we're too alike, you and I."

"I'm just so much looking forward to the time I never have to see your scaly face again."

———•———

The divorce should have made them happy. They never argue now, for they don't talk. Death and Life live in a house built in the 1920s—cornflower blue with crisp white trim, a wraparound verandah and a swing chair, in a side of town absolutely bristling with street-library cabinets—little shrines to goodness. The flashy threesome had a house built for them in a part of town that was wasted as a public park.

It's got the usual musts for their class: infinity pool, indoor full-size bowling alley and squash court, the wellness spa, and an ironic 1958 drive-in burger joint in the basement next door to a hyperrealistic inadequately equipped emergency ward for role-playing Epidemic.

Each would have hated the other's new home so much, they wondered how they'd ever managed to live together—and for practically forever, too. Divorce should have solved everything—if only everything had been provisioned for. What was needed was this recognition to keep the peace:

One takes the town. The other rides out.

What should each one care that the other was in town? Being separated only increased each other's individuality. Neither had ever been the yang of a couple. It was pointless to compete, yet that was all the talk.

Competition between these two pulled the town apart like two dogs who'd found a rope of taffy.

It hurt jaws all over town. The rivalry between the two households was the prime topic of gossip, though Death and Life never gave interviews and were only quoted in the type of hearsay that only stands up in paid-off courts.

The talk had all the thrills of bad shit happening to someone else, which should have inoculated it. But it also had a strange power. It made people in the town personally worried for their own safety.

Nobody would admit it, but there was a strong sense of panic building. Irrational foreboding. Nothing specific, mind you. More like worrying if the cops are gonna look in your basement, or if the IRS is finally gonna audit you. Or if the musical chairs will stop and you'll be sitting in the house you just flipped while it falls down the market's black hole. Those and the more specific ones: Is my job being advertised? I can't afford cover. I can't afford to get fillings, so I'll have to get my teeth yanked, but will the dentist take a personalized poem for pay?

Fear spread like a disease, transmitted by air. Soon many people in the town wanted the divorced couple in their separate households, to clear out of town. People just wanted to go back to old times when the feuds and spite and evil deeds were done on the screen. When reality was fake.

One group of outraged residents met at House of Pancakes for the 10:00 to 11:00 Seniors Pancake Special. They had planned to canvas lotsa plans, and indeed, spoke with the bravado of drunken retired pirates' accountants, about their plans for vacations. They did, however, compose a note that the craftiest of the lot desktop published two copies of and the most adventurous posted anonymously from the next town: Property valuations set to plummet. Sell now!

It didn't work.

Nobody could shift them through gentle nudging, and sure as hell nobody told them to pack their bags.

And nobody knew them well enough to act as a falsely sympathetic shoulder.

This threesome and twosome were like that family that moves in next door that you don't know. Every Saturday she must do something to rile him because you can hear them. and it could be very nasty for you if you interfered. And you certainly don't want to make things worse for her.

The town's zoning couldn't settle things. Nor could the sheriff nor the Freemasons nor the book clubs nor the golf club nor the local branch of the NRA.

The chief negotiator from every church in town had as much effect as if the parties were all human.

An intractable situation, to be sure.

So, surprisingly soon, because the situation became the new norm, that feeling of unease that stalked the town, that feeling of impending doom that hung over everyone—was normalized into the general awfulness.

It was getting on time for Thanksgiving.

Thanksgiving is an odd holiday for Life. It's when everything good gets picked. Pumpkins growing so big, they're due for their first teeth, have their life support hacked off. Apples are plucked. Turkeys so deformed they are all breast, suffer their final indignities.

And in the Life and Death household, Death was into his bbq. This was Death's first Thanksgiving, and he was having the time of his life, preparing. His smoker was a work of supreme craftsmanship, and his touch with meat, something else.

Life was all rawfood, nothing killed. So pecans good, peanuts bad (droppeth from the tree vs. duggeth from the earth). Apples are too confusing (is an apple plucked from the tree, alive or dead?).

The menu was imbalanced in terms of deliciousness, but the efforts could have been human, they both went to so much trouble in preparation and expended so much wasted worry re accommodating guests, for when are relatives guests?

Death, in his Life-loving reformed state, wanted no one to remind him of his past, so he insisted to her: "The only relatives should be yours. Invite all you want. I'll just slaughter more pigs."

"Great," said Life. She wasn't being sarcastic. She loved his bbq as much as anyone honest would. They first ate it together while binge-watching movies about pigs who talk. Afterwards, Life told Death about her involvement in using pigs as organ banks for people. "People will soon be able to watch their gardens of guts grow, so to speak. No, it's true."

"But will these transplants work?"

"They should extend life."

So a pig could hardly be thought of as something truly alive. "Got room for another rib?" "Always! Oooh, crispy and gooey."

Thanksgiving Day arrived on time, having no choice. It rebelled, however, as it always does, by doling out black ice, plane cancellations, flu, and enough anxiety and dread to give the world's greatest negativist indigestion from overindulgence.

The Thanksgiving table at Death and Life/Life and Death's house groaned appropriately.

At one end of the table sat Life. At the other, Death.

He'd been looking forward to this day so much. He had cradled an irrational wish: that Life's relatives would warm to him once they knew how sweet he really was. And now they were finally here, on both sides of the long table.

Life had never talked about her relatives. Death had never felt sure of himself to ask. Now, poised with his carving knife over the obligatory turkey, he looked down this tableful of guests, and froze, not as a model for a Norman Rockwell painting update but with fear and shame. He had no idea how to serve out conversation entries.

Just as well. The only way he was likely to catch anyone's eye was if he went fly-fishing for their eyeballs.

"You can only express yourself illegibly," said Literature to Music.

Vengeance and Spite were whispering in each other's ear, their faces a picture of anticipation.

Forgiveness, dressed in a once white dress smelling of a bestselling drugstore perfume and underarm sweat, cc. 1970, ate slowly and deliberately, making Death's skin crawl as the sound of her crunching celery sticks and tearing open apples with her teeth. When her cheeks hollowed, she was sucking clots of apple flesh dry.

Mercy didn't eat at all. Because her sad smile would have cracked? Death was feeling guilty for not having the social skills to put her at her ease, when she said, "I forgive you" as if there were a 'you' she was talking to.

Suffering made Mercy look like a girl who just wants to have fun. Her back rigid against the chair, the metal on it was making loud reports as it turned white with frost.

Not all the relatives were scary. Rhyme was a party animal, fun and obnoxious in equal measures. Drama was a bore. Color made death wish he had more rods and cones, or whatever was needed to see like a bee, an octopus, a human who could see the full human spectrum.

But for the most part, Life's relatives embarrassed him. "Naive," he mumbled. "I sure am."

How could he have expected them to all be wonderful?

⸻

"What?" said Life.

"Nothing."

She couldn't object to his obsession with her. That was all good, but he could be so annoying. This habit he'd developed of looking at her out of the side of his face when he thought she wasn't looking—it rather put her on her guard, which irritated her. For what was there she could ever do that she would be ashamed for anyone to see, or that she wouldn't know about. Yet he looked at her as if—

As if I only have eyes in the front of my head!

The thing is, it didn't matter which light he caught her in, she looked beautiful and smelled fresh. He'd tug on her hair when she was asleep. It was not a wig. Her nails with their crescent moons but absolutely no glitter, were as much a part of her as were her teeth. Her breath was fresher than a sea breeze.

Yet at that Thanksgiving table was: Corruption. He was thick as thieves with Greed, both of them eating and what looked like planning.

And it wasn't as if they were uncles who you can't help but have. Or just the two she'd shacked up with on the rebound after Death.

They were Life's.

Her kids.

A compounded sound came out of Death: either 'ghosts in my itches' or a geyser fixing to blow.

Pestilence would have been riled enough to imitate, punctuated with spit—but it cut no truck with Life. "Who'd you think I'd invite?" she asked. "The town's dry cleaner, pretending he was mine?"

"Well, I just thought 'Thanksgiving'. Parents, grandparents, cousins. You never told me you had children."

"Who else would have had them?" she laughed. "You slay me, Death. YSN."

He grinned involuntarily, which happened every time she used that acronym she'd made. It stung less than "You're so naive," but it still made him feel as if he'd been born yesterday. Yet there was no denying its beneficial effect: *I feel so young again.*

Death was dying to know who her first marriage was to. She didn't talk about it. *Did she have a marriage or was having kids a hobby? She hadn't had any since they'd hooked up, but would I know?*

That was another thing about her that he loved, when it didn't slightly miff him. He didn't think she tried to keep secrets, but *Life is so much more complex than Pestilence.*

⦿

The town's life continued around these households, as any town's life does. A checkout person after a typical day was driving home to the only rental available, given his credit rating, when the co-owner of VapeAway swerved his bicycle in front to teach this carhog a lesson about bikes—they have just as much right to rule the road.

He didn't live to find out if the driver agreed. The mess the car made of him was so definitive and the road so deserted, the driver sped off, the only witnesses being Death and a Great Horned Owl who was cruising by in this area of scattered businesses born to die, billboards that say "You can rent this billboard" and plots of frost-hardened weed skeletons poised like gangs against broken-down concrete.

Pestilence was only kept moderately busy with her usual flu season (more oldies got shots this year) but things got lively at Steiner Elementary, with a lovely touch of measles. Pestilence had fun this year by sending flowers to the parents of the unvaccinated dead. *It's petty, I know,* she told herself, *but I must get my kicks where I can.* She didn't know, however, that all the parents got so many of these florists' Sympathy Flower Deliveries that they rarely opened the cards. The few who did, just chalked up Pestilence's Thank You to a mix-up in cards.

What she didn't know about couldn't bother her. What did, however, was the revelation that the measles outbreak wasn't something for her to celebrate but someone Corruption couldn't stop talking about. "You're the activist," he told her. "Skepticism can't effect change."

So true. *Healthy skepticism was just a stick-in-the mud.* But Corruption had taken to praising Skepticism so much, Pestilence knew he was two-timing, stepping out with this creature on the sly, perhaps attracted to Skepticism's fresh-faced glow. Damn that healthy look! To have this happen twice!

And Skepticism must have been attracted to Corruption because that measles outbreak, Skepticism was ashamed to admit to herself, caught her by surprise.

Pestilence felt stabbed. She began to worry about Greed's faithfulness, though he seemed so simple, she felt silly.

She did, however, gather enough courage to contact Skepticism and ask to meet for a coffee or something at Domino's. Somewhat to her surprise, Skepticism agreed, meaning either that Skepticism didn't know enough to have jealousy issues. or was waiting, fruitless plans at the ready, to kill Pestilence.

Skepticism was in no state for either. Pestilence could only admire the job Corruption had done. Skepticism looked as if Pestilence had treated her, only awaiting Death to land the coup de grace. But it was all Corruption's doing, and Death was nowhere in sight.

Pestilence was almost sorry for Skepticism, so was quite happy to talk shop as if that was the real reason Pestilence had asked to meet.

They both had a lot of work in Yemen. But neither could take credit for the initiative which fell as it often does, to that hogging superstar, War, who is so popular that everywhere he goes, he has a minder who keeps fans at bay, and proffers wetwipes to him if he deigns to shake someone's hand.

They bitched about War as everyone does. He's so much more popular than they could ever hope to be. And the most maddening—his success is built on the most ludicrously shaky structure. "He's lazy and gets rewarded for it!" Pestilence groused. Skepticism nodded, unable to answer verbally, what with the coughs and wheezing.

They parted with a hug. There's nothing to assuage jealousy better than knowing your rival is weaker than you. Still, that sneaking bastard! Death had never two-timed Pestilence, hadn't even found someone on the rebound. Life had to be a genuine love, found well enough after the divorce for Pestilence to know this wasn't some dalliance of Death's. Besides, Death had never been frivolous.

Jealousy was too weak a sentiment. What Pestilence felt for Life was hate.

She got, with the help of that bemused couple, Corruption and Greed (sometimes she thought they were the couple and she, just the resident cleaner and Mom), a condemnation by the Council, of the premises where Death and Life lived, on the basis of a bad smell that must be emanating from an uncharted sewer gas buildup.

They moved, but not out of town.

She, again all through the offices of Corruption and Greed, got the town dog pound turned into a puppy mill that sold their prolific end-products to the dogfight industry. Life's address and email were published, and instead of a wreath on L&D's front door, dog feces was smeared, till they moved again, this time to the town's haunted house—a place with such a bad vibe that though anyone could walk in through the bashed back door, not even the stray dogs would shelter there in a blizzard. Hell, the place repelled dust itself.

As haunted houses usually are, the place had countless rooms and had been built by a crazy rich person. So it was on Main Street (as it was built when rich people lived in Main Street houses close enough to smell the greenbacks in the banks), much closer to the center of town (with its ghost of a well, and more recent ghost of a pump and horse-watering station) than the house of Pestilence, Corruption and Greed (so far away from the center, you were either poor or rich).

The ghosts in the center of town salivated as they never had before in all their ghostly lives. They smelt smoke, the hors d'oeuvre of a shootout.

———◆———

Dust rumbled unlucky lottery tickets down the dusty drag. Starlings made filthy whoopee under the protection of the rain-ravaged eaves of the boarded-up Roxy. Joseph T. Johnson, owner of Solomon's Jewelers, hung an Engagement Ring Special banner in his window, with as much hope as the barber next door had, of attracting anyone under 60. Johnson the jeweler did best with his Golden Anniversary Special, for that always got them in. Trouble was, the only followup you could hope for from those customers was a repeat sale when they hit Platinum, but by then, the couple was usually half dead.

As in all town's Main Streets in the center of town, the discontented tended to look out. Out to the center for excitement.

Maverick Dispatch's hauler was running late from Arapahoe, Nebraska. The driver had to get the load of cattle to Dodge City, Kansas, before 4 o'clock. They'd supposedly broken through the yard just before he had arrived to load them, and once out, they were filled with the joy of escape. He could have left it up to the farmer and his useless sons, but that would mean he'd still be waiting while those cattle went on the rampage, trampling fields and jumping over or just crushing some of the sorriest excuses for barbed wire fences he'd ever seen. He ended up commanding the roundup. The farmer said he was sorry but you could see he hadn't learned a thing. The trucker wanted to hit him when the cattle were finally in the rig. They hadn't been deliriously happy and merely carefree to escape. They'd been starving. He wished he could take off his belt and have that farmer feel his buckle around the ears, but he had to eat, too. And a fucking customer is always right. He did say, when handing over the docket, "Stick to soy ranching."

By the time he reached intersection of Main and First, he was ready to blow. No music had soothed his savage chest. He put his foot down hard when the light turned yellow, and would have made it through, but for the tanker.

Death is always on call, but that was some emergency rush. The ghosts of the town center had been expecting him, but not for this. There was no drama.

Pestilence didn't pitch up. But she did hear of the crash on the police radio Corruption loved as only a fan can, one who'd as "Corinna78" awarded it 5 stars and a review: "THE best radio station evah! It never recycles 'hits' and always has something up to the moment, but yet classic."

The crash, its fireball, the certain but as yet unknown toll of life came through in a mixture of loud followed by exaggeratedly calm euphemisms on the police radio. Pestilence could hear sirens rushing past as background ambience. She would have loved to rush to the scene of devastation, hide under the boardwalk and watch Death work, but there was only a boardwalk ghost. Absolutely useless, but…

But while he was so busy, the opportunity of a lifetime told her to knock. She patted her hair, and rushed out to confront Life.

Life was in the kitchen, talking to a bowl of oysters when Pestilence burst in.

She looked up and took off her apron. "You look terrible," she said. "Tell Mommy all about it."

Well, if the town had only known, it would have voted for a bypass. This Mother and daughter brunch shot to hell the prospect of that shootout between exes at high noon.

Pestilence was not only confused, but her skin crawled. "Why didn't you stop me marrying Death?"

"Why should I have?"

"Don't you care that your husband . . . my father—"

"Where'd you get that from?"

"Did you have a previous marriage?"

Life closed her eyes. The conversation seemed to tire her. "You young ones. Why are you so conservative?"

"So he's not my father? Who is my daddy?"

"You've gone too far. I am Life!"

"So?"

"So what makes you think I need anyone?"

Pestilence couldn't wait to slink away, but didn't know how to ask permission. This was so humiliating. Worst of all is that she'd always thought of Life as being the hag she had to be, but either this was the best case of plastic surgery evah, or Life looked frustratingly vulnerable. If only Pestilence could knock Life off her perch, she would cover that fresh face with pustules, fill those flowerlike armpits with stinking suppurating buboes. And drag out the result. The bloody cough, the long slow choke of throat cancer that immobilizes while being licked by a dozen cats teeming with toxoplasma gondii. If only—the image of her indecently gorgeous, heartless mother dying of multiple causes while being turned into a crazy cat lady was starting to soothe her ravaged—

"Off with you," her mother said. "And if you come sniveling here again, it should be for a reason. Don't you think I have enough to do without your dithering? You think I have 72 hours to find out what you want? You expect me to take a swab? You never did tell me what you wanted."

Pestilence left in confusion, shame, shock, and elation. Life is a bitch.

That bit of excitement in the town center came and passed, and the town no longer felt uneasy at the tension between two households. The reason for this could have been that the tension was all on one side.

Life had never given a hoot about Pestilence, any more than she could afford to, the private lives of Joy, Sorrow, Mercy, Compassion, or cockroaches. She couldn't afford to give them a thought once she'd had them, any more than a termite queen can, her offspring.

Pestilence was so shaken, she went into a period devoted to work. There was always so much to do, and she had to travel so much, she actually got upgraded once to Business Class.

A presidential election combined with widespread distrust of everybody got a Doctors Without Borders overrun in a place where she had just planted Ebola. This disrupted her plans, but only insofar as people helped her far more than she helped herself. She came home more rested than she had imagined she would. That was just as well, for the ministrations of Corruption and Greed were beginning to irritate her. They were so chummy with each other, she felt extraneous.

Life never told Death about Pestilence's visit. So he had no idea that Pestilence had harbored any feelings about him after the divorce. So many people say "I felt dead," after a divorce. If Death had had an ECG just after the divorce, it might have shown that he was more concentratedly himself than ever—in an intense state of Death.

Physiologically therefore, it is no surprise that his attraction to Life was inevitable.

He carried on working as usual, happy enough to get home for her massages, her fresh beauty, and her fragrance—so unlike those of Death and Pestilence, whose body odors had always thought they were making beautiful music together. As she massaged, he tried not to wince at her rather insensitive but honest putdowns that she couldn't help of his naivete.

Much of his work was odd-job quickies. Mr. Otis Bribiesca, 65, self-employed painter and plasterer, had just installed a stuffed Santa peering into a fake chimney on his roof when he slipped. Miss Adelaide Fern Randles, 82, retired teacher, tripped on her landline phone cord after washing the kitchen floor. Rachel Orland, 15, ninth grader with a 4.0 GPA, died on a rainy Sunday afternoon, officially of a heroin overdose, but the dealer had gone short on the heroin and long on fentanyl.

Then there was the type of job that filled so many wards of the public and private hospitals—those passing through the last weeks of a long life. The end was inevitable, the only differences being the Cause officially recorded, Long Enough Life not being Acceptable Practice.

He did his work and went home. Work and home. He was now embarrassed by his early escapades post-divorce when he was trying to aspire to Life's standards by taking on the comfort-dog persona. He was no comforter. Nor was he creative. He had to face facts. He was merely a garbage collector with as little power to decide who dies, as a garbage collector has to decide what people throw out.

Death wondered what Life saw in him. She, who created constantly.

He was trudging home feeling as tired and unsatisfied with his existence as an Amazon fulfillment center worker when something made him stop on the sidewalk and look in the window of a house. A young woman—more of a girl—was sitting up in a hospital-type bed in what had to be a living room. The curtains had been pulled askew so she had a shocking lack of privacy. She was looking in his direction, so he looked behind him. There was nothing there.

Something hit the window from the inside, so he turned around. Her mouth was making gasping fish movements, and she was still looking in his direction.

Not only that, but those mouth movements had to be: "Help."

He'd always laughed at stories where people see Death. Never in his experience of our human lifetime, had anyone ever seen him, much less talked to him.

He walked up the verandah steps, opened the door and up to her bed where she held out her hand. He took it and felt its warmth.

"Please," she said, and her eyes closed in a spasm. A woman in uniform was sitting on a couch on the other end of the long nave of a living room watching a shopping channel on a wide-screen TV. The girl in bed began to talk to Death. She had hardly any lung power, and the loud product-praising ecstasies coming from the TV would have made anything else impossible to hear, let alone the breathless girl, but Death's powers of hearing had improved no end since his stint as a dog.

Still, it took quite a while, for her pain came in waves. She said she'd had all the treatment they said was possible, but it was still going to kill her in, they said, twelve to twenty months. She never specified what it was, and he didn't ask. (As for whether they were right, he didn't know because that was too far in the future for him to have received the equivalent of a job sheet.)

Meanwhile, she had palliative care. He could see how well that was working. As she talked to him, the room started to fill. Mercy came and sat at the foot of the bed. Suffering tried to push her way in between Death and the girl, who didn't see either of them, but did have more severe pain attacks when they sat themselves down.

The girl, who must have considered her name irrelevant by her stage in life, told Death, "It's criminal in this state if I even look up how to end this. And I can't have someone else charged with murder . . . (a long delay here while he waited) But they can't convict you."

A fresh breeze stirred the curtains, and Life appeared. "Just what do you think you're doing?" she said to Death.

"I don't know," he said, for he didn't. "She needs my help."

"What? Don't be ridiculous. She's not dying now." She bustled in, plucking his hand away from the girl's. "Bug off."

"But—"

"But nothing. Life is above all. You most of all should know that, or haven't you learned anything? She'll live as long as I damn well please."

"But look at her."

The girl reached out to him, crying, mouthing Help. He snuck his hand forward.

"Get away from her!" screeched Life.

Her delicate nostrils quivered as a foul wind fluttered the curtains.

"Get away from her, you bitch," growled Pestilence.

Life jumped back, stepping on Mercy's toes, who hit Suffering mid-skedaddle.

They fell in a snarling knot.

Pestilence blew it away with such force, the shopping channel yelped once, and shut up. The blessed silence was cut short by a whimper, yelp, then silence—of Suffering, Mercy, or who knows—Life herself?

Pestilence turned to the girl. "This'll be quick," she said, and gave the girl a kiss.

Death got an odd lump in his throat.

"And as for you," Pestilence said. "I've never stopped loving you."

GALLAHER CALLS

Samuel M. Moss

Gallaher calls on my sister and me once a month to relay the status of our finances, any notifications of which we should be aware and to drop off our goods for the month.

Before they died all contact with my parents was channeled through the medium of the finances, those large holdings that have passed down through our family for four or five generations, which—like a tumor attached to a vital vein—grow and shrink somewhat over time, causing a great deal of concern and worry, but which cannot be excised or destroyed without causing grievous damage. My sister and I were granted use of this house, and upon the subsequent passing of my parents, were granted their other holdings of various forms, many of them artistic works, all overseen by a grand and complex trust.

Of the tenets of the trust there are thousands, perhaps many more. Written in the style of The Method of Totality, the tenets of the trust tend to be very abstract, covering every potentiality, addressing every meager legal option. For this reason the tenets of the trust are rarely applicable to our day-to-day lives, though occasionally one arises that requires some output of energy, demands some nontrivial alteration of our habits. For the most part the trust was written as a document in itself, a thing that exists primarily for itself, and which takes my sister and me—and our family's fortune—into account only as a peripheral concern.

Over time, I admit, we have grown weak with regards to the trust. I have never read the document in full, but rather rely on Gallaher to inform me of its relevant points. My sister read it immediately upon its release, is adequately versed in its requirements, subrequirements, addenda, appendices and amendments. She passed through it in a single monumental stretch which demanded some seventy-two hours of her undivided attention. It was one of the great weakenings of her life. For the trust, being read in full, inhabited a part of her, cut off and established a permanent domicile within her psyche. The trust lives, as it were, inside of her, dormant, silent, waiting to escape. This sacrifice of hers is one that I cannot respect enough, and which has since set her in my heart as a beautiful and selfless creature. This allows me—with my work which is far less important than her own—to pass on through life without giving the trust a single thought, by simply responding to Gallaher (or one of his ridiculous stand-ins) when he arrives, making the few small changes for which he asks and then moving on back to my work. Often, I simply shirk the changes, in-one-ear-and-out-the-other them, and find that my sister, sometime in the night, has sacrificed even more of herself, of her strictly limited energies, to implement them.

The goods Gallaher brings are regular: four boxes of Mellinger's Blood and Liver Tonic Tarts (frozen). Twenty-one to a box. Once a week, on Sunday, a box comes out onto the counter to thaw. Twice a day I remove a Tonic Tart for myself and cook it in the toaster for fourteen minutes. It comes out piping hot and I eat it with butter and marmalade. Source of my lifeblood, source of my strength. Once in the morning I prepare a tart in the same way for my sister. In this way, my sister and I are complementary: she eats the morning meal, I eat the afternoon and evening meals.

The Mellinger's tarts are hard to come by these days, what with our region's strict health regulations and changing tastes. Only a few small grocery chains in the South still sell them, mostly to invalids and old timers ridden with carbuncles, those who need six-thousand calories daily in order to get some nutrition after their tumors have fed. In some fetid backwaters, whole legions of hookworms are fed off of these pies, last malarial guests agog and gorging on the tart's remnants. I cherish the lard rich crust, the last great tart of our country made in this hallowed style. Plus the pig's blood is high grade and the liver finely chopped. No vegetables or fillers to get in the way, just gut greasing pork that goes down slick and hot. The packaging is antiquated and bare, nothing to get in the way of a proper meal.

Though Gallaher only calls on us sparingly I have recently come to find that his smell, an acrid reek of stale cigarette smoke, has come to persist in the house, has permeated itself into the boards and blinds themselves. I scrub and scrub to get it out but, as of yet, to no avail.

How did they make their money, my forebearers? They traipsed once down the tobacco road at a fortunate time, that is all. They found some new way to pound the leaf, sold it as "A Fortifier", along with some dubious medical claims. It was eaten up by old women with gout and the men that took care of them. "McHeller's Fortifier, the grease between your joints!", "McHeller's Fortifying Agent, take it twice and feel nice!", "Fortifying tobacco blend, the chew of choice for Bomgard's Minstrel crew!" All the operations run by the family for years, for a time the money accruing in berms and banks. This fad in chewing and spitting quickly passed out of fashion and lingers on now only in certain forgotten, threadbare fields along the gulf coast.

I tried it once, pulled the powder from a screw top tin, and nearly retched.

The company was dirty work, damned down in the dumps work. Now it is all hunkered in a bombed-out little warehouse in Ponte Claire, our hands washed of it. Not the sort of thing for my sister and me to take up. As you well know, as you so well know, we are thinkers. Ponderers. At the forefront of our fields, forging new ground.

Gallaher came by today. He arrived without warning but with a great deal of fanfare. Gallaher is a hideous man: a gray woolen suit worn in all weather, a thin mottled frame, his face creased, pinched, stricken with sebum. His hair—gray and slightly yellowed—falls in a ring around a perfectly bald crown, nearly to the shoulders. He always carries some law book in his hand, wielded like a cudgel, waving it about the house, using it to point and gesture as if his bare finger was not suitable for the task, hiding behind the law, a force to which he ascribes a power no less grand than that of God himself.

While I have never seen him engaged in the act, I know for a fact that Gallaher is an inveterate smoker. I suspect he smokes one of those strange, dead brands: Tereyton or Corvell, with their obsolete marketing gimmicks, their long-refuted claims to health and palatability. Surely my parents forbade him from smoking around us, some strange and strict condition of theirs: another hold out of their power, another grim reminder of their presence in our lives.

Gallaher not only stinks of smoke, he has the visage, hands, skin of a smoker. He can only be in the house for two hours at a time for want of his habit. When he first arrives, Gallaher is kind, effusive, cordial. As time wears on he becomes terse, businesslike, then, as his craving for nicotine peaks, he barks out each word, berates us for our shortcomings, channeling the anger of our parents, channeling the hatred and disappointment of our parents and society both. Then, something snaps within Gallaher. He halts midsentence, straightens his jacket, sits up, and excuses himself, softly.

So Gallaher arrived, as usual, his maroon Jaguar clattering across the gravel. He always takes his time in the car. I could see him through the kitchen window and he saw me. He did not wave. Did not nod. No recognition. He simply sat, motionless. Three minutes, five minutes. What was he doing in this time? What was he thinking? If he had been smoking in there I would have understood. If he were pulling from a flask, steeling himself for the experience of stepping inside of our home, then I might have understood.

At times I wonder what Gallaher's life is like outside our home. I see him sitting in dingy bars in the middle of the day, sitting in the back, a booth all to himself, picking at those awful boils on his neck, picking at his ears and his cheek, pulling at the stubble on his chin, a warm glass of Noilly-Prat Rouge or Cream Sherry before him. Flies hovering, dotting the surface and sticking, going drunk from touch, kicking then drowning then sinking to the bottom. Some meat thick law book before him, cracked at the spine, open to an esoteric section, a menial, rare aspect of elder law that he fawns over. The issues of the dead and dying, the laws of the dead and dying, some tricky point that he will never come across in real life. He takes a sip and the sugary stuff runs down his chin and he mops it with the lapel of his coat (he never removes it, no matter the heat) so absorbed as he is in the legal problem. Later, Gallaher alone in his home, the wallpaper peeling, as stained and yellowed as he is, the walls stacked with piles of law books as high as his chest, neck, chin. Gallaher, drunk, tipping over a pile of those books, the books falling on him, crushing him under their weight. Paralyzed, Gallaher wastes away and dies, not to be found for months.

Gallaher knocked softly at the front door. I was so lost in my thoughts, in thinking about Gallaher's life outside of my home, I had not realized that the man himself was trying to enter. He always knocks so quietly, as if afraid to enter. A man of weakness through and through. As if he fears us, my sister and me. As if we present some threat to the integrity of Gallaher's world. As if my sister and I—my ineffectual hermit sister and my own bland countenance—could cause more harm to Gallaher than the weight of his own God-forsaken books coming down on him.

I cross out of the kitchen, moving the third table out of the way, crawling over the Melitsos bronze, beauty that it is, through the hallway and thence into the foyer. Over my sister's papers, stacked high and atop a cushion of rubber mats to the main pathway which extends thus to the front door. The bolts on the door are numerous, and as I unset them Gallaher stops his knocking. There is little difference between Gallaher knocking and Gallaher not knocking. Gallaher knocking is so soft, so ineffectual that it may as well be not knocking. This is, in fact, an interesting question to me (perhaps the only interesting property that Gallaher has): where does Gallaher's knocking end and the silence begin? I have planned a sculpture to address this question for a few years but have hated every attempt at it. I have faith that a great sculpture will emerge while answering this question, someday.

So, I unset the locks and opened the door to Gallaher standing there in the light rain, emotionless, smoke-stinking. I always open the door a crack before letting a visitor in. Anyone. Even if my own sister were to knock on the door—if she were to leave the house, which is unthinkable—she would receive this same treatment.

"Hello," Gallaher said, in his tentative way.

This is Gallaher, always: tentative. Every utterance, every action, every hesitation and silence held back and waiting for something else. What, Gallaher, are you waiting for? What are you wondering at, you hapless scourge?

I pulled the door back, allowed Gallaher to enter. Regardless of my hatred for the man, my parents, each of them, drilled into me the importance of hospitality.

Even to your own worst enemy, my father would say, *Open the door wide and set heavy the linens. Gloss the walls in your most subtle art for the eyes of a guest. For a flattered enemy is an enemy no more, and a flattered friend is a friend forever.*

These were his pronunciations, usually sent out in the true white heat of an ether session: *Stately groom your casements, and gird them with lengths of holly,* he would say—this was a spiritual endeavor for him—*For a guest well entertained is a guest whose heart will land back at your doorstep and whose blessings will be brought to you again and again.*

"I see you've cleaned." Gallaher said.

You see now the hatred he has? How horrible this sort of man is. Not only Gallaher himself, but all men in the same vein. For Gallaher is not just an individual, he is a symptom, a stamp from the mold. Every day we are surrounded by Gallahers. So many men have crossed our threshold, have tried to sneak their way into our homes with this attitude of false grace. I smell it out in an instant, and Gallaher is given passage only because he was chosen by my mother.

"And your sister?" Gallaher said.

I gestured with my chin to her room.

Gallaher nodded, rapidly.

There was a silence.

Gallaher tapped one of Farquar's pieces from her minimalist phase—a parallelogram of forest green shag carpet—with his toe.

My anger surged.

"Is there any way we could get more light in here?"

The curtains were drawn. I shook my head. Gallaher always demands this when he comes over. My sister needs this for her work. Light, she says, disrupts her thinking. Gallaher has always held a pathological distaste for everything we need and have needed. An innate dislike for our tendencies. Fundamental. My sister and I both have tendencies and needs that we have cultivated over a long period of trial and error. We have figured these out like a puzzle, parameters for our life and work that are finely tuned. Years of experimentation, a process at once collaborative and adversarial. Each object has been set into the house in its rightful place in order to cultivate an environment of absolute calm, of total peacefulness. Of absolute, unclouded wakefulness at every moment. We are permeated here by a history of complete art, a tradition of finished thought. The works of Schiller and Leahy take absolute primacy, have become first order objects in our subtle carnival of ideas. The placement of the prints, the sculptures, the scores and furniture integral to this effect. All of it. True, some on the floor, but is not the floor just another valid surface, like the walls and ceiling? Cannot the floor hold art just as well as the ceiling holds a chandelier? These works are placed about our home in order to form a kind of semantic shell game *to which we alone know the solution.* Walking through this house I see nothing. This would be true for my sister as well, even more so in her case. Though she does not leave her room, she is so sensitive that the atmosphere of the house affects her even from a distance, through the walls, from their very proximity to her being. We see nothing and feel nothing but a kind of diffuse, kindled light. The light fills us at each moment and allows our barriers to fall away, allows the walls of our mind to sink away into the objects.

"I come bearing poor news." Gallaher said, abruptly.

This was one of the few moments of mirth I have had in Gallaher's presence. His presence which is itself to me poor news. Gallaher who is as a stream of interrupted obituaries, bound one to the next.

I nodded.

He continued, "The Bertrand-Smeller investments have been found to be," he cleared his throat, "Found to have been in a sense, in a certain sense," he paused.

I felt my sister moving in her bed, adjusting her position in order to listen more closely. She is, obviously, always disrupted by Gallaher's presence, her work broken for the rest of the day, sometimes for a week or more, by his setting foot in our home, his egregious displacement of our perfect environment.

"These investments, into which your family placed so much of their hopes, within which your family imbued so much of their future, to which they had been loyal and supportive through so many years, have been found to have been, as it were, corrupted to a total and existential degree."

This name—Bertrand-Smeller—is one with which I am somewhat familiar. I try as hard as I can to keep the goings on of these vague and distant things out of my mind. I revolt against the endless stream of names and places and numbers and situations. I labor each time Gallaher visits us not only to scrub the seat and carpet of this man's smell—a smell which is so powerful as to persist in spite of my efforts—but to cleanse too the presence of the names and signifiers which he brings, from my mind and from the manifestation of our minds which is our home. So, when this name is mentioned, I must wrack my brain for its significance. They come to me, from a vast distance, their vile, benthic forms resolving sluggishly as through a noxious fog.

"The investments have been found to be tampered with, starting some years back. Some moneys mislocated, others dropped into spurious corporations within backward states. Now," he reached out as if to console me, touched me with a damp hand as if this were some condolence. "You see the investments have, in a way, consumed themselves. Seem—in spite of the work which had been so studiously done in the name of your family and your dear, brilliant parents—to have fallen into themselves. While very rare, we have a name for this. *Financial Autophagy* we call it."

Gallaher said all this with a mock gravity, an act of nauseating melancholy. Was he drunk? He gripped my bones with his sweat slicked hand, left a residue of tar on my knee's cloth. He looked at me long and deep and I could tell that when this was all done, when his absurd visit was over, he would go home and laugh at us, would barely make it out of his car before breaking out into a surge of braying.

"These investments meant so much, *so much*, to your father. Even more to your mother who was a dear, dear friend of Smeller's, who, as you may or may not have known, attended the Academy with Smeller from a young age, who once even, I believe, had a short affair with Smeller while still a student, long before your father came along, and still harbored nothing but the fondest feelings for the man up until her death. Her faith in their organization was of the utmost strength. Unimpeachable. And you have carried this on valiantly after the untimely death of your parents. All this, I assure you, makes this moment one of the highest tragedy. Financial as well as personal. Bertrand was found dead at his estate by his own hand. Smeller, as I understand it, has absconded from the country with a great deal of money, has likely fled to Macau or Cote d'Ivore from which the possibility of extradition is precluded. No one among your family, least of all you and your lovely sister, can be blamed for this misfortune, not even a whit."

Gallaher looked around the house, as if expecting my sister to appear. Looked toward her room as if she would suddenly alter her character, the practice of solitude and absolute silence which she has cultivated since earliest childhood, and break down at his feet. This insipid man, who seemed to believe that his news, this news that could not hold less interest for us, in light of our continued, unbroken work, would warrant some sudden exclamation or reversal. The epitome of delusion, this man, this Gallaher.

Gallaher—and this should be no surprise—is a godawful liar.

What are we working toward? What an asinine question. The work is only found when it is arrived at. Our process is a wandering, a picking out of adequate passages. We work methodically, my sister and I. We search through every permutation, every dead end and blind alley of thought. Even if we see immediately that a way will be closed off to us, we pursue it, *for its own sake alone.* Passage through the labyrinth of thought is a work all its own. Only when we arrive at the end, after having disgorged every fruitless path, will we know that we have achieved what no one else has, or could. Only when the tree of thought has been totally searched through will our work be complete. This was a style and method imbued in us by our parents, who referred to it as 'The Method of Totality.' It is the greatest method of thinking, the greatest path towards thought and consciousness.

All other artists and thinkers sit down in the morning, before their easel or canvas and struggle for an original idea. They try to look deep within, hoping that inspiration will strike, but they look ever into an empty well. The barren well of the self. This notion fills me with a morose mirth. I cast aside the fallacy of inspiration and the fallacy of the self the same day I cast aside the fallacy of god. Each as vacuous and as useless as the other, each the crutch and construct of a stifled mind. No the Method of Totality provides us, each of us equally, with an illimitable source of work, a boundless path to glory. To see our spaces, my own studio and my sister's desk, would be to see a mountain of achieved permutations.

My sister's endeavors are characterized, solely and specifically, by an exertion of the mind. All day she alternates between sitting at her desk and lying on her bed. That ancient bed of hers. She will sit for a while, head in her hands, then lie. Sit, then lie. All day, alternating. It is a sort of exercise for her, physical, yes, but even more so an exercise of the intellect. Her movements in this time are of the utmost grace, planned out far in advance so as to be as efficient and brief as possible.

She sits and she lays and occasionally, very infrequently, will she write. A half dozen words once a month which she adds to a manuscript she has been developing since childhood. These words? What poetry. No, she does not let me read them, does not let anyone read them. Ever since she was a child this manuscript has been locked away in a great wooden chest in one corner of her room. Written on cast-off receipts, envelopes or scraps of wrapping paper with that indigo pen of hers.

I know when she is writing: the sound of the nib on her indigo pen is unmistakable. From across our home, even as far away as my studio in the carriage house, I can hear its sound. A great fluttering occurs then in my heart, a great rising up. *She has spoken,* I think. I well up with emotion. I know each utterance of hers is greatness because she spends so much time thinking, so much time running through every iteration of words, every possible permutation.

She holds a thought in her mind like a predator grasps its prey. Though in her physical form she is frail, so utterly and tenderly frail, no taller than a child, and thin, almost emaciated, intellectually she is like the most striking predator. A leviathan or roving beast of the earth. To hear her work is to witness a great beast pursue its prey: coursing over field, overtaking it, playing with it, batting it around, finding the most tender flesh, the most wholesome spot. Then, once those great jaws of hers have clamped down, they never again fully release. She grips an idea and lovingly tortures it, extracts everything from it, every gasp, every scream, every drop of blood and lymph and bile. She grips it tighter and tighter until it is on the verge of death, then releases just a bit, just to the point that it might take a breath, allowing the life to flow back and persist a moment longer.

This is the game she plays. Working over her words, treading her theses. Only then, only when she is satisfied, only when the lower bones have been eaten, the blood stopped up and the last breath gone from the thing, does she dart to her desk (ah, she spends so much time supine that her muscles have wasted away, she makes this transit in something like a four limbed crawl, I believe) and places her words upon the paper, only then does she move to secure her thoughts into this wan and vile world.

When she writes her words she writes them flawlessly. Her six-word phrases come out without a further thought, revision or hesitation. Perhaps this is one of the reasons I love my sister and hate our lawyer Gallaher with equal passion: where Gallaher is hesitation personified, an endless jolting, jarring jerk which never truly moves, my sister is all action, a steady release of energy which no force could stop.

Where my sister's work is all intellectual, my own work is without a single thought. I set my hands to my medium and work without my mind once asserting its presence. My own studio, situated in the great carriage house, is filled with my finished branches, dozens, hundreds of sculptures which vary in only the slightest ways, which differ in ways that only another adherent of The Method of Totality would recognize and appreciate. Two sculptures, finished or forgotten, would seem to the uninitiated to be identical. It is not uncommon for me to work for hours at a time and only come to, only really become aware of my surroundings, as I finish and fall exhausted into the chair in my studio.

In place of my father came my great teacher, Esterhazy. His life, beyond reproach. He grew up in a factory society, had for many years labored in some munitions mill, handling the bomb's hearts, gingerly lacing these hundred-pound loads into their skins, knowing that at any moment he might blow himself right into the world of ideas. Four fingers on one hand, three on the other and all of those remaining just scar ridden stumps. This never interfered with his work or his practice. He learned quickly to work around this disability, even to include them in his practice.

Long dead now, Esterhazy, but still ever with me. We would sit in his studio, he before his plinth, that bent and shrunken man, his nakedness covered only by a twill cloak, for hours. A master of Totality and its minor branch, Staticism. Long disused, long forgotten, this hunchbacked and deformed man would stand before a lump of raw material and rest before it, utterly. He would spend hours in absolute indolence before a piece of work, allowing the little particles of inspiration to pass through him, stilling himself beyond stillness so that the greatest ideas would lodge in him *and in the inchoate work* at once.

Esterhazy and I would sit, stand or kneel for hours in his studio, the busts of great Staticists looking down on us, the studio unlit, almost to the point of darkness. So as to add to the power of the work the positions we assumed with our bodies would be chosen in advance with the utmost care. At first these positions would be as comfortable as any other, were in fact chosen for their initial comfort, but as time progressed our bodies would begin to ache, the joints and muscles keening out as they reached their limits. Only when the strain had been passed through to the true point of numbness, only when the body had been conquered, could any work, any true sort of work, conceivably be undertaken.

It took me years as an apprentice to come to this point. Esterhazy would sit with a tarred bramble beside me, swinging it any time I moved.

"Stay static," he would mumble in his broken mouthed way (Esterhazy had been in some bland, pointless, Eastern war, had assumed wounds that stuck with him through life, were in fact the impetus for his practice as movement caused his rotten body to bloom with pain) "Eschew movement," with a swing, the words falling from his cracked and swollen lips.

So in this way I learned from him, from this man who could hold a position for hours, days, weeks. When Esterhazy worked my only task was to pour a few ounces of well water through his parted lips. For days on end he would perch before his work, his head cocked to the side, one arm held high. The strength of this man was unbelievable. To hold these positions for so long required a bodily strength only found in the most extreme athletes: summiteers of Everest and crossers of the Atlantic. Esterhazy's best blows caused one to pass through the bounds of pain and glimpse momentarily the spiritual realm.

Hours, days would pass, and then Esterhazy, sensing that pure moment, would strike with his tools, his own rough spade and spatula, a knife held between middle and ring finger, a point in the palm. He had to hold all his instruments at once and act on the material in much the same way as a calligrapher does, the movements flowing from him like boulders loosed from a precipice. Three or four quick, fluid strikes and the moment would end. This was all it took Esterhazy: a few slashing movements and the work was done, the idea realized, the question addressed.

"When is the work done?" Esterhazy would always ask me. One of his unanswerable questions. He would turn to me and ask this and every answer I could provide would be swatted away.

"When is the work done, when is the work done?" Said like a wind-up doll. He would shout at me, berate me "When is the work done? When can the work be done!"

A question or a statement, Esterhazy?

"What is a finished work! What could possibly constitute a finished work!"

Esterhazy had a handful of English phrases he used with me, the only ones he knew.

One day I came upon Esterhazy in his final position, perched above his greatest work. His breath had slowed to a minute's long sighing, his fingers grown cold and locked in place, the implements stuck permanently in his hand. But here, this time, they were lodged too in the work, inextricably caught in the medium. He had become, in that moment, a part of the work. The sculpture here, his greatest sculpture, joined—body, material, idea and spirit—in union. I flipped on the fan and dried it, threw it in a kiln at the lowest setting and, ten days later, pulled it out. The part that had been his body had reduced to a rough black column, the metal of his tools cleansed bright by the flame, the material itself cast into a low, hard brown. That clay which had gone in a shapeless mass emerged a perfect rendition of Esterhazy's soul: the sculptor cast in the light of God. I have it now, stored away in a safe place near the house. The rest of the world—those few anyways who had heard Esterhazy's name—believe that he returned to his home country to live out his days in deepest obscurity. But he lives on, those two linked columns, forever engaged in his art, transmuted into his art: the true stone Esterhazy beside that feeble column of carbon that once held him.

❦

I feel as if Esterhazy is looking over me now. Since Gallaher's last call I have gotten no work done. I spend my days scrubbing and scrubbing: the walls, the floor, the works of art. Every time I start toward my studio I get a whiff of that ashtray stink and I pick up the rag and bleach and try to hunt it down. Now it's here, now there. I think I have cleaned one place and it seems to pop up in another.

The lights have gone off, and I can barely see what I am scrubbing. I was working on a section of wall in the early dawn and as the sun came up I saw that I had cleaned the gouache right off of a Terrandoa. Right down to the canvas. A shame.

His smell is in everything. His essence in everything. In myself even.

——◆——

Today something dressed as Gallaher came into our house. This has happened occasionally throughout the years, some assistant or fraudster comes up our gravel drive in a vehicle appointed to seem as if it were Gallaher's and Gallaher's alone. This imposter steps out in their cut rate costume, no doubt picked up at some Mummer's supply corporation, affects the voice and tone and smell of Gallaher. They come to our door and knock in that ineffectual way—carefully practiced—and step inside and ask us some news on the progress of the investments, on the state of the trust, on the decisions of the trustees. They moan and cajole and wheedle us for an hour or two and then depart. What they are searching for, I cannot say. Some minor piece of information they could use to blackmail us or otherwise rip our fortune from our hands.

So today, as well. This one hastily adorned and wretched. I caught sight of it out the window. I hesitate to say 'he' or 'she' as I question its very humanity. Its Gallaher's wig askew, its Gallaher's suit sideways and patched together. It was a head and a half shorter than the true Gallaher, hunched and emaciated, writhing within its stained suit coat. On opening the door I sputtered and choked at its hideous smell, some sort of Gallaher's perfume sprayed on far too thick.

I heard my sister tossing in her bed, aching to cry out. We had to humor him, this ersatz Gallaher. It was written into the trust—in some far away place, locked behind faux-wood doors—that any Gallaher that stepped into our home needed to be treated as if it were the True Gallaher. That even the most atrocious Gallaher substitute was to be afforded all the humility and recognition of all previous and genuine Gallahers.

I obliged, though grudgingly. My sister and I were so faithful to the tenets of the trust, knew that our lives depended on the full and outright execution of the trust until its time of expiration, or of our own expiration. We knew that any Gallaher that came to our door was to be respected and listened to, though we had no obligation to answer or follow 'his' instructions.

When I let this Gallaher in I saw its face was covered in clown's makeup. A thick mat of white and red and black in approximately the form of Gallaher's own. It danced around the foyer, humming some carnival tune to itself, putting on airs of gaiety. Shivering and twitching as it went. It kept its head down, its body turned in on itself. Where Gallaher normally stands tall and erect—far too erect as far as I am concerned, the sort of erectness meant to affect authority—this imitation Gallaher wandered the house hunched and creeping, pulling his knees too high, its elbows all out and akimbo. I sought to gaze into its altered face, to see what lay beneath. With the one good look I got I found that it was barely human, just layers of makeup one atop another, some small polished face covered thick and uneven by the heaped-on white.

He joggled over to the great room, making a fool of himself, making a fool of our own home. This Gallaher sat in the overstuffed Howell chair, patting itself convulsively, dusting itself off, making little squeaks and grunts. It couldn't sit still, couldn't stop moving, wouldn't lift its head to face me. I sat across from it. All I saw was the crown of its head, some cheap grey wig set sideways, the peach plastic of the pate discolored and cracked with age. It hardly sounded human. As a rule I never speak to any Gallaher, real or fake, unless absolutely necessary. To speak to a Gallaher is to encourage him, to further his goals. It is to open your door to the thief, to cry out to the murderer. By not speaking I keep a Gallaher's worst intentions at bay. By not speaking to a Gallaher he says less, does less, thinks less and leaves sooner. His destructive effect on my sister and her thinking are significantly mitigated.

It kept its head down, its whole body jittering. Playing the waiting game. But I excel at waiting. Stasis is my realm, utterly.

After an agonizing time spent watching this horror show the ersatz Gallaher broke down. It squeaked out a few perfunctory phrases, words Gallaher might use on a normal visit, but spit these out one after the other in a meaningless stream: 'trust,' 'execution,' 'sister,' it said, 'bylaw,' 'signatory,' 'liability,' 'covenant,' stuttering here and there, 'addendum,' 'appreciation,' 'cosigner,' 'duplicate,' 'arbitration.' These words, and a few others like them, came out muffled, distorted, in a broken squawking voice, tacked one to the other in a meaningless slop of legal jargon and stern advice. As if this thing had listened to the man himself speak without comprehension and figured that mere regurgitation would sufficiently confuse me.

This went on for a few minutes. I nodded my head softly, letting this Gallaher get what it needed to get out so it would leave my sister and me to our work. I found myself wishing for the presence of the real Gallaher, who would at the very least recognize when his presence had become tiresome, who had some rudimentary sense of his impact on my sister's state and would attempt to minimize this impact to some degree by seeing himself out.

I suspected then that *this was in fact Gallaher himself* beneath all of that make-up. That the cheap wig and the soiled suit were somehow covering up Gallaher himself, wearing a suit of himself. I suspected that this was Gallaher hiding as himself, putting on an act of himself, trying to fool me into thinking that he was himself while not being himself. I, of course, would not be fooled. It was clear that, at best, this was Gallaher wearing a Gallaher suit, wearing makeup approximating Gallaher's face, Gallaher altering his voice as if to sound *as if he were something else affecting Gallaher's speech*.

The worst case scenario was that this was in fact something else attempting to be Gallaher. But this possibility was extremely unlikely: to affect Gallaher's mannerisms, suit, hair and wig would do no one any good at all. To affect the state of Gallaher would assist no one and no thing in any way, would allow them no benefits or rights. Gallaher has no special powers, no significant traits, no useful credentials. All Gallaher can do is convey the tenets of the trust to my sister and me, the trust which is immutable and eternal. On the other hand, Gallaher has good reason to imitate himself. Gallaher knows these things about himself, he is well aware that he is so low, the lowest even, on the ladder of life, that he exists at the very bottom rung of all traits. He must believe that by imitating himself, poorly I must add, he might dredge up some sympathy in me.

After some time spent spitting out these Gallaher-words, the false Gallaher—like some gear driven toy—grew quiet and still and slumped over in the Howell chair. I watched it for a long time, even as it grew dark outside. I was glad, I'll admit, that it had stopped its pointless speech, but I had hoped that it would see itself out, that we would be freed from its presence.

As it grew dark in the great room the Gallaher's features became indistinct. Its face grew dark, its suit dark too. Its outline joined that of the piled detritus that spreads in an even layer throughout the house.

Standing, I examined the Howell chair. There was nothing notable there, just an old mop head, a scuffed mannequin, a bolt of flannel and an empty pack of cigarettes.

Today seems to be the last day in our house that will be marked by the consumption of Mellinger's Tonic Pies. The box from Gallaher's last visit ran out a week ago. I found an old batch from the Fall, all frosty and hard, forgotten in an ice chest down in the cellar. I rationed this: one pie a day for myself, and for my sister one pie cut in half.

We keep expecting Gallaher to call on us, to bring some of his news, some fresh goods, but each day passes without him.

I do not know what to make of this. Even an ersatz Gallaher would know that its death has no effect on the true Gallaher. Even more so the true Gallaher! His absence then is unacceptable, and will result in a most stern rebuke.

Each time I have come to my sister's room with her morning ration she has pounded violently on the door. Most unlike her. I have tried to assure her in a measured tone that violence will not get her anywhere. She let out a string of obscenities which came muffled and distorted through the door.

In spite of her meek appearance my sister has at times been known to suffer from an irrationality, a widening of the spirit and endless anger at everything around her. She once trashed a gallery in response to a meagre refusal and at great cost to my family. These locks on her door, it must be made clear, have been instrumental in keeping myself, but also her, safe. The locks were necessary for allowing not only my own work to continue unabated, but especially her own work. Were she able to leave her room every time she fell into the grip of one of her tantrums we would hardly get anything done!

Today her pounding began in the morning and proceeded all day without end.

Very unbecoming.

I spent the afternoon moving my effects out of my room in the East wing and into one of the old servant's quarters in the South wing. This room was full of crated works and old books—but after some rearrangement, and a small fire outside—I cleared a space near the door just large enough to hold my desk and bedroll. I hammered a line of deadbolts into the lintel, just to be sure.

Just enough room to read and sleep, in the quiet, which is all that I need.

I should be comfortable here.

———◆———

My sister has come out from her room.

I woke to a sound like gunshots as the locks on her door were ripped from the wall. I rose from my bedroll and bolted the locks on my own door.

The sound of her moving came thunderous: wet flesh pouring through a bladed sieve, slickrock bowling over itself in a torrent. Her sound. The way it grew suggested she was looking for something—perhaps, I had to wonder—for me.

This change in form is not unheard of. The Method of Totality creates a strain on the mind that is in proportion with the power of that mind. If every avenue is completed, that is if Totality is reached, that strain has no outlet. The Method grows so immense that it bursts forth from the feeble confines of the body and becomes something altogether different. For a mind like Melitsos the strain bloated his body into a great misshapen mess. Yes, those endless swallow tongue pies washed down with Bordeaux did contribute, but it was the Method itself which, upon reaching Totality in his final years, caused him to balloon, crack and seep out into the gelatinous mauve puddle in which he ended his days.

So my sister, with a mind unlike any that has existed before, this mind which rips ideas utterly asunder, must have generated a force of unrivaled strength. The strain too of the Gallahers: the true and the false, the visits in such close succession, the rumor of our financial situation, may have sent her even further over the edge. Judging by the sound, her body has grown so large that she just barely fits through the hallways.

I had hoped that moving to this room would mitigate her disruption of my work. I fear now that by leaving the room I will place myself squarely in the cone of her wrath. This room too is so crammed with precious work that escape through a window is impossible.

I pulled a spackle knife from a nearby box, jabbed it at the ceiling, sent plaster flying, and opened a hole just large enough to pull myself through. My sister had grown briefly quiet, perhaps trying to locate me. I pulled myself up and though the ceiling and found myself in the crawlspace that runs above all the rooms in the house, crisscrossed with heavy beams, rank with must.

There came, to my surprise, a vague light, glowing soft around the corner of some brickwork. I crawled toward it. As I moved I heard my sister come rushing and rumbling through the hall below.

Coming around a corner I found the source of the light: a dusk caked desk lamp set onto the floor of the crawlspace and there—illuminated by its light—a low form on the ground, mustard yellow, ovoid and pleasing. I drew close and it resolved into view: a pile of hundreds, perhaps thousands, of cigarette butts, laid out in a mat nearly four feet around, its edges raised up, mortared together by what may have been dried saliva, ash heaped here and there. Then I saw its shape: a nest, like something a swallow might make. Propped on the edge: one of those cigarettes, bent but still burning.

With three pounding hits my sister broke down the door to the room in which I, moments before, had lain. There was quiet, then the sound of her turning.

I crawled into the nest, pulled my knees to my chin. The boards beneath shook with the sound of her approach. I picked up the cigarette, held it between two fingers like I imagined Gallaher would.

The light flickered, then died.

In the dark there was only the orange ember-glow of the cigarette.

How static, I wondered, *could I keep?*

When, I wondered too, *is the work truly complete?*

I took up the cigarette to my mouth, pulled from it deeply, listened to her sound and wondered.

THE RIDER

Victoria Dalpe

She'd dreamt she'd died. The details, like how exactly she died, she couldn't remember.

She just knew that she'd died. In the morning, after the dream, she wasn't certain that she'd ever woken up. In fact, from that morning on through the days and weeks that followed, she never felt that she had woken up. Strangely though, she adapted to this new dream-state and lived as if she was a ghost. She was seen but overlooked, heard but often misunderstood. Almost invisible. *Almost.* She could be touched, but the sensation never sunk past her outer clothes or skin. Numb and grower number all the time. And cold, always a little cold. She imagined the sensation was akin to freezing to death, a slow creep into the void. First devouring fingertips and toes, then up the limbs, till that chill got to the heart, freezing it mid-thump into a hard rock.

It wasn't until Andy, short for Andrea, was riding the bus to work one day, a few weeks into this death-state, that something changed. She had headphones in, though what song played she couldn't say, she wasn't so much listening as she was not listening to anything else. She held a book in her lap and read the same line at the top of the page easily a hundred times. Since she'd "died" her morning routine had been like this. Waking as if still dreaming, tired no matter how much sleep she'd had the night before, her coffee barely denting the sensation of treading through water. She'd ride the bus, she'd get to work, she'd sit until it was time to go home. Then back on the bus, home, and bed. Over and over.

Suddenly, the bus lurched, the brakes squealed and everyone fell into each other. Those standing pitched forward, tripping over the seated passenger's legs and rolling into the narrow aisles. Bags toppled, purses emptied. Andy noticed a metallic tube of lipstick, resembling a bullet's casing, roll by her feet. When the bus stopped, there was a moment of confused silence. She was fine, having been packed in tight between two sizeable people. Other passengers were helping those on the floor, gathering their things, all had a dazed look about them. Outside the bus there was yelling and crying, a siren could be heard farther out. Andy took it all in, interested, mainly because it was something different than usual. She wasn't scared though and knew she should be. She gnawed her lip, trying to find some life inside of her, some fear of death or injury. *Was she suicidal then?* That was when she noticed the petite woman across the aisle was staring directly at her with wide crazy eyes and a funny quirk to her mouth. Not a smile, but close. The eye contact lasted long enough to be uncomfortable and Andy blinked first.

At that moment, the bus driver, who'd run outside, came back in with a police officer. The bus driver was ashen, his eyes red-rimmed. The cop called out, "Everyone okay here? Anyone need medical attention?" Someone toward the front waved and Andy could see an old woman cradling her arm. "Okay, folks stay put, I'll send EMTs in then we will get your statements and get you on your way. Call work, make your arrangements, this may take a little while. Thanks."

The bus driver mopped his face with a handkerchief and followed the cop back out. Through the bus's windshield, it took a moment for Andy to understand the smear of red on the ground. She tracked an EMT to a woman who was on a stretcher, her body broken and her pale dress soaked with blood. Andy saw the moment they zipped up the body bag. She saw white dress and red blood turned to black vinyl. As if he could sense it, the medic looked up and met her eyes. His expression was stoic, but his eyes were sad. Then he turned away and began rolling the gurney. Movement beside her pulled her attention back into the bus. The strange woman from across the aisle was now sitting beside her, same intense stare, same quirked lip, now inches from her face.

"What?" Andy said, whispering, though she wasn't sure why she kept her voice low.

"I needed to get closer, to you, to tell for sure, but now I know."

"Know what?" Andy said, mouth going dry, this woman was clearly off, possibly deranged. Though her clothes looked clean and normal and in any other situation, she would be considered pretty, her eyes were crazy. They were large and a deep chocolate brown, almost black, the darkness of them swallowed the pupil and made her look like a shark, or a rodent.

"*You're like me*. I wasn't sure, but you are, I can tell." And then, without warning, she reached out and touched the skin on Andy's chest, above the neckline of her shirt and just below the clavicle. She used two fingers, like the blessing of a priest. It was the first touch Andy had felt, truly felt in a long time. The woman from across the aisle had cold fingers. Her touch was so cold it burned. But the sensation wasn't unpleasant, it was more startling than anything. As she'd *felt* so little of anything for so long. Andy came to her senses and knocked the woman's hand away, not hard, but forceful enough to show intent.

"I know how it is, to just exist. You're new to this aren't you?" the woman said.

"To what? What are you talking about?" Andy said. But a part of her knew what the woman referred to. That she was dead inside. All this time she thought of it as a deep depression, this persistent feeling of being dead. But a stranger had seen her and knew, not just knew but saw a shared affliction.

"I'll tell you, but not here, come on." The woman stood, slung her purse onto her shoulder and stuck her hand out to Andy. Outside it had started raining. The lights off the emergency vehicles lit the drops on the windows up like rubies.

Andy stood without taking her hand, "What about our statements? They aren't going to let us just leave an accident."

The woman turned back to Andy, piercing her through with those nearly-black eyes, "They aren't going to *let us* do anything. They don't even matter. You'll see." Before Andy could protest further the woman had grabbed Andy's wrist (that grip, solid and ice-fire like before) and marched past the other commuters, down the steps and out onto the rainy street.

Then without much ado, the woman just started walking away.

Andy took in the scene, the blood on the grille of the bus, a chunk of hair fluttering there. She saw a crushed stroller, looked for a baby. The bus driver wept on the curb. The crowd watched on the other side of the barrier, seemingly indifferent to the cold misting rain. Andy felt the twin sensations of wanting to see the horrors and not, like a child peeping through covered eyes. Then the yank at her sleeve by the woman and she was off down the street. The police officer finally noticed them, a small woman with dark skin who looked barely old enough to drink. She called out and came to them. "Ladies! We'll need your statements ladies, please, stay on the bus."

All it took was the dark-eyed woman catching her eye and the policewoman's face fell, blank as a mannequin. The woman dragged Andy, still staring at the unresponsive cop, down the street, past the barricades, and away.

"How did you do that? She looked hypnotized." Andy said, breathless, confused and exhilarated. The accident, the stranger, and now the world, unfolding into an unfamiliar pattern. There was something exciting in the surreal quality her day had taken. It felt good to feel excited, to feel anything frankly. "Where are we going?" Andy asked after they'd walked quite a few blocks and the rain had gone from sprinkle to deluge. The woman turned, her chin-length brown hair plastered to her wet face. Her lips had a blue tinge. The rain sluiced down Andy's collar, ice cold. Her feet were numb and squelched with each step. It had been some time since she'd been so uncomfortable and like the excitement, was most likely why she kept following.

"Not far now, Andy. Just a little further." She smiled. The woman had very white teeth, small and spaced apart like the milk teeth of a small child. A shiver snaked up Andy's spine, from the cold, from the woman's odd teeth, from the fact that she knew her name. A name she'd never given. Two or three blocks further and they reached an alleyway. The rain hadn't let up for a moment and the visibility was so poor Andy could barely see two steps in front of her, let alone orient herself and find a street sign or shop to help her. She followed the woman into the alley, feeling both terrified and curious by the prospect of what came next. Even fantastical scenarios like organ harvesters and human trafficking held an illicit thrill, not that she wanted either of those horrible things to befall her, but she loved feeling something. She'd felt nothing for so long that even fear felt good.

The alley dead-ended in an overflowing dumpster and a graffitied wall. There was a handle-less door. The woman knocked on it. No special knock, just the standard knock, a few seconds later the door cracked and she whispered something into the sliver of darkness inside. Andy squinted but neither saw nor heard anything from inside, the rain was too loud. The door opened and the woman went in, swallowed up by the dark. Andy took the moment to debate running away, leaving the alley, getting to work, and continuing on the way she had been. Or option two, where she followed a stranger further down a rabbit hole out of her ordinary life and into something unknown.

She stepped through.

The hallway smelled musty. The walls and door were thick and once closed, muted the rain to a mere whisper. The hall was dimly lit by an industrial bulb on an extension cord, the walls were cement. Andy reached out and ran her fingertips along them, they were rough and dirty. The woman did not speak and after a moment Andy realized there was no one she could see ahead of them. She'd never seen whoever opened the door and the fact that they were gone now sent a zing through her.

They rounded a sharp corner and came to three doors, all drab gray metal and identical. The woman went to the furthest and opened it, as she did she caught Andy's eyes and smiled. "Welcome home, Andy."

Home. Home, Andy realized when she stepped inside, looked to be a large and mostly empty storage room. Water stained drop ceilings overhead and flickering fluorescents looked down on scuffed linoleum, an unlit corner had stacks of old pallets, and the other side had a few fold-out tables. A circle of unfolded metal chairs was arranged in a ring in the center of the room.

"Home?" Andy said her voice a mixture of disbelief and disappointment. The woman only smiled and removed her wet jacket. She gestured for Andy to do the same. She did, but it was like skinning a rabbit, her coat positively glued to her body from the rain. The woman draped their coats over the pallets and the *plup, plup, plup* of them dripping on the floor was one of the few sounds in the cold room.

"Have a seat, here. The others will be coming soon. You probably have a lot of questions." The two women sat in the circle of what, Andy counted, was twelve chairs. In the center, she noticed a black circle drawn on the floor in what appeared to be sharpie marker. The circle was smaller than the circle of chairs so that her feet were just at its outer edge.

"What is this? Who are you? And how did you know my name?" Andy said, her hunger for adventure curdling to annoyance the longer they sat quietly in the dingy space. The woman slicked her hair back and squeezed out the extra water on the floor beside her, a gesture more common at the beach than an abandoned warehouse or whatever this place was. She was clearly in no rush to answer Andy's questions, nor did she seem deliberately provocative. She just wasn't in a hurry. Andy got the impression that this woman, whoever she was, wasn't one to take orders. Only after she'd wrung out her hair and shucked off her low-heeled pumps and trouser socks, spreading pale pruned toes, did she answer.

"My name is Melora, and I'm like you. We are the same. All of us," And she nodded to the empty chairs, "We are the same. A tribe. Rare and valuable. I'm happy to have found you. As the others will be."

"And… what are *we*? What is this lost tribe?" Andy asked, the words feeling ridiculous in her mouth. Was she merely indulging a delusional woman's fantasies? With a shock Andy realized she didn't care whether the adventure was real or in Melora's head. What did she have to lose? She'd felt more in one morning than the last few weeks combined.

Melora paused, chewing her lip, "It's different for all of us. But you probably experienced something, some moment, where you ceased to be the person you've always been. Like suddenly, someone turned the volume on your life all the way down."

"I dreamt I was dead, that I died in my sleep. That no one knew or noticed. And when I woke I still felt dead. I have ever since, it's like the dream never ended." Melora's eyes lit up and she smiled revealing those unsettling baby teeth again.

"Yes. That was the moment you left being one of them and became one of us."

"And what exactly are you? Since I thought it was called being 'clinically depressed' all this time." Andy's joke fell flat and she regretted even trying to make it.

"*You did die*. Or rather, a part of you died, let's call it your human soul, it died. And you've been living, or existing, as a husk ever since. Like you are a reverse ghost, a body but no spirit."

"A reverse ghost? And you are like that too? Your tribe are a bunch of… zombies?"

Melora shook her head the way a scolding mother would, "You aren't very funny, Andy. I think it better you just be honest and stop making jokes. No, we aren't zombies. We experienced a spirit death. Most stay in that state, the one you are in now, and can't transcend if there isn't a guide to take them through."

"Into what?" Andy asked.

"Into what comes next. You have a hole in you, your spirit died, and we need to fill that with something else. Or rather, someone else." Melora reached out and took Andy's hand and the twin sensation of burning and freezing mingled on her skin. "I'm sure you want to ask the next question."

Andy swallowed, trying to wrap her head around it all, "Who?"

It was strange eating pizza and drinking cheap white wine out of a paper cup with the other members of the "tribe." As she and Melora chatted, the others slowly made their way in. The others. They had brought the pizza and boxed wine. Andy had a hard time understanding this group or what it all meant. As absurd as it sounded, Andy did believe Melora that she'd died that night, or something in her had. She had felt the sensation of barely existing in all the time since. She wasn't even sad enough to be sad most of the time, or to care if she were in danger, or be suspicious of following a stranger out of a crime scene to points unknown.

Now the others were there. The tribe. There was little to unify them as a group. They looked different, various ages and backgrounds represented. There was even a child, which Andy found a little shocking. The child was a small stout Asian boy with thick coke-bottle-glasses who couldn't be older than ten. She knew she was staring, but she couldn't help it. He came to her and stuck out a hand, fingers still chubby with baby fat.

"Name is Drake, or this body's name was Drake. *We* are Centurion."

"Centurion is our leader, or as close to one as we have, as there isn't much need for hierarchy here," Melora said as she sipped her wine.

The group had twelve members, one for each chair. They had to drag a thirteenth over because Andy was there. They ate and chatted quietly with each other, all sparing her curious looks, and with time each individually or in pairs came to introduce themselves. Andy was not good with names normally, but this group she pressed into her mind like a stamp.

Centurion, the boy leader. Melora small teeth and dark crazy eyes. Then there was Xavier who was round and milk-pale with a shaved head and Neve who was his opposite, head shorn as well, but tall and whip-thin with the darkest skin Andy had ever seen. They held hands and seemed a couple. There was Thierry, who had a gray beard and only one eye, the other a cluster of scar tissue, and Mark, who was a lanky teen with long brown hair that hung in his face. Liz with copper skin and platinum hair, she wore a glinting septum piercing and a vampy Marilyn Monroe dress. Dolores was a stooped old woman with an elaborate bouffant wig. Damien, a classic goth type with dyed black hair and eyeliner, whose appearance she found the most incongruous. Andy couldn't put her finger on why, but when he sat beside her, his talismans clanking, his patent boots creaking, he felt like someone wearing a costume.

"Welcome, Andy. It's so nice to meet another member of our tribe. I know how lonely it can be out there." Then he patted her hand and it was an almost fatherly, or even grandfatherly, gesture. She watched him walk toward the pizza, curious. Candy was next, she had huge boobs, an inch of makeup covering bad skin and tons of hair extensions. While she was dressed like a stripper and a cheap one at that, no one seemed to bat an eye. Candy reached out a hand with long sparkly blue nails and Andy shook it warily, but while garish, the woman was kind and soft spoken. The twins were next, Zora and Zoe. They were early twenties with straight brown hair, and they moved and acted like mirror reflections. And last, because he was late, was Darren. Darren was tall, dusky skin, muscular under his flannel and jeans, and had a mop of black hair. He was strikingly handsome and when he came to introduce himself, Andy felt a flutter in her gut she thought was long dead.

"Welcome fellow Rider."

"Rider?" He brushed his damp hair back and smiled at her, like something out of a romance novel cover, "Guess we haven't covered that yet. Yes, we are all Riders. Empty vessels that can share our bodies with those who want to walk this earth but can't for one reason or another. Make sense?"

She laughed and it surprised her to do so, it had been so long, "No, that makes no sense I'm afraid." He patted her shoulder and she could feel his hand through the thin fabric of her blouse, ice cold and burning. "It will all make sense soon, Centurion is a good teacher and guide." The boy nodded, graciously, in thanks.

"Now that introductions have been done, let's finish eating and get down to it. I'm sure Andy has a thousand questions." Melora said. Andy looked at the group, trying to sense anything about them besides that they were all so different from one another. Did she feel any sort of kinship? If this was a scam, what was it? Was this all a much longer, stranger dream? She wasn't sure. She'd said earlier that she felt her dream had never ended, that she was still dreaming. Perhaps that was true.

Centurion stepped into the center of the circle. Everyone instantly stilled and turned to him. While he looked like a boy, when he spoke the idea that he was a child instantly vanished. His body language and voice were that of someone quite dignified and much older. "Now that we've had introductions and some lunch I think we should get down to it. Welcome Andy. I do mean that from the bottom of my heart, as Riders are a rare breed. Too often they go undiscovered and end up in institutions or taking their own lives before being brought to one of our enclaves. I'm happy that Melora found you." He and then the entire group bowed their heads in welcome. Andy sat ramrod straight, hands in lap, unsure what it was that she was supposed to be doing in return. It was only when she caught Darren's eye and his welcoming smile, that she relaxed.

"Riders have the rare ability to take on another in their own bodies. Negative and misrepresented examples would be those possessed. You've seen *The Exorcist* I presume?" Centurion crooked one eyebrow up and waited for Andy's response. "Good. Yes, so if a Rider was unaware of their ability and left themselves open and unoccupied, entities can take advantage and come in, in a way that essentially hijacks the body. A possession. But I don't want to scare you. And that scenario is very rare. I just wanted to start on common ground. To show you may be more familiar with Riders than you think. Moving on."

Centurion described a secret society that had existed for centuries, a group of individuals able to share their bodies and lives with other entities.

"So… these entities, that you are talking about, are they ghosts? Or demons?"

"All kinds." He answered flatly, and Andy had to wonder about demons being real. But Centurion continued before she could ask more.

"And many are entities from other worlds and planes, travelers who cannot bring their physical bodies into this world. We allow them entrance into our bodies to learn and explore and we in turn learn from them. There is no more intimate coupling in the known universes, than to share your body with another, on the inside."

"It's like a marriage." Melora said with a smile.

"Do any of you have… someone with you right now?" A small ripple of laughter followed, causing Andy to frown. "We *all* have someone with us. All but you." Centurion said.

Andy looked quickly from face to face, trying to understand any of this, wondering again if this was an elaborate and bizarre hoax. To what end? No one was trying to get a credit card number from her. Centurion continued, "This boy, the body I inhabit, was a Rider nearly from birth. He was so empty that he was labelled severely disabled, unable to speak or walk. I'm an immortal entity, formless here in your world, and so decided to move into the boy and settle in for his lifetime. There was so little soul inside him that my occupation caused his to vacate, besides the barest of whispers. I am the exception. All others here have a more balanced coupling."

"How can you expect me to believe any of this? It's absurd! That you are some immortal creature from another world?" Centurion cocked his head to the side, studying her and his pose was decidedly un-child-like. Andy squirmed under his attention.

"You think it's more likely that a ten-year-old boy hosts these meetings? That Melora just approaches strangers on buses and brings them here? We know who and what we are and we know what you are. That truth may take longer for you to reach." Centurion sat down, crossing his arms in a huffy fashion that Andy found a bit immature for a thousand-year-old alien or whatever he was. The group was silent, avoiding her eye, and it was clear that Centurion set the tone for these meetings.

"I know this all sounds crazy, Andy," Melora finally said. "But believe me it's all true. I was alone and empty for so long. In and out of hospitals, look." She lifted her wrists and pulled back her sleeve revealing zig zags of old scars. "I wanted to die. I felt dead."

"You were dead." One of the twins said and she took her sister's hand. "We all were. But now we are more. Oliver and I have shared my body now for three years. We have the best conversations, he was a philosopher and poet. A magician, in his time. And we teach each other and care for each other."

"Melora isn't my name." Melora said, covering her wrists again. "I was so empty that when she entered me, I let her take the lead for the first year and I just rode in the back. I let her rename us. In time, through her coaching and friendship, I've found myself and came forward."

Andy stared at each face in the circle, her mind reeling. It was all so fantastical and so bizarre and yet a part of her, the lonely depressed part, yearned for it all to be true. But if it were true and she was a Rider, did she get to choose who went in or kick them out?

"How? How does this all work? How do you pick who you get, or do you? Or is it just whatever ghost is floating around?"

"You—" Centurion cleared his throat, interrupting handsome Darren, who closed his mouth and sat back in his chair.

"This circle here, is a basic summoning that brings attention to a vessel looking for an inhabitant. Think of it like fishing, you are the worm, the hook, the spirits are the fish."

"Do I get to choose who it is?"

"In a way, this is a partnership between two beings. And, if you do not summon one, you have few options besides succumbing to the slow and cruel death of a body that has lost its spirit. Or an involuntary possession, which is like rape. You've been a shadow, living a lie, yes? Don't you want that the end?" Centurion pushed on, not allowing space for her to answer, "Step into the circle and become whole."

Andy stared at the circle, it was still just black magic marker on old linoleum tile. She could feel their eyes on her, anticipatory. The circle wasn't the issue as much as the reality that no one knew where she was, and these people clearly believed. As silly as a magic circle seemed, she inched her feet back from it. Thinking back, she'd never even let so much as a toe into the circle. Choosing to walk around it. She'd avoided it for reasons she couldn't name. And now they wanted her to just jump inside and let someone move into her body.

"It seems a little fast, no? Don't I get some time to think it over and decide?"

"Centurion, maybe Andy is right and we are rushing her. Can we at least give her a few minutes?" Darren said. "We all forget, but we've all been here. It's a lot. We are expecting a lot of trust." The group watched their small leader and although he clearly disagreed, he finally gave a curt nod. Andy released a breath she hadn't realized she'd been holding. Darren stood and walked over to her, crossing the circle on the floor without hesitation. Even seeing that, Andy kept her feet tucked tightly under the chair, as far from the line as possible.

"Take a walk with me, please?" He held his hand out, like a prince on a romance novel cover, and she let her hand slide in, cold skin against cold skin. Safe and secure. Andy could feel everyone's eyes on her back as he led her away from the circle and out the door. It was only once they were in the hallway that some of the tension bundled at the back of her neck released.

"He can be intense, but he's really a good guy. Well, for as much as he is a guy."

"What is he, really, an alien?" Darren glanced back at the door they came from and shrugged.

"I suppose you could say alien. A traveler of worlds. He's seen so much, experienced other planets, other creatures. He's truly amazing, if you give him a chance. If you give us a chance." Andy hugged herself, still cold and wet and wondering if she would ever be warm or whole again. She realized she hadn't been warm since the dream that she died.

"Are you cold and numb all the time?" She asked.

"I was, before, when I was empty. I don't feel it now." He lifted her chin and met her eyes. His were almond shaped and a soft brown with long thick lashes. "I like you Andy. I feel a connection here, don't you?"

"It's like… we've met before." She wanted him to kiss her and wondered at the impulse. He was a stranger after all and a possibly delusional one. But when he leaned in she mirrored him and their lips touched. His mouth was cool, even on the inside, and she wondered if hers felt the same. As much as she wanted the contact and wanted to relish the feel of his hands along her body, it was, like everything since she died, far away. It felt like it was happening to someone else. She could feel his mouth and hands but they didn't sink past the surface. Why would they? She was dead after all. She broke the kiss, sad.

"That bad?" He teased, but she sensed no malice or hurt pride. "This is why you must let them in, otherwise you're cursed to walk around living life in gray. Alone. Feeling nothing."

"Who is in there with you?" Andy said, her hand on his chest. He paused, looking away, as he chewed the inside of his cheek.

"We have a complicated relationship. As Centurion said though, without a host spirit you are basically dead on your feet."

"Does it hurt? When they come in?"

Darren thought for a moment, clearly weighing his words, "It doesn't, but it is strange. For me it felt like someone trying to fit inside a sweater I was already wearing. Uncomfortable. But then you merge, you meet, you talk, you bond. And then, you feel again." He brushed her lips with a fingertip.

"I don't have a choice, do I?" Andy stared at the closed door and could picture them waiting on the other side for her. All of them. She wasn't sure if she meant they would never let her leave, or if her life was over either way. It didn't matter.

"You want to continue on as you are? The living dead? You don't have a soul anymore Andy, only the memory of who you were in a body that forgot to die. And there are those who are only spirit, who need a body. Become complete." Darren's cool hand was on her arm, firm. She wanted to be more scared, but if she was honest, there was so little of anything in her. He was right after all, she was dead.

"Okay."

*

Then, she was outside the circle, the tribe around her, watching eagerly. Centurion, in all his smallness and boyishness, stepped inside of the circle and beckoned her to follow. Andy felt fear, real fear, for a moment. She believed stepping inside would do something. She met each Rider's eyes and each nodded back, and none looked afraid for her. Melora nodded and put her hand to her heart. Darren smiled wide and how she wanted to kiss him again and to feel real desire. She wanted more. She wanted to be alive again. For food to taste and hands to touch, to laugh, to cry, to hope.

She stepped into the circle.

Inside, the pressure was different. There was the sensation of supercharged air, like during a lightning storm. Raging winds deafened her. She could feel the hairs on her body lift, feel her heart trip as her lungs begged for more air. The Riders standing in a circle were blurry as if through fogged glass. The pressure pressed on her and she felt as if at any moment, the wind could catch her and carry her up into the air, like riding a storm. Centurion took her hands and the contact grounded her. She tried to look at him, but was unable, there was a halo of blinding light around his head, and his eyes glowed an eerie blue. This must be the true Centurion, she thought, a creature of light and energy.

"Can you feel them? How hungry they are for you? They all want you." He said his voice all the stranger in the circle, it was layered, one-part boy, one-part something else. "Can you feel them pressing in? Fighting to get to you?"

Andy nodded, the sensation of many feather light fingertips touching her all over was unsettling and exhilarating. Tears fell from her cheeks. "Give in, surrender yourself, and the right one will come. Much like a single sperm reaching an egg." She wanted to ask how, but as if he could read her mind, he continued. "You're a Rider, just let go, let them in. Your body knows what to do."

She closed her eyes, getting a welcome relief from the relentless pressure and Centurion's searing light. It was as if she'd stepped into a tornado. Only Centurion's hands kept her from flying away. *I want more,* she thought to herself, *I want to feel again, I want to live again. Help me.*

Ghost fingers grabbed and pulled at her body, her clothes, her hair. Rougher now and more urgent. They probed her eyes and ears and lips. Even with her jaw locked shut tight, those fingers were scratching at her teeth and gums. She shook her head, trying to keep them out, but Centurion was whispering to accept them. Heart in her throat and dripping with fear sweat she eased her lips and jaw. Suddenly forceful fingers, more than fingers, what felt like an entire choking arm was in her throat and she was gagging, drowning, and something was inside of her now. It inflated her ribs, scrabbled in her lungs, it was snaking around her guts. She wanted to scream but couldn't. No air, no room to gather air. Flailing, she fell to her knees. She wanted to pull it out, but there was no way, apart from turning inside out. It was in. It was running around beneath her skin, exploring her. She was aware of it flipping through her mind and memories. A violation.

"Who are you?" She said, aloud, or in her head, it didn't matter anymore. She was sprawled on the floor, limbs jerking, nails scratching. Voice swallowed by the deafening wind. Andy felt corrupted by the thing inside her, keenly aware of it settling into every cell. Alarm bells clanged all over her body, the sensation was like a burglar, a trespasser, a thief: we've been invaded.

"Not invaded. *Welcomed.*" Said a voice, whispery, sexless and chittering like an insect. Out of her own mouth. The sensation of being puppetted chilled her to the bone. "You welcomed me in. And here I am."

"Who are you? What are you?" Andy said, unnerved by the sensation of hearing her voice inside and outside. All around them the wind raged on.

"Your friend, if you let me. Your master, if you fight me."

———◆———

Ten minutes later Andy opened her eyes and stood, she smoothed back her hair and clothes, then surveyed those watching outside the circle.

"Any issues?" Centurion said.

"Nothing major, she has a little fight left, but it won't be a problem." Andy's hands ran all over her body. "I like this one, young. Fertile." She looked at Darren and winked.

"It's nice to see you back in this reality. I missed you." He said with a smile.

"You too, all of you. It's a shame when a body dies, hell of a time getting back to you. Tell me all that I've missed." The thing that was Andy stepped out of the circle and Darren put his arm around her, pulled her in, and they kissed deeply. Then, the Riders talked and caught up, a lovely reunion with a lost member. And all the while, deep inside, behind the smiling face, like a stowaway on a ship, was the last remnants of Andy. Able to see and hear, but do nothing. The creature that had invaded her was remarkably strong, with a will like iron. Although the body was Andy's, the thing evicted her easily. What remained was little more than a shadow of the girl that had been.

Andy wondered if she'd been duped, or just lacked the strength of will to fight, maybe whoever was stronger won the body and the other became the Rider. The creature ignored her questions and she realized she may never truly know. Cursed to watch someone else live her life.

Leaving her little more than a ghost that had forgotten to die.

A STUDY IN ABNORMAL PHYSIOLOGY

Eric Schaller

I. *"Everything about you screams the news"*

Although Darwin's most visible supporter, in truth I saw him rarely and so took an immoderate delight in our dinner engagement at the Hotel St. George. But I was late—late!—and properly chagrined. Even the weather was no excuse. Hadn't Darwin traveled all the way from Kent in the same downpour? I passed my sopping overcoat to the doorman and then, leaving the maître d'hôtel in my wake, shoved open the door to the private dining room his trajectory indicated. There was my good friend Darwin, feet propped before a warm crackling fire.

"Darwin," I cried.

He swung round and my heart slipped a measure. Neither his smile, for all its genuine affection, nor his unruly side-whiskers could camouflage his ashen cheeks and glistening forehead. He must be having one of his spells. Yet, for my sake, he had evaded the protective web of his sweet wife Emma to make the journey to London.

"Pardon my tardiness. I hope you were not inconvenienced."

Darwin dismissed my concerns with a wave of his hand. "My dear Huxley, think nothing of it. I have plenty to keep me occupied in here." He tapped his balding pate. He then added, smile turning mischievous, "Besides, unless I miss my guess, congratulations are in order."

I must have blanched. I thought to brazen it out but realized that every tarried second confirmed Darwin's supposition. "How did you know?" I asked. "Nettie only told me this afternoon." In truth, she was so early in her pregnancy that we had agreed to wait at least two months before sharing the information.

"My dear friend, everything about you screams the news."

"How so?" I pulled up a chair.

"Firstly, after Leonard was born, you said that you looked forward to a goodly brood, so I knew more children were in the offing."

I nodded.

"Secondly, you were late, something quite outside your character and which not even the weather could explain. So a matter of importance must have occurred today."

I nodded again.

"Furthermore, you gave no excuse as to why you were late. And so the cause was such that you wished to conceal it."

I ventured a sally. "Surely that is not enough to build a theory on?"

Darwin pressed his fingertips together. "There are also more tangible evidences."

"Tangible?"

"The pollen on your vest."

I glanced down and saw the faintest of yellow smudges on my lapel.

"Roses, naturally, for love. But also the anemone, an unusual choice but, within the language of floriography, the symbol for expectation. I recognized their co-mingled scents immediately."

"That's all?"

"That's enough."

"Really," I said, trying not to sound aggrieved, "I don't see how you do it. I admit you are right, but based on such fairy dust"—I brushed the pollen from my vest—"it seems more a matter of luck than reason."

"True, by itself each item presents a world of possibilities, but summed together, first one, and then the next, and then the next thereafter, but this single theory suggested itself. Have you an alternative?"

Darwin's eyes twinkled as if he were playing the grandest of jokes, and I wondered if there were additional clues, perhaps excruciatingly obvious, he chose not to reveal. Nevertheless, Darwin's method for reconciling mysteries was of relevance to my upcoming debate with Robert FitzRoy, and, in attempting a rebuttal, I seemed to inhabit the skin of my future antagonist. But before I could produce another viable theory, we were distracted by a commotion in the main dining hall.

The maître d'hôtel, his figure muted by the frosted glass, gesticulated and rudely latched onto the shoulder of a woman. She freed herself and cried, "But really I must see them." Then the door burst open and she stood framed before us, the maître d'hôtel wringing his hands behind her. "I am so sorry," he said. "This woman barged into the hotel and asked to see the X Club. I explained, quite properly, that your dining club did not meet today and, furthermore, even in the event it did meet, she would not be welcome. But then I let slip that you and Mr. Darwin were here for a special engagement and, after that, there was no restraining her. I will escort her off the premises if you see fit."

Judged by her clothing, the object of the maître d'hôtel's derision was a young woman of the working class. But she was wrapped in so many layers, and these were so wet and disordered, that her form was more amorphous than feminine. Nevertheless, her eyes compensated for these deficiencies of her sex. Green, overlarge, and desperate, they burned with a feverish intensity.

"Stuart Hopkinson," Darwin said, addressing the maître d'hôtel by his given name. From his tone, I understood the anger he felt to see any woman, regardless of her station, so mishandled. "Water with a drop of brandy would be more suitable. And a warm blanket."

"Thank you, dear sir," the woman said. She fell to her knees at Darwin's feet. "When I heard that you and Mr. Huxley were here, I knew that God had answered my most fervent prayer."

Hopkinson, the significance of Darwin recollecting his name having not gone unnoticed, straightened his shoulders as if called to military attention. "Really, sir?"

"What are you waiting for? Drinks and a blanket for our friend."

"But she's so wet. The upholstery…" Hopkinson wrung his hands as if he wished to wring every contaminating drop from the woman's clothing.

"These should recompense you for whatever troubles you might encounter." Darwin dropped several thick coins into Hopkinson's ready hand. "Our friend has waited long enough for the most minimal of comforts."

Darwin had a grandfatherly way about him that soon set the woman at ease. Indeed, she was quite presentable once she had rearranged her cap, brushed back her wet hair, and, after taking a seat, sipped sufficient brandy that the blush returned to her cheeks. I nevertheless found her features unsettling although I could not decipher why. "Thank you again," she said, her face aglow with renewed vitality. "I am at my wit's end and you are my last and only hope."

"I'm afraid you have us at a disadvantage," I interjected. "You know our identities, but we do not know yours."

She looked to Darwin for guidance. He nodded. "Marjorie," she said, "But call me Jo."

"Surely you are blessed with both a Christian and a family name?" I said.

"You'll pardon me if I don't reveal my full name. Through it you might trace my master. He is a good man, and highly respected, but my story could do him a public disservice."

"Then Jo it is," Darwin said. He quieted me with a look. "By what means may we assist you?"

"I fear, dear sirs, that I am losing my mind."

II. "*An entertainment more marvelous than anything from* The Arabian Nights"

"It's my dreams," Jo said. "They've turned into a waking nightmare. I never used to think I had much imagination. I went to bed to sleep, and sleep was like the blowing out of a candle. I don't know if I dreamed but, if I did, I forgot my dreams upon waking." She heaved a sigh. "If only I could forget these dreams so easily."

Darwin laid a hand on her shoulder. "Please continue. When did the dreams begin?"

"Perhaps four or five months ago. One morning I awoke with a dream of flying that lingered in my mind. To fly! How strange, how wonderful! The airy world of my dream had no edges, no bottom and no top, and so I never feared a fall. There was just a feeling of weightlessness, of gliding about in a greenish light that darkened and paled around me. Most significantly, in recalling this dream, I realized that I had dreamed of flying before. I had in fact been having the same dream every night for weeks on end.

"At first I did not find the dream so horrible. I have little imagination, as I said, and it now seemed I was to be rewarded for those long dark years with an entertainment more marvelous than anything from *The Arabian Nights*. I looked forward to sleep as I never had before, and my dream responded. As my skills at flying improved, so did the substance of my vision. I discovered a vast palace of stone arches and circuitous hallways. Every night, I explored the palace but I never reached an end."

Darwin interrupted. "Did you tell anyone else of your reoccurring dream?"

"Only my master. He said that I should accept it as a gift, which put my mind much at ease."

"But you no longer feel at ease."

Jo lowered her distinctive eyes and nodded. "The more time I spent in this dream world, the more exhausted I became. But like an addict I longed for its nightly return. My bones, my muscles, my head ached. I could hardly drag myself out of bed in the morning. The stairs to my master's quarters rose like mountains before me, higher and higher each day, but still I climbed them and performed my duties. My master told me that I needed rest. But I would have none, for I have never lost a day to sickness in my life. There then occurred the event that convinced me I had lost my mind.

"I went to sleep as usual, knowing full well the enrapturing dream that awaited me. But I had a goal this time. I was resolved to reach the furthest end of a winding corridor, to press forward until I reached a boundary to my vision. In doing so, it seemed I flew backwards in time, sweeping past the brickwork of our age, then the stone arches erected by the Romans, and, toward the end, the somber monoliths once raised by savages on our moors. At length, I arrived at a cavern hollowed from ancient rock. This cavern narrowed into a cave, and the cave into something less, but still I had not reached its end. At last, my strength failing, I realized I must return to the waking world.

"Fear overtook me. I felt I had ventured too deep into the unknown and, like the princess in a fairy tale, must pay a price if I failed to return home before the cock crowed. The safety of my room was a distant memory, my arms were limp with exhaustion, but I flew like one possessed. A greenish light beckoned me homeward. But from behind, darkness grasped at me. Ice-cold tendrils slithered past my toes, my ankles, my knees, my waist, my very heart.

"I must have screamed, for the next thing I knew I was awake in bed and shivering. My master held me. He told me everything would be all right. He was wrong. My nightmare was far from over for, in the cold morning light, I saw that rank water had soaked through my nightclothes such that they hung like leaden rags from my limbs. Foul strands of algae tangled my arms and legs. I knew then that I had not been flying in my dream but swimming, and doing so in water that I could breathe as easily as I might air. Most horrible of all, this demonic dream had pursued me into the waking world.

"Is it any wonder that I question my sanity?" Jo's eyes brimmed with tears.

"When did this last dream occur?" asked Darwin.

"Two nights ago. I have not slept since. I am too afraid."

"You are certain that you were swimming in the dream, not flying?"

"Yes. But I have never swum before in my life. I've only waded in the Thames."

A church bell sounded in the distance and Jo started from her armchair, throwing aside her blanket. "I must return home or my master will wonder at by absence." She looked imploringly at Darwin with her overlarge green eyes and added, "But I have more to tell."

At Jo's recommendation, Darwin agreed that we should meet again the next day at a public house called The Crown and Anchor, convenient to her morning shopping route. He then pressed some coins into her palm, more than were necessary for the cab fare home. "I recommend finding alternative accommodation for the night. A change in location will do wonders for your sleep, and for your dreams."

After Jo left, Darwin asked if I had noticed the obvious. I nodded, for I had now identified what aspect of her features disturbed me so. "She is unique in my experience," I said. "I cannot place her as being Xanthochroic, Australoid, Negroid, or Mongoloid, nor some admixture of these types. Perhaps tomorrow, if she will allow it, I will apply my calipers to her skull and so resolve this mystery."

I thought for a moment that Darwin would do me the indignity of laughing, but his outburst was smothered, whether from sickness or politeness, and emerged a cough. "Good old Huxley. You are the most observant man I know, but you are also sometimes the least perceptive. Did you not notice her many layers of clothing? Did you not notice how she tidied the blanket to camouflage her belly? She, like your dearest Nettie, is with child. I estimate about six months along."

"Pregnant? She said nothing about a husband."

"You, friend Huxley, are more knowledgeable about worldly matters than I, yet even I have heard of a pregnancy occurring without the benefit of marriage."

"That could go hard on her." I felt an immediate gratitude for the good family to which I belonged. Then, remembering the strange passions that had possessed my own Nettie during her first pregnancy, I said, "The onset of these weird dreams coincides with her pregnancy. Do you think they may be a delirium brought about by her situation?"

"I hope you are right. My fears suggest otherwise. We shall know better tomorrow."

III. "Is she dead?"

The next morning, the previous night's downpour having dissipated into a charitable drizzle, Darwin and I met at The Crown and Anchor. I tucked into a full breakfast while Darwin drank tea and nibbled on a cold triangle of toast. He muttered a plague on the diet regime proscribed by his doctor. Jo was late. At first we thought nothing of it. One bell rang, then two bells after the hour. Darwin shifted from tea to snuff, never a good sign. At three bells, he accosted the manager and asked if a young woman had inquired for us earlier. The manager, more intent on the racing form than on his guests, shrugged.

Darwin furrowed his brow and glared at the floor as if he hoped to decipher the hotel's history from its scuffmarks. "What a fool I am?" he suddenly cried. "Did you let a room to a young woman last night? Brown hair and about so high?" He held his hand at level with his chin.

The manager again shrugged. He had been off duty at the time, but he did have the hotel register. Six rooms had been let but there was not a Marjorie or a Jo among the signatories.

"Bother the names," I said. "A single room. One woman. Arriving late."

"A Dorothy Hopkins signed in last night at five after ten."

"Has she checked out?"

"No."

"That must be her."

We dragged the manager up two flights of stairs and pounded on the door. No answer. "I really should not be doing this," the manager protested while producing the key. He quieted when he tried the knob and found the door unlocked. The door swung open to reveal a tranquil room with a narrow bed, a nightstand, and a single chair set against the far wall. A woman occupied the bed. For all appearances she slept, wrapped in sheets and blankets, her head propped upon a pillow. "That's Jo," I said. Darwin called to her. Jo neither moved nor spoke. Her face was deathly pale. In two strides we were beside her. Darwin shook her shoulder and her head lolled to the side. I, putting my medical training to use, touched my wrist to her chill forehead and then fumbled for her pulse but found none.

"Is she dead?" the manager asked.

I did not answer but peeled the bed coverings away. A pool of blood, centered about Jo's hips, had soaked through the dress she still wore from the previous night and spread across the lower sheet.

"Her pregnancy," I said. "She has lost the baby."

"A baby?" said the manager. "But where is the baby?"

This was, in my estimation, the first intelligent remark he had made during our brief acquaintance.

"Perhaps she was assisted," said Darwin, his voice dour. "You remember how the door was left unlocked." I knew immediately to what he alluded. A woman, finding herself with an unwanted pregnancy, might resort to drastic measures for its termination. The doctors who catered to this dark practice often gained additional recompense by selling the fetuses.

The horror and pathos of the situation struck us all. The manager muttered a prayer and tugged at his neckerchief. "Fetch a doctor," Darwin said to the manager. "And the police. Huxley and I will remain with the corpse."

After the manager disappeared at a stumbling run, Darwin turned to me and said, "This is an ugly business. I do not accept the coincidence of this poor woman's death so soon after her meeting with us."

"You do not think she died in childbirth?"

"I think the process was orchestrated. Are there not methods that can be employed to induce labor?"

I kept up with the medical literature although I had not recently practiced. "There are physical means, such as the rupture of the membranes, a method commonly employed by midwives. An article in *The Lancet* also reports promising results when women are injected with a pituitary extract from female dogs."

Darwin returned to the dead woman and, with a whispered apology, hiked her dress up past the waist to expose her abdomen. He pointed at a small puncture on her left side crowned with a glistening ruby droplet. "I believe the second method may have been employed here, perhaps in conjunction with the first. Note also the consistency of the blood." He flicked the skin adjoining the puncture. The bead broke and trickled down her side. "In Herefordshire, two summers ago, a dozen cows hemorrhaged and died. The causal agent was traced to mildewed hay. A grain of the compound produced by that fungus is enough to prevent clotting so that even the smallest nick is life-threatening."

"Then it is murder. Of both a mother and her child." A rush of anger blinded me. I could not help but imagine my dearest Nettie in a similar position.

"I fear it is something even more horrible. I suspect the child was delivered prematurely and stolen from Jo at the intentional cost of her life."

"Why?"

"Undoubtedly for some evil end. But if the child still lives—and I think it might—there may yet be a chance to save it." A haunted look came over Darwin's face and he wiped a frail hand across his forehead. "We must save the child."

I bowed my head, awash with the memory so recent and so painful of my own son Noel's death. I remembered his funeral, his cold body lowered into a hole from which he would never rise. I, like Darwin, do not hope for reunion beyond the grave. Darwin, however, had suffered three times over in this respect. I still do not know how he stood the sorrow. "For Annie," I said, naming his favorite daughter.

"And for Charlie and Mary, and for your sweet Noel."

"Cannot the police arrest this fiend?"

"The culprit, even if we knew his identity, has covered his tracks so well that there is no evidence of foul play beyond our own conjectures. An unwed mother. A botched abortion. The situation is far too common."

"What can we do?"

"Do you have your calipers?"

Caught off guard, I nevertheless patted my coat pocket.

"You said that Jo's physiognomy disturbed you, and I think there is still time, before the police arrive, for you to make your measurements. In analyzing the data, you may disregard the time you spent aboard the HMS *Rattlesnake* as Surgeon's Mate studying oceanic invertebrates. Your more recent studies on the lobed-finned fish are most pertinent."

"And then?"

"I believe you have an impending debate with FitzRoy. Or have you forgotten?"

IV. *"Show me a gemmule"*

My opponent in the debate at the Workingman's College was the same FitzRoy who had once captained the *Beagle* but who now implored adherence to Biblical creation. In truth, although I attempted to uphold my popular sobriquet as *Darwin's bulldog*, my mind was not on topic. I kept recalling the decrepit bedroom scene from that morning and the story, disturbing and most mysterious, that my calipers told. I wondered if Jo had been once employed as a fishmonger. Might she have acquired her Piscean features through a Lamarckian process, akin to how dog owners take on the characteristics of their pets? I wondered what further researches into the matter Darwin pursued, alone, while I entertained the restless crowd.

Perhaps I was more distracted than I imagined. How else to explain the ease with which the mundane FitzRoy ambushed me? I was attempting to explain how Darwin's theory of gemmules enabled traits to be passed from one generation to the next when FitzRoy, a malevolent glint to his eye, extended his hand. "Show me a gemmule," he said.

I was flummoxed. To say that a gemmule was too small to be seen by the naked eye, or even by aid of a microscope, seemed a prevarication. I hemmed. I hawed. Then, as if sensing my discomfort, a member of the audience stood, raising himself with the aid of an ebony cane, and asked if he could relate a relevant example. The man was large, of about my age, and with an unsmiling mouth that lent his utterances a weight commensurate with his frame. "Within man himself, during his growth from fetus to adult," he said, "do we not see dramatic changes take place that span but a single generation? We do not know how this happens, but just as assuredly it does. Similarly, rather than argue the existence of a mechanism for transmutation, should we not instead seek it out by all means at our disposal?" With that final question ringing to the rafters, he settled back into his chair, forcing a squeal from its strained supports.

The stranger's example raised my dander back to a fighting pitch, and I concluded the debate strongly. "To be a man one must think, truly think, otherwise one is much less than an ape"—I speared FitzRoy with a glance—"one is nothing but a noisome fly that buzzes about laying the maggot of an idea hoping, merely hoping, that it might someday take wing." Then I was down among the audience, shaking hands, pounding shoulders, and accepting congratulations on my performance.

The weighty stranger did not step forward into the crush but stood to one side, casting a cold eye on the proceedings. In truth I found the stranger's attitude more disturbing than FitzRoy's ignorant bravado, for it seemed that buried within his corpulent frame lurked an alien intelligence that looked upon mankind and found us all wanting in some fundamental respect.

V. *"Do not turn around"*

I did not rejoin Darwin until that evening, responding to a message to meet him at an address on Park Lane and which ended with the admonishment to, "bring your stick." The walking stick in question was of stout oak, its handle a snarling bulldog cast from bronze. Darwin's request suggested imminent trouble.

The Darwin I discovered was so coifed and pomaded that I hardly recognized him. Darwin swung us out of the current of pedestrians and we took position in the shadow of an awning. He reached into his jacket pocket, extracted a packet of calling cards, and passed these to me. I looked at the top card. The first line read, *Lawrence C. Wilderman.* Beneath that was the suggestion of a business, *Goshen and Wilderman, Proprietors.* And then, beneath that, the brief description, *Purveyors of the Finest Clamps, Forceps, and Specula.*

"Who is this Wilderman?" I asked.

"That, my friend, is you. I am your business partner, Frederick Goshen. I had the cards printed this afternoon."

"For what purpose?"

"To effect an entrance. Legally," he said, eyeing my cane. "Keep your eyes on number 12." I squinted in the direction he indicated and was met with a sharp elbow to the ribs. "Try to be less conspicuous."

I rubbed my side. "Who lives there?"

"That is the residence and practice of Dr. Paul Monroe, the employer of our late friend Marjorie Constable."

The doctor's name was vaguely familiar. "Monroe? Are you certain?"

"Ninety-nine parts out of a hundred. I learned his identity within the hour of our separation this morning although, as I said, most of my time was spent on the tedious task of establishing our pseudonyms." He located my ribs again with his elbow. "I insist you refrain from displaying an obvious interest in our quarry."

I shifted position so I would be less sorely tempted. "How did you learn his identity?"

"Do you remember why Jo came to the Hotel St. George?"

I thought back to the events of the previous night. "To find us?"

"In a way. But how many servants would know to look for us at the Hotel St. George? More curiously, according to the maître d', she had in fact come in search of the X Club. The existence of your dining club is hardly a matter of public renown."

I nodded. "I have done my best to keep our circle a secret known only to initiates. If I follow your reasoning, Jo must have learned of the X Club from her master. Moreover, given the nature of our club, he has a scientific bent and has acquired some stature in society. But surely there is more?"

Darwin smiled. "Even though she did not intend to reveal it, I knew within seconds of our meeting that Jo's master was a physician, most likely with surgical leanings. Did you notice her perfume?"

"Perfume?"

"Women are well acquainted with the use of aromatics for attraction but there are few, perhaps none, that consciously choose ether. That is a scent peculiar to the medical profession, and one only acquired by a woman when she is in close contact with such a man."

"Contact? Do you mean…?"

"I do not use the word *contact* lightly. Yes, I suspect her pregnancy derived from the relationship she intimated with her master."

"Then the physician who presided over her death, the man who stole her child…" The bloody scene recalled itself to me in all its horrid detail.

"That was her master. The unborn child—his child—was more dear to him than her life. I shudder to consider why."

I shook my head, stunned that such a beast roamed our city. "This man, this creature, how can you be certain it is Dr. Monroe?" The name burned like bile in my throat. "Surely there are hundreds of physicians in London?"

"True. But before she died, Jo revealed her master's address."

"She told you?"

"Nothing so exact. But she chose our meeting place at The Crown and Anchor, and indicated it was along her shopping route. Significantly, the manager gave no indication of knowing her. Based on this I concluded that The Crown and Anchor was close enough to her home to be familiar but was not a business she frequented. A range of five blocks, with the public house as its epicenter, seemed a good starting point for my search. There were also a few minor clues that further narrowed the possibilities." Darwin seemed about to expound on these when, without changing tone or tempo, he said, "Keep talking as if we are just two friends out for a pleasant stroll. Most of all do not turn around. A messenger has arrived at number 12."

It took all my self-control to resist the temptation to peek. "A messenger?"

"Although I am all but convinced that Dr. Paul Monroe is our man, there is still that one chance in a hundred that I am wrong. This is the final test. There! The door has opened. The messenger has been admitted. We will soon know. You may turn around."

The door to number 12 was closed and I might have thought the messenger a figment of my friend's imagination but for the flickering of shadows in the transom window. After five minutes, the door opened. I held my breath. "It is only the messenger," said Darwin. "His work is done." The messenger's departure was followed by another five arduous minutes. Then a hansom cab pulled up to the opposite curb, blocking our view. Darwin grabbed my arm, and we perambulated a dozen steps until we once again held an unobstructed vantage point.

The door to number 12 swung open. A heavy gentleman shuffled into view, backlit, in his one hand a leather bag weighted with the implements of his trade, in his other hand an ebony cane.

"Dr. Paul Monroe," hissed Darwin. "Our quarry has taken the bait."

I gasped. I recognized the doctor from my debate with FitzRoy. He was the audience member who came to my aid when I stumbled over the concept of gemmules. What's more, I now also remembered when I had previously heard of Paul Monroe. George Busk had recommended him for inclusion in the X Club but, unable to command a majority, had dropped his petition. "I know that man," I said and—while the footman assisted the doctor into the cab and then, with two flicks of the driver's whip, the cab rattled down the street—entertained Darwin with my short tale. I concluded with the question, "What message could possibly incite the doctor's convenient exit?"

"Would it help if I told you the messenger is named Erasmus?"

"Your brother?"

"The same."

"Then, unless I miss my guess, you wrote the missive and can enlighten me as to its contents."

"It was merely the report of a birth, one I thought our doctor might find of interest, of a child born with a vestigial tail. In Fobbing."

"Fobbing? Then the doctor will be gone for hours."

"That is my hope."

VI. *"One scent is missing"*

The door opened at Darwin's knock and the footman, reminiscent of a fox with his sly eyes, pointed nose, and wisps of coppery hair, leaned out. Darwin presented his card and I did likewise. "Goshen and Wilderman, purveyors of the finest clamps, forceps, and specula," Darwin said. "We have an appointment with the esteemed Dr. Monroe." Darwin withdrew a velvet roll from his jacket pocket and, patting it, elicited a muffled jangle. "Our instruments are imported from the four compass points, even from so distant as the Orient."

The doorman looked stricken. "I am sorry, but Dr. Monroe was called away on an emergency. I do not know when he will return."

"We would be happy to wait if you would show us to the sitting room." Darwin passed him a shilling and, not for the first or last time, I marveled at how the seemingly inexhaustible fortune of his family greased the wheels of protocol.

Two more shillings and we were established on a stiff-backed bench in a claustrophobic room at the far end of the hallway, our only comfort two glasses of a mediocre sherry. The room held an empty coat rack, a desolate shelf, and a table that under better circumstances would have supported a copy of the evening newspaper. It was not a room reserved for esteemed guests and my mind turned, as it would, to the missing comforts of home. I wondered how my wife could ever forgive me for abandoning her so soon after her confidence of the previous afternoon.

"I have a question," I said.

"Are you still troubled by the manner in which I uncovered your wife's pregnancy?"

This was indeed the question that preyed on my mind. In spite of Darwin's noted acumen, the clues he had paraded before me seemed too meager to warrant their conclusion. But I refused to grant Darwin the satisfaction of having so closely followed the current of my thoughts. "What is in your pocket roll?" I asked, hoping to resolve this mystery at least.

"Some tableware from the hotel. I don't know what would have happened if our man had demanded a closer look. Kindly crack the door ajar so we may keep an eye on him."

The footman returned twice to check on our comfort, or lack thereof, before disappearing downstairs to the kitchen. This gave us the opportunity to sneak upstairs. I followed close behind Darwin, taking two tense steps to his one, my cane at the ready. The first two doors were locked but the third opened into the doctor's consulting room. This was dominated by a massive desk and towering bookshelves bowed beneath the weight of musty volumes. A coal fire smoldered in the grate.

"This is more to my taste," I said, eyeing the comfort of an upholstered chair.

Darwin shook his head. "There has to be more. What do you smell?"

"Books. Tobacco. Coal smoke."

"Exactly. One scent is missing: ether. Where does our doctor perform his surgeries?" Darwin paced the room, muttering to himself. "There has to be an entrance in here somewhere. He would want to be proximate to his library." He now stood before the bookshelf, nose inches from an embossed spine. He pulled out the volume, passed a finger across the top to test for the dust that was noticeably absent. "Aristotle's *History of Animals*. And over here…"—he pulled out another volume—"Saint-Vincent's *Dictionnaire Classique d'Histoire Naturelle*. A most interesting choice of reading materials for a physician."

"Not just his reading materials." I pointed to a skull that served as a bookend. "An orang-gutang, otherwise known as the wild man of Borneo."

"He has souvenirs from all over the world." Darwin rapped on the carapace of an armadillo and, although I am sure he would disavow such a random act as initiating his next train of thought, I cannot but think that the hollow echo was the impetus for his immediate response as well as much that came thereafter. "What a fool I am," Darwin cried. "There must be a door, a hidden door!" He proceeded to rap his knuckles against the walls. Of greatest interest to him was a space at one corner of the room, a yard in width and adjacent to the bookshelf. This space was empty save for the ceramic sculpture of a snake twined around a Negro. "The sculpture has been recently moved," Darwin said, pointing toward a circular indentation in the rug. I had no trouble lifting the sculpture and, in accordance with Darwin's observation, found that the base precisely fit the impression in the rug.

But there we were stymied. Although Darwin continued with his rappings and tappings, the expression on his face shifted from hope, to irritation, to, at last, simple befuddlement.

Giving up his pet hypothesis, Darwin wandered the room. He pressed and pulled on knotholes, lamp fixtures, any protrusion he found. I followed suit but met with an equal lack of success. He then turned his attention to his own forehead, drumming his fingertips as if to jog his brain into activity. This may have done the trick for Darwin, with a small cry, returned to the empty corner and, dropping to his knees, ran a finger along the join where the baseboard met the floor. "Yes! There is a gap of at least a quarter inch. Note also the abrasion to the wood." He then rose to his feet, grasped the edge of the bookshelf, and pulled. A large section, a yard in width and extending from floor to ceiling, dislodged and slid along the wall.

"By Jove," I said. A doorway was revealed and a winding stair leading down.

VII. *"It moves"*

A grayish light suffused the circular stairwell, sufficient to discern each step and thereby avoid mishap. I took the lead in our descent, brandishing my cane. The light originated from concealed crevices that opened into the house proper. Most interesting were a series of lenses set into the walls by which we could spy on what transpired in the neighboring rooms. We passed from the first to the ground floor, and from there to the kitchen level, where we discovered the red-headed footman, like a fox in the henhouse, romancing the kitchen maid in his master's absence. The steps then passed below the basement level, the light dimming and the air becoming still, and came to an abrupt halt before a windowless door.

Darwin almost bumped into me. "We're here," he whispered.

I cracked the door open and peered in. I was met with the blackness of the tomb. Only my nose proved up to its sensory task, alerting me to the caustic odors of the chemist. "Should I fetch a lamp?" I asked.

"I am sure the doctor's laboratory is provided for."

I fumbled along the wall and, coming upon a knob, turned it clockwise. Light flared from a dozen lamps and illuminated two long tables sheathed in metal, a glistening palace of interconnected glassware, and shelves congested with flasks of all shapes and sizes. Darwin and I explored Monroe's secret laboratory. I was not sure what I hoped to find, but it was all morbidly fascinating. The body of an executed criminal, or so I surmised from the mark of the rope around his neck, was spread-eagled on the nearest table. His chest cavity had been cut open and his organs, some still attached, exhumed and placed in trays containing a yellowish liquid. Two bloody stumps on his right hand revealed the positions of amputated fingers. I lifted the disfigured hand, stiff with death, and was met with an unexpected shriek alongside my ear. I whirled, cane raised. Ghostly fingernails skittered along my spine. I pulled a velvet drape aside to reveal an ornate cage and a pet budgerigar. I wondered what purpose it served but then, on closer inspection, saw the bird's legs had each been removed and replaced with a human finger. Monroe's avian experiment gripped its perch with the white-knuckled ardor bequeathed by the dead criminal.

I transferred my attentions to the shelves and discovered canisters containing a zoological menagerie, some desiccated, others preserved in spirits. A cabinet door opened to reveal glass baubles that entombed a succession of human embryos. These demonstrated more clearly than any display I had ever seen how an embryo passes through developmental stages approximating its own evolutionary history. A pinkish embryo no longer than my finger joint mimicked a bug-eyed minnow with gills. Another appeared amphibious with its webbed hands and feet. From there, they took on more generalized mammalian forms: a nude mouse, a curled piglet, and, finally, hunched and naked primates that aspired to humanity. To my consternation, however, I perceived greater variability among the embryos than I would have suspected possible.

I called to Darwin. "Would you look at this?"

"What do you have?"

"A fetus. Human, I believe, but unlike any I have seen."

"How so?"

I paused so that I might describe the creature more exactly. By my estimation, based on its size and development, it was six months old. However, it still preserved characteristics of an immature form. Pinkish membranes spanned the digits of its hands and feet. Gill slits parted behind its ears, revealing downy frills crimson with oxygenated blood. It lacked obvious genitalia, suggesting a female, but I could not be certain given its erratic development.

"I would describe it thusly," I began. But there I halted, my senses taking flight like game birds at the huntsman's blast. What I saw was clearly impossible. The left hand of the fetus shifted. I hypothesized it a swimming motion, perhaps attributable to a current within its aquatic prison, only the movement was so perfectly executed that it brought the fetus face to face with me. Then, and for this I conceived no possible explanation, the lids of its eyes sprang open to reveal irises of the deepest, most captivating blue. "It moves," I croaked.

Darwin was beside me in an instant. He clapped my back. "Our efforts are not in vain. The water baby lives."

"Water baby?"

"Yes. Jo's child. The result of Monroe's experiments. Through injections and drugs he halted the development of her fetus, maintaining its aquatic physiology. These treatments also had the side effect of inducing the changes you observed in Jo's physiognomy, affecting not only her bone structure but her mind. We must rescue the poor innocent before Monroe returns." Darwin hoisted the crystalline globe from its shelf and thrust it into my arms. The child within turned a back flip—I noted that fins decorated its arms and legs—and beamed, positively beamed at me. Bubbles trickled from the corners of its lips.

We were already too late.

Even as we turned for the exit, I heard a sarcastic harrumph. Dr. Monroe stood in the doorway, his ponderous bulk more impenetrable than the door itself. The red-headed footman leered over his shoulder.

"To what do I owe the pleasure of this visit?" Monroe said, his voice thick with evil. "You have taken the names of Goshen and Wilderman, but I wager those names never passed the lips of your mothers. Why do Darwin and Huxley, two esteemed members of the Royal Society, prowl my laboratory uninvited?"

Before Darwin or I could make rejoinder, Monroe seized the footman's lamp and hurled it in our direction.

VIII. *"I have a confession to make"*

"Look out!" I cried, but I mistook the missile's trajectory. It burst among the glassware, destroying several flasks and spattering flaming oil. Unbalanced, the towering ensemble of beakers, flasks, and tubing swayed, then crashed among the flames. Acid fumes fogged the air and fresh spirits fed the blaze.

"The door," I gasped, thinking only of escape. My eyes and throat burned. I pulled my neck cloth over my mouth and nose, following Darwin's example.

"Closed and locked," said Darwin. Our captor had fled, leaving us to die. The inferno was already beyond hope of control. Cabinets erupted. Jars exploded. The budgerigar emitted a horrendous shriek, flapped its smoking wings, then tumbled from its perch still aflame but silenced forever.

"We are not finished," cried Darwin, "Help me with the carpets." He tugged ineffectually at the corner of the one nearest him. His weakness had returned.

"The carpets?" Their oriental patterns danced with flame.

"Yes. There must be access to the sewers from somewhere in this room."

I moved to his aid, but our efforts revealed only stonework. Another carpet met with the same result. "What makes you so sure?"

"Jo awoke from her dream soaked with water. She certainly did not wander through the streets in her nightclothes. Also, Monroe had a means to dispose of his dissections. Indeed, the proximity of his laboratory to the lost rivers beneath London was key to my locating…" His voice broke in a hacking cough.

I peeled back another burning carpet to no avail. Sweat trickled down my temples and spattered on the floor. I sucked at my singed fingers.

Darwin wished to communicate one last item of importance. "I have a confession to make," he said. Those terrifying words, if nothing else, convinced me that the hour of our demise had arrived at last.

"Yes."

"I must tell you how I deduced the secret of your wife's pregnancy."

"A final clue?"

"I am ashamed to admit it…" He paused, glanced about the laboratory as if a spy might lurk within its fiery embrace, then blurted: "I was told the secret."

No man, most especially Darwin, would fabricate a lie under our dire circumstances, but I found his revelation more impossible to credit than his earlier deduction. I had only learned of my wife's situation the previous afternoon and, such is her sanctity, that she would have informed no other. "You were told?"

"Yes."

"By whom?"

"My brother Erasmus."

This only compounded the mystery. Was all London privy to matters of my bedchamber and my heart? "How would he know?"

Another fit of coughing, but nothing can dissuade Darwin once the arrow of his mind has been loosed. "Just as the lost rivers permeate the subterranean levels of London, unseen and oft forgotten"—he pulled at a carpet and in doing so reminded me once again of the urgency of our situation—"so too does information race along those avenues least noticed."

Fire skipped along a shelf. Glass vessels exploded into blue flame. Half blinded by smoke and acid fumes, I kicked aside the rug with which Darwin wrestled. Nothing. I wanted to remind Darwin how Nero fiddled while Rome burned, but forced my impatience into a semblance of temperance. "This is no time for riddles."

"The servants. Your housekeeper noticed the signs of morning sickness in Nettie—how could she not given her proximity? Once a servant learns of a situation, so too do her friends, and the friends of her friends, and so on…but there, I have made my confession and now we must return to our task." Darwin spoke in a hoarse rasp as if the fire had taken root in his throat. He fell to his knees and crawled about the floor, head tilted as if gripped by dementia.

It has been too much for him, I thought. What little faith I still possessed, like my anger at being duped, turned to ash. Nevertheless, I continued my efforts with the rugs if only because it had been Darwin's last wish. Monroe's laboratory enclosed us in its Hellish mouth, licked at me with tongues of flame, choked me with its smoky breath. I pulled feebly at a rug, no longer remembering why.

A whisper, barely discernible above the roar of the fire, stopped me. "Over here," Darwin croaked. His head was pressed against a flagstone, his knuckles raised in a cat-like stance. Then I understood his strategy. He was rapping on the floor as he had recently done on the walls of the consulting room. "It was not under a carpet, after all," he said. A broad stone shifted in its setting and slid aside.

"Nor is our adversary so imaginative as I had credited him," I said. But my hopes were immediately dashed. Under the flagstone was an iron grating. And the iron grating was locked. "Can you pick it?" I pointed at the hasp lock, large as my fist and with a keyhole into which I might have poked my little finger.

"No time."

Can you imagine how I felt? Freedom, life itself, was only inches away. I saw the metal rungs of a ladder that descended to the sewers. I felt the cool up-rush of air, heard the delightful trickle of water. But none of this was for me. I would roast in the horrific oven of Dr. Monroe's laboratory.

Then, like Venus appearing to shame the darkest night, I heard these words: "Your cane."

Of course! My cane swung from a loop at my waist. I set aside the globe that contained the water baby. Its glass was warm to the touch. Its charge implored haste with innocent eyes. I inserted the oaken shaft of my cane into the grate and leaned my weight upon it. Metal creaked but did not give.

"Not the hinges. The lock."

I shifted position. Pressed down. Metal squealed, then popped. A stud flew free. Another. The lock tumbled into the shaft and, from deep below, I heard the ecstatic plunk of its entering water. I swung the grating back. The abyss was a stairway to Paradise. "After you." I gestured for Darwin to precede me.

He did not budge. "You did the lion's share of the work."

"This is no time for chivalry." The fire roared.

"But you have charge of the water baby. "

There was no arguing with Darwin. I did as he bid. Ten feet down, the metal rungs came to an abrupt end. I kicked at air but found no support. Unbalanced, I fell not knowing how far below the lost river ran.

IX. *"Follow my voice"*

I landed on my back, the water baby's globe cradled safely in my arms. The depth of the water was a mere three feet but I could not avoid dunking my head into that stench-filled slime. I righted myself and wiped the muck from my face. "Take care," I called to Darwin, his form silhouetted by flames. A portion of the inferno detached itself and, descending toward me, revealed itself to be carried in the hand of Darwin: a chair's leg, one end populated by flame.

Although popularly known as the lost rivers, this name is a pleasant-sounding holdover from history, a suggestion that what was once a river shall always remain so. Nowadays, rife with the daily waste of three million Londoners, these underground tributaries yield a dank trickle, thick as molasses, that only aspires to join the majestic Thames. Nevertheless, I detected a faint current in that ooze. "This way. Follow my voice." I waded through foulness. Darwin slopped along behind, his torch casting a dispassionate light that revealed all too clearly his haggard, limping form. Darwin seemed a ghost of himself.

"Are you all right?"

"Yes. Make haste. The danger is not past." Darwin's voice was a faint croak.

I do not know how long we traveled. A wearisome hour, most assuredly, but it may have been many more. Nor do I know the distance we covered. Our steps seemed to demark the intestinal tract of a gigantic serpent that wound its way beneath London, an Ouroboros who, should it ever awake, could suffocate the city in its mighty coils. Moreover, sometimes this serpent split into a many-headed Hydra intent on deception. But no matter the temptation of a larger corridor, always we followed the current, however miserable it might seem, knowing that it must flow to the Thames and our eventual freedom.

Darwin's torch gave out. At first I thought we moved in utter darkness, but that was only the after-effects of the flame. As my eyes adjusted, I detected phosphorescence from the fungi that encrusted the ancient stonework. Revealed were the strange greenish arches and hallways, the labyrinthine magnificence that Jo had referenced from her dreams. Still we journeyed and, eventually, I beheld a sharp point of light that was no bedazzlement of the senses. It persisted no matter how I blinked or rubbed my eyes. A star! Yes, a single lonely star spangled the night sky at the far end of our prison tunnel. "Almost there," I cried. I hoped my beleaguered friend would take heart. I hoped even the water baby, whose globe I encircled with my arms, might recognize in that spark an end to our trials. But then, just when our safety seemed at hand, from behind came a roar like a steam engine pulling into the station. The earlier warning from Darwin came back to me in force: "The danger is not past."

I turned and saw a sight to blind even the Pope's jaded eyes. A seething wall of water bore down on us, flooding the sewer from floor to ceiling. The bowed form of Darwin was but a miserable insect cowering before it. The rage contained in our approaching doom seemed the very spit and venom of our adversary made manifest. Indeed, I have no doubt the flood was the work of Dr. Monroe: he had opened a sluice gate upon finding us escaped.

I had only seconds to react but, in that elastic time, I saw to my right an iron ring set in the wall. I flung myself at it. A skeletal hand barred my way. Death come to lead me from this mortal coil? No, only the remnants of a prisoner once chained and left to drown in the rising tide. I knocked the bones loose and slipped my arm through the ring, gripping it fast in the crook of my elbow. Safe. Or safe as anyone could be when trapped like a rat in a world intent on his drowning.

Darwin was not so lucky. Like me, he turned to the wall for succor but, unlike me, he found no protrusion to offer relief. He scrabbled in vain. His eyes widened in fear. At the last moment, he gulped a lungful of air and dove, seemingly into air, but the water reached out and grabbed him in its fist. Then, as if disappointed, it batted him aside. His body somersaulted toward me in the foam, and I swung myself out and toward the oncoming wave. One arm tethered me to the iron ring, the other reached for my friend. The water slammed into me so hard that I wore its bruises for a week but, wonder of wonders, within its crushing embrace my fingers made contact with the twisting, churning fabric of Darwin's coat. I was not so much pulling Darwin to safety as holding him against the vengeful flood.

I saved Darwin. But at what cost? In so doing, the globe containing the water baby slipped from my hands. There had been no decision involved, no weighing in the balance the life of a friend, a fêted scientist who had experienced all the good and the ill that can span fifty summers, compared to the life of a child, an innocent who had respired upon the earth less than fifty hours and this only as the captive to a madman. I simply reached out in blind hope to aid my friend. But, although the world might condemn my actions, although I lost the living, breathing object of our adventure, I would do the same again if given Hell and all eternity to decide.

Darwin safe in my arms, I watched the lost globe as it sailed away upon the receding wave, a crystal bubble aimed at the stars. For a few haunting seconds it seemed it might survive intact. Then, as if compelled by a demon's hand, it spun toward a protruding buttress and shattered. The water baby—a flash of pink against the gray—slipped into the murky stream, and left not a ripple to mark its memory. I do not know how long I watched in vain for it to reappear, but my attention was only diverted when the cold weight of Darwin proved too much for my arm. "Careful," he cried, finding his footing on the newly scrubbed sewer floor. "I believe the Doctor's tricks exhausted, but it is foolish to tarry."

X. *"Welcome"*

We stepped forth from the sewer into a night like any other, I suppose, but never have the stars in the sky and the lights of our city seemed so beautiful, for they announced our escape from the underworld and the renewed possibility of hearth and home. Yet we were cold, wet, and tired beyond all endurance. We stumbled along a stone path bordering the Thames and, a little ways down, on the lee side of a ramshackle structure that leaned dangerously far over the river, I saw the friendly glow of oil lamps and heard the voices of my own countrymen raised in joyous fraternity. There, I resolved to take our chances and our rest.

No grand enterprise will set foundation near the noxious fumes of an open sewer, and our destination proved no exception to this rule. Indeed, in all my travels, never have I discovered so strange a domicile. From a distance I assumed it a cottage. On approaching I thought it a shack. Up close I was hard pressed to call it anything but flotsam cast up by the Thames. Pressed against the moldering apartment building was a derelict pile of wave-polished timbers and barrel staves, tattered sails, pottery shards, an upended basket, and even, I am convinced, the skeletons of a dog and a gigantic rat. Nevertheless, the edifice assumed a vaguely domestic shape. Most strange of all was the name affixed to the splintered board that overhung the canvas door: *THE HOTEL ST. GEORGE.* Yes, it had the same name as the public house where we had first met Jo. In height, the door was a little below that of an average man and we stooped to enter. I blinked my eyes against the unaccustomed glare.

"Welcome."

I recognized but could not place the voice.

"What may I offer you to drink?"

The man's angular silhouette was also familiar.

"Be warned, the only choice is beer, unless you have brought something to share."

An expectant scrape of chairs as the other occupants of the low room, a half-dozen in all, leaned in to listen to our conversation.

I shook my head. "We have nothing." I pulled the soaked pockets of my jacket and pants inside-out. "Nothing." And now, to my dismay, I recognized our host. He was the same man, or else his very twin, that served as the officious maître d'hôtel at the uptown Hotel St. George. Any hope I had for charity disappeared.

But this man was as like, and unlike, the other maître d' as it is possible for two brothers to be. His eyes sparkled. His voice was animated. His hands fluttered like a dove's wings. Then, as if to both confirm and deny his identity, he said, "You paid handsomely for your friend's comfort. Whatever I have here is yours."

"Thank you." These words could not express the emotions of my heart. I extended a hand. "Thomas Huxley, forever at your service."

He returned the favor. "Stuart Hopkinson, as ever, at yours."

The other occupants were all scavengers from the flats—mud larks, I've heard them called—their clothes caked with the pungent muck of the Thames, and these rearranged themselves so that we might be seated in closer proximity to the coal fire. I wrapped Darwin in the towels Hopkinson fetched and applied myself to rubbing life back into his inhospitable frame. Hopkinson entertained me with his observations about the world, circumstance, and the collision of the two. I have not space to repeat all that he said, and will content myself with the following, which, I believe, unriddles the mystery as to why two establishments named The Hotel St. George exist in London, so different in all respects save the commonality of Stuart Hopkinson. "There," said Hopkinson in reference to the uptown Hotel St. George, "no matter the quality of my suit, I will always be in service to another. Here, although the circumstances be not so fine, I am and will always be my own man."

In these convivial surroundings, augmented by a medicinal draught of beer, Darwin made a rapid recovery. The morbid gray of his cheeks was replaced by a pinkish hue, like roses blooming by a factory wall, and the furnaces that stoked his eyes were lit once more. He pushed the towel shrouding his head back to his shoulders. "I hope to never repeat such a water cure," he said. "Yet, against all odds, we have survived."

I, now that the danger was past, felt only a burgeoning sense of failure. The death of Jo. The loss of the water baby. Doctor Monroe's escape. Each was a dagger to my heart. "We accomplished nothing." I pounded my fist on the table.

"Nothing? Imagine what would have happened if we had not been here."

"He murdered the woman who loved him." In saying this I knew it to be true, and thought of how love had doomed many a good woman.

"Monroe's laboratory is destroyed, his work discovered, and now he must flee."

I rose from the table, almost bumping my head on the low ceiling. Perhaps something could still be accomplished. "Let us call the police before he escapes the country."

Darwin motioned for me to resume my seat. "What are we to do, tell the police that we broke into Monroe's house, rifled through his belongings, and stole from him? Would you trade these warm lodgings for a prison cell?"

"Stole?"

"Monroe would count the water baby as among his possessions. Even if the police followed our lead, all evidence has been destroyed in the fire. No, we must take our satisfaction in knowing we have put a stop to his predations."

I took a bitter drought from my mug. "Do you really think the threat of Monroe is over?"

"For now," Darwin said. "But in a world absent of God and the devil, I am afraid his kind cannot resist the temptation to assume the form of the deity and, in doing so, take on the aspect of a demon. He will reappear, although perhaps under another name." Darwin's voice trailed off as he tried out various permutations of our adversary's name, "Martin, Marlowe, Montrose, Moreau…"

"But what of the water baby?" The pain this question engendered in my breast took me by surprise, and I wondered if Darwin noticed the tears that flooded my vision. I, like Darwin, am not a religious man. I grant neither the existence of God nor of an afterlife. To have failed the water baby was to have failed utterly in our task, and to have failed also the memories of our departed children.

"Monroe is an evil man, but did he not create something of beauty, of wonder, in spite of his evil?"

I nodded. In my mind's eye I saw once again the sweet child with her pale blue eyes, sensitive mouth, and gills that flushed crimson. I saw the delicacy with which her tiny hands and fins fluttered against the water in her crystal globe. And I saw, and could not shake, that final image of her lithe form slipping from its shattered prison to disappear into the wave that almost drowned us. "Do you think she might yet survive?" I am not given to prayer, but this question was nothing else.

"I believe the water baby will seek the sea and there find others of its kind."

Darwin's vision astounded me with its audacity. Not one infant, but many, a tribe of naked children prospering in the same waters that held sharks, squid, and any number of carnivores, not least of which were blood-thirsty fishermen with their hooks, nets, and harpoons. "What makes you think that others of its kind exist?"

"To go from none to one is infinite in conception. But now, having seen an example of one, it is but a small step to conceive of two. And if two, why not three? If three, why not more?"

"I follow your logic, but do you really find this plausible?" I wanted to understand Darwin, to have him brush aside the cobwebs of my stubborn disbelief. His response, for the first time in memory, disappointed me.

"With some things," Darwin said, "it is not a simple matter of reason." He picked up a charred stick and stirred the fire. He seemed afraid to meet my eyes.

I stared at the tiny flames raised from the guttering chunks of coal. In those fire-sprites I saw Annie, Charlie, Mary, and Noel, robbed from us when they had burned so brightly and been extinguished after so short a time. But, although I might dwell on loss, in my heart I knew that Noel would not wish it so. Had I not two other children among the living, and another on the way, all of which deserved my love?

I could not suppress a smile in remembering Nettie's belly warm beneath my tentative palm—had this really occurred only a day ago?—as I sought to decipher a heartbeat, too early I knew but I optimistically persevered and demanded in vain for Nettie to hush her laughter and joyful tears. In thinking of this tiny life growing within Nettie, soon to take its place in my arms, it seemed that I better understood the water baby. She too, for now I could think of the water baby as nothing but a she, had embraced the waves, reaching out to them as to her natural environment. She entering the water without a backward glance for the world she abandoned. Rather than witnessing a death, I had witnessed a birth, a beautiful, miraculous birth such had never been witnessed in all the eons of man.

As if reading my thoughts, Darwin said, "Consider what you and I survived this night. Fire, water, and a monster intent on our destruction. No matter the dangers, I will never take odds against life."

ROOT AND BRANCH

Jen Downes

"She's dying." Julia Chen's eyes glazed as she concentrated on the datafeed. The cranial implant hummed faintly, like positive ions buzzing in the back of the skull on a windy day.

Ten meters west, alone at a slender parapet with a view over a forest canopy unbroken before the nearest skytower soared upward, Roy Thorpe didn't see Julia's data, wouldn't have understood it if he had. The gulf between bioengineer and health inspector yawned too vastly. "Impossible. Run your numbers again." He frowned at Boronia, the next city, a kilometer high, twenty kilometers north, hazed by blue distance. Beautiful, graceful in its own way, a shimmering aggregation of a thousand substances, spun, woven, grown in situ, just as cities always grew. Cities didn't die. Julia watched him dismiss the idea with an impatient gesture, and sighed.

She blinked out of the interface, gave her head a little telltale shake as she disengaged from a realm of raw information and joined Roy in the reality of Concord Park. Green stretched away behind and on all sides. Above, a vault of windswept sky reached beyond mist-hazed horizons, broken only by a single white, fast-blurring contrail charting the course of a lander from the docks at High Five. The descending vapor column would dissipate in minutes.

A thousand meters above the forest, Julia and Roy were alone. Concord remained closed, at Community Health's insistence. Every major data conduit terminated here, under a service hatch she had opened an hour before. Prying, curious eyes were the last thing Waratah Citizens'

Committee wanted. Better if the public remained ignorant until the problem could be corrected; then, a polite if vague acknowledgment of two hundred power outages scattered across this city in the last week, a pledge that all faults were remedied

"I rechecked everything." Julia's small, fine hand clenched on the parapet. "I check it all every day, Roy, same as I reported to your boss and *her* boss. I'm telling you, Waratah is quitting, like… a plant you forgot to water, or over-watered till you drowned its roots, or forgot to feed it."

"For godsakes," he remonstrated, "Waratah's not a houseplant. She's as alive as you or me, or any tree in this forest. A city! She can't just quit."

"She's not *just* quitting." Julia took a breath, cultivated patience she didn't feel. Roy was a good guy, but no Community Health monitor possessed any real foundation in bioengineering. In their minds, cities like Boronia, Waratah, Acacia and three thousand others seeded across the world were immutable. They grew, they'd always grow, like oak trees with lifespans measured in millennia: they didn't die. *Couldn't.*

A bioengineer knew better. Julia dropped a hand on his forearm to catch his attention. "Anything alive can die. It's the one factor all living things have in common. People used to call this 'the secret of life'… It ends. And Waratah is ending. *Will* end," she rasped, "if we don't find a clean, unambiguous diagnosis and—"

"Fix it." Roy turned his back on the view. "So, any ideas?"

She hesitated. "Clues. Nothing firm enough to base a judgment on."

"At least give me a bone to feed my boss." A pleading tone sharpened his voice.

Julia could well imagine his reluctance to approach Counselor Eleanor Rinaldi with a handful of smoke that, to ordinary nostrils, reeked like the very effluent Waratah recycled into food and fuel for growth. Rinaldi had forged a caustic reputation. Roy could earn a thick wedge of pay demerits, punishment for being gullible enough to buy into crap. Julia wished she had handed him such rubbish, but numbers didn't lie.

"Any living system can contract a disease," she said slowly. "Something's gotten into Waratah, down deep, maybe right at the roots. She's dying, no question about it. I just don't know why."

"Yet," Roy added. His brows rose, creasing his forehead. "You're looking for it, yes?"

"Looking," she allowed. "Finding is another issue. It's never happened before. No city ever got sick, much less terminal." She pointed north. "See Boronia, healthy as the day she grew big enough to accommodate a population. Two hundred years, Roy. She's far older than Waratah, nurturing ten percent more people."

The thought inspired a chill. A million humans lived, studied, worked, played, romanced, bore and reared children, grew older at an ever-decelerating rate afforded by gene therapies, right beneath their feet. Julia looked down, trying to imagine them teeming in this kilometer-high, kilometer wide living structure, with its vertical forests on every wall, internal rivers and cataracts pumping and recycling water and waste every second, every day; generating surplus power with every square centimeter exposed to light and wind; raising food crops even as she wove structural members to grow ever stronger.

The latest census, just three days earlier, showed Waratah's population as 998,986, with 163 women in stage-four maternity care. Every soul depended on Waratah. Beyond her walls, centuries-old forest lay dense as jungle, tangled, largely inhospitable to humans save for sporadic cleared zones where a handful of people who cared to ever 'go outside' vacationed.

If she were to die—

Even Julia's mind tried to reject the idea. Roy was right, cities didn't die. Or, not yet. "Had to be a first time," she murmured. "Just my luck to drop in for the fun."

"So what do I tell the boss?" he pressed. "The city's come down with some ailment, you're diagnosing it, you'll cure it?"

The oversimplification dizzied her, but it was exactly what Rinaldi wanted to hear. "Say anything you need to keep her happy—buy me time." She pinned him with a glare. "But understand, Roy. Diagnosis is a long shot, and as for a cure?" Julia shook her head. "I'll make no guarantee. But I know who to call for help."

The breeze wafted freshly, cool, slightly humid, fragrant with the earthy, sweet-rotten scent of Waratah's skirt of forest. Animals cried, trumpeted, growled, far below; birds fluted across Concord Park, called from above and far below. Earth sprawled, green as far as one could see, punctuated only by the great skytowers where so many generations of humans had lived for so long, any other way had passed out of living memory.

If Waratah died, a million people had nowhere to go. Other cities reported themselves at capacity, each growing slowly according to ancient biological processes, to accommodate an infinitesimal yet inexorable population growth. Earth was green once more; its skies had never been so clean since hominids walked these hills. No one ever imagined a city could die. Julia had rerun the data twenty times before she could no longer refuse to believe the truth.

"Look, I gotta work," she told Roy. "Keep Rinaldi happy. Keep your Council happy. Tell them we'll get to the root of the problem, fix it, if they'll bear with us. A week or two."

"So long?" he mused doubtfully.

"If you know a way to work faster, don't keep it to yourself! Two weeks, max," Julia sighed. "Because if the rot goes any longer, it's all over. You know what 'point of no return' means, in a living biosystem?"

The way he changed color assured her that he did. He tugged his tunic, ran both hands through his breeze-disheveled hair, and got moving. "I'll let you work. As for me, I've a bundle of lies to tell to a woman who scares the crap out of me." He flung Julia a grim glance as the elevator opened. "Wish me luck."

"Luck," she said dutifully, though her mind had already moved on. She must message thirty specialists, call in numerous favors, fast. Even the deciduous trees, shifting restlessly in the park's perpetual wind, had begun to change color as if this were autumn. Those fall colors were ten weeks early. Every tree snaked its roots deep into the wellsprings from which Waratah's life energy flowed, and—

With a pang of dread, Julia Chen hurried back to the lab.

———◆———

Francine Merton and Ranjit Gupta flew in from Banyan; Ed Silva and Tonia Romano from Sequoia. Bioengineers from every city traded favors. Calling them in was more arduous than Julia had hoped, but four specialists could escape their own projects to reach Waratah within a day. The rest analyzed her classified data at a distance and confirmed what she knew.

Three times Julia's age, far more experienced, 'Frankie' Merton settled into one of three labs and immersed herself in VR to catch up fast. Ranjit—small, thickset, with perennially suspicious eyes and an abrasive personality which masked brilliance—preferred to digest information at a slower pace, over liters of coffee. Silva and Romano, Julia knew the least well, and let both choose their own space and method. Eduardo Silva was tall, gaunt, born and raised on the L5 city of Aldrin and proud of it. He came to Earth just five years before, as a post-grad at University of Sequoia. By contrast, Antonia Romano had recently retired from Sequoia's immense faculty and vaguely recognized Ed as an anonymous face in her lecture theater. They'd never worked together, and at once Julia felt their sparks of competition.

She made every byte of data available, let the four ingest it through whatever means. Three hours later, she locked both doors on her lab's staff lounge and deliberately shut off all surveillance for complete privacy. They could hardly fail to notice, and Frankie Merton observed aridly,

"You haven't informed Waratah Citizens' Committee." Not a question.

Julia suppressed a shiver. "You want a million people panicking?" She gestured at the display, where current data updated without pause. "She's dying. We better find out how, while there's a chance to turn this around. This is why I asked you to come here. It's too much for my staff, and I don't trust half of them not to blab to the media, if they see the numbers. I'm terminally short-handed."

"And we don't have much time. All right." Silva leaned over the table. "Bottom line is disease, transmitted from outside. Trace the vector back to source, you'll at least know what you're dealing with. I'm surprised you haven't already done this."

"Maybe because she's not so complacent," Ranjit Gupta snapped, brittle as always. "I suspect failure somewhere within the biosystem, not contagion. More similar to organ failure in mammals. There's no plant disease on Earth a city could contract. Immunity was engineered in my great-great-grandfather's day." He frowned at Julia. "You're examining every sub-system, I assume?"

"*And* searching for a pathogen," she affirmed. "It's more work than ten of me could hope to cut through in the time we have left, and I trust only four of my staff to maintain the confidentiality we need to prevent citywide panic."

Huffing a protest, Merton pushed to her feet. At such great age, even the newest therapies were less than efficient. Age had begun to overtake her, and she knew it. Useful, productive decades remained ahead, but she must be aware of 'running down the clock,' perhaps trusting in some radical new biotech to eventually avert the inevitable. "In other words," she said tartly, "stop bickering: *work*." She gave Julia a bare hint of a smile. "Divide our attention between three possible causes. Contagion, system failure, or deliberate attack."

"Or—*what?*" Romano echoed.

"I said, attack," Merton reiterated. "This data is equally consistent with an assault on Waratah. I suggest, Julia, you examine your domestic security."

The concept hadn't occurred to Julia but, once spoken, it was horrifyingly obvious. Her mouth dried. "Immediately."

Three minutes later she sealed her own office and frowned at Roy Thorpe's worried face in the comp. "Get up here," she told him. "There's stuff that's far closer to your area than mine. You know these channels better than I ever will. And no, I can't say word *one* on open send."

"But, Julia—" Protesting, busy, reluctant.

"Get here!" She waved a hand through the display field to cut him off.

———◆———

Exhaustion had a way of siphoning optimism and enthusiasm, leaving behind bleak thoughts, corrosive pessimism. Julia sat on the couch in her apartment, sixty levels below the labs, regarding another handful of peps and a mug of bitumen masquerading as coffee. Eyes closed, she concentrated on the data streaming through her implant, but the only thing it yielded was a headache. Roy sat at the circular dining table, working five palmtops at once, with a face like a thundercloud.

"Nothing?" Her voice had grown croaky. Peps and coffee did that, if one indulged too much, too often. Not since student days had Julia relied on them, and many decades later it seemed the more mature body rode the chemistry grudgingly. She blinked out of the interface and the apartment spun slowly, rich with the golden hues of Waratah's native constructional materials, burgundy carpets, ivory blinds. The single room was sparse, the futon rumpled, heaps of clothes abandoned beside it. Only the shelves opposite the window wall remained orderly, each bearing a piece of history: mementos of generations of Chens who'd called Shanghai home when the region was inhabitable.

Figurines, a vase, a brazen incense burner, reproductions of Ming era paintings, family pictures revolving endlessly in the player frame.

His fair head shook slowly. "Security's tight as a drum. I tasked an AI of my own—on a secure server with enough encryption to hide a whole pod of blue whales, don't worry—to review the feeds from eight thousand cameras, around the clock, over the last month. Doctor Silva's tracked the onset of this…what? Disease?…back twenty days."

Power outages began ten days ago, but long before this Waratah showed multiple subtle signs of sickness which went unnoticed. Automatic systems patched over them with relentless efficiency, reporting minor mishaps to City Health monitors like Roy who, failing to know them for what they were, saw no reason for concern.

Then came the complaints about water quality on Level 48; scores of maintenance calls on 50 through 220, South Side, where light levels were inconsistent; soon, sporadic reports from all over Waratah— temperatures too high, too low, sodden air steams from the inner-building ducts. Robot tech gangs scurried like worker ants, correcting cascading system failure, until at last some nameless plebe at City Health called Bioengineering.

Julia remembered the call: a young voice, high pitched, hesitant, even apologetic as an unknown girl said, "Sorry, Doctor Chen, but something's wrong. The city's gone—I dunno. Squirrelly? Can your department look into it? Our maintenance 'bots are spread so thin now, I've got folks on 122 through 275 saying their water stinks like mildew or sewage, and I don't have a techbot gang free for assignment till tomorrow. Can you help?"

Something's wrong, she said. The understatement made Julia's bone marrow congeal. Resignedly she swallowed the peps, trying to remember when she'd slept last. It seemed a vampire confronted her from the mirror. As a natural insomniac, Frankie Merton handled the hours better than any of them. Silva and Romano were bloodshot, haggard.

"Nothing on any security feed." Julia hauled to her feet at the window wall, gazing over the vastness of forest.

The sky's inverted bowl burned blue to the east while marching squalls darkened the west. From this altitude, storms showed themselves a full day before they struck. Birds were rare so high up, but a scattering of commercial and private craft cruised leisurely between cities—many freighters, airships on the import-export trade, delivering exotic commodities specific to one city, craved by another. A few craft were unmistakably civilian. One held a direct heading and, like anyone, Julia knew it on sight.

At dusk the showboat would illuminate, garish with the animated signage of *Carnival Capricornia*. The troupe of sky-travellers played Waratah every January. Tickets were scarce, prices high, but the wild, weird, ragtag company drew adoring audiences. In minutes the airship—long, lean, gorgeously contoured—would dock, dolphinesque flanks rippling through greens, golds, ruby and amethyst. She was immensely old but in pristine health, as alive as any city, biological down to her hollow bird-bones, the synapses in her living brain and the multi-hued hide stretched taut over her helium cells.

The travellers took a day to set up their arena in Concord Park, but even before they docked anyone in Waratah who possessed an implant knew they were in town. Julia blinked into the interface, eyes closed, and smiled as the commercial ran. She'd booked months before, and keenly anticipated the performance. Now, she deliberately forced her mind away from the showboat as Roy said,

"Security shows *squat*. Which doesn't mean we *weren't* attacked," he warned. "Doc Merton's hypothetical aggressor might be too smart for the cameras."

Her head drooped. A chair scraped, the weight of his arm fell across her shoulders. "We'll find it. There's time. Merton's only covering all bases with this theory of attack. Three to one odds, it's disease, not assault."

"Says who?" She leaned against him, grateful for the support, tired eyes lingering on the graceful, lovely traveler showboat. *Capricornia* drifted overhead, out of sight, like the embodiment of freedom.

"Eddie Silva."

"Huh. He's been harping on disease, contagion, vector, since we started."

Roy gave her shoulders a hug and released her. He stood a head taller, almost twice her weight, chronologically twenty years younger, biologically a few years older. He seemed happiest in his mid-thirties. Like so many women, Julia's fancy was for late-twenties. When oceans of time raced under the bridge, age ceased to matter.

"Silva could be right," he mused. "If Waratah were human, I'd say she had 'flu. Full of aches and pains, creaking, groaning, fevers and chills, and the runs."

The analogy was shrewd. Julia chugged the coffee and set the empty beside his palmtops. "Keep searching. Anything out of the ordinary." She knuckled dry, sore eyes. "You looked into that other matter...?"

A question too delicate to be made public, though it must be asked. If Waratah died, where could a million people be relocated? His face shadowed. "Our folks will scatter on the winds. Fifty thousand here, twenty there. We might find enough space for all, but it'll be tight. Forty K can resettle in Apollo Central on Luna, if they fancy the mining life. The new Gagarin City at L5 can take sixty K more—problem is, it's so new, they haven't shaken out the kinks. Buggy as an ant farm, so I heard. They haven't even spun her up to gravity yet, so the toilets don't flush."

Tech gangs, regiments of 'bots, could hammer the job into line in weeks; mechanical issues were not the problem. For two centuries Earth's own residents had enjoyed a green, growing world beneath blue skies, rich in wildlife, with abundant fresh water and oceans of surplus power. No Waratah citizen would happily relocate to a 'tin can' parked at a Trojan point, or a billet in a subsurface mining town where water and power were rationed, and constant recycling turned the very air metallic. Only small pet animals lived on L5's twenty cities and the forty Luna settlements. A few birds, portly 'apartment cats,' toy-size dogs. No wolves or tigers, wild horses, buffalo, giraffe, deer. No city off Earth boasted open range, forest where long-extinct, re-engineered species surged through burgeoning, resurrected wilderness.

Humanity had neatly divided itself: those who took to space when the going got seriously rough—too hot, stormy or dry, too thirsty, hungry or flooded; and those who stayed, sheltering from the elements inside old, refurbished buildings which generated their own power, recycled every drop of water and waste, until new-generation tech birthed the living, growing cities. In fifty years the world greened; in a hundred, wildlife thrived again from wood to steppe to jungle. People who'd kept their feet on the ground through the bad years claimed the new, green world as their inheritance—

Move them *en masse* to the sterility of L5 and Luna? Julia shuddered, imagining the riots. But they must go someplace, or perish. In time some might return, though a city capacious enough to embrace a million souls took many decades to grow. Waratah herself was well over a century old, Sequoia, almost two.

"It's not the best way," Roy sighed, "but if we can trust recent stats, I found space for half our population. So long as they don't mind living rough for a while."

"A while?" she echoed. "How long before they get back to the comfort they know?"

He could only shrug. "How long's a piece of string? Beggars can't be choosers. Nobody chooses to be a beggar, but—"

A chime from the comp interrupted. Tonia Romano's voice said tersely, "Doctor Chen, come to Biotech 5. Quickly, please."

Heart beating a tattoo at her ribs, she grabbed Roy by the elbow, hustled him out, and ran. Data rushed through her implant as fast as she could run it, giving her the gist before an elevator car arrived.

The four stood around the big display, too mesmerized to notice the door, which immediately security-sealed behind Roy. Rotating slowly, the display seemed filled with glorious abstract art. Each rotation, its view changed to a greater or lesser magnification, but an illusion of art remained, even when Julia made sense of what she saw.

At last Merton looked away, clearly taking no pleasure in the discovery. The old face settled into grim lines. "Here's your gremlin. Before you ask, I've never seen anything like it. I doubt anyone has. It's so new, no city could be immune. Which means we slam the doors on Waratah *fast,* before it escapes."

Quarantine. The word burned in Julia's throat. "And the people?"

"Lockdown is lockdown," Roy said hoarsely. "Let anybody out…" He shook his head. "Gotta tell my boss, Doctor Merton. Layman's version, please, quick and simple. What *is* it?"

Ed Silva shoved hands into pockets and glared into the display. "A bastard third cousin of something nastily like tobacco mosaic. A virus. Single-strand RNA, jumps readily from species to species. In most plants it'd stunt growth. Not kill the plant outright, but smother it into a deformed little weed."

"That's… good," Roy hazarded, grasping blindly. "If it won't kill—"

"A city isn't a bloody geranium!" Silva snapped, glaring Roy into silence.

"Eduard, for heaven's sake," Merton remonstrated. "Look, Mr. Thorpe, it's far more complex than a layman can expect to grasp, but I'll tell you this: a virus that stunts whatever it touches has gotten into the brains of Waratah. You know these cities are biological, right down to their circuitry. They're alive, in every sense of the word. Humans live with them in elegant, beautiful symbiosis. We provide the waste products to feed them, the carbon dioxide they breathe. In return they grow and function according to grand designs programmed into them before they're rooted. Their living brains don't think like yours or mine, of course. If a banyan tree could be said to have thought patterns, they might approximate the 'thinking' of a city like Waratah or Sequoia. Make no mistake, there's a biological AI at the heart of every city, governing each smallest function, from pumping and filtering water to controlling temperature, growing complex building materials to buttress the structure…*everything*." Her brow rose. "Now, introduce a stunting virus into the living control center we'll call a brain for want of a better term."

She waited for Roy to think it through, but it was Julia who whispered, "It's as if Waratah has galloping Alzheimer's." She glanced at Gupta, who had originally suspected sub-system failure akin to organ collapse in mammals. He nodded. "Then, our biosystems are healthy. They're malfunctioning because they're receiving gibberish instructions."

"Exactly." Silva had calmed, though muscles twitching in his jaw betrayed stress. "We can't know if this virus can or will spread to sub-systems, of course. Technically, it could get into anything."

The lab fell so silent, Julia heard Roy swallow. "I'll inform Community Health right now. Institute lockdown. Nothing in, nothing out, till this is fixed."

He left on those words and Romano groaned. "Meaning us, too. We're all stuck here."

"Where else would you be?" Merton stooped to peer at the graphic of the virus and its suffocating effects on the beautiful, tree-like forms of the city's brain.

"My grandson's birthday, in two days, perhaps?" Tonia suggested sourly.

The senior scientist regarded her with suppressed anger. "I should have thought preserving your grandson's life would trump a birthday party." She gestured at the images. "This disease gets out, my dear, and every city will be dead. It'll take a while, but extinction is inevitable. You look forward to wrestling apes in the forest for fruit? Some of us would survive. The strong and young, those cut out for hunting, killing, tribal behaviour. The rest—? No more biotech or gene therapy. By tribal standards, everybody in this lab is geriatric. We should have expired long ago. You want to live in a world where science collapsed and a few survivors compete for dregs shipped down from the space cities?"

"No," Ranjit Gupta said quietly, "I don't. So we put Waratah in lockdown and we fix this." He glared at each face in turn, in particular Silva and Romano. "Enough bellyaching. Let the city authorities do their job…and for the love of *anything* you care to call 'god,' let's do our own!"

With an effort of sheer willpower, Julia battened down the trembling and pulled a chair up to the nearest workstation.

———◆———

Two hours after Community Health broadcast the announcement, protests began, blossoming into full-scale riot within a day. Julia had known it must happen but still her mouth dried as she watched the security feeds. On Waratah's lower levels, crowds rampaged—not that these people ever desired to 'go outside,' but the instant that the privilege was denied, they demanded it. Most had never left the structure in their lives. They were born, educated, worked, paired off, played, bred, raised offspring, in sunlit spaces where clever landscaping, window walls and holograms created a sense of infinite space. They foraged in forty retail megaplexes, flocked to countless theaters, twelve sports arenas, four major universities. Most citizens never had reason to even ride the skytrain to Boronia for a day. But they valued highly the liberty to do it, and when their rights were curtailed—

Every police 'bot the city possessed deployed at once; reinforcements trucked in from every city within a hundred kilometers. Lockdown would always be ugly and this one careened into violence before nightfall. Mayor Wei spoke from the Civic Center, begging for order and calm: the problem was minor, it would soon be righted, but in the interests of other cities' health, the people of Waratah must be realistic, be calm, settle and wait. *Carnival Capricornia* had just opened, and for the first time all tickets were refunded, every show would be broadcast free to all citizens. Wei diplomatically omitted to mention the showboat was equally imprisoned. The sky-travellers lived under identical quarantine regulations, albeit aboard their own ship in Concord's free winds.

A week of peps, coffee, insomnia, work and dread left Julia strung taut, nerve endings frayed to tatters, patience threadbare. Concentration steadily eroded till she feared she might see the right answer and not recognize it. Every lab on Waratah's science and tech levels had been commandeered, running on isolated power cells and unnetworked processors shipped from Boronia and Bayobab. Any machine connected to Waratah's brain steadily regressed into disorder, chaos, painfully reminiscent of the chronic neurodegenerative diseases which had once beset humans.

"It's highly contagious," Gupta sighed over tea, rubbing his aching neck. His eyes squeezed against the early evening sun flooding the window wall. He massaged the back of his skull, where his implant must be raising a nagging throb. "It's also slow to develop, so early stage symptoms were overlooked. The fact there's no vector we can isolate makes it deadly. It's in most of Waratah's slaved AI networking now. If we don't disconnect the lot, there won't be a comp or conduit viable in another week."

"Shut down the entire network?" Roy whispered. "Every datafeed quits, Waratah goes offline. We'll have riots we can't begin to control."

"Still, it'll have to be done." Gupta's face might have been granite.

"We've worked around a lot of systems," Tonia offered. "We're scrambling to control power, water, sewage, using old fashioned cyber gear—chips, cables. Trash hardware no one's seen on Earth in centuries, but thank gods Luna dropped us a shipment, or the situation would be critical already. We're functional, to a point. People won't suffocate or go thirsty. Food reserves are good for two weeks. Longer, if we instate rationing."

"Rationing?" Roy echoed. "Damnit, Tonia, you'll see rioting you can't even imagine!"

"It's been done before." She frowned at Frankie Merton, by far the group's oldest. "You remember. You were there."

Dark, bad days: environmental collapse, weird roiling skies, breather-masks to supplement oxygen as vast tracts of ocean perished, monstrous corrosive storms gnawing away structures, human and animal populations crashing in months while lunar industry expanded exponentially and cities raced into production at L5 so fast, several suffered fatal flaws.

For a moment every one of Frankie's vast years haunted her eyes. Then she visibly shook herself, dragged herself back to the moment. "In those years, desperate people accepted stringent measures. These folks, in modern cities? They're soft, spoiled, demanding, petulant when they don't get their own way. Oh, yes, expect them to retaliate if you crack the whip."

The lab lapsed into sullen silence until Julia said softly, "If my numbers are right, we have three days, four at longest, before we pass the point of no return. After that, we shore up what we can with any antiquated hardware we can get from Gagarin, Armstrong, whoever'll help from L5 and Luna. Mars is too far away. We use the time to start ferrying refugees to Acacia, Boronia, Sequoia—"

Roy made negative gestures. "Lockdown, Julia. Quarantine. Anyone and anything leaving Waratah could act as carriers. No city on Earth will take them. Ironically, the only ones that will are —" He nodded upward, toward those 'tin cans' where so many generations of humans had lived in partial gravity and incredible synthetic environments, deigning to return to Earth only as curious, mildly appalled tourists. "I petitioned every L5 government. We can offload a quarter million, allowing for tough living conditions at destination. The rest stay put, make the best of what's left."

"Die," Ed said bleakly.

"Eventually." Tonia looked away. "We'll stave off the end as long as we can keep vital systems stable, but Waratah isn't growing now. No structural repairs, no new conduit branching or root-cabling. Inevitably, there's only one way to contain this virus. We all know it."

She must be destroyed, to the cellular level. Julia's heart squeezed. "Three days," she repeated. "Experimental Antivirus 27 is simulating right now. Six hours to get results." She blinked away from the data flow, rubbed her skull where the implant buzzed uncomfortably, and heaved to her feet, hands pressed to her lumbar. "I'd say I gotta sleep, but I couldn't if I tried. I," she said acidly, "have actual arena tickets for *Carnival Capricornia*." Blindly, she reached toward Roy. "Interested?"

He took her hand, squeezed it. "Be a genuine pleasure."

A release, to leave the lab for a few hours, shut off the implant, silence the datastream—stop talking and thinking about it. The end had begun to race toward them. Impossible to imagine a world without

Waratah, but the day loomed close.

They were waiting for the elevator when a chime caught Julia's ear. She listened dully. An exhausted, harassed voice from City Council said, "Apologies for intruding, Doctor Chen. We've been trying to unload these cranks for days, but they won't quit. You got a minute?"

Groaning, she returned to the lab. "What kind of cranks?"

"Students, Doctor. They insist it's important, but—"

"I'll take it. Audio only." Julia looked at Roy and mouthed, "Two minutes."

He nodded, tired enough to sink into a chair and close his eyes while a young, high voice stumbled, "Doctor Chen? My name's Hannah Myles. I have some data—you better see it. Can I transmit?"

"Data regarding *what?*" Julia's mind refused to focus. Too many peps. She needed fresh, open air, sunlight, green grass, wide skies—

"The, uh, disease in the, um, city," Hannah muttered. "I'm pretty sure…that is, we, uh—"

"Say it, child, and be done," Merton snapped impatiently. "We've better things to do than listen to babble."

Hannah's tone hardened. "Okay. It was us."

A static charge ricocheted through the lab. Julia jerked awake. Even Roy sat up straight, eyes brightening. "What do you mean?" She peered through the haze of the display into Merton's grim face.

"We're in third year virology," the girl said bitterly. "It's a project. We're splicing genes, plant viruses, looking for ways to accelerate crop growth. You know how our population never stops growing. They're always warning about famine next century. This was supposed to be huge, we'd be rich and famous." She paused to breathe. "I guess we made mistakes. Don't know where we screwed up, Doctor Chen. We've spent a week trying to figure it. We've been calling for *days* but the bastards shut us out. Can we—"

"Transmit." Julia joined Frankie and Ed on the other side of the display to watch. Her implant kicked in, humming in her skull.

Silva groaned as numbers, charts, images, unfolded. "Oh, yeah, there's your vector. Explains why no other city's reported—*yet!*—any infection. The fricking thing started with us. We're ground zero. But this, here, is the original strain, and I can tell you right now, this bugger's mutated ten times since it got into Waratah. Knowing there is no vector is comforting, but zip I can see here helps cure the current strain.

Best we can hope for is containment."

"But it develops so slowly at the outset," Frankie reminded, "it could've escaped long before Waratah manifested symptoms. Any city with a physical connection back to us could present symptoms within seven to ten days."

"They all commenced diagnostics when we identified it," Ed growled. "They're seeing nothing so far. Wonderful, isn't it, finding yourself reduced to prayer? All right, Miss Myles. Report to your authorities. Lodge a full statement. Wait for a hazmat squad to collect your materials and decontaminate your facilities. Where are you working?"

"Level 225 North Campus," she said, gloomy, embarrassed, mortified at once. "Are we in trouble?"

"For a genuine mistake?" Julia sighed heavily. "Your work will be examined. If your methods were slipshod, you'll be in serious trouble. If you observed every precaution…" She glanced from face to face. "Mistakes *do* happen," she said to her colleagues. "Fact: it could happen to any of us."

"Happened to me," Frankie confessed tartly. "Eons before you were born— took thirty years to live it down."

Roy had been busy. He gestured sharply for attention. "Hazmat's *en route*. I traced their project, logged in campus records. I just ID'd those kids. They're not going anywhere, if the Citizens' Committee wants to crucify them."

"For a professional blunder?" Julia suspected it might happen anyway, but history's bitter lessons burned through her brain. Thalidomide, asbestos, Minamata Disease, CFCs, so many mistakes costing lives, almost destroying the world.

Unable to grapple with the situation another moment, she pushed away from the desk. "Knowing where it started isn't a cure, and if I don't get a break, I'll be cuckoo tomorrow. *Carnival Capricornia*. Give me a few hours to get my head together, I'll do better when I haul myself back. Roy?"

In the elevator they embraced, each chill with the knowledge an L5 'tin can' city awaited them, a place where plant viruses were of no consequence in the sterile environment of space.

"Jule, darlin', you lookin' like crap, what you doin' to yourself?" Cass was in stage makeup, kohl around his eyes, flecks of gold scintillating across eyelids and cheekbones. The long black corncob braids were his own, like the deep bronze complexion of one who spent his whole life under the sun. He owned *Capricornia*, which floated at her gantry, the only ship on South Terminal 4.

Often, Julia envied the sky-travellers' footloose life. Their airships were as living as any city. They grew from seed pods the size of melons—generated, pumped and balanced their own helium as well as yielding every erg of power needed to cruise the free sky as long as they lived; and their lives were so long, no one yet knew what their longevity might be.

At the heart of every traveler 'skyboat' was a biological AI similar to Waratah's, and Julia fretted about infection. For a fleeting second she fantasized about going aboard, telling Cass Diarmid to run while the showboat had half a chance to escape this insanity.

But either Waratah or a nearby city would launch a squadron, force them back to face criminal charges as well as the madness begun by too-young, well-meaning, innocent, ignorant Hannah Myles and her study group. The fantasy evaporated. If *Capricornia* perished with Waratah, Julia would mourn no less than Cass. She grabbed him by both big hands, hugged hello. Four months since she's seen him, when she caught his show on the skypark at Cedar.

"There's trouble," she began.

"I saw." He fended her off, held her by both shoulders to study her. Towering, clad in loose, gaudy silk and a lot of jewelry, ready to wrangle a show, he looked over her head at Concord's unmistakable fall colors. "Is a total buggeration, ain't it?"

"Understatement." She stepped back. "This is Roy Thorpe, from Community Health, liaising with us while we…get this fixed." *Optimism,* she told herself. *Never stop believing.* "I've been working for days. Need a break before I jump my track, and—here you are,"

"Here we be." He gave her a white-toothed grin. "We's on camera this year, some kinda sop to your folks. Keep 'em quiet a few hours."

"Lockdown's a bitch." Roy offered his hand and Cass shook it.

The traveler beckoned toward the open-sky arena which had sprouted from Concord's grass. "Got the best seats for you, Jule, darlin'. Take a rum or three with me after."

"One," she agreed. "Then—work. This thing is bad."

"Tell me 'bout it." Cass surveyed the brown trees with a sigh. "Ain't just droppin' leaves for autumn, they's dyin'. Not dead *yet,* though. There's time." With a familiar lopsided smile, the perfect host, he ushered his guests to the best seats as sunset began to blaze.

Equal parts circus, vaudeville, ballet, burlesque, concert, opera, the show constantly evolved, never the same from season to season. Julia had watched thousands of hours of recorded entertainment from Waratah's centuries-deep archives, but live performers possessed something else. Glitches were inevitable; lines might be flubbed, blue notes occasionally struck, but this was *life,* not prerecorded, artificial perfection.

Singers, dancers, acrobats, a tightrope walker, stand-up comics with old jokes, balladeers with ancient songs, harpers and flautists, three miniature pet tigers the size of sheepdogs, romping through a joyously disobedient performance—Cass with his magic tricks and master stage presence. Two hours sped by while the sky darkened to velvet black and the stars assumed a diamond glitter. The Milky Way provided a backdrop for the last songs, stories, and when Cass deftly produced three white doves from thin air and released them, the stage lights faded to black.

Moments later lamps flooded Concord once more, bathing *Capricornia* in ever-shifting hues. Cass stepped down from the stage. He wore a gleam of perspiration as Julia went to congratulate him.

"I should have flowers," she apologized. "If only I'd been thinking."

"I've rum," he reminded.

"A *small* one." Perhaps to mourn Waratah? She took Roy's hand, followed Cass backstage to tents the public never saw. A troupe of thirty who all doubled as roustabouts, riggers and airship crew milled in companionable disorder.

The pet tigers wove around his legs like enormous house cats as he ducked into his own tent, fetched a tall brown bottle and three glasses. Through the open flap, he regarded the floodlit trees sadly. "Aye, a buggeration. I guess we were just damn' lucky."

"You weren't." Roy sampled the rum. "Did no one tell you? Lockdown went into effect after you moored. You're quarantined with the rest of us."

"Mm," Cass agreed, "till she's all better." He tossed back his drink and poured another. "We's playin' Waratah till month's end in any case."

Julia closed her eyes, dreading what she must say. "You don't understand. Waratah's *dying*. As for being 'all better'—dear gods, I wish."

The showman frowned at her. "Cure her, why don't you?"

"Because there *is* no cure." Julia took a second small rum. "The best in the world have been working till we're almost out of time."

His frown deepened. "I'd swear its the same ailment she got herself, four years back." He gestured at *Capricornia*. "Aye, she damn-near died before she found her own cure." He tapped his skull. "Is in here. Brains go cockeyed and all else follows. So, what's Waratah's trouble?"

"The same." Julie shared a glance with Roy. "Cass, are you saying *Capricornia* fell sick with something like this?"

"So she did." He sprawled on a futon, gestured with his glass. "Dementia—and it was catchin' as any pox!"

"She healed herself?" Julia scarcely believed it.

"Took four months," Cass allowed. "All that time, we didn't dare dock nowhere. Hung up high like a plague ship, didn't know if she'd live or if we'd be settin' a torch to her."

Julia pressed her face into both palms, wondering if rum or impossible data were fogging her brain. "Where were you, when she fell sick?"

His brow creased in memory. "Way south, where is all labs and *facilities* and tech-heads. We played a gig. Needed the work. Place called… yeah, Amundsen-Scott, cold as all hell, mind. Didn't wanna go, but we scored the work and, hey, gotta follow the cash in this game."

It was a research and hazmat containment facility located in the cool southlands, right at the pole. And it had earned a notorious reputation Julia knew too well. She turned a dark face to Roy. "Those bastards develop bio-weapons, store trash they don't even know how to destroy, left over from wars so old, they outstrip living memory, which is saying a lot." Her mind raced. "How much d'you want to bet, Miss Myles and her pals retraced the steps of some madmen centuries ago, committed some student blunders, stumbled on a virus so similar…"

"Damn." Roy could barely speak. "Could Waratah find her own cure?" He searched the showman's face for answers.

But Cass only shrugged. "Maybe, maybe not. She's pretty far gone."

"Worse than *Capricornia* was, when…?" Julia hazarded.

"I'd guess so," Cass judged. "See, *Capricornia's* way different. She's old, wild and wise, bred from original tree stock, ain't somethin' total artificial, lashed up in no lab, hundreds years back and supposedly better cuz of some canny new design. *Capricornia*'s old as any god; wiser than most. Waratah's young, like all your cities. They's bred from artificial stock. Traveller skyboats just…grow. They's still got roots half-way in the dark earth."

"Damn." Julia stood, hands clenched into her hair. "Let me think. *Think!* Cass, do you have data?"

He chuckled. "Me? Ain't no tech-head!"

"Then, does *Capricornia* have data?"

"Dunno, darlin'. Never asked." He stood, frowning at her distress. "If *Capri* died, she'da been her own pyre, fine Viking funeral. You wanna feed a root into her mind, interface, download what she knows?"

Julia's heart slammed her ribs. "Understand: interfacing increases the chance of contagion a hundredfold."

"She's immune, like gettin' over 'flu and not gettin' it again." Cass shrugged. "Do what you gotta, babe. Can't promise naught, but am tellin' you, the sickness sure looks the same."

She grabbed him in a bearhug, for a moment, inhaled the scents of cologne, makeup and rum, then steered Roy back to the elevators and ran.

———◆———

Again, every display roiled with maelstroms of data, cranial implants burred, thrummed with the rate of the feed. But this time she and Frankie were wide awake, running on surges of their own adrenaline. Ed and Tonia hung back, terminally skeptical until the comp modeled both viruses, Waratah's and *Capricornia*'s, and rotated them side by side.

Not identical, but so close. Julia took a deep breath. Frankie Merton peered at the images, then at Julia. "Amundsen-Scott, you say?" Julia nodded. "Well, crud," Frankie said sourly. "I should've bloody known."

"Meaning?" Ed prompted.

Frankie eased aching spine into smart-mold chair and glared at the display. "I've been messaging a bastard called Alec Silkin for the past week, begging for a skerrick of data or at least some processor time, since we're underpowered and overtasked."

"He's dodging you." Ranjit leaned his knuckles on the desk. "You showed him our scans?"

She nodded soberly. "And ours will be so friggin' similar to theirs, right now they're wetting themselves, wondering how garbage from Amundsen-Scott jumped eight thousand K's to Waratah, put a million souls in death's way." Her hands clenched as if she were wringing Silkin's neck. "I'll try again, but don't count on help." Frankie looked from Julia to Ed and back. "Pick *Capricornia*'s brains. Hunt for an antigen, something to induce an immune response close *enough* to catch that stupid little girl's pathogen as well."

"Hardly stupid," Ranjit argued. "Those children managed to recreate the work of brilliant specialists—"

"Of *idiots* who should've know better," Frankie barked, "and in the process put a whole world at jeopardy." She clapped sharply. *"Move, while there's time!"* She held out a hand and Julia took it, helped her rise. The workload had begun to exact a toll no body of Merton's age could support for long. Raw fury powered her, an unhealthy substitute for true vitality.

"Rest," Julia insisted. "We might still do this."

"Rest?" Frankie scoffed. "I'm going back to your office, and yell into a comp till a certain fat-bum bastard at Amundsen-Scott picks up!"

She plowed away, stiff, noticeably uncertain on her feet. "Stay with her, Roy, watch her." Julia waved him off. "You can't help here —and do *not* alert your boss till we grasp something firm. Bureaucrats understand none of this. Throw them a bone, they demand miracles… and you know," she added quietly, "it's still a damned long shot."

His face shadowed. "The only shot we'll get." Then he followed Frankie and the lab sealed behind him.

———◆———

Little of Waratah's brain functioned, but even now she retained rare lucid moments. Wires, chips, L5 cybertech, shored her up until she discovered enough clarity to handshake with *Capricornia*, communicate haltingly, stumblingly, with such agonizing slowness, Julia could have wept for her.

Hours dragged while Frankie repeatedly called the Antarctic facility, shouted herself hoarse. When Alec Silkin replied at last, he might have been a brick wall. A pale, mask-like face glared from the display and every word was clearly scripted, memorized. On behalf of IDR Amundsen-Scott, he denied all knowledge of any virus; stated officially that *Capricornia* had at no time been endangered, and claimed his processors were at capacity with their own research.

"Bastard liar," Frankie accused to his face, but she knew an official firewall when she saw one. Her hand jabbed into the display cloud to cut him off.

Well out of vid-pickup range, Julia heaved a weary shrug. "We're modeling five possible antibodies right now, sims'll run all night. There's maybe two days left, I think."

"One," Frankie rasped. "Over-optimism serves no purpose." She reached out. "Help me."

She made it to the futon under the window wall, stretched out, head on a pillow, half-closed eyes on the canopy of lush forest far below, the glorious vault of blue-white, cloud-laced sky, the gorgeous shimmer of Boronia, rising like an Olympian edifice, misted by distance.

"I'll get a medic," Julia began, but Frankie's head shook.

"Don't. Just tired… old," she added, gravel-voiced. "I remember this world when it was a cesspit. I was young in those days, though you probably can't imagine it."

But Julia could glimpse the girl trapped in the senescent shell, and felt a deep sadness of loss. "You were there at the rebirth, when the first cities grew. You watched industry banished to Luna and Mars, and the sky cleared."

"It's been my privilege." Frankie's eyes closed; her breathing shallowed. Julia took a step closer, blinked into the interface to access coms, but the old voice chuckled. "Away, child. I'm not dying. Not before this job's finished, one way or another. If we lose Waratah—we learn from such blunders. We might save a fair number of our population and still maintain quarantine protocols. Survivors always go forward wiser, stronger. Now *git*, let me sleep."

Julia set the comp to observe her, with directives to summon an EMT crew at any hint of failure, and crept out. Central Control would certainly salvage a quarter million lives, liquidate the rest along with Waratah and stoically term it *containment*. But who qualified for a ticket out? Social scientists had argued this question since the catastrophic mid-twentieth century. The debate raged on in simulation, as if some global authority, perhaps Infectious Diseases Research itself, actually predicted a day when arbitrary, draconian plans must be initiated.

Nauseous, too tired to sleep, too fretted to work, she fled to Concord, ran in the free, open air until fatigue shook her limbs. "Enjoy it while you can," she rasped, sprawling in the grass among drifts of dead leaves. She rolled onto her back, shaded eyes on deciduous trees growing skeletal in high summer. Only eucalypts—tenacious water-misers whose ancestors evolved in the Eocene—hung on.

A day, Frankie said, before too little of Waratah remained viable. Her tech and science community would score relocation to L5 or Luna. No city on Earth would accept refugees, no matter how rigorous the quarantine protocols: the danger was too horrifying. Something in Julia's brain clicked into gear, mentally sorting what she might take, what must be left. Passengers might be allocated perhaps twenty kilos of dead-mass, so she could carry only necessities. A change of clothes, a few mementos of family, keepsakes to cherish in the dark decades while a new city grew.

And if Waratah's refugees returned at all, they would come home bearing the stigma of disgrace: the fools who killed a city.

"Hey, darlin', good to see you out'n runnin'. Just done workin' out meself. Gotta stay in shape for the show, y'see. Look damn' fine on stage while I's pullin' rabbits outta hats." Cass Diarmid's shadow fell across her as he sat in the grass at her side. "How's Waratah doin'?"

"No news." Julia pressed the heels of her hands into her eyes, conjuring tides of blood red.

"S'not like *Capri* tells it." He sounded surprised. "She don't much like dancin' with no cyber circuit and hot metal wire, but I told you, she's old and wild and wise. We asked her nice, she said—okay. Was chattin' with her not an hour ago—" he tapped the back of his skull, over his implant "—before pumpin' enough iron to sink a skyboat."

Befuddled with exhaustion, Julia peered at him. "What are you talking about?"

"Auntie Beau Dee," Cass chuckled. "Who'n hell's this Auntie Beau Dee, like *Capri* keeps talkin' about? With a name like that, I'd hire him—or her. Sounds like an hermaphrodite opera diva! Man, s'what this show needs: big beauty singin' through seven octaves, tricked out in stuff like spun moonlight and tight black leather." He gave her a teasing wink.

She watched him yawn, stretch till his joints crackled, bare to the hips, bronze, sweat-slick, corncob braids tied off at his nape and every muscle pumped. Careless of the drama exploding in the kilometer below, he stretched out, head on one forearm, two meters of superb black panther at rest. Half asleep, half hypnotized, Julia imagined this fabulous diva of Cass's, next season's superstar and public sensation on the showboat circuit—

Auntie Beau Dee, so *Capricornia* kept saying. Auntiebeaudee.

She shot bolt upright. Life and energy surged through every muscle like a supercharge of adrenalin.

Cass blinked up at her. "Whazzamatta, darlin'? You's jumpin' like you been shot."

She felt that way, shock passing ricochet-fashion from synapse to synapse. "*Capicornia's* been talking to Waratah?"

"Aye, since midnight." He sat up. "Hadda wheedle her, mind. She don't like none of your machine trash, like you's spliced in, but we explained, gotta be done, keep Waratah thinkin'. So…"

"My gods," Julia whispered, perhaps a prayer. "She's not saying *Auntie Beau Dee!*" She swooped on Cass, smacked his full lips with a kiss. "She's saying *antibody!*" She took off for the elevators fast, all trace of exhaustion expunged.

❯━━❮

They swarmed like locusts, eating the rot as if it were the most delicious fodder for their kind. In their wake, fresh tissue extruded as tenuous, hair-thin tendrils, rapidly meshing, weaving, spinning complex nets sparkling with constellations of energy. Living thought. Merton, Sylva, Gupta, and Romano held their breath, watching, but Julia was sure. *Capricornia* was so sure, she was as complacent as Cass Diarmid, who'd turned his attention back to the show, and some new acrobatic routine that wasn't working out.

Silva subsided into a chair and dropped his head into both hands. "If I were the praying kind, I'd be thanking somebody's god right now for sweet mercy."

"Thank the travellers," Frankie snorted. "Their biotech is light years different, grown from different stock, in different soil, back in an age of cowboy entrepreneurs when every man and his uncle could tinker in the shed. You can believe me, they birthed some monstrosities! They also," she mused, "brought into being some angelic forms of life. *Capricornia* has more in common with a yew tree than anything developed in our labs. Also something in common with the brain structure of a mud wasp, amplified a trillion times. Does she think? Not as we do. But it's a mistake to believe all knowledge and memory spring from the brain. They're rooted in every cell in your body. Those are your great-grandmother's ears you're wearing: you don't know it, but your body does." She shook her head in wonder, watching swarming antibodies wage war upon Hannah Myles's accidental pathogen. "So much to study, so much that's new."

"I intend to," Julia said so softly, she might have been talking to herself. "Why don't you stay on here, Frankie?"

"Possible." Merton considered the western view, where the sun set in oceans of crimson, gold and silver. "I like it here." Her eyes glittered with humor as she considered Julia. "I did *Carnival Capricornia* last night. They're rather good. I haven't seen a live show, from a showboat, since I was a girl."

"Get out more often," Ranjit told her. "It's good for you."

"But first," Frankie said with malicious relish, "I'm going to ream a bastard called Alexander Taylor Silkin a very large new one, and watch him change color when he realizes we cured EP-105d. Oh yes, it has a name. One of a suite of bio-weapons developed by several major players in global politics in the decades when industry went offworld and humanity made its choice: go to space, or huddle in ramshackle, tumbledown buildings we were patching up just faster than the environment took them to pieces. You couldn't even go outside without protective gear and a breather mask, yet a gaggle of patented bastards in every major capital city funded programs to develop some 'doomsday bug' to kill a city. As if," she spat cynically, "it would only kill one city—always *theirs,* never *ours.*"

"Doomsday weapon," Silva said disgustedly. "Still tanked at Amundsen-Scott, goddamnit."

"And they sprung a leak somewhere in their quarantine routines," Tonia added. "*Capricornia* was infected. What, containment breach?"

Merton only shrugged. "They're wise to it now. They'll have tightened up their act, and besides—" She chuckled. "Vast amounts of our dear 'Auntie Beau Dee' will be cultured in a thousand labs. Every city gets the vaccine. IDR can retire EP-105d. Still, I'll enjoy rubbing Colonel Silkin's nose in it."

Fatigue crept over Julia like a thick, quilted blanket. She sat on the couch, sunset behind her, while their voices receded, the lab faded to gray, on into black, and she slithered into dreams without realizing she'd fallen asleep. Even in dreams, she'd begun to plan. She had a favor to ask, but already knew what he'd say.

—•—

"You really are leaving." Roy made no secret of his disappointment. "I thought you'd change your mind."

Across Concord, the deciduous trees were winter bare but the eucalypts thrived, and in spring the northern hemisphere species would burst back into life. Most were healthy *enough;* for them, autumn had simply come early this year. Julia gazed with a smile at South Terminal 4. The showboat idled on standby; tents and arena had vanished. The inevitable mob of fans hung on, harassing the charismatic stage master and magician before *Capricornia* uncoupled from her moorings. Cass signed programs, show posters, images, a woman's bare chest, with promises to return next January with a bigger show, new acts, holographs, fresh music.

"I'm leaving," Julia told Roy, not without a thread of regret. "Frankie's taken over my position, you won't miss me."

"I will," he argued.

"I meant, in the professional sense." She took his hand. "I'm easily replaced."

"Not to me." He kissed her fingers. "But I know you have to go."

"So much to learn—like going back to class." She mocked herself with a chuckle. "I asked Cass to let me talk to *Capri*, and she agreed to let me study her. She's so different from Waratah, it's like comparing humans with the great apes. Oh, we're brothers on the evolutionary bush, but look at the difference a tiny percentage shift in DNA makes: human and gorilla."

At her feet sat the remainder of her bags. Gallant to the last, Roy shouldered them and walked her to the pylon, by blue pacifica and oleander, roses and camellias, all bee-busy in the early February sun. Cass had escaped the mobbing fans and waited for her in the lift, clearly ready to go. *Capricornia*'s vast green-gold helium cells had swollen for maximum lift; she tested every control surface as Julia watched. She too was ready to move on, always the traveller, only at home in the sky.

Roy dumped the bags by Cass's bare feet and gave both hands to Julia. "Keep in touch."

"I will," she promised. Cass's thumb hovered over the control panel. "Besides, this is a showboat. She's always back, every year."

"New acts, new music—hologram horses and lions," Cass promised genially. "Hey, Roy, take care, man. Next year, huh?"

"I'll book early," Roy promised, and stepped back.

The lift rose swiftly up the gantry. Moments after it reached the top, *Capricornia* cast off and rose away, elegant, exquisite, fluorescing in the morning sun.

ANEMONE
Jake Marley

Delight in the night.

My girlfriend believed in a god with a name like someone clearing their throat, but I didn't judge—I was never the religious type. I used to wish I could believe in something like that. In the early hours before dawn, staring up at the chipped ceiling of my lonely apartment, I would wish so hard that there was more to this world. My chest would ache and my heart would ache as I thought about how my wish wasn't being heard by anyone or anything, not now, not ever, so I might as well just roll over and try to sleep.

I never slept well, but my girlfriend did. Cara slept like a worn-out puppy, loose-boned and puddled, taking up most of my small bed. It was like she'd spent all day running around the park, chasing the squirrels and geese. When I'd prop myself up on my elbow and watch her dream, she was always smiling in the dark.

Cara's real name was Jennifer Anne Carapace, which I discovered after seeing her driver's license when she was carded on our seventh date. And she was always Cara to me, even if her name never sounded quite right in my mouth. She liked long cozy sweaters and thin leggings and untied sneakers. Her hair was a bedhead mess, but it took her almost an hour to get just right. I loved her, as much as I could love anyone at the time. As much as I understood what love was. She loved me, too, but not as much as she loved her god. And who can blame her? I couldn't really hold a candle to omniscience.

I was never the religious type, like I said, but I went to church with her a few times. This was a shadowy building, abandoned some time ago—a warehouse or forgotten storage space, accessed through a small, windowed office that Cara called a narthex. Cara had described her church as if it were a grand cathedral before I joined her, so the reality was a let-down. It was strange for me, following her in, looking around at the cobwebbed corners and the dull, gray concrete floors. But it was no worse than any other place of worship, I guess. Every church I had ever stepped in felt so small, so pathetic. These were the houses of god that belonged to tiny people with limited imaginations, not a divine, unknowable being. Most of these parishioners never bothered to even think about it, they just accepted the lies from their parents, their ancestors, their heritage. They built temples and raised their hands to the sky, but they didn't understand that there were no mighty deities in the clouds waiting for their voices, their songs, their love or praise.

Church made me ugly.

Cara was smiling, filled with joy, and she grabbed my hand and showed me around. The others there all had the same dreamy look on their faces—well-rested, cheerful, and sweet. Sometimes when they spoke their eyes bugged out or their tongues got in the way of the words they were saying, but I always understood that their devotion was from a place of mad love. Of obsession.

At the time, I wasn't self-aware enough to realize how envious I had been. How jealous.

The Church of the Unpronounceable Cough, as I called it in my own head, was filled with odd ducks and broken birds. People who didn't much belong anywhere else, as far as I could tell. They fluttered and swayed, singing their warbling siren songs and holding hands, offering up their voices, their love, their manic-fluted calls, to the leathery thing on the altar that looked a little like an egg and a little like a sea anemone. Cara would look at me troubled sometimes, and I'd realize that I was just saying "anemone, anemone, anemone," over and over again because I liked the way it sounded in my head and on my tongue. It was a fun word in my mouth. I'd snap my jaw shut and I would hang my head and apologize, and Cara would smile in that forgiving way she had and say, "It's not a problem, darling."

At first, I didn't like the "darling" part, but Cara said it all the time and soon enough, it made me feel loved. It made me feel, if just for a little while, like there really was something greater than all of this noise and mess and grease. That perhaps the world might just be the product of compassion and swelling beauty. Then I'd get embarrassed and go sulk and I wouldn't call her back for days and I'd text that I was too busy if she wanted to hang out, even though I knew I was hurting her feelings.

Love was like that—at least it was for me. Love brought happiness, and happiness brought guilt, and guilt brought out something darker and meaner in me, and then I felt shame. Shame was easy to understand, and it was comfortable. It was the black swarm that buzzed and skittered in my mind, and I wouldn't be able to see Cara until the swarm subsided.

"I missed you, darling," she had said.

And I'd lie, because lying was easier than telling the truth. "I missed you, too."

Cara's church never frowned on our relationship. She didn't have the same hang-ups about drinking or sex or swearing or anything like they have in other religions. She was allowed to be exactly herself, to do exactly as she wanted to do. I don't know why, but sometimes I found it infuriating.

Cara dreamed peacefully and I slept fitfully, and we both woke to the same empty, hopeless world.

She liked to clean my little apartment. "Tidying," she called it. She'd hum to herself and ask questions, as if she were trying to dig into my heart and see what was inside. "If you don't work, how do you afford this place?" Or, she'd say, "Who's that sour-looking woman in the picture by your bed? Is that your sister or your mother?" Or, once, Cara stood in the center of the living room and said, "Darling, I just noticed you don't have any books. Isn't a life without books kind of dreary?"

I let her play house as I cowered on the sofa and punched nonsense into my phone and pretended that everything was going to be alright.

———— ◆ ————

There was a plan in place. My belief had nothing to do with it.

———— ◆ ————

When we went to her church on Tuesday nights the parking lot was always crowded with older cars, dusty and in need of a wash. There were no kids at Cara's church so none of the dirty back windows of the cars had dicks drawn on them, or WASH ME scrawled in wobbly, elementary school letters. There were a few faded bumper stickers on a couple of the cars, like they'd printed them up special a decade back. They were dull yellow stickers with black writing. DELIGHT IN THE NIGHT, they said.

I read it once or twice, walking through the parking lot, holding Cara's hand. And I repeated the phrase, under my breath. I liked the way it sounded in my mouth.

"Delight in the night, delight in the night, delight in the night."

It was like anemone. A mantra, of sorts. It felt right.

The others at Cara's church started to recognize me, and they would come right up to me and shake my hand and say things like, "Hey, buddy, you're looking good!" or "Great to see you again!" or "Here he is!"

I always pulled my hand away from them, tucking it into my pocket. Or I would hide behind Cara, trying to smile, trying to be polite, but knowing that a scream was rising in my throat. My actions only encouraged them, and they'd laugh like we were both in on the same joke. They'd laugh until they couldn't breathe, until their faces turned red. Their eyes never laughed, though. I had seen eyes laugh before, sometimes, especially when I was a kid, before the sickness of adulthood got hold of me, but the eyes of the congregation never, ever laughed. Their eyes darted from me to Cara, slick and rolling, as if they were coated in desperation-sweat every time they blinked.

As if those eyes were keeping secrets.

"Ease up, darling," Cara whispered to me. "You're crushing my hand."

The service, like all church services, was intensely dull and hollow. They sang to their god and rushed forward to touch the leathery thing on its altar, and I would sit with my mouth shut, feeling numb, feeling lost, feeling alone, as life quickened around me and the jubilant congregation celebrated regardless of my inadequacies. Stay or go, they didn't care what I chose to do. They could delight in the night with their mighty anemone, and I could sit in the far corner, arms crossed, hating them.

I knew I shouldn't resent them . . . and I knew I shouldn't be surprised that I did. Regardless of desire, I was never the religious type.

———◆———

It was a sequence of events, one after another. There's a word for that, I know there is. It's on the tip of my tongue.

———◆———

At breakfast, one Wednesday morning, eating wobbly fried eggs and wobbly bacon and wobbly toast, Cara said I looked ill. I said I hadn't been sleeping so great and she did one of those little aw-sounds of sympathy and called me darling, again, and I knew right then I was going to break up with her. Every Tuesday night I skulked home with her and cowered in bed, shaking as she slept, as if I were poisoned by her faith, and every Wednesday morning I was hangdog tired and I woke with what felt like a hangover. Cara and her fellow parishioners could rejoice and revel in the misshapen thing on its altar, their Unpronounceable Cough, but their secretive eyes told me I was left out of it. They worshipped, while I hid from the immeasurable weight of their watchful god.

They slept easily, while my thoughts raced and shrieked.

I had to be rational, that was the fundamental problem. I had to see the world as it really was, not as I wished it could be.

There was no god. That was the weight hefted onto my shoulders, the profane knowledge.

If Cara could sleep untroubled while I carried that burden, then our relationship was probably doomed anyway.

"You feel clammy, darling," she said with a hand on my forehead. "We've gotta perk you up! Want a fresh cup of coffee?"

"No," I said, pinching the bridge of my nose. "I want you to get the fuck out of my apartment."

———◆———

Ritual.

The word is ritual.

Cara cried when we broke up, but I didn't. She asked me why, she asked me what happened, she asked me how she could fix it. All the while, the words on that dusty yellow bumper sticker rolled through my skull, over and over again, haunting me. *Delight in the night, delight in the night, delight in the night.*

It was a long weekend full of desperate phone calls and sorrowful messages. Once, Sunday night, Cara returned to the apartment and shouted and pounded on the door, demanding an explanation.

"I love you, darling! Can't you understand that? Don't you know how important you are to me? I know you better than you know yourself! You need me and you need this. You need this more than anyone I've ever known!"

She kicked at my door, making a spectacle of herself. She cried out dramatically. She begged me to let her back in, to open the door, to open my heart.

"You're everything to me, darling," she said.

My forehead was pressed against the door, only inches away from her shouting insistency. When my mouth moved, my lips pushed against the wood. "Anemone," I whispered. "Anemone. Anemone."

Then she stopped calling and stopped coming around and I was allowed to once again find my own form of peace.

On the first of every month, my mother called me with her questions. She had a bright voice and a false Southern accent.

"Are you sleeping well?"

"Of course," I lied. Every night I stayed awake, afraid of the night outside, afraid of the weight in the clouds, the unstoppable gravity of our hidden sun, praying for dawn. And in the mornings, I would make myself shitty eggs and shitty bacon and shitty toast and I would stare at the walls of my shitty apartment and wonder at how it got so filthy so fast.

"Do you still have my picture by your bedside?" There was a hum behind her voice, like she was calling from a party. People cackling behind her, people calling her over, calling out her name.

"Of course," I said. *That sour woman*, Cara had called her. In the photo she was so young, but so upset by the world that she forgot how to smile. She never wanted to be a mother. Not now, and not at sixteen, either.

"I'll know if you're lying," she said, and someone drunkenly started singing to her.

"I know, Mother."

"You're not lying, are you?"

"No, Mother."

"You've had a woman over, haven't you? Are you in love?"

"No . . . I mean, yes, I've had a woman over, but no, I'm not in love."

Mother clucked her tongue. "You should be ashamed of yourself."

I said nothing. We both knew how I felt. We both knew about the black swarm, and we both knew that shame was my oldest friend.

"Don't lie to me," she said.

"I wouldn't."

"Mm-hmm," she said, doubting me. "Then don't lie to yourself."

I didn't know what to say to that.

"Hon, you there?"

"Yes, Mother."

"Is your allowance adequate, or should I make another phone call?"

"I have what I need," I said, looking around my hateful little apartment. No, there weren't any books. It was dreary.

"Are you eating? You know how you get when you don't eat right."

"I'm fine," I said.

"And . . . I hate to ask, but you know I have to . . . you're not going to show up again here, are you? You're not going to embarrass me like that?"

"No, I won't."

"Because when you do, it complicates things for me, hon. It scuffs them up."

"I know, Mother."

"I'm still a young woman, and these people in my new life, they don't understand you. They don't know where you fit in. They *can't* understand, and when they look at me and they look at you and they try to do the math, their noses wrinkle up in that way that makes me know they think less of me, and it hurts me. It cores me out. And you don't want me to feel like that, do you?"

"Of course not," I said.

"Of course you don't, praise God. You're a good boy. I'll tell Rick to send you some extra cash this month."

The Reverend Rick was my mother's latest conquest. He'd won the lottery after a vision from Jesus, and he'd used the money to start a church. Every Sunday the pews were filled with the same kind of blank-eyed zombies that spend hours at a time slipping quarters into slot machines, praying for the jackpot that never comes.

"You don't need to do that," I said, meaning it.

"Nonsense. A little extra spending money, and you can take that girl out for a proper meal."

"Thank you, Mother," I said, because it was the right way to get her off the phone. I sat shaking for a long time after that conversation, burying my face in my hands, trying not to scream . . . and then I realized it was Tuesday.

———•———

A sequence of events, one after another.

And belief had nothing to do with it.

———•———

I watched from across the street until everyone went inside and the service started. The dull yellow moon was caught in the powerlines. I'd bit one of my thumbnails to the quick, and it hurt and throbbed, matching my racing heartbeat.

I tried to ask myself why I would do this, but I couldn't come up with an answer, so I ran through the parking lot, past the dusty cars and their yellow bumper stickers and I snuck into the church. The usher at the front was a toothy man in a shiny black coat with bright red rosettes high on his cheeks. "You're here!" he said, and I heard genuine happiness in his voice. "Aren't you a sight for sore eyes."

He held the door for me, and guided me inside.

There were only twenty or so people in the church. Cara said it used to be much larger, much grander, but the world was moving on without them. She never said it with the bitter sadness I expected, but with a general understanding that this was part of the process, that one day that wheel would turn and they would be whole once again. Still, it was easy for me to hide in the back row, away from the leaning believers, away from their unnerving altar.

I didn't know their songs, and I couldn't follow their stories. My brain always slipped away, chasing its own thoughts, its own tail, until they all rose up and walked to their altar and touched their living god—that leathery egg, that sea anemone. A coral crown had grown upon it, sharp and organic, and more than one of the believers pierced their hands on the jagged points, leaving faint drops of blood. A small sacrifice to their living god.

I didn't go up there. I remained seated, but I wasn't the only one. Up in the front row, off to the side, sobbing into her hands, Cara was shunned as the others smiled and laughed and rejoiced in their service. They showed their wounds to each other. They giggled and kissed their bloody palms, then shuffled back to their seats.

I watched Cara for a long time, expecting to see that familiar smile, that peace around her eyes and the corners of her mouth, but she kept covering herself, kept wiping away her tears. She was utterly without delight. The others grinned at each other, big mouths, big teeth, but their eyes never smiled. Their eyes shared secrets and derisions. Their eyes were full of panic.

If they saw me, they never let on, and I wondered if I was being shunned, too.

———◆———

Delight in the night.

The tip of my tongue wiggled and writhed, but it was caught by the needle and bound by the thread and sewn to my lips and—

———◆———

After the service, Cara caught me in the parking lot as I was running away. "Why did you come back here?"

I shook my head. "I don't know."

"You're a shitty person."

"I know."

"You hurt me."

"I know."

"I'm stronger than you think, though. I don't need you."

"I know."

"But you came back here. I brought you here . . . I shared this with you because you were special, do you know that? Can you understand that's how I saw you?"

I said nothing.

"I don't just play around with boys. I don't fuck random guys and bring them here. I'm not like that."

"I never said you were."

"But you don't care, either! You just told me to get out. You wouldn't even talk to me, but now you're back here, and what? What are you looking for?"

"I'm sorry," I said.

"You don't get to hurt me like that. Nobody does."

"I understand," I said.

"I'm stronger than you think," she said.

"I understand."

"You don't . . . I wish you did, but you don't."

My mouth was dry. I hung my head and my hair covered my eyes. I couldn't look at her.

"Look at me," she said.

"Cara, I'm—"

"*Look at me.*"

I breathed in, breathed out. I opened my eyes. I raised my head.

"You think you're unlovable because you're broken," Cara said. "But what you can't get through your skull is that I loved you *because* you were broken. I never wanted to change you or fix you, I just wanted to be there for you. And you threw me away. You hurt me and wouldn't speak to me and you… you came back here. Was that to hurt me, too?"

"I don't know," I said. "It was Tuesday, and I—"

"What? You were bored? You were lonely? You wanted to see what kind of damage you did?"

I shook my head.

"Then what?"

I threw up my hands, useless. "It was Tuesday."

She turned away in disgust. I ran to her, meaning to turn her back to me, meaning to tell her how much I missed her, how much I needed her. I'd tell her about my mother and my allowance and my unbeliever's heart. I'd tell her everything I never told anyone else. I touched her shoulder, grabbed her arm, and I impaled my hand on something sharp, tangled in the wool of her sweater. I yanked my hand back, examining the meat of my palm in the orange glow of the lights in the parking lot. It felt like a splinter in there, something rooted deep and already sore. There was no sign of it, though. No divot or pinch, no bruise or blood. Still, I sucked at my palm, thinking swirling, bizarre thoughts of snakebites and harpoons, of anesthetic needles and rusty nails and I backed away, hurting.

I thought of a coral crown and grinning faces.

Cara had stopped walking, but she wouldn't look at me. Her voice was roughened, tight with emotion. "Are you going to come back here?"

I didn't answer.

"Did you find what you were looking for?"

I didn't answer.

She glanced back at me, just the once, and she saw me sucking my smooth palm, and she said, "You will know how loved you are, and you will know you don't deserve it."

———◆———

The true gods of our world are small, tangible creatures, kept alive by belief. They quiver with vulnerability.

And sometimes they die . . . just as all creatures die.

———◆———

I stumbled through the city, hoping my head would clear. There was a tension behind my eyes—a dull, constant ache like I was swimming deeper and deeper underwater, like the pressure was building. I opened my eyes and caught snapshots of civilization. A bone-thin woman grabbed a toddler by the hair and screamed into his little face. A man with bruised eyes dragged a limping dog by a chain, cursing the whimpering beast. Two white-haired ladies took turns screaming at passing cars as they tried to cross the street. A broken cat twitched pathetically in the gutter.

"Have a blessed day," a woman said, leaving a coffee shop. She bumped into a much taller man, barking into his phone, and she nearly spilled her drink. "Go to Hell!" she screamed, and the man jerked away from her like she was radioactive.

It was too much, and I had to sit down. I found a fountain splattered with pigeon shit and algae-green floaters drifting along the pool, and I slumped down onto the edge and buried my head in my hands. The noises around me—cars, birds, and the mumbling, hateful voices of humanity—grew louder and louder until I wanted to shriek.

I smelled him first—old food, piss, stale beer. A homeless man with a scab over one rolling eye. "Motherfuckers believe in a man in the sky, but they don't believe in taking care of their kids. Don't make no sense. I'm a rational individual. I'm rational as fuck. But I don't know how you rationalize morality. How do you half-believe in something, man? You say, yeah, there's a god, no doubt, no doubt. But then you turn around and say, all of you who are different have to die. You don't look like me, so you have to die. You don't live how I live, so you have to die. You don't believe in my god, so you have to die, am I right? What the fuck is that, man? That's hypocrisy, that's what that is. Duplicitousness. First, they lie to themselves, then they lie to each other, and then they cover up the lies they know about and the lies they worry about and the lies that might or might not be truths, and you know what that gets you, my brother? A fuckin' world full of liars, and a world where God's just another lie, ain't it? If the big man's believers can lie, then they can lie about believing."

And I said, "My girlfriend believes in god."

The homeless man scoffed. "Yeah? Which one?"

I tried to say the name. It came out sounding like a cat's hairball.

"Is that one the real deal?"

I shook my head. "I don't know." Then I shrugged. "I'm not the religious type."

———— • ————

I fell through the door and launched myself at the ringing phone, thinking, *Cara, Cara, Cara*, thinking, *Don't stop ringing, don't stop ringing*. I fumbled it, nearly dropped it, didn't even glance at the screen. And when I said, "Hello," the man on the other end of the line laughed a deep, preacher's rumble.

"You've strayed from the light," Reverend Rick said. He had the Southern accent my mother was trying so desperately to adopt, but he'd earned it genuinely by growing up in the sticks of Arkansas and the hills of Tennessee. He was the only man I'd ever heard use the phrase, *The South will rise again.*

"No, sir," I said, trying to hide my disappointment. Cara's name still fluttered in my head like a thousand-thousand wings.

"You callin' your mama a liar?"

"Not at all, sir," I said.

"She's worried about you," he said.

"I never meant for that to happen."

"What's that?"

"I never meant for her to worry, sir."

"Uh-huh. You remember the rules we talked about, don't you, son?"

My skin crawled when he called me son.

"Of course I do, sir."

"Of course you do. Uh-huh. And yet, your mother is cryin' at night." His voice became mocking, high-pitched, "*He's strayed from the light of Jesus. He's strayed.*" Then, gruff once again, "You think I'm lyin'?"

"No, sir."

"You get an allowance because of the rules."

"Yes, sir."

"You don't come around."

"No, sir."

"We can't have people think she's seeing some young buck on the side, can we?"

"She's my mother, sir."

"And who knows that, huh? You and me and her. So we can't have that, can we?"

"No, sir."

"And you're not to upset her, are you?"

"No, sir."

"And yet—"

"I would never—"

"*He's straay-aayed.* Shit. Cryin' herself to sleep like a mewling toddler, worried about her wayward boy and his premarital affair."

"It's not like that."

"Then why's she cryin' about it?" The Reverend boomed into the phone. He was sixty years old and his voice was made for amphitheaters and stages, not phones. "Why's she sayin' that you're lost? And why's she so worried you're going to try to come down here again, hmm?"

"I'd never, sir," I said. "You told me not to, and I won't ever—"

"Uh-huh," he said, interrupting me.

There was an angry red welt on my palm where I'd been sucking and sucking at it, trying to get the splinter out. I tucked the phone under my chin, wedging it with my shoulder, and I started picking at my palm with my thumbnail, trying to get at the shard inside of there.

"There were rules for a reason, son."

"Yes, sir."

"Simple rules, I thought."

"Yes, sir."

"And now I'm thinkin' you didn't get the message," Reverend Rick said.

"Sir?"

"I'm thinking you didn't get the message about the rules, son." I could hear the sadistic smile in his voice.

I stayed quiet, and my thumbnail tore into the skin of my palm.

"You hearin' me?"

"Of course, sir."

"I'm thinkin' maybe we need to change things up a little."

"Sir?"

"I'm thinkin' maybe we need to cut you off. No more allowance, no more free rent, no more free rides."

"Sir?" Panic in my voice, I couldn't stop it if I'd wanted to.

"Uh-huh. That's it. That's our solution, praise His name. You're a big boy, now, God bless you, and you can learn to take care of yourself."

"Sir, I'm—"

"You interrupt me again and I'll drive up there and beat you down myself, you hear me?"

I bit my tongue and tasted blood. I dug into my palm, watching the skin stretch and tear.

"Well, do you hear me?"

"Yes, sir."

"Uh-huh. You'd better, son. See, that's the one thing I miss about being a prison guard, praise the Lord. Not enough ways to kick some-one's ass out here in the world. Plenty of reasons, though, and you're one of them, boy. You're the number one pain in my backside. I told you before, boy—you don't want me as an enemy."

Before I could stop myself, I had to ask for clarification. "Anemone?"

"An enemy."

"Anemone?"

"An enemy, damn it all. You don't even fuckin' listen."

"Anemone," I said.

"What's that? You're being smart, huh? Well, say it once more, you little shit-for-brains. I fuckin' dare you."

I didn't think. I just opened my mouth.

"Anemone."

"A—"

"*Anemone!*" I screamed into the phone, then I hung up on him and threw the phone against the wall, smashing it to pieces.

Nobody came to evict me, and nobody came knocking, asking where I've been. I lost track of hours, days. I didn't shower, I didn't eat.

Something was bad wrong inside of me.

My gums bled, and one morning I woke up and choked on a tooth that had slipped free. Moaning and scared, I left my apartment, trying to get out between the ticking seconds of my watch. I didn't wear shoes, and my scabrous toes jittered on the sidewalk. There was a yellow film on my teeth and I bit at the air, at my reflection in strip-mall Plexiglas, at passing cars. My fists clenched and unclenched spasmodically. My left eye twitched.

Sometimes I ran, loping at an angle. Or I hobbled between street signs and crouched behind bus benches. The sky was damp silver, threaded with bruised violet. The town was bled gray, static and hollow. My skin crawled, and I only stopped to scratch at it when I was in a hedge or pressed up against a wall. My fingernails came away coated in blood. The world tasted like oil and grime.

I whimpered at the feeling that Cara's god was watching me, and I howled when I knew that it wasn't.

I had never felt so alone.

Reverend Rick's church used to be a Circuit City, and I knew it was a Sunday when I saw all the nicely-dressed people milling around, shaking hands, smiling. A woman squealed as I pushed past her, and she shielded her children behind her wide hips. A deacon with slicked hair and a bolo tie tried to stop me, but I crashed into him and sent him sprawling on the sidewalks.

I screamed for my mother and caught a glimpse of her wide, horrified eyes before the man at her side peeled away, red-faced, and rushed toward me. Reverend Rick shucked his jacket and threw it at my mother, and started rolling up his sleeves. His red face turned purple, but it paled again when he was only a few steps away. His eyes got big and round and he said, "Jesus, son . . . what's happened?"

And I held out my hands to him, begging for salvation, for sanctuary, and I screamed, "*I don't know.*"

———◆———

My mother was crying, and Reverend Rick was trying to calm her down.

"I called a doctor, honey, and I've said prayers over him. He's God's child as much as yours. Jesus will watch him."

I'd never heard him speak with that calm authority, with genuine love and care, and I knew that whatever happened he would take care of my mother.

I was soaking wet, slumped into a chair in Rick's office, his coat draped over my shoulders. "What'd I do?" My voice trembled.

Both of them turned, but they didn't get any closer than they had to. It was only the three of us in that room, and my mother clutched her husband like a drowning woman clinging to a lifeline.

"You went for a dip in our baptism pool, son," Reverend Rick said. Here, in person, the meanness I'd heard over the phone was stripped away.

"Were you *trying* to drown yourself?" Mother asked.

"Of course not," I said, but I wasn't fully sure.

"You're burning up. I think you've caught a bug, or an infection in that hand of yours. Now, like I told your mama, I've called a doctor, and—"

"Do you feel God here?" I asked.

"Pardon?"

"This place," I said, standing. "When you're here, do you feel God's presence?"

"Of course I do," Reverend Rick said. "I built Him this house, to praise His name and to thank Him for the gifts that He's bestowed upon me."

"And you?" I asked my mother.

She nodded. "Every time I step foot within these walls, I feel the Lord is with me."

I had no more questions. They couldn't stop me from leaving. I don't really know if they even tried.

⸻◆⸻

I broke into Cara's church using a fist-sized chunk of concrete from a broken parking stall. I was worried I would be followed, at first, but the wound in my hand kept me safe and protected from curious gazes and prying eyes. I sank to my fingers and toes, scuttling through the narthex, listening for good-natured cheer, for a "There he is!" or a "You're looking good!" or a "Great to see you again!"

All was silent in that house of worship.

My tongue felt too thick for my mouth, so I let it tumble out between my lips, drooling a thick, phlegmy liquid down my wrinkled shirt.

On the altar, the leathery thing that looked a little like an egg and a little like a sea anemone started to pulse with an arrhythmic heartbeat. *Ba-bump-ba-ba-BUMP, ba-bump-ba-ba-BUMP. Delight in the NIGHT, ba-bump-ba-ba-BUMP.*

Here, at last, was a tangible god. There was more truth in that heartbeat than in any sacred text or benediction.

The rhythm of the heartbeat matched the words in my head, and I let them out as if I were lancing a blister. "Delight in the night," I said, my voice rising. "Delight in the night! *Delight in the night!*"

The pulsing god on its altar was three times the size of a watermelon. I tore off its crown of coral, flinging it aside as it cut me, and when I dug my fingers into the god, its leathery skin crinkled and peeled away like an eyelid. The thing under the delicate leather was smooth and jellied, smeared with bright red blood. I scraped at it with my fingernails and saw something the color of marbled jade beneath the blood, glistening milky green. I felt its heartbeat under that smooth flesh, and I heard it scream in my head as I curled my fingers and clawed into it, gouging the meat of it and scooping it into my yawning mouth.

Oh, god, I thought. *Oh, GOD.*

It was thick and chewy, rubbery and gritty. I choked on it and it gagged me, but I forced it down, swallowing every stringy bite. It tasted of the ocean and of bitter insects. It tasted of raw, spoiled meat. It tasted of a roadkill harvest squirming with maggots. Under the foulness of it, though, there was something unexpected. With every bite, I tasted lives on my tongue and prayers between my teeth. I swallowed sanctimonious sorrows and unfettered joys. The gore of the living god coated my chin, my arms, my chest. I snorted blood into my sinuses as I plunged my face into it, chewing, chewing, searching for that beating heart.

Connections came, and for the first time in my life I wasn't alone. I screamed into the cavity, pulling apart the threads and tendons of a malformed beast. At last I found its thrumming heart and I devoured it bite by bite.

I fell onto the floor, rolling on my back and staring up into the rafters of Cara's church, as my own tears of joy spilled from my eyes.

I spent most of the day digesting the thing from the altar, until I finally rolled over and stumbled down the aisle. I washed the gore from my head and hands in the bathroom, staining the countertop in reds and greens and making ghoulish faces at myself in the smudgy mirror. I laughed, afraid of what I had done, worried that the abyss of loneliness would return to my tarnished soul as the experience faded away. I tried to hold onto it, feeling the heaviness in my gut, seeing the smeared mess I'd left in the bathroom, scared that it was a squirmy, fleeting thing.

Belief was so much harder to do than I ever expected.

But as each moment passed and my faith clamped its teeth into my soul, I almost wept with relief.

"Delight in the night?" I asked, and I walked back to the altar and shoved the carcass from its place of power. I wore its crown upon my head and I crawled up and stretched out on its altar—on *my* altar—and closed my eyes.

Before that moment, I had never known such peace in sleep, and I had never felt so safe and so shameless.

The ritual began as I slept, and I woke to their songs. My eyes were heavy and unfocused, but I blinked back my bloody tears to once again see the rafters of that shadowy church. I felt their hands on me, holding me down, communing with me. Everyone wanted to touch me, and in every hand and fingertip I felt their joy, their ecstasy, their praise. The walls of deception were gone, and ideas were transferred through touch. Language and social anxieties didn't exist, and I felt their thoughts. They knew all about me. Cara most of all.

She was congratulated and embraced. I felt her love and peace and faith. "Oh, darling, isn't it magnificent?"

Her delight lit up the world.

They stripped my clothes from me and put me back on my altar. They had needles and thread, and they sewed my tongue to my lips. They tied my ankles together, tied my knees to my chest, and sewed my skin at each bend to keep them tight. They wrapped my arms around my head and sewed my fingers together, right hand to left hand. My heart pounded furiously against my ribs. I looked upon their faces, their wide, feverish eyes, their beatific smiles, and I felt the world thrumming with energy, with power, with knowledge.

I saw their secrets, now, and I saw how scared they had been. Their god had been dying, and so had their church, but things were different, now. Things were so much better.

I felt their love as they sewed my eyelids closed.

"Delight in the night," Cara said, and I wanted to call out to her, to thank her for choosing me, for showing me how marvelous the universe could be, how full of unknown joy.

"Delight in the night!" my people said, and their voices rose to a scream. No cathedral was better for this moment as I felt the delicate leather stretching over my head and shoulders, over my bare back, over my body. "Delight in the night! *Delight in the night!*"

And it was good.

I WILL FIND YOU,
EVEN IN THE DARK

Jessica Landry

I

The world is static. Lines and waves and noise that crowd your vision like an old VCR, the one where you had to adjust the tracking to get a clearer picture. I found one of those once, a VCR, in an expired man's house. Took it home, cleaned it up nicely, and started the tape that was stuck inside. A home movie played back, one from a time when people had hand-held cameras, when the world only began to record their memories.

The man was much younger and leaner than how I'd found him. He smiled at the camera, shoving his face into the lens, then ran off into the water behind him, splashing some screaming children. The picture was pixelated but the colours were vibrant—greens and golds and yellows. Colours that didn't exist anymore, not in this neon red landscape. I sat there, watching them play over and over again as though I was the one behind the camera, living this moment with them, this man and these children my own.

What happened to them? To the person behind the camera? Where were they when I went to this man's filthy apartment, when I scraped what was left of him off the floor, his body left to decompose for months, his chip the only tangible piece left of his withered corpse?

Who knows.

But that's why I was there when no one else was.

It's my job.

II

The call came in early Thursday morning. I was the on-call supervisor, sitting at my desk, flicking through case files and filing reports. I had sent my skeleton crew home to get a decent night's rest before the calamity hit—the requests mostly came later in the mornings, when the sun had risen high enough to rouse the smell of expired bodies. Usually it was the neighbours who called it in, older people crammed like sardines into rundown apartment complexes called Commons. People without family. People biding their time until their bodies expired and the only thing left of them was their chip. People called the unwanted.

As a cleaner, it was my job to be first on the scene after an unwanted was discovered. I'd go in, usually to Sagashi City, a small town designated solely for the unwanted—retirees with no family, no money, people simply waiting for their bodies to be done with them. After removing what was left of the bodies into the organic matter incinerator, lovingly dubbed OMI by my team, we would get to work removing the unwanted's earthly possessions. I'd let my workers pack trinkets, sort through items to be resold, and do some cleaning in the main rooms, leaving the body and any of its leftover stains for me.

I'm sure the kids who worked under me might've thought I was being selfless by taking the worst part of the job for myself, and I certainly didn't correct them otherwise. But if there's one thing I've learned in my thirty-odd years of existing is that no one does anything out of the goodness of their own heart.

And that's why I steal memories.

We all have chips implanted in our skulls, just below the ear. A long time ago, people got tired of carrying around useless items that would only weigh them down, so someone decided, hey, might as well install a port into your brain so you can upload, download, erase, duplicate memories as you please! I'm sure it's a little more complicated than that, but that's the gist of it.

Thing is, everyone thought the idea was great. No more lugging around a cellphone. No more owning a computer and having it go blue-screen-of-death on you. No, simply insert a chip into your new port, undergo a slight corneal transplant to access your retina screen, and voilá, you can now document your whole life at the blink of an eye.

"Open," I said, digitally signing off on my reports as the neon blue message icon popped up on my retina screen. Next door neighbour called in, complaining of a distinct smell. The landlord got into the apartment and found the body. The woman had expired about a week ago, late 80s, no family to claim her or her belongings.

"Responding: Elena Wasureta, six-oh-five-two," I said, transmitting the message back to dispatch. "Going solo on this one, sent the rest of the crew home."

"Wasureta, six-zero-five-two, confirmed, syncing in now," replied Shonji. She worked at the head office downtown. I had never met her in person, but we sometimes bantered back and forth through the waves.

A solid blue dot appeared at the top corner of my retina screen, letting me know Shonji had linked to my chip, allowing her to record the job. This was common practice these days, your employer accessing your chip and watching your routine. It's how they keep everyone in line.

"Sync confirmed," I replied, flipping myself off. "Hey Shonji, how many fingers am I holding up?"

"Very funny, Elena," she said, dryly. "All looks good on this end, thank you."

"Any day." I stood up from my desk and stretched. Fluorescent lights buzzed overhead. Another day, another expired.

"Hey, Elena?" Shonji's voice crackled over the static.

"Yeah?"

"Bring extra supplies for this one."

III

I pulled up to the address in the company van, an overcrowded Common in Sagashi City overlooking Lake Pacific. The bright lights of New Vancouver some thirty clicks away shone from across the water, the city's reflection rippling like a million little pieces of shattered glass. I always found it funny how such a rundown neighbourhood had such an amazing view.

I gathered my equipment from the back and I logged onto the company's file server waiting for it to load, gazing up to the very top of the shitty Commons that I'd been at already twice this week.

The apartment number flashed on my retina screen: 1142. Next to it, newly uploaded, the photo of an old woman with dark, curled hair and tired eyes: Ms. Oboeru.

———◆———

That first step into someone's home is always surreal. Everything's how they left it, to them, not more than a moment ago. A once-hot bowl of noodles now ice cold and mouldy. A book stuck in a middle of a chapter, the words never to be finished. A fork and knife set on the table, a napkin wedged between them. It always looks as though I'd stepped into the house of someone who'd run out to the corner store.

What sets it apart is the smell.

Ms. Oboeru's body was slumped over at her dining room table, her skin black, her body crumpled at the waist as though she'd started to sink into herself. A who-knows-what of black liquid pooled around her corpse, running down the metal legs of her chair. The same black liquid seemed to streak down what was left of her face.

Her file said approximate date of expiration had been ten days prior, but she looked as though she'd been gone for a few weeks.

I scanned the room, ensuring that my feed—and Shonji—saw the whole apartment. A small dining room and kitchen area, an open door to her bedroom at the back, and a sitting room with the sliding doors ajar on my left, something brightly coloured inside catching my eye, even in the dark.

I pushed both the sliding doors in, the light from the kitchen dimly illuminated the room's contents: children's toys.

They looked ancient, from a time when screens and chips and ports didn't exist. I knelt and picked one up. Though it was dusty and some of the paint was peeling, I was sure the colours were as vibrant as the day they'd been painted on. This toy had a square frame painted bright red with five metal poles inserted from side to side, each with ten or so beads of varying bright colours on either side. I tried to yank one of the beads off, but it seemed they only followed the path of the poles.

I placed that toy down and looked at the others: an old rotary telephone on wheels with a smiling face, a plastic cash register with half its stickers peeled off, and a small instrument with colourful metal slats.

What looked like static caught the corner of my eye near the end of the room, the part where the light didn't reach. I peered into the darkness as something seemed to flutter behind the stacks of boxes that filled the rest of the room from floor to ceiling.

"Wasureta, six-zero-five-two," Shonji buzzed in my ear, causing me to startle.

"Christ, Shonji," I buzzed back, my hand over my heart. "You scared the shit out of me."

"Yeah, sorry. Just wanted to get you back on track. Can't keep looking at relics all day. I've got a backup crew en route to you as we speak to assist with bagging and tagging all those items. I told you to bring extra supplies."

"Great, thanks," I said through grinding teeth. With backup on the way, I'd have to hurry.

I stood up and brushed myself off, the dust already collecting on my coveralls.

"Hey, Shonji, this unwanted didn't have any offspring, did she? Any grandkids?" I buzzed as I moved to my supplies.

"File says no known relatives," Shonji replied.

"Yeah, that's what I thought," I said, making my way to the front entrance, to the same position I stood when I initially scanned the room.

I closed my eyes.

When I opened them, the simulation started.

The scan of the room I had done earlier adapted as I moved, projecting a simulated reality that transmitted through my retina screen. The blue light pulsed as Shonji and whoever else was watching ingested what I was feeding them. They were none the wiser. They never had been.

To keep the finger pointed away from me, I didn't do this with every expired. There were often tell-tale signs of the kind of life a person had lived based on what their apartment looked like. Some led straight, boring existences. Others, like Ms. Oboeru with her old children's toys and boxes upon boxes of items, had secrets meant to be discovered.

I crouched beside Ms. Oboeru's body, examining what was left of her: she had no jewelry, nothing of importance on display. Her nails had been painted a deep red, the black of her decomposing flesh creeping in around them.

As the simulation ran me tending to Ms. Oboeru's remains as per company protocol, I tapped my index finger against the table. My fingernail lifted—one of my many homemade modifications—exposing a hacked Red Market chip to switch with Ms. Oboeru's actual memory chip.

I brushed away several loose strands of her curly black hair, letting my gloved fingers poke at her skin for the feel of metal. Just below her ear, I felt the plate to her port. The skin had fused around it so deep that it took several tries to cut the plate loose.

The same black substance dripping onto the floor had found its way into her port, solidifying around her chip.

I carefully reached out, getting the tips of my fingers around the edge of her chip. It stuck a little, but some elbow grease got it out.

I looked it over before I put it away, noticing that this wasn't the standard gold and black chip that we all had. This one was entirely red and looked fairly new.

I placed it under my nail for safe keeping, then took the fake chip and placed it in a metal box marked DO NOT DESTROY, the standard practice for any chip extraction.

I caught up with the simulation, which now had me feeding what was left of Ms. Oboeru to OMI. I closed my eyes, pretending to yawn.

When I opened them again, the sim stopped and I was back in realtime, alone in a dead woman's apartment.

IV

I used to live for an expired's memories. There are legal, government-sanctioned trips that anyone can take—a dog named Sparky here, a family experience there—when you've done them all a million times over, you want something more. Something different. You yearn for it and it yearns for you. I mean, wouldn't you want to live a hundred different lives if you could?

I'd often found myself going back to the same trip, one similar to that VHS tape I'd found years ago, one with blue skies and green grass and children laughing. One where I was the person holding the video camera.

I still enjoyed the occasional unsanctioned trip though. And by 'occasional,' I mean every day. I would go under to experience horrible things, things that I couldn't shake after I'd logged off.

I'd been clean for three years, staying away from any sort of memory, including making any of my own. But that didn't mean I didn't think about it all the time.

I sat at my kitchen table the following night after cleaning Ms. Oboeru's place, unwashed and still in my pajamas, flipping her red chip between my fingers. What was so special about this woman that I couldn't shake her?

Bring it to the Market, I tried to reason with myself. Let Carn take a look at it. She lives for this type of thing.

It made sense. But I hadn't seen Carn in years, since that last trip. We hadn't exactly parted on good terms.

But she was good at what she did. No chip could keep her out; no mod was too much. She was the one who'd helped me mod myself, who'd shown me the opportunities available on the Red Market. She could take an expired's memory and flip it around in the Market for public consumption within a day—three days faster than anyone else—clearing it of any traceable code or any viruses.

I got up from my chair and went into my bedroom closet, pulling out several small boxes from the floor, letting my fingers trace the wall. Finding the thin line where drywall split, I pressed my thumb against it and a tiny door popped open. Inside were a few things no one ever needed to find: a silver ring with an infinite symbol engraved on it, a chip of old memories that I had no desire to remember, and an external port, one that acted as a firewall between the user and the unfamiliar chip, should that chip be contaminated.

There, in my closet, I linked myself up to the external port and tried to insert Ms. Oboeru's chip, but it wouldn't fit. The red chip was too big.

"Shit," I said, unlinking myself and tossing the port aside.

Still, something tugged at me, something urgent. I knew it wouldn't work, but I brought the red chip to my own port with a hesitant hand, finding the extra slot. It clicked in, as though it had always belonged.

Three years of clean living. And it all went down the drain when I closed my eyes.

"How do I know it's working?" says a voice in the darkness.

"You'll know," a second replies.

Static. Then, a woman's face. Young. Dark, curled hair. Dark, round eyes filled with uncertainty. She regards herself in the mirror.

"Everything looks the same," she says, touching her face.

"Try looking at the top right corner."

She does, looking up to the ceiling. When she looks back at herself in the mirror, a neon blue light pulses at the top of her vision. When she looks to it now, she doesn't move.

"I see it," she says, voice weary. "Now what?"

The other woman in the room chuckles.

"Now you go home and continue on with your day. There's nothing else you need to do."

"Really? That's it?"

"Mmhmm."

"What about maintenance or cleaning or, I don't know, general hygiene of the hole you made in my head?"

"You should receive a message in a few hours after you've been entered into the system. That message will explain everything to you in further detail."

"You can't tell me anything more here? I mean, this is kind of a big deal."

"We only do the implants, sweetie. Sorry."

Hints of static creep into the woman's vision.

She leans forward, focusing on the blue dot as the static grows thicker.

"Is it supposed to do that?"

Static consumes the screen.

She's following a path through the woods, some place quiet and serene. A lake is on the right. Trees all around. Birds chirp. Someone beside her laughs.

"Aggie," a voice says.

Then, running.

She's running hard down the same path, the sound of her breath pounding in her ears. It's night now. Trees zoom by. She turns to her right: the lake, blue and rippling, a small wind.

Static licks at the edges of her vision.

There's something floating near the shore.

She runs harder.

Then, a black screen.

Error 2202_please contact system administrator.

I sat back in my chair, catching my breath. No trip I'd been on had jumped from memory to memory without a prompt, and I'd never encountered an error before.

I had to take this to Carn. There was something in these corrupt memories that she'd be able to fix. I had to see what else was on them.

I wiped my sweaty palms on my pajama pants, bringing my fingers to my port, getting the tips around Ms. Oboeru's chip.

But when I pulled, the chip didn't budge.

I tried again, wiping my hands more thoroughly.

It didn't move.

I got up, my legs weak and unsteady. I found my way into the bathroom, positioning myself in the mirror so I could see what was going on.

There was something black spilling from the chip, thick like paste. It had wedged itself between the chip and my port, acting as a superglue to keep the chip in place.

"Fuck," I muttered, terror and adrenaline coursing through my system.

"What are you doing?"

The voice came from behind me.

I spun around, nearly dropping to the floor, and saw a young girl, no more than ten, standing in the doorway. Her curly black hair framed her thin, pale face and made her dark eyes look like two dark holes in her skin. She stood motionless, waiting for a response.

"Uh, can I help you?"

The girl said nothing, only regarded me with dead eyes.

"How did you get in here?"

Her little body swayed slightly, as though a light wind had passed by.

"I'm lost," she finally said, almost like an afterthought.

"Do you live around here?"

She didn't answer.

"Where are your parents? It's really late."

"Where's Ms. Oboeru?" The girl looked up at me. "I need to speak with her."

Silence hung over us like a heavy cloud. She moved away, into the kitchen. I followed, slow as to not startle her, seeing that my front door was wide open.

"How did you—?" I started, one foot in front of the other. "What's your name?"

"I need to go home," she said, stepping out of my apartment. "Please, take me home."

I ran out after her, onto the eleventh-floor balcony.

But there was no one out there, in any direction.

I was alone.

V

I took the next few days off, citing stress from the job—an acceptable excuse that I often used.

I spent the better part of the day in bed, not wanting to open my eyes. If I did, would she be in the room with me, that little girl, huddled in the corner? Would she be floating over me, her dark eyes on mine?

Maybe it was stress after all. I'd cleaned up hundreds of expireds in my time, most of them old folks with no one left. But there had been the occasional few that were younger than the rest, the youngest being a 30-year-old woman. No family. No loved ones. She'd died by her own hand in the Commons. When I stepped into her apartment, the carpet had squished under my boots.

I rolled in bed and, on a whim, opened my eyes. The world outside my bedroom greeted me, and not much else. By that time, it was already early evening, not that there was much of a difference between night and day anymore—for the better part of the last 20 years, the city of Toksan had lived under a low-floating cloud of smog that veiled any attempt the sun tried to get through. During the day, the city was hazy and hard to move through. At night, it was a neon jungle. The low-hanging cloud above acting more like a ceiling, keeping the city and all its inhabitants contained like a dirty snowglobe.

Still, on some nights, the haze that covered the Pacific Lake cleared, and if you found the right spot, you could see the clean air that surrounded New Vancouver.

That was the dream—to someday move there, away from the slums and the sick and the dying. Away from the only city I'd ever known to the city across the water that I'd stared at my whole life.

And I was close to getting there.

After showering, trying again without luck to remove Ms. Oboeru's chip from my port, and having an internal battle on whether or not to go see Carn, I sat on my couch, half expecting the girl to pop out again. But all was still. My things were still, random things like dolls in glass cases, an old hammer with a wooden handle, a first-generation retina calibrator, and a small toy called a Beanie Baby. Things I'd collected over the years. Things that I'd taken from expireds.

My way of thinking had always been that I was doing them and the world a favour by taking some items off their hands and off the list for incineration. That's what we did at work with all the undesirable pieces left behind: put them in an orderly queue for burning. There were so many things that others seemed so careless with that I couldn't bear to watch burn, so I always took a little something home. Whether that was all for me, or that some part of me didn't want all the expired persons I had come across to simply vanish into thin air, I wasn't sure. But it was funny to think that when my time came, the only things left of me would be things I stole from everyone else.

As the early evening dissolved into the neon glow of the night, I became restless, going back to my 2000's television set and even earlier VCR to rewatch the old cassette that I'd found during one of my first solo jobs. It was a wonder both still worked being as old as they were, but my knack for electronics had served me well, old TVs and my own personal body mods included.

Distorted faces slowly started to appear through the static: the man, smiling. Children running around him. Colours that didn't exist any-more. I pulled my blanket tighter around me, nearly feeling a smile creep on my face. I watched them splash in the water, a green, lush for-est behind them; crystal blue water up to the man's knees. The two kids were having the times of their lives, splashing who I had now come to believe was their father, the smiles on their faces telling of their day.

"Come here, you," I said a split-second before the dad did on screen, giving chase to his youngest, a little girl in a blue watermelon bathing suit. She screamed and ran from him as fast as her little legs could carry her. He caught up to her in no time, grabbing her tiny body and tossing her into the air.

I smiled at what was coming next—he would embrace her, and she him. And it would just be the two of them living in that moment. A moment long gone for him, and maybe for her too, but alive and well for me, a voyeur of this private memory.

As the moment approached, the tracking on the TV started to wors-en, the grey and black static lines licking the corners of the television.

It grew worse as the moment played out, until it became so thick that I could hardly see the picture.

I went over to the VCR and tried to adjust the tracking, but it didn't seem to make a difference.

"Come on," I muttered, stopping the tape and yanking it from the slot. I pulled the top plastic piece back to examine the film, expecting it to be twisted and gnarled and unwatchable.

But it was fine.

I sat back and clicked off the television, and it was then that I saw the little girl in the screen's reflection.

We stared at each other through the reflection, my breath caught in my chest. Hers so silent, there was nothing to hear.

When I turned around, she had lowered herself to my level. Her face was perfectly smooth, perfectly round, perfectly pale. There was an innocence to her, a curiosity in those dark eyes, but something about her seemed off. Her clothes were dated and heavy, like they'd been wrung through the wash without being properly dried.

"Who are you?" I managed to get out.

She regarded me with her dark eyes, then said, "Have you seen Ms. Oboeru? I need to speak with her."

"How did—how do you know her?"

"She's my friend." The girl's expression didn't change, as though her answer had been pre-programmed.

"What's your name?"

"Aggie."

"I'm Elena."

She nodded and turned her eyes downward.

"Where are your parents?"

She cocked her head slightly, then replied, "Have you seen Ms. Oboeru? I need to speak with her."

"Aggie."

"I want to go home."

"Aggie," I said, forcefully.

She looked up.

"Have you seen Ms. Oboeru? I need to speak with her."

I reached out for her then, I'm not sure why. Maybe to try and shake her out of it, maybe to try and shake myself out of it.

Either way, my hands went straight through her.

She was a sim.

A ghost.

A virus.

Ms. Oboeru's chip was infected and I had inserted it into my port. The fact that her body had been black and secreting—I should've known better. But I let my impulses get the better of me, just like old times.

I shot up and ran to the bathroom, positioning myself in the mirror to see the chip. The dark tar that had covered a portion of it yesterday had spread throughout my port, spilling out onto my skin.

With everything in me and more, I pulled. I pulled and pulled and pulled. I wiggled, I used my palm, I even put my hand in a fist and tried beating the chip out.

It didn't budge.

"Please don't do that," Aggie's soft, sullen voice echoed from behind me. I turned to face her. The look she wore on her face nearly drove me to tears. "I need to remember."

A single tear spilled down her cheek. Aggie turned to static then, disappearing into the air before my eyes.

VI

I ran out into the evening haze, my bomber jacket pulled tightly around my body. The wind tossed my choppy black hair about as I kept my hands securely in my pockets, their contents critical to where I was headed.

The Red Market was no secret to anyone who ventured to it—not the legal part of it anyway. It was on the street, on the main drag, a bazaar draped under the red neon lights of downtown Toksan, the true Market hidden in plain sight.

Nestled in between stalls selling authentic New Vancouver air were countless others offering memories of all kinds. Some were government sanctioned, okayed by the head honchos and the bigwigs hidden in tall buildings that stretched above the polluted clouds. The okayed experiences were all happy, pleasant ones—memories of puppies and kittens, blue skies and kites flying on windy days. Things that helped us remember how life used to be. Things to keep us in check.

But some people wanted different.

Some people wanted to live full lives outside of their own, submerging themselves for years into memories.

Some wanted to hurt others.

Some wanted to watch others hurt.

I was not without blame for the spread of unsanctioned trips, but I was not the first to contribute to it, and I wouldn't be the last. Supply and demand, the Market called it. And demand was high. My job paid my rent. The demand let me save up for my dream.

I stopped at a booth selling maps and snowglobe holograms of Toksan—a real tourist attraction. The Market was quiet this late, most of the usual lurkers already in their trips and most of the tourists gone back to their hotels from the night.

"Dropping off?" The stall clerk stared at me with age-ridden eyes and a half-smile, like I was a child and she was my grandmother, ready to scold me for something I was about to do. I'd encountered her once a week when I came by to drop chips off for Carn, our middle-woman, but didn't know her name. I wondered if I'd come across her one day in the Commons, and what sort of memories she had inside her.

"Carn still back there?" I asked.

The woman's smile faded. She looked me over through squinting eyes. "I'm Elena Wasureta. We're old friends."

She muttered something under her breath, then disappeared behind the flaps of her stall's tent.

I turned to her wares while waiting, having never been around the stall long enough to see what they sold. I picked up a snowglobe of Mount Fuji and shook it from its base. Simulated snow floated down around the image of the old mountain, or, at least, of what it once looked like before it was lost to the shifting seas and tectonic plates. I pressed a button on the base and the mountain began to rumble, shooting smoke and ash from its spout, forming its own blanket of embers.

I wondered if that's how it had looked as the sea swallowed it whole—one last display of its powers as it fought to stay above the waters. As it fought to be remembered.

The old woman poked her head out from the curtains.

"Follow me," she said. "And leave the globe."

———◆———

We ventured down an empty back alley, the thoroughfare that connected all the stalls and that lead to the real reasons why most came to the Red Market. The alley had no protection from the buildings around it, so the neon red light was ever present on the smog above, forming its own sort of red canopy. It was almost suffocating.

At one point I had known the way to Carn's office, but I'd removed that memory a long time ago. Carn and I had set up shop down these back ways, our business an instant success thanks to the memories I was able to procure from my job. After I left Carn and all this, I still supplied the chips to keep the operation going but kept my distance. It's funny what money can do to a person.

We turned a corner, went down a slick set of stairs, and underneath a building through a dank tunnel. At a nondescript section of a brick wall, the old lady popped off her pinky fingernail revealing her own modded black and gold chip and inserted it into a small slot that would go unnoticed to anyone passing by.

As she did, the right side of the wall flickered but remained.

"Go on," she said, her nail going back on. She started away, not even turning to meet my eyes.

"Thanks," I muttered as I stepped through.

Junk was everywhere. Well, junk to everyone else, useful items to her. The cold, concrete walls were covered with old notes and photos and hologram posters that played clips from old bands. A thin line of frosted windows had been installed at the very top of the wall, where it met the ceiling, looking onto the ground of the back alley I had followed the woman down moments ago. The neon red found its way in through these windows, pulsing its vibrant colour into the cold room. Old tech, new tech, obscure things, modern things sat around me, there was barely any room to walk through. She had beds set up to test new trips in, she had several mod stations, and at the far end of the room was the hub, her desk lined with computers and ports and chips where she put everything together.

And that's where she sat, with her back to me, her shoulder-length brown hair swaying as she bobbed her head to some music.

I made my way through the rubble and peeked over her shoulder. She was editing a trip, filtering through a memory to piece together something more cohesive, more intimate. A sunny day on the beach, a couple holding hands. A love experience.

"Carn."

She spun around, eyes full of suspicion.

"I honestly thought someone was playing a joke on me," she said, her face flat as stone. I nodded. She continued, almost hesitantly, "I didn't think I'd see you again."

We existed in silence for a moment, then she stood, her figure thinner, her clothes hanging loosely off her frame. There was something stiff about her posture, something more mechanical. She bore a silver ring on her finger, etched with an infinite symbol.

There'd been a time when she was the only face I'd see for days at a time, when her face was the only one I wanted to see. As her familiar vanilla scent reached me, I felt my stomach twist into a million knots. She regarded me, waiting for me to say something other than why I was here. I wanted to see you again too or I missed you. Even though those statements were slightly true, they couldn't erase what had happened, whatever it had been. I'd stored that memory away too, the only thing left was the knowledge of knowing she had done something unforgiveable.

"I need your help," I finally said, still fighting the urge to run out the door and never come back.

Carn forced a smile. "What's the problem, sweetie?"

———— ◆ ————

Carn stared at her screens, at the blue numbers and codes that flashed, her eyes darting back and forth, searching for something that I never understood. She was a genius, though she'd never admit it—she had a way with technology, just like technology had a way with her. I figured she was probably somewhere around 70% modified now, given how she moved as we walked to one of her mod stations.

"This is fucked," she said, scratching the back of her head, the noise sounding a little more metallic than it should've. "I can access the code, but not the files themselves. I tried rerouting the operation, saving the code to a new chip, nothing's working."

She spun in her swivel chair and looked me dead in the eyes.

"You had this in you when it fried?"

"Yeah," I said from the chair I was laying in, looking at the numbers and code like I understood them. "After that, it covered my port in this black goop and I haven't been able to get it out."

She scratched her head again and took a deep breath. "Elena..."

"What?"

"I've never..."

"What is it?"

"These memories," she said, spinning back to the computer, pointing to a line of code that meant something to her but nothing to me. "It's like they're forming new ones."

"Meaning?"

"This sequence, this code...it's not a virus. It's self-aware."

I sat in stunned silence, the neon red glow from outside pulsating against everything in the room. "How is that possible?"

Carn shook her head. "I don't know."

"Can you try to extract it?"

The look on her face said it all. It was one of disappointment. Of hopelessness. But still, she said, "I can try. I just...I can try. What's happening in there with that chip?"

"There's a little girl. She shows up asking for the woman...I think she's her daughter."

"What?"

"Ms. Oboeru must've done something with her chip, some sort of memory implant. But the memory consumed her. Now Aggie's in me, and she wants to go home."

"Aggie? The ghost has a name?" Carn asked, genuinely intrigued.

"Of course she has a name, she's a child—was a child," I corrected myself.

Carn moved forward in her chair, as though she meant to reach for my arm, but stopped herself short when I looked down at her.

"I feel sorry for her, for both of them," I started before I could stop, my voice cracking. "Can you imagine having someone you love beyond words, beyond feelings, taken away from you? Can you imagine being so lost without them that you mod yourself just so you never forget them?"

Something changed in Carn's eyes then. A shift, subtle but there.

"No," Carn said after what felt like ages. "And for this sim to become self-aware, it's just...this is unheard of."

"You need to get her out of me. I can't live like this. I can't live with a ghost."

We sat still, both holding our true emotions from spilling out. I started to open my mouth, to be the one to break the spell, but Carn stood up before I could.

"Just...hang on one sec," she dashed behind a door, closing it behind her.

I stood up slowly, alone in Carn's office, surrounded by an endless array of gizmos and gadgets. Alone in a room of empty things. A woman with no one to love, with no one to love her. A woman alone in a world that moved on without her. A woman destined to live in the Commons when the world decided she wasn't worthy of living among it anymore.

I paced around her office, haphazardly flipping through scattered papers, eyes darting her wall of photographs and finding none of myself, running my finger along the shelves of chips that she stowed away, the labels of some faded, others marked in fresh ink.

One slot in particular was empty, one labelled FEB_22_22.

"Excuse me?" A quiet voice said from behind.

I jumped, spinning around to its source.

The room was empty.

It was then that the lights cut.

The room pulsed neon red, illuminating in little flashes. One minute, it was black. The next, red.

"Have you seen Ms. Oboeru?" The voice said, closer now. I turned and saw nothing before the room went to black.

"Carn!" I stumbled toward the door she'd gone through, banging my knees against her mod tables.

Red.

"Have you seen Ms. Oboeru?" Right behind me. "I want to go home."

"Stop it," I cried. "Leave me alone!" I fell to my knees and crawled, using my hands to push things out of the way. The door was within reach.

Black.

I tried the door handle, but it didn't open.

"Elena," the voice said into my ear.

Red.

I turned.

Aggie was in front of me, hovering in the air. Her curls floating around her as though it were caught in a breeze. Her tattered clothes did the same, pushing and pulling away from her body. She looked as though she were swimming.

"Aggie," I said, as though saying her name might make her stop.

She opened her mouth.

"I need to remember," she said.

Then, the room turned black.

A light buzzed on overhead. The door opened, and I fell backward onto Carn's feet.

I twisted to her in pure terror. She saw it in my eyes, saying nothing but looked around the room with apprehension.

Carn dropped the stuff in her hands and knelt down to help me. "Holy hell. What's on your face?"

Confused, I sat up and looked around the vicinity, finding a reflective piece of junk.

Dark spots streamed down my cheeks as though I'd been caught in a black rain.

I tried wiping it off with my sleeve, softly at first, then with enough force to break my skin.

The streaks remained.

"Jesus," Carn said, placing a hand on my shoulder. "Now what?"

My chest heaved. My heart throbbed. I knew what I had to do.

"I bring her home."

VII

Carn insisted on coming along. I was too weak to put up a fight, though I still felt uneasy around her.

We walked in silence through the streets of Toksan, the red glow always hovering over us.

By the time we got to Ms. Oboeru's old apartment, the clouds beyond Pacific Lake had cleared slightly, allowing the bright lights of New Vancouver to run across its waters.

I stopped and watched the lake, the cool breeze soothing against my skin, the air filling my lungs fresh and crisp.

As I stood and watched a life that would never be, I felt a cold hand find its way into my own, its fingers wrapping around mine. It squeezed, a squeeze that said everything's going to be all right.

I squeezed back, even though I knew it wouldn't.

"Are you ready?" Carn's voice said from behind.

I turned around and saw her standing a few feet back, her hands tucked into her pockets.

———— •• ————

Ms. Oboeru's door was unlocked. It opened slowly, the faded red light from downtown mixing with the yellow streetlights from below allowing a dimmed view into the now-vacant abode.

I stepped in first, Carn nervously following suit, flicking on the kitchen lights.

They buzzed into action, illuminating the empty room and the black stain where Ms. Oboeru's body had been slumped over. Everything else had been cleared out.

The doors leading to the sitting room were closed, the light unable to penetrate them. But behind them, something moved.

"Aggie?" I called out, stepping toward the doors.

"Hey," Carn grabbed my arm, holding me back. "Are you sure about this? I could always try to remove your port, see if that helps."

"And then what? I'd start over with no memories?"

"You've done it before and turned out fine," she said, pulling me closer. "We could start over. Start new. I...I miss having you around."

"I can't do that," I said, pulling away from her and reaching for the handles.

The sitting room was unchanged. Boxes still lined the walls, old toys still sprawled out across the floor.

Aggie sat in the middle, a small shadow among colourful toys, her legs pulled up to her chin.

"Where's Ms. Oboeru?" she sniffled as I moved closer, taking a seat across from her. "She's not here. She's not at home."

"Aggie," I started, unsure of what to say next. "Ms. Oboeru isn't here anymore. She's...she died."

"Oh," the little girl replied, the news not hitting her as hard as I expected. She looked up at me, dark eyes reflecting the pale red glow from the world outside. Dark eyes full of so much life for a sim.

"I'm sorry, Aggie," I choked, unsure how I would tell this little girl that I needed her gone. "But I don't know how to help you. You can't... you can't stay here."

She moved toward me then. Her cold, little hand found mine, and a blue light started on my retina screen. I closed my eyes.

She's following a path through the woods, some place quiet and serene. A lake is on the right. Trees all around. Birds chirp.

Someone laughs.

"Aggie," she says and turns.

A little girl's face smiles back at her, black curls bouncing along.

"Mama," Aggie says.

"Come on, I'll race you to the lake."

She's running hard down the same path, the sound of her breath pounding in her ears. It's night now. Trees zoom by. She turns to her right: the lake, blue and rippling, a small wind.

Static licks at the edges of her vision.

There's something floating near the shore.

"How do I know it's working?" says a voice in the darkness.

"You'll know," a second replies.

The woman looks back at herself in the mirror, hints of static creeping into her vision.

She leans forward, focusing on the blue dot as the static grows thicker.

"Is it supposed to do that?"

"What?"

"Be all staticky."

"Yeah, it's a part of it, sweetie."

She runs to the shore, her heart pounding in her chest.

Aggie's body bobs in the still waves of the lake.

Leeches cover her skin like little black rain drops.

The water as black as tar under the light of the moon.

The woman leans back and looks herself over once more.

"Okay, and when will I be able to see her? When can I see Aggie again?"

"As soon as you want to, Ms. Oboeru."

When I opened my eyes, the room was quiet, our hands still locked together.

"She could only remember the bad parts at first," Aggie said through tears. "She would cry every time she saw me. But it got better."

"Hey, it's okay," I reached my other hand out to her. "It's okay."

Aggie was solid now. I could feel her coldness. I could feel the way her body trembled as she cried. I could feel her tears as they fell onto my arms.

She was no longer a ghost. Not to me.

"Elena?" Carn's voice startled me. Her shadow from where she stood in the sitting room doorway loomed on the wall in front of me, tall and dark and hollow. "Are you okay?"

"Yeah," I managed, the quiver in my voice betraying me. "Listen, you should go."

I felt her shift behind me, uneasy with my words. "What?"

"I mean it, Carn. You need to leave." It came out harder than I meant it.

"Why?"

"I have this under control."

"Do you?" She hesitated. "You came looking for my help, and now you're telling me to leave."

"I was wrong," I said, though I wasn't wrong in asking for her help. I'd only been wrong in thinking that I could look past what she had done to me all those years ago. Even though I'd taken that memory away from myself, it still stuck with me enough to know to stay away. "I'm sorry I brought you to this place."

"Whatever," her voice shifted from concern to anger. "Do what you want. You always choose wrong here anyway, sweetie."

I listened as the sounds of her soles on the floor became fainter and fainter, until she slammed the apartment door behind her, shutting out the neon red glow of the city.

Shutting out the smog that hung over us.

Shutting out her last words.

The lights flickered off as Aggie and I sat hand in hand in the sitting room.

"Will you stay with me?" Aggie asked.

"I will," I said, pulling her into my arms.

As her cold skin pressed against mine in the darkness, the corners of my eyes filled with static.

About the Authors

PAUL L. BATES was trained as an architect; is happily retired from a career in construction management; swims distance; lives on the shore of a small private lake in Western Massachusetts with his two girlfriends, one of whom is a cat. He is the author of the novels  *Imprint* and *Dreamer,* from the late lamented Gale FiveStar. Writing credits include short fiction appearing in *Vastarien: a Literary Journal,* issues 1.1 and 2.2, and in the anthologies *For When the Veil Drops, Twisted Boulevard, Darker Than Noir, Arcane* and *Mark of the Beast.*

CHRISTOPHER BURKE grew up in Cincinnati and received his MA in Literature from the University of Louisville. His previous fiction has been pub-  lished in *Nightscript, The Yellow Booke,* and on *The NoSleep Podcast.* Criticism and interviews are available at weirdfictionreview.com and most recently in *Thinking Horror, Vol. 2.* Christopher lives in Rhode Island with his partner, Cassandra, and their cat, River. More information can be found at www.christopherburkewords.com

VICTORIA DALPE is a visual artist and writer. Her short dark fiction has appeared in over twenty-five anthologies and her debut novel, *Parasite Life,* came  out in 2018. She is a member of the HWA and the New England Horror Writers. Victoria makes her home in Providence, RI with her husband, screenwriter and director Philip Gelatt, and their young son.

Jen Downes trained as a beautician and has worked as a copy editor, commercial artist and care-giver to the frail aged. After more than fifty years as an avid reader she now writes with the same enthusiasm. She has traveled extensively in Alaska, Canada and the UK, and lived most of her life in and around the city of Adelaide, South Australia, where several future stories will be set.

From the day she was born, Bram Stoker Award-winner **Jess Landry** has always been attracted to the darker things in life. Her fondest childhood memories include getting nightmares from the *Goosebumps* books, watching *The Hilarious House of Frightenstein,* and reiterating to her parents that there was absolutely nothing wrong with her mental state.

Since then, Jess's fiction has appeared in several anthologies, including *Tales of the Lost, Twice-Told: A Collection of Doubles, Monsters of Any Kind, Where Nightmares Come From, Lost Highways: Dark Fictions from the Road,* and *Fantastic Tales of Terror* (which includes her Stoker award-winning story, "Mutter"), among others.

Her debut feature, *My Only Sunshine,* a coming-of-age horror film set against the harsh prairie winter, has been called "a sharp and precise slow-burn horror story" by the Black List. Jess has also written several other screenplays, including a handful of Lifetime movies. She is a member of the Winnipeg Film Group and OnScreen Manitoba, and currently sits on the Board of Trustees of the Horror Writers Association.

Your best bet at finding her online is jesslandry.com and on various social media channels (@jesslandry28) where she often posts cat gifs and references *Jurassic Park* way too much.

Jake Marley's fiction has appeared in *Resist and Refuse, Unnerving Magazine*, and the *Writers of the Future* anthology, Volume 33. His short story, "Acquisition", won the Golden Pen Award in 2017. A Southern California native, he now lives and works in Western Oregon.

Samuel M. Moss is from Cascadia. His work has been published or is forthcoming in *Dim Shores Presents, Vastarien* and *decomP* among other venues. He cohosted Hespera, a quarterly reading series in Minneapolis concerned with the distant and ineffable and is an associate editor and web lead at 11:11 Press. He travels between, lives on and writes within North American public wilderness land. More at perfidiousscript.blogspot.com and on twitter @perfidiouscript

Chiara Nova writes stories in various genres, ranging from fantasy and science fiction to the darkest of horrors. She loves to get lost in other worlds and has turned an entire room in her home in The Netherlands into her personal library. She is currently writing her first novel.

Jonathan Raab is the author of numerous short stories, veteran advocacy essays, and novels including *Camp Ghoul Mountain Part VI: The Official Novelization* and *The Hillbilly Moonshine Massacre*. He is the editor of several anthologies from Muzzleland Press, including *Behold the Undead of Dracula: Lurid Tales of Cinematic Gothic Horror* and *Terror in 16-bits*. He lives in Colorado with his wife Jess, their son, and a dog named Egon. You can find him on Twitter @jonathanraab1

Jane Sand is a pseudonym the author happened to have lying around. She has previously published stories in The Fantasist and Golden Visions online magazines. Her hobbies include writing, drawing and decapitating Orange Lantern dolls to give them different heads. She has a blog at jaynsand.wordpress.com, but it is rarely updated and mostly about political embroidery instead of writing, so you should probably not go there. She is a health care worker in New York.

Eric Schaller's debut fiction collection, *Meet Me in the Middle of the Air*, was released in 2016 from Undertow Publications. His stories have appeared in various anthologies and magazines, including *The Year's Best Fantasy and Horror*, *Fantasy: Best of the Year*, *The Time Traveler's Almanac*, *Wilde Stories*, *Nightmare Magazine*, *Black Static*, and *The Dark*. He is an editor, with Matthew Cheney, of the on-line magazine *The Revelator*.

Richard Staving writes and plays and records bass for various music projects. He and his wife live outside Pittsburgh, PA. He struggles with online technology on facebook.com/Richardstavingwrites and on Twitter and Instagram @richardstaving.

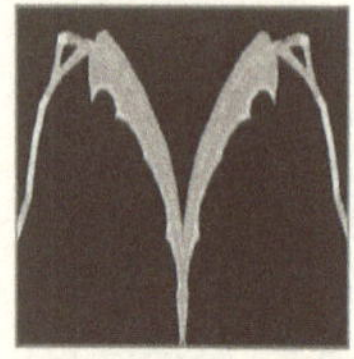

Anna Tambour's stories have appeared so far this year in the Swan River Press anthology *Uncertainties*, Vol IV, edited by Timothy Jarvis; and *Weird Fiction Review* No. 10, published by Centipede Press and edited by John Pelan, and the Decameron Project. A WFA-award finalist (novel), Tambour's latest two published books are the novel *Smoke Paper Mirrors: A short saga for our times*, published by Infinity Press; and the collection, *The Road to Neozon*, published by Obsidian Sky Books.

DIM SHORES PRESENTS
VOLUME 2 / WINTER 2020

*The second volume in an ongoing series
spotlighting an array of today's
cutting-edge speculative fiction authors.*

Featuring new stories from

Mike Adamson
Randee Dawn
J.W. Donley
Timothy G. Huguenin
Jennifer Loring
Avery Kit Malone
C.M. Muller
Mari Ness
dave ring
Erica Ruppert
Michael David Wilson
Jake Wyckoff

Coming in late 2020